RETURNED FOR NOW

Bob Howard

ISBN-13: 978-1-945754-06-7

DEDICATION

This book is dedicated to the first readers, Julie Cowell, Drew Howard, and Dawn Howard. Julie is my second child, so she always gets mentioned second. This time she gets to be out front. They put up with the mistakes, the typos, and the things that didn't make sense. I could not imagine the final project being completed without their help. All three of them have really sharp minds and are brutally honest about letting me know when something isn't written well. I'm incredibly lucky to have their help.

1

Rebuilding

Guntersville - Year Seven

Things have changed.

When I consider how much of an understatement that is, I realize if I had said the same thing on the first day of the infection, it would have been just as ridiculous. I guess I had gotten used to the "new normal" existence in the Guntersville shelter that made me feel like we were finally at peace in this horrible new world.

In the six weeks since we watched the Chief lead away a caravan of our best friends, life has almost been boring, but no one has been complaining. I still cringe when I go outside for sunshine and fresh air if I see a spider web between trees. I know they aren't the same spiders we left behind in Charleston, but spiders are spiders. I tell myself anyone would say the same thing.

Jean and I want the kids in the shelter to grow up with a healthy fear of the infected dead, a fear of strangers, and a careful approach to the unknown, so we make sure they all visit the village above the shelter and the woods on the farthest sides of our mountain. We've made it safe enough for them here, but like I said, things have changed.

Two soldiers arrived this morning from the Mud Island shelter. No helicopters, no vehicles. These two were worn out from six hard weeks of travel through hostile territory. There were eight soldiers in their squad when they left their shelter, but only two of them made it from the east coast to the northeastern corner of Alabama. It was lucky for them that they stumbled into one of our routine rescue operations in the city of Guntersville, or they might not have made it the last few miles.

Patrols have only been sent into the city when there are reports from the night watches that lights were seen during the previous night. We're always interested in knowing who is nearby, and if they're friendly people, they're welcome to join us. Sometimes they aren't so friendly, and we avoid them if possible, but we deal with them if we have to. The last visitors had been unfriendly, and if any of them survived, they probably won't be coming back anytime soon. Today's patrol had gone out heavily armed and extremely cautious just in case the last visitors were back.

The local Walmart was like a magnet to almost everyone who ventured into the city. Even after more than six years, people checked the store for supplies just in case something had been missed. For that reason, we left a small cache of survival gear and food along with instructions on how to make contact with us. We change the means of contact once a week on the off chance that someone with bad motives considers setting a trap for us. Sometimes the supplies have been taken without an attempt to contact us, and once there was a thank-you note from someone who appreciated the gesture but didn't want to be part of a group.

Today's instructions said to go to the Wells Fargo bank and find a way up to the white steeple on the roof. A lantern had been left there for someone to safely light at night. It was a long way from our shelter, but we could see it well enough at night. When the light appeared last night, a patrol got ready to leave by dawn, but their insurance policy was the two highly skilled scouts who were sent out in advance to take up overwatch positions on the church across the street. It was built like a castle with rampart towers and had plenty of cover for both snipers.

Our cautious plans paid off for the two soldiers from Mud Island when they stumbled into the middle of the intersection between the church and the bank. They knew the shelter was somewhere in the area, but they weren't really sure where, so they were hoping to be found. The risk was that they could also be found by the wrong people.

The patrol from the Guntersville shelter was still a few blocks away and moving on foot toward the Wells Fargo bank when the overwatch reported movement in three locations. The squad had left their vehicles a few blocks short of their destination so they wouldn't drive into the middle of something. Our advance scouts reported that someone was in the tower above the bank, but someone was also on the roof of the convenience store across the intersection. Whoever it was, they appeared to be providing overwatch for the person above the bank. It was a poor location for an overwatch to be in because there were so many higher places to occupy. The church was one of those places.

There wasn't time for the patrol to reach the intersection and find out who the people were in the tower or on the convenience store roof, but the two men in the intersection wore shoulder patches on their uniforms that had been designed a few years ago by our own good friend in the Army, Captain Jim Miller. Each patch was white and shaped like home plate on a baseball diamond, and they had either an FS for Fort Sumter or an MI for Mud Island sewn in the middle. He chose that design because that was the shape of Fort Sumter.

When the overwatch passed along that piece of information to the squad that was moving in their direction, the leader decided the other two locations must be hostiles and gave the order to eliminate the overwatch on the roof of the convenience store. Even if they weren't hostiles, they were taking aim at two friendlies and generally being rude guests.

There was a moment when it felt like we all held our breath. With the order given and acknowledged, everyone had to hope that our overwatch shot first because the soldiers were exposed.

High above the street the two church snipers only exposed a short length of the barrels of their Barrett M82 rifles in case someone was watching their positions. They had decided ahead of time with a coin toss who would shoot first, and while one watched the bank tower, the other took aim at the hostile. He exhaled slowly as he squeezed the trigger. A split second later the man on top of the convenience store bucked into the air a few inches and then fell motionless.

In the control room of the shelter hidden inside Green Cavern, we were all quiet and still as if any movement would cause our people to be too late. The radio chatter we were monitoring between the patrol and the overwatch was nothing but static as we waited. Then the report came through.

"Green squad alpha, Owl has eliminated the mouse."

The combined release of tension in the room along with the choice of words from the overwatch caused a fair amount of laughter.

"Owl?" asked Jean. "When did he come up with that?"

Jean didn't appear to have aged at all over the last six years, but the laugh lines around her eyes were a touch deeper. They were showing up now because the radio report was so unexpected.

I didn't have a clue, but our old friend and shelter physician, Dr. Bus, explained it between fits of laughter.

"That's Gahan out there on the church tower. He's been complaining about radio security and thinks we should be using call signs and code. He's the Overwatch Leader, so he's the OWL."

"I can't say I disagree with him, and I imagine it makes sense to give himself that call sign," I said. I had to admit, it was appropriate even if it was funny.

The radio came back to life with the response from the squad. There was laughter in the background as the squad leader said, "Affirmative, OWL. What about the other mouse?"

The second overwatch reported that the person in the tower had gone to ground as soon as their overwatch had been shot. From the tower, the roof of the convenience store was completely visible, and there was no misunderstanding about what had happened to their plan to trap our squad from the Green Cavern shelter.

The soldiers in the intersection mustered up what little strength they had left and used it to get as close to the church as possible. They heard gunshots from that direction above them, and they couldn't see where the shooters were, but they knew it would be hard for someone to shoot straight down at them.

I keyed the microphone and quickly told the squad and the overwatch to begin hailing the soldiers on all channels in case they were carrying radios. It would be senseless for anyone else to get shot. The squad was quick to report that they had contact with the two soldiers and were moving into position to protect them.

The second overwatch followed with a report of his own. "Green Squad, be advised that OWL needs to eliminate that mouse again."

Our expressions were blank at first, but then it dawned on us that the man on top of the convenience store had turned. It wouldn't be much threat to anyone, but it was a good idea not to have it crawling around after falling off the roof. It also wasn't a great idea for the overwatch to fire a second shot without explaining why. Moments later the second shot did its job and permanently eliminated the infected dead.

Within the next ten minutes the squad reached the church and set up a perimeter as the squad leader and medic cautiously showed themselves to the two men who had managed to survive long enough to find us. They were holed up in an alcove that covered a side entrance to the church. We got the good news that they weren't bitten or otherwise injured even though they were exhausted and in need of a good meal.

An hour later our squad returned to Green Cavern through the village entrance. Bus wanted to give them a more thorough examination, but he gave in when I insisted they could give us their report while he was doing his job. Within minutes, I knew why things had changed, and I wished there was some way to contact the Chief and the rest of the group that had traveled north to see what had become of the rest of the country.

******

Chief Barnes - Six Weeks Earlier

The weather turned against the caravan before the end of the first day on the road, so it was good that they headed west to reach I-65. If it had been the old days before the infection, everyone in the group would have been fighting for the steering wheels and enjoying the drive on the country roads between Guntersville and Huntsville. The twists and turns through the mountains down into the foothills would have been exciting.

Something about the way the temperature dropped was the reason for the last minute decision. It was fair to say that they were all experienced with the outdoors, but it was Hampton who threw up a hand and gave the signal for a stop. Until they knew what was ahead in this new world, they would keep radio silence, so they had a complete set of signals that seemed to grow every time they practiced them. There was no disagreement that a big storm was coming. When it started, the hail sounded like rocks, and they ricocheted through the open cabins of the RZRs.

The Chief had taken the time to do extra modifications on each of the RZRs. They were off-road vehicles that could get through mud and overgrown terrain, but they were far too open when it came to protection from the infected. The passengers were also too easy to shoot, so steel panels could be lowered from the ceilings when they needed more defense, but they weren't lowered soon enough, and it was a painful lesson. One chunk of ice hit Tom in the mouth, and he needed a couple of stitches in his upper lip.

The Chief asked him if it was his kissing lip. The comment earned him a long stare from both Kathy and Iris, but Tom almost pulled the new stitches loose trying not to laugh.

The modifications made the vehicles heavy, and heavy meant more fuel would be needed, but they would still be fast enough to outrun anything in rough terrain except a dirt bike. There was some concern that they would be top-heavy and likely to roll over easily, but if the weight changed anything, it made the RZRs hug the ground better.

They had been right to stop just before the hail began because they were in Tornado Alley, a place famous for its thunderstorms and funnel clouds. They were only a few hundred yards from an overpass when they saw the dark sky extend a finger toward the ground, and they were quick to start their engines and get rolling again.

The four RZRs were forced to change directions over and over as they zigzagged between the cars and trucks that sat on their flat tires and rusted until they fell apart. The wind blew swirling debris into the air, making it harder for the Chief to see the next clear path, and their biggest fear was that there would be no way through. A dead end would take on a new meaning if they drove into one.

A moment of clear sky was all they needed to see that the funnel had touched down only a mile or so from their location, and it was following I-65 straight toward them. The race was on to see if they could reach the overpass before the tornado. If they lost that race, they were too exposed to hope for survival.

The Chief had no choice but to roll the dice and bet on a narrow gap that was part of a massive pile up. It was so big that it was possibly the wreck that had backed up traffic on the Interstate for miles. If that was true, the Chief was betting that beyond the wreck it would be a clear path all the way to the overpass. The RZR shot through the gap at full speed, and metal screamed in protest on both sides of the all-terrain vehicle. It was a good thing that they still had the metal plates lowered, or they would have been hit by the rust-red debris that scraped at their sides. The Chief couldn't do anything for the three vehicles that followed him into the gap. He could only hope they hit the opening the same way he had and that none of the debris he hit was knocked into their way.

The funnel was a black monster that grew in size as it churned up the debris ahead, but the Chief had guessed right. The road ahead opened wide, and he saw a clear shot from the median onto the highway that led straight to the overpass. He came to a stop as soon as he reached the concrete supports under the overpass, and above the noise of the approaching tornado he yelled for Iris to run. He somehow managed to climb out and grab his bug-out pack and M4 with one hand.

From the underside of the overpass, the view ahead was gone. It was nothing but a swirling black wall. He risked a glance backward and saw the other three RZRs behind his own. He didn't have time to find out if the rest of his friends had already run for cover, and he only had seconds before it would be too late for him to do the same. He put all of his physical training as a SEAL into motion, and his powerful legs pulled him up the steep concrete incline where they would be most protected from the wind. The visibility dropped with every second until he blindly stumbled into the narrow spot where his companions gathered. They held onto each other as if they could keep the funnel from sucking them out of their hiding place. The Chief felt something hit him in the middle of his broad shoulders just below his neck. He concentrated on the spot, willing himself to not feel the sensations that would mean he had been hit by something that had torn through his clothing and ripped into his bare skin.

The deafening roar made it impossible to hear each other, but there wasn't anything that needed to be said. In the minutes that followed the arrival of the tornado, all they could do was pray. Then, after what seemed like a much longer time than it was, it was quiet again. Light flooded into their dark corner as small bits of debris floated down all around them. They covered their mouths and noses to keep from breathing in the dirt and junk that had coated their clothing.

One by one they helped each other into a standing position on the steep incline, and as they surveyed their surroundings, they saw just how lucky they had been. The median and the road under the overpass had been swept clean as the suction from the tornado had pulled everything it touched into its vortex. If they had stayed on the interstate they would be dead. The Chief sat back down on the concrete slope and watched as the dirt in the air settled to the ground. He was the first to speak, and even to him his voice sounded far away. The roar of the tornado had made them all slightly deaf.

"I need someone to check my back. I got hit by something."

"That doesn't surprise me," said Iris. "You were covering me so well that I knew I wasn't going to..."

Iris didn't finish her sentence because she was trying to understand what she looking at. She leaned closer to the Chief before turning her confused expression toward the rest of the group. Kathy was the nearest to her, so she moved closer to Iris and turned the Chief slightly so everyone could see. Hampton let out a low whistle.

"What's the verdict?" asked the Chief.

Kathy reached up with both hands and gripped the Chief's coat at the shoulders.

"Let me help you get your coat off, Chief. I think we need to do that to get a better look at your shirt."

"My shirt? Did something cut through my coat?"

"You might say that," said Cassandra. She took the coat from Kathy as soon as she got his arms out of the sleeves. She spread it out on the sloping concrete wall below their feet so the Chief could see what had gotten everyone's attention.

It wasn't what he expected, and even though it was obvious to him what the object was, it was hard for his mind to accept what he was seeing. He leaned over and studied the dirty but perfectly aligned row of teeth. He was so occupied with the discovery that he momentarily forgot there were seven friends examining his back. It was their collective sigh of relief that reminded him that the teeth were embedded in his coat. He lifted the heavy garment in the air and flipped it over to the inside. The teeth were protruding through the material.

Sim clamped a hand on the Chief's left shoulder.

"You must be blessed, my man. You have more lives than a cat."

The Chief wasn't ready to celebrate until he heard what the verdict was on his shirt.

"Did they get through the shirt?"

Iris said, "Let's check the skin underneath to be sure."

She unbuttoned his shirt for him as if he needed help, but it was mostly for her and that she wanted him to move faster. They pulled the shirt down at the collar and saw the beginning of a black and blue bruise, but the skin wasn't broken.

Iris moved back around in front of him and grabbed his head in both hands. From only three inches away she stared into his eyes and said in a firm voice, "Would you please stop tempting fate?"

"All I did was cover you," he said defensively. "If I hadn't, one of you might have been hit with those things."

Tom used his rifle barrel to poke the dentures out of the material and mumbled something about wondering where the owner of the teeth was. Before he could finish the thought, he had a coughing fit like he was choking on something. He was coughing because he tried to speak too soon and got a mouthful of the fine dust that still floated in the air. Between gasps for air and coughing, he managed to get out a couple of words about the RZRs.

"Save your breath," said the Chief. "I know they're gone."

As he said it he gestured to the place where they had parked the RZRs. All of that work. All of the hours they had spent modifying their transportation, and it only took one day and one stroke of bad luck for them to be walking again. They were gone, and even if they found them down the road, they would most likely be heaps of scrap metal.

Kathy sat down heavily next to the Chief. She handed him his coat as he finished buttoning his shirt.

"If you try to take the blame for this, we're going to have our first real fight because you didn't make that tornado."

"I'll second that," said Iris as she sat down on the other side of him. "It's not all on you, Chief."

He shook his head. "That's not what I was thinking. I was thinking that the RZRs were a bad plan all along. It didn't occur to me until now that even if we had only lost one of them, we would still have a problem because there was no way we could carry everyone in the other three without leaving supplies and gear behind."

Kathy held up a hand to stop him from going on.

"It wasn't a bad idea. It just didn't work out. We've walked before, and it didn't kill us. How far are we from Huntsville?"

"About twenty miles," said Tom. "The last few miles are over that small mountain, but it won't be so bad."

Tom had lived in northern Alabama with his wife and daughter, and he knew the area like the back of his hand. He knew that when they reached the highest point where the highway crossed the mountain they would be able to see Huntsville sprawling out in front of them. It had been the fourth largest city in Alabama, but their goal wasn't the city as much as it was the Army base attached to it. Redstone Arsenal had bordered the city for the most part, but it was also next to the home of the United States space program located at the Marshall Space Flight Center.

The small group of survivors didn't know what they expected to find at the NASA base, but it had been the main research and development center for both the Space Shuttle and the Saturn V rocket used in the Apollo moon launches. When they had talked about where they were going after they left Guntersville, Tom had suggested the possibility that the Army and NASA might have followed contingency plans to survive the apocalypse. Although he had never seen proof of their existence, there were rumors about a network of shelters on a highly guarded part of the base. It was worth checking out that rumor, and they had all the time in the world to explore.

They gathered together their gear, and the Chief was happy to see he hadn't been the only one with the presence of mind to grab his rifle and emergency pack. All eight of them remembered what was important to their survival. They may have lost their transportation far sooner than he expected to, but they had the things that mattered most. They hefted the backpacks by their straps and carefully eased their way down the steep embankment. The dirt coating the concrete made them slide and lose their footing, so they took it as slowly as possible until they were close to the bottom. A sprained ankle or broken leg wouldn't help them get to Huntsville any time soon.

Once they were on level ground again, they helped each other to secure the backpacks and fell into a walking formation without much discussion. It was something they had done often enough without having to be told what to do. There was only a brief question from Sim about whether or not they needed anything from the RZRs, wherever they were. Terrance Simmons, known as Sim to the rest of them, had been a flight navigator on commercial airlines. He had survived under worse conditions than he was facing on this new adventure, but he was still the least experienced one in the group.

"Nothing we would want to carry," said the rest of them in unison. They sounded like a choir that had rehearsed the line. They had needed something to lift their spirits, and that did the trick. Their eyes were already busy searching their surroundings for threats, but they still laughed as they settled into an easy pace for a long hike.

Charleston

The flow of infected toward Charleston continued even after the signal transmitter on the Arthur Ravenel Jr. Bridge was destroyed, and the dead followed each other until they dropped into the Cooper River. The harbor was choked by bodies, and the gases from their decaying tissues made them float on the current. A steady stream of tangled arms and legs locked together like a moving island of debris drifted toward the mouth of the harbor. Helpless to break free of the current, they moaned as if complaining about where they were going. The current where the Ashley River met with the Cooper River turned the island of bodies like a tugboat pushing a barge, and the next destination of the infected dead was the Atlantic Ocean.

Unseen below the thousands of bodies, the real winners of the battle being waged within the food chain were the blue crabs. They attached themselves to the underside of the living debris that formed a solid wall of bodies so dense that they blocked out the light, and they fed on the moving flesh even as they reached the open sea beyond the jetties. It was there that they were joined by the larger predators.

What had once been a sanctuary for hundreds of survivors, the Yorktown was now shrouded in a milky white and gray cloud of spider webs. For the people who weren't able to jump from the deck before being dragged down by the venomous brown recluse spiders, it became a torture chamber. They died slowly and without mercy, fully aware that they were being used as hosts for new colonies of spiders. Those people who were lucky enough to jump into the river measured their luck in seconds. Bodies rained down on top of them before they could swim away from the doomed ship. Some were knocked unconscious, receiving a merciful death. Some were driven deeper into the water only to fill their lungs with something other than air, and as they popped back to the surface they found themselves caught up in the other stream of bodies being pulled to the Atlantic by the current.

Hundreds of living people rode the current directly into the floating island of infected dead, and even as the infected were being fed upon by the crabs, the infected found one last meal when the living arrived. Screams for help and screams of pain went unheeded and continued until at last there were no more living beings coming from Patriots Point.

As a final insult to humanity, seagulls continually landed between the waving arms and legs. They tore away large strips of flesh and left quickly, making room for the next bird to land. Sometimes they plucked off the blue crabs that climbed above the water, and at least for a short time, they grabbed fingers and flesh from living people with their hungry beaks. The last of the bodies drifted out of the harbor and into the open sea almost a month later.

The harbor was quiet.

******

Fort Sumter sat and watched as the former members of the human race drifted into the Atlantic. The fort stood silently and witnessed the evil that mankind could inflict upon itself, and it continued to watch as all evidence of a human presence disappeared.

It was also nearly silent inside the fort, and within the massive shelter hidden below, there was the faint hum of machinery that continued to function after the evacuation. Machinery that powered positive air pressure to the lowest levels and machinery that bathed the rooms in white light. Machinery that kept the water pumping through the network of pipes and kept the security cameras online. How long the hum of the machinery would last was not something Captain Jim Miller wanted to think about. It only needed to last long enough for him to figure out a way to get out of the shelter alive.

As the highest ranking representative of the US Army, he had gone to great lengths to know every inch of the shelter. To most of its occupants it was just a safe place that protected them from the infected. They were fed and given jobs that helped them to forget the world outside and what they had lost. To Captain Miller the shelter was the future and the survival of the human race. His knowledge of the shelter had saved most of the inhabitants, but there hadn't been enough time to save everyone. Seeing them drift like monsters through the hallways of the two levels immediately above his was a constant reminder of what he considered to be his failure. He saw familiar faces and said their names out loud.

On that day when Phillip Corrigan committed his act of domestic terrorism by releasing a deadly pathogen into the HVAC system, Captain Miller had known when the moment came to give up his efforts to save everyone. He would fall on a hand grenade to save the life of one last soldier or civilian, but he recognized that his death was not going to save one more person. With only seconds to spare, he had used his knowledge of the shelter to make a safe haven for himself on the bottom floor.

He activated an auxiliary ventilation system that served as a backup for the main system. He increased the output until it reversed the direction of airflow in the HVAC system and created positive pressure on the bottom floor. That kept the powder from reaching his level. Satisfied that he had bought himself some time, he ran for the supply rooms that held the hazmat suits. He felt his ears pop in response to the change in air pressure, and he hoped that it would keep him alive long enough for him to get his suit hooked up to an oxygen cylinder. Once he was safe inside a suit, he carried the oxygen tank over to a workstation where he logged into the security system. He skimmed through the many different views, and what he saw was painful to witness. He had missed people on two levels, and they died as he watched.

What Captain Miller didn't know was that the agent released by Corrigan was supposed to totally eliminate the infected. What no one alive knew was that its effectiveness was temporary. Two days after the poisonous powder killed the people he hadn't been able to warn, they pushed their bodies from the floor, stood up, and walked through the corridors in search of living flesh. The grand plan of the people at Patriots Point had drawn close to a million of the infected dead into the Cooper River, but the plan to exterminate them with the deadly powder would have failed.

There were too many questions he couldn't answer, and his lack of information was what made him stay on his floor of the shelter. In the first two days, while the bodies remained scattered on the floors above him, Captain Miller did an inventory of his supplies and an assessment of his situation. He found there was enough food to last several months, and he was relieved when he discovered there was bottled water that would last even longer. He figured if he rationed the supplies, he could stretch them out for a year. So much for immediate needs, but the long term plan of escaping from his floor wasn't so easy without knowing what the powder would do to him.

He entertained the idea of wearing the hazmat suit as he climbed the stairs all the way to the top floor, and he would have at least given it a try if he hadn't discovered the small tear near his left shoulder blade. He realized he had possibly exposed himself to the powder without knowing it, but he still felt fine. At least there was a reason to be optimistic, and he tentatively released the seals of the suit. He held his breath when he pulled off the hood, and when he finally inhaled, he nervously waited for the spasms he had seen the others experience on the security cameras. The increased air pressure on his floor must have worked.

He found some duct tape in a tool chest and made a quick repair of the suit, but before he could take a chance and trust the suit to protect him, he decided to test the strength of the material. It seemed to him that he could avoid tearing it again, but he wasn't so sure it would protect him from teeth. His last check of the security cameras revealed a large number of the infected were in the stairwell. Someone had propped the door open on the next level up, and the noise from the infected had echoed loudly. Others were drawn to the open door until there were too many for him to get by.

Captain Miller held up the bright yellow material of the hazmat suit and bit down on the area where his forearm would be. He didn't use nearly as much force as the infected would, but when he released it from his mouth, there was a neat row of holes where his teeth had gone through. The suit was big and bulky, not made for fighting the infected, and a small hole would compromise the protection he needed against the white powder Corrigan had put into the HVAC system.

"So much for that."

His own voice startled him, and he involuntarily glanced around to see if anything had heard him. There wasn't a reaction from any of the rooms nearby, but being startled was just what he needed to get him moving. He realized that he had only assumed there was no one else on his level, and he didn't know if the elevators were still working. If they were, and if they happened to open on his floor, the air inside could deliver the powder from another floor. There was also the possibility that there would be infected dead passengers.

Thirty minutes later he stepped back and appraised his work. He didn't know if duct tape could hold an elevator door shut, but since he had no way to test it, he just kept adding layers until every inch of the line between the doors was covered. For added protection, he pulled a large tarp from the supply rooms and taped it over the entire opening. He eyed the other elevators and picked up his pace.

After another hour of stretching duct tape and sealing the doors, he was finally satisfied with the job. If an elevator full of the infected came down to his floor, and if the tape didn't hold the doors shut, the tarp would hopefully resemble any other wall to them. With any luck, the doors would close again, and they would ride back to the floor they had come from.

He went back to the workstation to check the security cameras again, and that was when it occurred to him that he was on the same floor where the Senator killed one of the kids. He thought of it that way despite the fact that it was Whitney who was forced to shoot Perry after the Senator had bitten him. Captain Miller wasn't the type to let past history haunt him, but he was having to face something new, something different. Since the beginning of the infection, he had never been alone. Now he was totally alone, and his soldiers undoubtedly thought he was dead. He knew it would be up to him to find a way out of the shelter. A drawer at the work station had a legal pad in it and several pens. He got comfortable in a chair and wrote down the names of the three soldiers he could see in one of the camera windows. He left that view open but brought up another view on the same level. There were several more soldiers, but there were also civilians. After recording their names, he went back to the first window to see if more had arrived since the last time he checked. None yet, so he moved on to a third camera. He knew it would take time, but he had to know what he was up against.

An idea took shape in his mind as he went from one view to the next and then back to the beginning. New arrivals were in some of the windows, and he added them to his lists. The lists were organized by camera locations so he could plan his escape route. He could only reach the top floors by using the stairwell, but the seed of the idea was growing in his mind. It wasn't going to be fun, but it was likely to be the only chance he would have, even if it was risky.

2

The Living

International Space Station - The Beginning of the Infection

In the weeks before the infection, the world of the living was much bigger than what was on the planet. With billions of people walking on land, floating on water, and traveling for endless hours in planes, it was almost easy to forget that a small group of exceptionally skilled people was orbiting the Earth at almost five miles per second. From the safety of their sophisticated home two hundred and fifty miles above the Earth they could do nothing more than watch the news feeds relayed to them from below. Needless to say, the ground control centers preferred they not be worried about another crisis on Earth, but the men and women of the different space programs were professionals. This had been part of their training. At least some of it was. They had taken classes about grief and loss and were well aware that they could suffer both while confined to their limited environment. When it happened they could grieve, but they could never forget their mission.

"Commander Callaway, this is Cindy Blair with the Canadian News Network. How are you and your crew members feeling today?"

The live interview on the TV showed a split-screen view of Adam Callaway floating inside the space station while the attractive news anchor on the screen to the left appeared to be smiling in his direction. He was grinning because it crossed his mind as he faced the monitor that in his world there was no up or down. They had even asked him to check the monitor so his feet would be in the right direction. It was easier for the viewers to understand that he was floating without the pull of gravity as long as he was right side up to them. His thick, black hair didn't float the way his Russian crew member's hair would, so he didn't have to wear a hat. When Natalia was on camera, she was forced to pull her auburn hair back into a ponytail.

"Hi Cindy, if you're wondering if any of us has had the urge to bite someone, we're feeling fine."

The flight team in Houston had also reminded him to behave himself. Adam was known for his quick wit and tendency to smile when he wanted everyone around him to relax. It was a useful tool in the astronaut program because his heart rate never got high enough to indicate he was anxious about anything. The problem was that someone like a news anchor might not be able to keep up with his sense of humor. Adam was also amused when he got someone in the control center to hold their breath during these interviews. His grin just added to his handsome features, and he could see it was working on Miss Canada.

"Well, yes Commander, that's what I was asking about. You have undoubtedly heard the news that there has been a disturbing number of reports from around the world related to attacks by seemingly rabid individuals. They bite their victims, and have even attempted to consume human flesh." The last three words came out slowly and sounded more like a question than a statement.

She made a show of shifting through a few sheets of paper in front of her for numbers she had most likely already committed to memory.

"There have been twelve hundred and fifteen incidents in forty countries, including the US. Over sixty major cities have reports of these incidents, and we have been informed that it will impact your work on the International Space Station. Can you tell us about that, Commander Callaway?"

As he listened to her question, his two fellow occupants of the ISS drifted into the compartment near the computer monitor. He had expected them to show up as soon as the interview started. Not so they could get on camera, but so they could make faces at him while he tried to be serious. His surprise when he saw their worried expressions wasn't detectable by Cindy Blair, but finding out from a news anchor that there was a program change wasn't his preferred method of receiving mission updates. Their casual attire of khaki cargo pants and navy blue polo shirts didn't reflect the tension they felt.

"I would be glad to tell you all about it, Ms. Blair, as soon as we get an official press release from Houston, but I imagine that a copy of the release would already have been given to you."

Adam tried to read the expressions on the faces of Henry Tisdal and Natalia Lebedev. He didn't see anything there that could be repeated even if he knew exactly what they were trying to tell him. He saw concern and urgency on two normally rock solid and confident faces.

The newsroom anchor had paid her dues by spending a few years in the field, so she knew she hadn't ruffled the feathers of the handsome and good natured astronaut even though she wondered why he had glanced away in the direction of something beyond her field of vision.

"Yes, Commander, I have been informed that the scheduled double launch from the Baikonur Cosmodrome in Kazakhstan has been canceled or at the very least delayed by these new developments. How will that affect you?"

"That's a good question, Cindy. As it stands, I would need to be officially notified by NASA of a change of plans before I can comment. We'll probably have to come back to that question during our next interview after I've been properly briefed."

Blair had her mouth forming the first word of her next question, which was undoubtedly the same question when her face froze on the screen. In real-time she was probably telling someone in the studio to get him back, but on Commander Callaway's end, Natalia had reached over and flipped the switch that cut off communications.

"I didn't think you would mind," she said.

"Houston will. I don't know why they'd hang me out to dry like that, but for some reason they didn't think it was a big deal to let me go on the air without all the information."

Henry Tisdal could say some of the funniest things with a straight face, but he wasn't kidding around when he thanked Natalia for cutting off the broadcast. Adam liked the Briton and found himself trying to learn a thing or two from him about how to keep a straight face, but so far the man had cleaned him out every time they played poker.

"Since Houston and Huntsville haven't given me the courtesy of a briefing, why don't you two fill me in. Normally I'd give them a call and tear up some butts for letting me get on the air without knowing as much as the reporter, but let's save some time."

The two astronauts and cosmonaut drifted together and pulled themselves into a compartment known as the Destiny module, the research section constructed by the United States. They were away from the camera that had been broadcasting, and it had been turned off, but they spoke in low, almost secretive tones.

Natalia handed Adam a printout. A quick glance showed him what he had already learned, and it made him resent even more that he'd heard it first from a reporter.

"Don't be too hard on ground control," said Henry. "It came across the printer literally seconds before you started the interview."

"But she had it already," snapped Adam. He regretted taking it out on Henry, but he was right. If they had time to give it to a reporter in Canada, they had time to stop the broadcast.

He saw that the report said multiple launch personnel had been attacked, and that the launches had been scrubbed while the crews were sitting on the launchpad. The two rockets were scheduled to launch only minutes apart, each one carrying half of the large crew that was to occupy the ISS.

"Well, it could've been worse," said Adam. "It could've been the resupply mission that had been scrubbed. That would have left us with a crew of six and no food. At least we got the food and sent the others back with the resupply capsule."

He was right. They had been lucky. They had been operating with a crew of six people for months on about eight tons of food, and the plan had been to increase the crew for some major experiments. More countries were involved, and there were some lengthy spacewalks planned to repair satellites that had been big investments for contributing nations.

To get ready for the unprecedented lengthy stay of a crew of nine people, a private company had sent two unmanned resupply missions to the ISS. Twelve tons of food had been offloaded, and three members of their crew had hitched a ride home in the second resupply capsule after helping to offload and store the supplies. The other was still docked at one of the airlocks. It had been hailed for the cooperation of so many countries and private industry as the future of space travel, but as it stood the unintended result was enough food for three people to last a very long time without another resupply mission. They weren't going to have visitors for a while, but that was just a delay, not a problem.

Adam knew they all understood the math, but he asked anyway. "We got twelve tons, right?"

Natalia picked up where he left off. "We only need four tons at full rations to last six months. If we want to be safe, we could go to half rations now, and we could live a year just on a third of the supplies."

Henry finished the thought. "We could survive three years at half rations without being resupplied." The stoic face of the Briton didn't give away a clue that an additional three years in space would be difficult.

They nodded agreement and felt fine with the idea of going to half rations even before talking with Houston because the likelihood was that they wouldn't need to survive three years anyway. They needed to conserve their food supplies because the delay in the combined program was going to shorten that mission. The longer they lasted on half rations, the longer they could extend the combined mission once it finally got off the ground.

"Okay," said Adam, "let's get Houston on the line and find out what's going on."

"What about your Canadian admirer?" asked Natalia.

"She's yelling at her producer about dead air right now. I can talk with her again when she's in a better mood."

The three crew members used handholds and closed equipment panels to pull themselves through the Harmony module into Columbus. Natalia settled in at a communications terminal and checked the time in Houston. It was 10:00 AM, so they should have enough caffeine in their systems to be able to deal with three space jockeys with attitudes. As soon as she tried to get Houston online, an unfamiliar voice came through the speaker and identified the location as Huntsville, Alabama. It was the Marshall Space Flight Center, and although they were always monitoring communications, they wouldn't reply for Houston unless something had gone wrong. Natalia acknowledged the contact and turned the call over to Adam.

"Ground Control, would you mind not letting me hear about a change in mission planning from a reporter?" Adam didn't feel like exchanging pleasantries with whoever it was that had dropped the ball.

"Uhhh, good morning Commander. I apologize for the lapse in protocol."

Adam didn't recognize the face or voice of the young lady who nervously adjusted her microphone. "This is Commander Callaway, who's this?"

"This is Gentry, sir." The young flight control specialist sounded uncertain about what to say next, but before Adam could help her, she added, "We seem to be short on personnel, sir. There were a lot of people who didn't make it in today, but we didn't expect to lose contact with Houston either."

Now it was Adam who was at a loss for words. A normal call into ground control was often friendly with smart comments that were intended to make everyone feel the human connection, but this gave him the feeling that no one was in charge in the one place where someone had better be. Instead, he was wondering how old this kid was on his monitor.

"Commander?" The young lady thought they had been disconnected because he didn't move for so long.

"I'm here, Gentry. Take a deep breath and then tell me what's going on down there. Let's start with your name. Is Gentry your first or last name?"

The Control Center had almost a hundred work consoles manned around the clock, but he could see only empty seats surrounding the new face on his screen. They had two birds on the launch pads only minutes ago, so they should have a full house in the United States nerve centers at Houston and Huntsville. The same number would be at their stations in Baikonur. Gentry seemed ready to cry at any moment, and Natalia placed a hand on Adam's shoulder. When he faced her, she gave a barely perceptible head shake, and he met her eyes just long enough for her to know he understood.

"It's okay, Gentry. We've already heard from a Canadian news source that the launches were scrubbed, so we can wait a minute with the details." New people talking with the ISS crew wasn't unusual, and sometimes the impact on them was like meeting a celebrity, but this was different.

"Thank you, sir." She sounded better, but her voice was still shaky.

"Gentry is my first name, and my last name is Campbell. My parents went back and forth between Houston and Huntsville all the time with the Space Program, and they're big country music fans, so Bobbie Gentry and Glen Campbell. I have a brother named Glen. They started having kids kind of late, but they're also stuck in the sixties when it comes to music."

She was rambling, and Natalia gave Adam's shoulder another light squeeze to remind him to be patient. Obviously, something was happening down there that was making her more nervous than she would have been if she had been drafted into service on a normal day.

"It's nice to meet you, Gentry. Is your family okay?"

Just when Natalia thought she had gotten her attraction for the Commander under control, she had to push back a sudden rush of warmth that she was sure would show up on her biomedical recordings. She made a mental note to talk with the Flight Surgeon before he said something about it.

"Handsome and sensitive in one place," she mumbled just below a whisper as she turned away from where she was floating near the Commander.

Adam thought she was talking to him and turned with her, but she busied herself with readings on a panel behind him. When he turned back to Gentry, she had her forehead resting on the palm of her hand and her elbow propped on the workstation desk. He saw she was doing everything she could to keep from crying. She seemed barely old enough to be working in a NASA facility, and her brown hair didn't hide enough of her face for him to see her red eyes.

"Commander, I'm switching your camera feed to the whole control center so you can see why you got stuck with someone who really didn't expect to be talking with you today."

Adam started to say that it wasn't necessary and to reassure her, but she switched the feed before he could say it. On his monitor the view was from the back of the control center. It was like standing up in the back row of a theater that wasn't showing a movie.

"Where is everybody?" asked Henry.

He had drifted over to Adam's other shoulder while Natalia returned to where she had been. The three of them all had the same slack-jawed expression. There were supposed to be launches today, and the crews were likely still sitting on top of their launch vehicles, but there was no contact with the main ground control center, and the backup control center was almost empty. Most of the consoles were dark, but the big screens on the front walls showed the status of ISS. One showed twin gantries on a dark background in Baikonur where the Russians appeared ready to send the crews into outer space. The sun had already set, and the gantry lights illuminated everything, but there was no movement near the launch pads.

Gentry switched back to her console view. "As you can see, things aren't going so well here, and to answer your question, I don't know about my family, sir. I can't get anyone to answer their phones. When people didn't show up for work, we started calling them immediately, and the ones who answered said they were on their way. Some of them eventually showed up, but most haven't."

"Gentry, this is Natalia Lebedev. Has the Flight Director scrubbed the launches, or has he just put the countdowns on hold?" It was the question on all three of their minds, but it seemed harsh to even utter the words when she considered the young flight controller didn't know about the safety of her family.

Gentry cleared her throat. "He's one of the people we haven't heard from yet."

They were all silent for a full minute that felt far longer than sixty-seconds. Gentry was waiting for them to tell her what to do, and they were each prioritizing what needed to be said next. As professionals, they were sorting through their thoughts, filing some away for later and pushing some toward the front. Lebedev and Tisdal would wait for their Commander to speak first.

"Okay, Gentry. Let's do this by the book. As much as I'd like to know what's happening in Baikonur, that's for someone else to deal with, and I get the impression you're not able to deal with that problem either."

Gentry was nodding as Adam spoke. She composed herself and listened intently for him to tell her what to do.

"The first thing we need to do is ensure your safety. How many security guards are there, and while we're at it, how many ground control people?"

Before she could answer, Adam surprised her by interrupting. "Forget doing a headcount. Gentry, I want you to get everyone you can into the control center. Bring the security guards inside too, then lock the doors just as if there was an active shooter event in progress. You've had the training. As soon as you're all secure, gather the most senior people with you at your console. We'll be waiting to talk with you then."

Gentry disappeared and Adam floated around to face Natalia and Henry.

"What are you thinking?" asked Natalia. "I could accept a problem at one location, but all three at the same time?"

"Whatever stopped the launches, it had to be bad, and with no Flight Director NASA isn't sending the rest of the crew up to join us," said Adam.

"I've run the numbers already," said Henry, "and that kind of delay after fueling the boosters is going to create an even longer delay before the boosters can be fueled again. They have to drain them and then pass all of the quality control tests before they can be refueled. We're already looking at two weeks because they've been on hold for hours."

"How did they even prepare for launch at the Cosmodrome without people in the flight control center in Houston?" asked Natalia. "Wait, don't bother to answer that. The flight control center at Baikonur must have started without them and figured they could do a handoff in time. Maybe we should be talking to them instead of this poor girl in Huntsville."

"I agree," said Adam, "but why haven't we heard from them? Let's see what communications she's had with them."

Adam turned back to the monitor to find they were waiting for him. Gentry was surrounded by a handful of people. Two uniformed men filled the view behind the small group of technicians.

"That's everyone in Flight Control?" He wished he had been able to hide his reaction a little better, but it was too late. "Did you lock the doors?"

"The doors are locked, Commander, and Mitch says there were some people outside that didn't look like they belong here." Gentry turned to indicate one of the guards as she spoke. He nodded at the monitor and wanted to add something, so she let him squeeze in front of her. He was middle aged and balding with a mustache.

"Hello Commander, it's an honor to talk with you, sir."

Adam didn't mind being a celebrity when someone recognized him out in public, but he always felt uncomfortable when it happened at work, and he wished he could be the kind of person who told someone to get to the point.

"Thank you, Mitch. What can I do for you?"

"Something bad's happening outside, Commander. There's a crowd of people that never should have gotten past security at the front gate, and they look sick like those people on TV."

"Are you saying the Flight Control Center isn't secure?"

Adam was piecing it together a little faster than Mitch and apparently faster than the others in the room too. No one was coming up to join them at the ISS, and there was no one who could man Flight Control to coordinate the effort to bring someone back to Earth. It wasn't as simple as just loading up and taking aim at the recovery area. They would need their telemetry or they might come in at the wrong angle. Too shallow, and they would bounce off the atmosphere and head for deep space. Too steep, and they would burn up from the heat generated by the friction.

"Yes, sir. That's what I'm saying. I have Ivan in here to help me, but the rest of security is out there." He gestured toward the other guard who was dressed like him.

Just as the words came out of his mouth Mitch and the others were startled by something happening at one of the doors they had locked only moments earlier. The two guards disappeared from view in the direction of the door, and the technicians all watched something Adam couldn't see.

The last thing the ISS crew members expected to hear was what Gentry yelled next, and it was followed by the unmistakable sound of shots being fired.

"Don't open the door! Don't let them in!"

******

The crew of ISS was forgotten as people pushed each other out of the way. They instinctively leaned closer to the monitor display and searched for Gentry in the sudden flurry of movement. The view switched back to the one Gentry had shown them earlier, and they could tell she was reacting much faster than the other people in the room around her.

She had apparently anticipated that they would want to see what was happening beyond her terminal, but more importantly she had a better grasp on the problem than her peers. They could see her withdrawing her hand from the console where she had just punched the button that switched their camera view, and in a smooth motion that underscored her athletic abilities, she threw herself over the terminal behind hers in a direction that carried her straight toward the steps that went upward to the visitors' gallery. The glass walls of the gallery were well above the floor, so no one could see her from the control center, but even better was the fact that the door could be locked from the other side.

Gentry was followed by a half dozen other people who for one reason or another figured they were safer with her. It was probably because she had been talking with the crew of the ISS, and that had given her some rock star status in their minds. They had no idea that when she had started her day at five o'clock, it was her third day in the backup ground control. She was so excited to be close to one of the nerve centers of the International Space Station even if she was still learning her job duties. She had been hired to monitor the communications and verify recorded data at key moments. It was redundant and below her level of skill, but it was where she wanted to be.

Over on the other side of Ground Control, it wasn't going well for the security guards and the four technicians who had followed them to the doors. The hallway was one of the most secure areas in the building outside of the room, and they assumed they were going to the rescue of the security guards on duty there because their distinctive shirts were visible in the crowd that was mashed up against the glass panels of the doors.

Mitch got to the doors before the others, and he recognized his fellow security staff members being pushed and shoved. Someone was pressed against the glass as he reached for the lock, and he saw it was Charlie Perkins, the man who just last week stood next to him at his daughter's wedding. Charlie was like her uncle, and he needed help. Nothing could have stopped Mitch from unlocking that door.

The door opened outward, and there was so much weight pressed against it that it was being held shut. Even if it had been unlocked, it would have remained shut because no one was pulling on it. No one heard Gentry's warning, and Mitch put all of his weight against it and pushed. They all pushed, and they felt the weight on the other side give a little. A gap appeared at the edge of the door, then six inches. Hands appeared along the rim, pulling as Mitch and his band of rescuers pushed.

Gentry and her followers didn't turn around when Mitch screamed. Unlike the people who ran toward the fight, their self-preservation instincts were greater than their desire to fight. Gentry held the door for each of them and then stepped inside before reaching down to twist the latch. She consciously fixed her eyes on the lock and then on all the glass that surrounded it. The door obviously couldn't be counted on as anything more than a first line of defense.

"Everybody listen," she yelled in a higher voice that she didn't recognize as her own. The others weren't that far away, but they were huddled together in a small group as if some kind of herd mentality had gripped them. She absently wondered about five of them being men, but the Control Center had never completely let go of the gender mentality that had dominated the early years of the Space Program.

"This door might not hold, and someone go check the other exit. Make sure it's locked, and then start blocking this door with anything that moves."

The group spread out and went to work, and the good news was that the second exit was a solid door in the back that was already locked, but the bad news was discovered just as quickly. The seats in the observation area were fastened to the floor like the rows in a theatre.

One of the men positioned himself against the back wall and used it for leverage. He managed to get both feet up on the back of a chair and pushed until the metal frame of the seat groaned in protest.

"Give me a hand over here," he yelled.

Working together in a row, four of them lined up and pushed with their feet. The seats broke away from their supports, and in a minute they were stacking broken chairs against the glass. The cushions of the chairs created an effective screen that covered the glass well enough to block the view from the other side.

"Everybody get down where no one can see us," whispered Gentry, her voice much lower than before.

The situation inside Ground Control grew even worse. When Mitch screamed, the pushing against the door from the inside stopped, and without the resistance from inside the force from the outside caused it to slam shut…with Mitch's arms extended through the opening. It would have been a second scream, but the first one had never stopped because he was face to face with Charlie Perkins. Mitch's old friend was viciously tearing away three of his fingers with his teeth.

Somehow the group of men gave one push on the door and a big pull on Mitch at the same time. Everyone fell backward into a pile and over the first row of workstations, with two of them trying to cushion Mitch's fall. The door slammed shut on fingers that either fell to the floor or remained where they were. Mitch reached for them as if he thought they might be his.

"Someone bit me," said one of the technicians who was separating himself from the tangle of men who had fallen together. "Me too," said a second one. "What's wrong with those people?"

"I don't know, but help me with Mitch. Someone really tore him up." One of them pulled his shirt over his head and wrapped it around Mitch's shredded hand. He was losing far less blood than he appeared to be, but the pale color of his face was a clear indication that he would be in shock soon if he wasn't already there.

The scramble on the other side of the door intensified, and someone was actually turning the doorknob. A face appeared briefly on the glass pane. There was so much blood smeared across the person and the glass that it was hard to tell if it was a man or a woman, but it was easy to tell they were yelling for help. The face disappeared, and for a few moments there was no pressure on the door as the mob in the hallway focused its attention on the person who had tried to get inside.

During those few moments of relative quiet, the small group of men sat in a half-circle around Mitch and watched the door as if they had gotten a reprieve. They learned soon enough that it was more like a stay of execution than a reprieve.

The door was made to withstand a fire, and the small pane of glass was reinforced with wire mesh. Across the inside was a panic bar so occupants could exit quickly if there was a fire, but by special order from the Director of NASA, the door had been fitted with a standard lock that had one purpose. In the event of an anomaly, the door would be physically locked so all evidence could be preserved. The anomaly that was anticipated was a launchpad disaster. Since the planned launches were still sitting on the pads, there had been no official order to lock the door.

The saving grace, if there was such a thing outside the door, was that the knob was round. If it had been a lever type handle, it would have been pushed downward even if totally by accident. It had turned for a moment when the unfortunate person tried to get through the crowd, but it hadn't moved since. Mitch had passed out, but the remaining security guard threw himself at the door and activated the lock. It couldn't be unlocked again from the outside.

When he returned to Mitch's side, he slipped the unconscious man's service pistol from its holster. It was a Smith & Wesson nine millimeter, so he ejected the magazine to see how many rounds it held. He was glad to see it was the full-sized magazine, so he had about seventeen rounds plus his own Glock. The others had all bravely followed when they went to the door, but when he held the pistol out to them, they all shook their heads. None of them had any idea of how to use it.

"It's not rocket science, and you guys are rocket scientists," he said. "I'll show you how to use it. All you have to do is point and shoot."

They eyed the gun like it was more dangerous than the people in the hallway, but one of them finally agreed to take it. Ivan showed him how to flip the safety off, but he left it on for the time being, feeling like there was a distinct possibility of getting shot in the back before the day was over. He took a moment to rack a round and showed the man one more time how to flip the safety. He could tell the man was surprised by the weight of the gun because he almost dropped it, and within seconds he found himself moving left and right as the man tried to get comfortable holding it.

"Okay," he said. "Two rules to follow. Don't put your finger inside the trigger guard until you're ready to shoot, and never point it in the direction of people even if you know it's not loaded."

The man nodded, realizing where it was pointed. "It's loaded now, right?"

Ivan told him everything again and noticed the other three technicians were watching closely. He knew they were smart and had jobs he couldn't do, but right now he wished he had been stranded in the room where the cleaning crew usually hung out. They didn't know squat about telemetry, but he bet they knew how to fire a semiautomatic pistol.

3

Stranded

International Space Station - The Beginning of the Infection

"Ground Control, come in please. What's your situation? We heard something happening there. It sounded like gunfire. Is Gentry still in the Control Room? Hello, Ground Control, come in please."

Adam's voice had been coming over the speaker at the workstation the entire time. When Gentry had switched the view so the crew could see what was happening in the whole control room, they had seen everyone scatter and heard the unmistakable pops, but something caused the camera to change back to show just the workstation. The noise from the hallway was still loud enough to drown him out, and it took a few minutes for the men to realize the voice was coming from inside the Control Room with them.

One of the technicians who had been helping to get Mitch's head situated on a cushion finally heard the Commander over the noise. He eyed the pistol in the other technician's hands as he got to his feet and went to the terminal. Oddly, he felt safer once he had some distance between him and his friend.

"Commander Callaway, this is Ground Control. You're still there. I'm sorry. I'm not really sure where Ms. Campbell went. We have a problem here."

"That appears to be an understatement. What was the commotion? Better yet, Ground Control. Start at the beginning. Who's in charge there and what is the status of the launches?"

"Ms. Campbell is the senior person here, Commander, but I think she went up to the gallery. Sir, we don't know what's happening. We have one man badly injured, several of us were bitten, and it appears there may be some dead in the hallway outside control."

To the ISS crew, every answer just added to the questions. Where was everybody? There should be close to one hundred people in Ground Control. Why were the launches on hold at the Cosmodrome? Who was injured and why? Several of them had been bitten? Dead people were in the hallway? Adam wasn't sure the technician knew where to start, because he certainly didn't start at the beginning.

The face of a different technician appeared on the screen. All three ISS crew members wondered why he had a semiautomatic pistol in his right hand, but even more importantly, he was gesturing with it as he spoke as if he was holding a laser pointer.

"We were already here this morning because ten of us were on the night shift, Commander. I'm Ford, sir. We spoke last night when we verified some telemetry from Houston. Anyway, we were here but never got relieved. Our relief never showed up. On the news they're saying stay home because the attacks increased. Someone in Baikonur didn't get the message I guess, and they prepared for launch, but we haven't been able to establish communications with them or Houston, so there's been no transfer of data."

Henry Tisdal said, "Ford, we haven't been able to raise the Russian Ground Control at all, but why do you have a gun. What's happening there? Where's Gentry?"

Ford held the gun up where everyone could see it. He regarded the black metal in his hand as if he didn't remember why he was holding it, and he turned his head in a slow circle as he tried to see where Gentry had gone. His eyes passed by the door to the gallery because from his angle he couldn't see that anyone had gone into the room reserved for guests. His eyes settled on the door to the hallway and all of the smeared blood on the frame. Two fingers still protruded from high up along the gap between the door and the frame, and a new face was pressed against the glass.

Adam thought Ford wasn't going to answer him and was just about to say more when the camera angle changed. Ford had decided to show the ISS crew rather than tell them.

In orbit above the Earth, the crew sat silently staring at the monitor. All three had their mouths hanging open, and no one spoke. The scene before their eyes didn't make sense. Eventually, Natalia just said one word. "No."

Henry asked the obvious question first. "Are those fingers?"

Ford said, "Yes, there were more of them a few minutes ago. I think they fell off."

"Ford, this is Natalia Lebedev. Do you think you could establish communications with Baikonur? They should be monitoring the crews on the launchpads and your communications with us, but they have not given any indication they are trying to speak with us. One other thing, Ford. You haven't answered the question about the gun. Where did you get it, and why do you need it? Are you all right?"

"I gave it to him," said Ivan. "I'm one of the security guards, Ma'am. It belongs to my partner, Mitch, but he got hurt when we opened the door."

"Hurt? I'm sorry if I don't understand, Ivan. How did he get hurt?" Natalia shook her head at her companions. She wasn't doing any better than they had.

"When we opened the door for one of the guards in the hallway, he bit three of Mitch's fingers off. Mitch is unconscious, so I gave his gun to Mr. Ford. I don't think Mitch is going to be able to shoot a gun again anyway."

"He must be in shock," whispered Henry.

Ivan continued, "We pulled the door shut, but Mitch passed out. One of your technicians got bit, and so did I, but we're okay. Hurts a lot, but we have a first aid kit." He held up a bare arm and showed them what was clearly the imprint of two rows of human teeth. One of the technicians behind him was wrapping a piece of gauze with a bandage. Even as they watched, the man leaned over and laid his head on a rolled up jacket. Large beads of sweat left trails on his face as they dripped from him.

"Ivan, stay with me a minute," said Adam. "You're saying you, the other security guard, and one technician were bitten. There's a second group of technicians. You think Gentry Campbell is with them, and they're holed up in the gallery."

"That sums it up, Commander."

"Can you get someone to check on them for me?"

Ivan no sooner nodded at him when one of the technicians called out that he was on his way. He was already going up the steps along the side of the main floor to the gallery. Mitch chose that moment to have a seizure, and the crew of the ISS was forgotten again as the group around the work station had to put their combined weight on him to hold him still. An eerie sound escaped from him that didn't sound human.

Natalia called out to Ivan repeatedly asking for him to tell them what was happening, but it was clear that he had his hands full. The astronauts knew they were busy, but the noise level outside in the hallway seemed to get even louder when Mitch made a sound that went from a higher pitch scream down to a loud groan.

The technician who had gone to the top of the stairs on the opposite side of the control room stopped a few steps short of the door. He watched as the others wrestled to hold Mitch still, but he had a vague feeling like Mitch wasn't Mitch anymore. His eyes moved back and forth from Mitch to the door they had just locked. The sounds from the other side of that door were strikingly similar to the sounds coming from Mitch.

From inside the gallery they saw the technician coming, and they tugged and pulled at the pile of broken furniture they had stacked in front of the door. He heard the scraping sounds and turned away from the wrestling match on the floor just as a gap appeared at the door.

"What happened to Mitch?"

Gentry could only get one hand through the door, and she couldn't see all of the technician, but she had a good view of the work station she had used to talk with the ISS, and during the moment she had glanced away, people had changed positions. Somehow, Mitch had gotten on top of Ivan.

Ivan had his arms extended as far as he could, and he was holding Mitch's throat. Mitch was dripping blood from his mouth onto Ivan's face, and the first thing she thought was that Mitch was hurt. Then she saw a chunk of something fall out of his mouth, and there was no mistaking that he was snapping at Ivan's arm. The bleeding gash in his arm was ragged, and the whiteness of the bone stood out in stark contrast to the red blood.

Gentry joined the others pulling the furniture away from the door to let the technician inside. As soon as the door was open far enough, he squeezed through and pushed it shut behind him. He grabbed a heavy row of chairs and practically carried them back to where they had been without any help.

"Wait. What are you doing? What about the others? We have to get them in too," screamed Gentry.

To her surprise, the rest of the people inside the gallery joined in with the man to barricade the door. It virtually disappeared under furniture in seconds, which was about the same amount of time it had taken for the remaining three technicians to break free from the tangled arms and legs of Mitch and Ivan. Once free they had slipped and fallen several times in all the blood that flowed from open wounds. They eventually reached the steps and ran up to the gallery door. Mitch and Ivan followed close behind them, but at a slower, lumbering pace. They didn't slip or fall, but they could only navigate the steps with obvious effort.

"Let us in," pleaded the frantic technicians. "Mitch killed Ivan. He bit off a piece of his arm and I think he ate it."

The words seemed to echo in the room as the people inside repeated them to each other. It was as if they had to confirm what they had heard, but even as they spoke they remained where they were, not attempting to remove the barricade for a second time. The men outside pounded their fists and rammed their shoulders against the unyielding door. One of the now crying men drew back his foot and kicked so hard at the lock that he fell backward onto the carpeted steps and barrel-rolled almost to the feet of the approaching security guards. They fell on the man before he could get away, and his screams pierced the walls of the viewing gallery.

Gentry felt the warm flow of liquid on her legs and absently thought it was bad timing for her to have her period, but then she saw she had released the contents of her bladder. She made a mental note of it, but she felt strangely unconcerned. Any combat medic would have told her she didn't need to be physically wounded to go into shock. She and the others inside the gallery slowly backed away from the barricade, putting distance between themselves and the screaming.

From where they were they could still hear the pounding and the curses coming from the men at the door, but they didn't have to witness what they knew was inevitable. They also wouldn't be able to watch it happen because their view of the control room was limited to the massive wall of monitors showing different locations and data associated with the forgotten launches of the large crews in Baikonur, Kazakhstan. Gentry's eyes fell on a screen she had ignored earlier because she had her own screen on the terminal where she had talked with the crew of the ISS. Their faces were closer to the monitor on their end as if it would somehow give them a better look at what was happening in the Huntsville Mission Control Center. She watched their mouths moving as they shouted, not hearing them but so focused on what they were shouting that it somehow allowed her to block out the real sounds on the other side of the door. The shouted curses and thuds of the fists stopped.

For a moment she wondered if it was over. She glanced at the people who had run with her to the safety of the visitors' gallery, and she saw that the technician who had joined them moments before was on his knees with his face buried in his hands. The others were loosely grouped behind him but still on their feet. It was while she was watching their silent expressions mixed with hope and fear when the screaming filled the brief moment of silence.

The thuds were different because they weren't the sounds of fists pounding or feet kicking. Bodies were falling against the door on the other side because there was nowhere else to go. The men had their backs against the door and their arms extended toward their attackers. The difference between the two groups was the way the attackers bit at the fingers of their victims and far too often closed their teeth on them.

It reached a fever pitch only a few minutes after it began, but to the people inside it seemed to go on forever. When the fighting stopped, there was another sound that was muted compared to the screaming, but it was vaguely familiar. Gentry turned at the waist and raised one finger to her lips. With the exception of the man they had let in, everyone nodded their understanding. The man was still on his knees, but he was staring at the floor.

Gentry moved quietly to the right side of the barricade and got as close as she could to the glass without giving away her position to anyone outside. The workstations in the last row by the stairs blocked her view, so she had to lean further than she wanted. At first she thought the stairway was empty because no one was standing there. Then she saw why.

There was a crowd of people below the workstations on the stairs, and they were moving. One man in a security uniform sat upright, and his milky white eyes were pointed straight at her. He opened his bloody mouth, and Gentry felt something leave her stomach and force its way into her own mouth as she threw up against the glass. Before she doubled over in spasms she saw the man stand up and walk toward her, immediately falling over the bodies on the floor.

Behind her there was a commotion as her fellow survivors reacted to her. The woman wasn't the only one who was crying. Two of the five men wept openly. She wiped a sleeve across her mouth as she hurried away from the window, and the thuds on the door began again. This time no one was yelling from the other side to let them in, and the noise wasn't as coordinated. As she joined the group still huddled together as if it would be safer, they all backed away from the door. Everyone except the man on his knees. He was sitting back with his weight resting on his legs, but his head hung forward as if it had become too heavy for his neck. Gentry thought she saw his hands twitch, and she saw that one of them had a ragged cut across it. The skin by the cut was oddly shaped like a big flap that had been lifted then laid back down.

His head came up slowly as he leaned forward and put his hands flat to the floor. He struggled like someone who had gotten too old to get up from the floor without help, but he eventually got his right foot under him. Gentry thought he was going to fall over onto his side because there didn't appear to be any strength left in his body, but she didn't make a move to help him. She wasn't sure why, but she backed away even further.

Everyone except the woman backed up with her and the men. Out of reflex she moved quickly to catch the man from behind, and she wrapped her arms tightly around his waist. What followed was something resembling a bizarre ritualistic dance as they moved away from Gentry and the men.

They took several steps forward as the woman tried to keep herself upright, but she wasn't releasing her grip on the man, and he appeared to be holding onto her arms in front of his body. As they fell forward she screamed louder than Gentry thought possible. The scream galvanized the group of men, and they rushed forward to help their fellow technician. Gentry's legs and feet felt too cold to move. Numbness made her stay right where she was as a grain of understanding grew in her mind.

Five men pulled at the woman's arms, and they weren't able to get her to let go of the man's waist. They didn't break apart until all seven bodies fell forward into the barricade of gallery seats. It was so sudden that most of them couldn't avoid the tangle of metal legs on the chairs that stuck outward in all different directions. Faces fell forcefully against sharp metal. Blood erupted as skin tore, noses were broken, and teeth were knocked loose. A chorus of moans replaced the shouting that had started as they first wrestled then fell. The woman was sobbing as her arms pulled free, and she held them in front of her face trying to make sense of the mess they had become. Both hands were torn and shredded.

Gentry was the only person in the room who wasn't bleeding, and her numb legs felt like they belonged in one of those nightmares where she would try to run but wasn't able to. They only let her back up until she reached the wall behind her. Once she was there, she slid along the wall for support, and she slowly increased the distance between herself and the bleeding crowd lying at odd angles on the furniture and the floor. The whole time she kept her eyes fixed on them, and her mind sorted out the reality of her situation. She realized she was inside the room with something that was going to kill her.

Six dazed and confused people pulled themselves apart from each other. The young lady with the damaged hands was still trying to make sense of her injuries. The man she had tried to help was face down on the pile of furniture. She could see that he was twisting his body from side to side in an attempt to pull himself free of a metal chair leg that had impaled him. Her hands didn't make sense, but she was more interested in the way the leg of the chair protruded from the man's back. She turned at the hips and saw Gentry across the room. She held her hands out toward Gentry. There was nothing Gentry could do to help her, but her pleading eyes locked on Gentry's. Gentry's eyes were fixed on a place over the young woman's shoulder where a man who had fallen with the woman had pulled himself free of the others. One arm had become dislocated at the shoulder, and it twitched to the right and the left as he attempted to reach for the woman's hair.

Gentry wanted to warn her, but the words wouldn't come out, and as she watched in paralyzed fear, the twitching hand found its target. It wasn't that the man grabbed her hair as much as he got tangled in it as she fell to her back. As soon as she felt something there, she tried to pull away, but the man just followed her down to the floor. Her screams momentarily got a reaction from the others who had fallen with her, but the impaled man had captured a leg by the ankle and pulled it toward his face. Blood erupted as another scream pierced Gentry's ears, and attempts to help the woman turned into attempts to escape.

She couldn't watch, and her hand somehow found the handle on the door of the other exit from the gallery. It never crossed her mind what was on the other side of the door. Whether it was a closet or a hallway, she didn't know or care, and to her a door was just a way to be free of the terrible scene that had unfolded right before her eyes. If the door was a hallway she could leave. If it was a closet, she would hide.

It was the hallway that was reserved for the private use of the Director and his guests. It was deserted today, undoubtedly because the Director and the people he would have accompanied to the gallery didn't even make it to the gates of the Marshall Space Flight Center. Gentry had never been in the hallway herself, and she didn't even know where the exits were. Worse yet, she didn't know what was happening outside or if she should even leave the building.

The hallway was windowless and curved away to the left and right. The carpeted floor absorbed every sound, and she couldn't hear noises coming from anywhere. Her breathing was ragged and sounded loud in her own ears, but as she got herself under control, the silence of the hallway closed in on her. She reasoned that since her back was to the gallery, the hallway to the left would take her toward the main corridor that went to the entrance of Ground Control and toward the front entrance of the Marshall Space Flight Center. From what she had seen, that wasn't where she wanted to be. The hallway to the right was unknown, but that seemed like a better choice.

Gentry wasn't consciously aware that she had made a decision or that she stretched her legs into an easy run. She ran right by an elevator door and had to come back to it to read the small plaque above the buttons. She had guessed right. It said the elevator was private and reserved for the Director. Her finger hovered over the button for just a moment until she realized there was no reason to push it. A small part of her made Gentry feel like she still had a job to do, and she considered going to the Director's office to tell him about the situation. He would want to know that the launches from Baikonur had not been made on schedule, and he would want to know that Houston hadn't handed off the launches to Huntsville. She told that small part of herself the Director could find out from someone else if he didn't already know.

She dropped her hand from the button and jogged down the hallway in one motion. If that was the elevator to the Director's office, then the hallway had to be the road to his private parking space. The slight downward slant of the floor led her to believe she would come to the secure parking garage under the building, and if she was lucky at all, she would find security forces had things under control.

The Marshall Space Flight Center sat along the perimeter of the Army Base at Redstone Arsenal. It wasn't unusual to see a squad of military police manning the gates on days when launches were scheduled, and this day was about as big as a moon launch to NASA.

Up ahead she could see that the hallway ended at some kind of atrium. A security checkpoint separated the hallway from the atrium, but she didn't see anyone at the guard's desk. A metal detector was on, and as she stepped through it, the light switched from green to red. She was so used to following the rules that she stepped back through it.

"What am I doing?" she asked herself out loud.

She gave the empty guard post an angry glare as if it had something to do with her stopping and turned toward the door at the middle of the atrium. When she pushed through the closed double doors, she felt like she was in an underground concrete bunker. It was brightly lit, and the only sounds were the echoes made by her footsteps. When she stopped, they went on for a couple of seconds and then faded away. It was quieter than the carpeted hallway, and she honestly didn't know which way to go in order to reach the gates to the outside.

The Director's parking space had a car in it that bore a US government tag and the NASA symbol. She had expected the space to be empty, and for just one moment she pictured the Director exiting the elevator and walking to the gallery. He would open the door and walk inside expecting to see Ground Control buzzing like a beehive. A few privileged visitors would be watching from the gallery, and they would stand when he entered the room. That sense of duty reared its head again, and she almost gave in. If she went back and saved his life, she would have done a good thing, but if he was in his office, he would already know something had gone wrong.

For a second time, she made the decision not to listen to that voice, and she passed by the car to the ramp that she guessed would lead to ground level. The soles of her shoes tapped on the concrete, and she felt the pressure on her shins as the pavement sloped upward and spiraled to her right. She came to a steel door across the entrance and wondered if it was operated by a remote in the Director's car, but then she saw the smaller door to the right side. It had a standard panic bar that was probably required by local fire codes. She ran straight to it and leaned down on the metal bar.

She didn't expect that much sunlight, and it blinded her. It was a good thing because her sudden stop saved her from running out into the middle of a desperate battle inside the security gates. The Army and NASA security personnel were shooting literally anyone that surprised them because the battle was all around them. There were people like the ones she had seen inside, like Mitch and Ivan who were biting people. From what Gentry could see, the ones who had gone crazy and were trying to bite people seemed to know who had not been bitten yet. She could tell which ones they were because they were the ones that were screaming for help. The ones that were crazy weren't screaming or running.

She saw that they didn't run, they didn't scream, and they didn't panic. They weren't yelling for help, and they weren't afraid of the guns that fired almost continuously. The sharp blasts had already overloaded her eardrums within the first minute after the door closed behind her. She could still hear them, but there was a constant high pitched ringing that drowned out everything else, including the voices that were yelling at her to go back inside.

A soldier turned in her direction and raised an M4. She put up her hands to defend herself, but she was far too late. The bullet passed by her cheek so closely that she felt its heat, and her hand came back to the spot out of reflex. The woman behind her was hit in the middle of her throat. She was knocked off her feet between Gentry and the door and landed on her back. There was blood……lots of blood, and the neck wound was too much for the carotid artery to be missed. Gentry felt its warmth where it splashed against the back of her hand.

She was torn between the soldier and the woman and didn't understand how he decided to shoot one of them and not the other. She also didn't understand why the woman was trying so hard to get back on her feet. She should be dying.

The soldier shot the woman two more times across her chest, and each bullet pushed her back to the ground, but she still seemed almost unfazed. Gentry stood with her right hand on her cheek and her mouth hanging open as if she was in the middle of saying something and had been interrupted. In her professional charcoal gray pants suit, she could have been a supervisor watching someone's job performance for an evaluation, and she was amazed by what she was seeing. She turned toward the soldier, and his eyes came up to meet hers. They didn't need words to know they were asking each other the same question.

"Do you see that?"

The soldier raised his rifle again, and this time Gentry moved more or less in his direction to give him room to shoot. As the woman sat up straight on the pavement, the bullet hit her between both eyes. The 5.56 mm round left a neat hole that was deceptive considering the damage it would do to the inside of her head. It slapped her head backward on her shoulders and drove her to the pavement one final time. They shared another unspoken agreement that he wouldn't need to shoot her again, and there was an understanding as to the reason why the last shot worked. They both nodded with eyebrows raised.

Gentry found herself immediately drawn to the side of the soldier as he turned away from her to locate his next target. He put himself between her and the action that continued to swirl between them and the front gates of the Space Flight Center. At first she wondered how many had gotten through the gates before they could get them closed, but she saw so many wearing NASA identification cards clipped to their clothing that she understood they were already inside.

The soldiers from Redstone Arsenal moved as a unit and slowly gained the advantage over the mindless, disorganized mob. It was hard at first, but once they were able to work together, they saw the opportunity to take control. The soldier shielding Gentry called out to the others to aim for the head. He sounded like he was a mile away from her even though she was close enough to touch his back, but his friends spread the word. Gentry didn't realize it before because there was so much mayhem and chaos, but there were a lot more soldiers inside the secure area than she had thought at first. They formed into a broad wedge and drove forward, keeping her and a handful of NASA employees behind them. Gentry was more than happy to be behind them.

The parking lot outside the garage door for the Director was littered with bodies, and for the moment no one was coming toward the soldiers. A series of hand signals were passed along the line of the wedge, and they changed directions. Gentry was impressed by how they worked together with little more than a few waves. The wedge backed toward her and the other civilians, and it became apparent that they were withdrawing.

They were only about a hundred yards from the front gates that Gentry had never seen closed before. There was a large chainlink gate on wheels that had been rolled into place and locked shut. Behind them along the side of the big building where she worked there was another gate that she had never seen open. She could see that the soldiers were escorting them toward that gate.

Through the ringing in her ears she could hear someone say something, but she was surprised to discover he was talking to her. It was the soldier who had saved her once already, and even though she couldn't really hear all of what he said, she could tell he was asking for her name because he pointed at the ID she had clipped to the lapel of her blazer.

Her own voice sounded far away and she had to shout just to be able to hear herself.

"Gentry Campbell," she yelled. "What's yours?"

She felt a little stupid for asking because she had to lean toward his face and watch his lips to understand his answer. She wondered if he thought she was trying to kiss him.

"I'm Manuel Calvo, Ma'am. My friends call me MC."

Under all of his headgear and streaks of dirt across his face, she had missed his Latino features, but when she figured out what he said the well-tanned skin made sense to her. She saw a thick lock of black hair poking out from the edge of his helmet. She also couldn't miss his big smile.

"Pleased to meet you, MC. Thank you for saving me back there."

Gentry allowed herself to be ushered through the gate with everyone else, and she felt safer having someone with a gun sticking by her side. Beyond the fence were mounds of earth as tall as a house, and she thought they were berms that had been placed around the building to give a small amount of privacy to the Space Flight Center. She was surprised when they reached the end of one berm and saw there was a big door built into the side of it. As a matter of fact, the berms were in rows, and there were doors at the ends of each of them.

MC put his hand gently on the back of her arm and guided her toward the door along with everyone else. She couldn't think of anywhere she would rather be than with these soldiers inside a safe place. She assumed the berms were safe because the soldiers all visibly relaxed once they were inside.

There was something like an atrium just inside the door, followed by a second door. It reminded her of the big steel doors on walk-in freezers, but it must have been way heavier because it took two men to open it. When it was wide enough to go through, they were hustled inside where they descended a steep set of metal stairs that went deeper and deeper into the ground. It didn't go down in a circle or stop at landings. This thing just went down at an angle and kept going so long that her shins hurt by the time they reached the bottom.

The ceiling over the stairs was so low that she couldn't see too far ahead, but when they reached the bottom, the ceiling jumped from being reachable by hand to a height of at least fifteen feet. They were in a corridor that was made from stacks and stacks of supply crates.

"What is this place, MC?"

"For the time being, this is home," he answered.

4

Cold War

Marshall Space Flight Center - The Beginning of the Infection

Gentry tried to make sense of the corridors that snaked through the big room with the high ceilings. The lights were from hanging fluorescent strips high above her, and the stacks of crates cast shadows over them as she followed MC and the others. If she had to find her way back out on her own, she would be out of luck.

MC glanced back and flashed his big smile as he kept up with the squad and explained the strange place.

"Did you see that all the other berms had doors too?"

Before she could answer he continued, "Each berm is a shelter just like this one, but I hear they're all connected to each other. After World War II they were built to protect the scientists and their families. Since the Army brought all the German rocket scientists here to work on the space program, they wanted to protect them from an attack by the Russians. Everyone was paranoid about another war because they thought the Russians would try to take us all out before we could develop long-range missiles."

It didn't make sense to Gentry because there was no way they could have rounded up all the families in time if there had been a nuclear attack, but when she had time to think about it, it was all part of the Cold War paranoia, and it didn't need to make more sense than that. What did make sense was the fact that it all still existed. It made sense because she knew the government mentality. Money had been spent making the shelters, money had been spent stocking them, and the government had a hard time letting go of it. After all these years, the shelters would be used for something, even if it was only for a short time. She was amused to see that some of the crates had dates on them, and that the crates had been stacked inside the bunkers in 1951.

They reached the end of the maze formed by the supply crates and were led into a processing operation that had been set up in a hurry, but it was functioning like a Red Cross shelter. There were people getting personal information from the civilians, and there was a Sergeant who was checking off lists of names given to him by squad leaders. MC explained to her that they were figuring out who had made it and where to assign them.

"You're leaving already?"

Gentry didn't know anyone else in the rush of civilians and soldiers that were all being sorted out and sent in different directions, and having his friendly face nearby was comforting. A lot had happened in a very short time, and she didn't feel like facing it by herself.

MC saw her worried look, and he told her to wait where she was. He went over and talked with the Sergeant for a few minutes, and when he came back he was smiling from ear to ear.

"The Sarge said nothing's permanent down here yet because the squads got pretty split up. The area is secure up top, so he was okay with me staying assigned to this shelter. Let's see the housing quartermaster over there and see about getting you assigned to a room."

Gentry felt the gratitude wash over her and couldn't help giving MC her own best smile. He led her through the crowd to one of the tables set up along the wall and introduced her to a Corporal who was assigning the rooms. She was amazed at how efficient the operation was considering the fact that less than an hour earlier she was inside the Marshall Space Flight Center and running for her life. She was given a room key with a number on it and a stack of papers to fill out.

"Have everything back to me by sixteen hundred hours, and we can get you a seat in the mess hall," said the clerk. "The PX won't be operational for about seventy-two hours, so you'll have to get by with this." He handed her a cardboard box that was labeled, "Emergency Supply Rations - Adult Female."

When she walked away from the table with MC following close behind her, she stopped and took in everything that was happening around her.

"This is happening inside all of the berms, all of the shelters around this one?"

"Yes, Ma'am. Like I said, the Army kept these shelters operational, so you should find that you can get almost everything you need down here."

Gentry suddenly felt very tired, and all she wanted to do was get to her room, wherever that was. They found it down a quiet hallway, and she was surprised to find how nice it was. It was more like a cabin on a cruise ship than a room in a bunker. It was small but comfortable. Most of all, it was quiet. There was a small desktop that folded down from a wall, and she could sit on the bunk to fill out the paperwork. MC promised to come back by thirty minutes before the deadline so they could get supper together, and he slipped out to find the rest of his squad. When the door shut behind him, the silence was only broken by the ringing in her ears that still hadn't stopped.

Gentry sat the box on the small table and opened it. There was an assortment of toiletries, a couple of power bars, a paperback book, and a flashlight. She had to wonder about the person responsible for packing the box because the book was a romance novel, and there was a sewing kit wedged in between a pair of white sweat socks and a washcloth. A mental apology was in order when she read the label on the kit. A little red cross was embossed next to the words SUTURE KIT. Gentry surveyed her room and wondered what would happen next.

******

Feeling forgotten as they circled the Earth, the crew of the ISS spent hours just trying to make contact with someone who could tell them what was happening. They could bounce their signals from one satellite to another, so there were never times when communications were totally blacked out. That made the silence from below even more unbearable. They each focused on different locations rather than one installation. Natalia was calling out to the Cosmodrome at Baikonur because she could talk in her native tongue with anyone who answered even if they didn't speak English. She alternated between the primary spaceport and the headquarters in Moscow. When she couldn't raise anyone at Roscosmos, the Russian headquarters of the space program, the usually upbeat and positive Cosmonaut became tearful and frustrated. Her family lived in Moscow.

Henry Tisdal was from England, but he represented all of Europe as a member of the European Space Agency. With twenty-two member states, he had his hands full and had to work from a list. All of the centers should have been monitoring the delayed launches in Baikonur, but the Guiana Space Center at Kourou, French Guiana had always been actively in contact with the ISS for as long as he could remember. As he tried to raise a friendly voice from their center, he thought of how often he had joked about them. He said he was sure they had someone with their hand poised above the send key at all times.

One by one the stations had been hailed, but there was nothing to hear in the static. It hurt to get no answer from Noordwiik, Netherlands, and he felt disconnected when he couldn't raise the astronaut training center at Cologne, Germany, but he felt the sting of tears in his eyes when they passed over his native land and he heard no response from Harwell, England.

Defeat didn't come easily to any of them, but when they finally gave up and faced the reality that no one was going to respond, the emotion was more like anger than loss. Something had happened to their respective space agencies, but for some reason they felt like they had to lash out at someone. The focus on contacting a ground control center had been so intense that none of them had thought to try the television networks again. When it finally occurred to them that the television networks were always broadcasting, it only became a matter of getting one of them to answer a call from the Space Station.

In the early days of NASA, the idea of watching television in space would have been ridiculous. At the very least, it would have been thought of as unnecessary, but as missions grew longer in duration, the value of binge-watching had become apparent. The final irony was that the signal from a TV program didn't have to travel far to get to the ISS because it was coming from a satellite that was closer to the Space Station than it was to Earth. As a matter of fact, most of the big communication satellites were in orbits over ten thousand miles further from Earth than the International Space Station.

Natalia located a station that was broadcasting in German. They all spoke a little of the language, and there was closed captioning, but they could tell what was being said just by what they were seeing. Crowds of people were throwing bottles, and rocks, and just about anything else they could find. Their targets were other people who didn't appear to care that they were being pummeled. They walked slowly with their arms outstretched toward the crowds that backed away even as they threw their ineffective ammunition.

The space crew's first reaction was to be concerned for the victims who were hit with the garbage. Glass bottles bounced away, and they could see that some were very well aimed direct hits that should have been devastating, but there were no reactions indicating that the victims even cared. They just kept walking forward. Even the ones that were set on fire kept walking forward.

Henry pushed buttons on a remote, and channels changed at high speed as he searched for the familiar channel where he stopped. The BBC logo was in the corner of the screen, and the camera angle showed enough landmarks for them to recognize London even at night. The scene matched what they had watched on the German channel, but they could understand everything the reporter was saying. The hysteria in his voice was enough to make the fine hairs stand up along the backs of their necks.

"...a horrific scene. There's no other way to describe it. A national curfew has been called into effect to stop further bloodshed, but there are reports of outbreaks in every city and town. Within the last hour those reports have been pouring in, and even the people who have locked themselves inside are calling for help as family members turn on each other like rabid animals."

Henry drifted closer to the monitor watching as if he expected to see someone he knew, but in reality he was studying the faces in search of an explanation. Of the three, he was the family man. Somewhere just outside London were his wife and children, most likely with his parents.

"Over there," he shouted. "Do you see that?" He put his finger on a spot, and the cameraman obliged him from over two hundred and fifty miles away by remaining still.

Adam and Natalia moved closer to see what had caught his attention, and they saw that a group of people had dragged someone to the ground. They could just make out that it was a large man who was carrying a few extra pounds around the waist from a lifetime without exercise. He was tall and had possibly been athletic in his youth because he fought hard to stay on his feet despite the fact that as many as eight people were pulling at his arms and legs. One had a good hold on his hair and eventually made him fall over backward, and as he did, the crowd fell with him and buried their faces into his oversized gut. Blood erupted through the man's clothing, and the faces above him were more like wild animals than humans.

The picture went blank, and Henry reacted like it was something wrong with the monitor. He slapped it on the sides like people used to do before they became solid-state circuit boards.

"Let me help you, Henry." Natalia kept her voice soft and was careful not to make Henry feel anything forceful in the way she eased him from the monitor. If it had been Adam who intervened, Henry might have reacted differently. It was clear that Henry was in the middle of a full blown panic attack, which was way out of character for him.

Adam had the good sense to catch the remote as it floated past him in the zero gravity. He flipped through the broadcasts in search of another feed from the BBC for Henry's sake. A special announcement was just beginning from somewhere inside a British government office, and the speaker was surrounded by well armed soldiers. He turned up the sound, and Henry immediately settled down. Natalia kept herself in position behind him in case he lost control. There was too much damage one person could do inside the compartment if they became combative.

"We are asking all citizens to remain calm. Return to your homes or find a place of safety nearby. Stay there until the situation is under control. Do not attempt to seek medical care. Call the emergency number on your screen and leave your contact information, and someone will come to you. Medical centers are not safe at this time."

"What does he mean they aren't safe?" asked Henry. His forehead was furrowed, and his anger was apparent. "Where would you go if you were injured like that one man was?"

Adam said, "It's too soon to know anything, but your Army will get control. We need to see if this is local or worldwide."

Henry shot an angry glance at Adam, but Natalia's hand on his shoulder was quick to make him realize he wasn't alone in the ISS, and he turned back to the screen in time to see a new camera view. This one was from somewhere on the east coast of America where it was still daytime. Early evening rush hour traffic meant the streets were full of cars, and the sidewalks were jammed with pedestrians walking or waiting at curbs for lights to change in the intersections.

There was no mistaking the city. New York streets were recognizable to people even if they had never been there. There was a stark contrast between the chaos of London and the controlled chaos of

New York. It wasn't happening there yet.

"Shouldn't we warn them?" asked Henry. His head swiveled back and forth between Natalia and Adam.

"They know already," said Adam. "It's just not their problem yet. Whatever is happening in London, it hasn't arrived in New York. Turn up the sound. Let's see if the reporters are saying anything useful."

The anchor on the network channel was in the middle of a description of what they were seeing on a broadcast from London and Berlin, undoubtedly the same things the ISS crew had witnessed, and she was asking the same questions as everyone else. She was relaying the information to her audience as fast as her producers could get it, and she said the network was standing by for an emergency broadcast from the White House. She repeatedly asked someone off-camera if it was possible to let everyone know that they should go home quickly and tune to a station for updates, but this was the story of the year, and the network wasn't about to tell their people to go home.

Blue lights in the distance drew the attention of the pedestrians as a siren increased its wail. Crosswalks full of people emptied as they scurried to be the last to get across before the traffic moved aside to let a police car enter the intersection. It was joined by three more as they came to a stop with their doors flying open. The uniformed officers spread out and immediately worked together to get the traffic flowing in one direction.

"They're evacuating the area away from the city center," said Adam. "My guess is that they're getting the traffic moving toward the bridges." He pointed at a group on the sidewalk and saw a cordon of uniforms holding back the pedestrians. "Some of those people need to cross to get back to their cars. They're out of luck if they have to wait for all that traffic to clear."

On the sidewalks the pressure of the crowds caused the line of blue uniforms to bulge backward toward the street, and more than one officer was pushed off the curb. The camera was somewhere behind the officers and about a block away, and viewers could see the crowd grow rapidly until it filled the sidewalks all the way back to the next intersection. The same scenes were being played out on every street corner within view of the camera.

Adam leaned in with a finger pointing down the street and said, "You can see that they're trying to get all of the traffic reversed by having them turn to the right and then turn again this way. There's nothing happening yet, but they know something is coming."

He knew as soon as he said it that he had spoken too soon. All three of them recoiled from the monitor as the dam on the sidewalk across the street burst. Police officers were pushed backward into the cars that had come to a standstill behind them. Most of the people who trampled them were being pushed from behind by others who appeared to be fighting each other. The blue line disappeared and anyone who could stay on their feet did a combination of hopping and running.

The news desk anchor cut in and said, "We have someone down there in the crowd. Maybe we can get some information about what's happening."

Adam wondered why reporters seemed to think they had to explain everything. From the view of the camera, there wasn't much that needed to be said. Traffic wasn't moving because everyone had inched as close to the next car as possible. Pedestrians were no longer concerned with waiting for the traffic light to signal that it was safe to walk, and every gap between the cars was immediately filled. There were so many people trying to move in every direction that no one could move at all. Horns blared and drivers screamed curses as people climbed over the hoods and trunks of the cars.

A camera and microphone went live in the middle of the mayhem as a young reporter tried unsuccessfully to stand in one spot long enough to describe what was happening around her. The cameraman apparently found a perch on the trunk of a car because he was able to keep the camera aimed at the reporter as she was swept away by a sea of people. After she disappeared under the swirling crowd, the cameraman stood up and bravely walked onto the roof of the sedan and followed the spot where she had disappeared as if she was a drowning victim.

From the closer angle of the camera, it was even more devastating to watch because the three of them could make out the faces. It was an understatement to say the people were afraid. It was impossible for smaller people to stay on their feet, and when there were enough of them on the ground, the larger and more sturdy people fell on top of them. Then came the others.

Up until now there had been chaos without an apparent reason. The traffic jam and the congestion on the sidewalks had been an attempt to maintain order in the face of what was to come, but it had only made it easier when the others came. There was a live microphone somewhere out there in the crowd that had been in the hands of the reporter, and the first screams might have been from her.

The screams rose, and the crowd parted for just a moment at the center. The ISS crew watched the same things they had seen in London, but this time they had a front row seat. The camera followed the place where the crowd split open and then followed the progress of a group of people who weren't trying to get away. They were covered with blood but were still reaching out with their mouths stretched wide and biting more people.

Shots were fired by police officers, but it wasn't clear who they were trying to shoot. It also wasn't entirely clear who was being shot, because bullets slammed into people with enough force to drive them to the ground, but they got back up and went about the business of biting people only seconds later.

"Here," said Natalia, "this woman here. She was shot and didn't get up again. There must be a reason why."

Natalia said it excitedly as if she had made a discovery, and she turned to the others for approval. It was so strange to see the terror happening in the streets of New York and the contrast of the excited expression on her face. Adam knew she would have an appropriate response to her own reactions after it finally sank in, but for now they were having to see and understand something that was terrible to watch and even more terrible to accept. Accepting it also meant they had to be witnessing the impossible.

"It's time to get some real answers from someone explaining whatever this is happening on camera," said Adam. "Natalia, is that Canadian station still in the buffer? Maybe we can reconnect with them and ask some questions."

Software was so much easier to use than dials and buttons, and Natalia scanned the list of contacts in the buffer history until she saw WCAN, the station letters for the Canadians. She clicked her cursor on the history, and the image immediately sprang to life. A producer let out an audible whoop that got everyone's attention in the broadcast room, and he was quickly replaced by one of the senior news anchors.

"Are we ever glad to see you," said Jonas Morante.

The gray haired anchor was well known throughout the world for his popular interviews with countless heads of state. Now he was smiling at them as he undoubtedly realized he had yet another scoop on his hands. He was quick to understand that the three faces looking back at him were the faces of three heroes who had yet to be told about the conditions on the ground.

"Mr. Morante," began Adam.

"Please call me Jonas," he interrupted.

"Jonas, we haven't been able to make contact with any ground control centers. All we've been able to do is tune in to a few TV stations and get sporadic reports. Can you tell us what's going on, and can you find out what happened to the rest of our crew? They were supposed to be launched from Baikonur hours ago."

Jonas Morante knew the gravity of what had just been said to him, and despite his many years of chasing the story, he had never had a story chase him. This one was coming straight at him, and it was almost more than one person could believe. A quick nod to someone off-camera, and he knew that it was being recorded. A second nod got the attention of a producer who knew instructions were incoming.

"Cheryl, contact every Russian news source we have until you can find out what's happening at Baikonur." She was gone as he finished the last word.

"Commander Callaway, we'll have some answers for you directly. While we're waiting, can you please tell us what you know?"

A seasoned reporter like Morante wasn't about to broadcast what everyone else already knew. Reporters around the world were already telling their viewers that mobs of people were attacking and biting living people. They were ravenously consuming the flesh of their victims, and they themselves appeared to be almost dead, if not totally dead. Now they were about to hear something from three very special observers.

"We lost contact with all of our ground stations while we were in contact with the Marshall Space Flight Center in Huntsville, and we haven't been able to raise any of our stations worldwide. The last we heard from Huntsville, the rest of our crew was still on the ground inside two launch vehicles waiting to join us."

That was exactly what the anchor wanted to hear. Something no one else already knew. In a whirlwind of activity, the newsroom set the stage and had the cameras rolling with breaking news being sent out to their viewers. The ISS had lost contact with ground support, and with perfect timing Jonas Morante broke the news to the viewers that included Adam Callaway and his crew. The twin launchpads at Baikonur were the scene of a devastating accident that had caused the destruction of the two Russian launch vehicles. There were no known survivors.

The video was grainy and was obviously shot from a mobile phone.

Other than the lights surrounding the launch areas, it was very dark. A voice spoke in Russian, but Natalia shrugged her shoulders in response to the unasked question written on Adam's face.

"It's gibberish, or the man is out of his mind. The only thing I can make out is that he says it's the end of the world," said Natalia.

"Someone get confirmation of that," yelled Jonas.

Natalia didn't realize the mic was open, or she would have waited to comment, but her interpretation was hardly the topic of concern as gunshots rang out in the immediate vicinity of the launchpads. It was the staccato rapid fire of an automatic weapon, probably military, and tracer rounds lit the night between the tall boosters.

"Are they crazy?" Adam's and Natalia's voices overlapped each other as they helplessly watched the battle move closer and closer to the rockets.

Adam finished for them both. "Just one of those hot tracer rounds could detonate both launch pads." He didn't care that the Canadian station was hearing him and broadcasting his words to the world. He had a vague hope that they would hear him and somehow stop the shooting.

Against the ink-black background of night, the Cosmodrome was already a spectacular scene. The tracer rounds turned it into a hellish display of fireworks as superheated bullets hit equipment near the launch pads, and every flash of light made them flinch, sure that the next flash would be the one that ended it all. It didn't keep them waiting for long.

Everything seemed to slow down, but the explosions destroyed everything in seconds. There was always a feeling of hope mixed with despair when a comrade from any country was lost in a space tragedy, and the slowness was caused by the high speed flip of the emotions. In one split second there was hope that the space pioneers would survive. In the next split second there was the sinking feeling that there was no chance whatsoever that they could.

The light blossomed from a large glowing ember at the bottom of the launchpad and climbed the side of the massive Soyuz-FG rocket like a lightning bolt. Adam, Henry, and Natalia all wished for the man-made explosion of the jettison devices that would blast the Soyuz capsule from the top of the rocket. In seconds the crew would be drifting safely to the ground under parachutes, unhappy that something had gone wrong with the launch but relieved to know the escape rockets had worked.

The controlled destruction of the rocket by the escape system didn't happen, but the lightning fast explosion from below blossomed until it blinded them all. The sound cut off, but the video feed continued, and when they could see through the first explosion to the second launchpad, it was only in time to see the second Soyuz capsule blast away from where it had sat perched upon its launch vehicle. Half of their hopes had been realized.

They weren't even aware of the voice as the Canadian anchorman described the tragedy. Not since the American Space Shuttle had exploded had there been the loss of space explorers as dramatic as this, and Jonas Morante called the action as noteworthy as the description of the Hindenburg disaster. His voice carried all of the emotion to do it justice, but the three crew members of the ISS didn't hear a word. Each of them felt the rush of meaning this had to them as well as the personal sorrow at the loss of life. This meant their mission was over. There would be nothing left to do but await new instructions from mission control.

Working together for so long in training and then in space, the three friends had many moments when words weren't necessary. Sometimes there wasn't even the need for eye contact. This was one of those moments. They didn't need to see each other to know what they would see. As a matter of fact, this was one time when it would be better for them not to see the pain in the eyes of their shipmates. They still felt the presence of the others floating in the module, but silence was what they needed. That was how they finally heard the voice of Morante.

"Do you hear me ISS? Come in, ISS. I still have video, but do I have audio? Both rockets have been destroyed, but we still have radio contact with Baikonur through a network satellite, and mission control at the Cosmodrome says there are multiple reports of cannibalistic attacks by hundreds of people inside the launch area. We believe the second Soyuz capsule landed well outside the Cosmodrome."

They could see it all for themselves, but they had been so focused on the rockets that they didn't consider why there had been tracers being fired in the first place. There weren't usually people around a launch pad when rockets were fueled and ready to go, but there had been the shadows walking between the two rockets right up until the time of the explosions. The launches should have happened hours ago, but the number of slowly moving people walking around the restricted zone, added to what they had already learned from Huntsville, was enough for them to know they would not see the arrival of the six friends they had trained with for over two years.

"We hear you," said Adam. "We saw it all."

There wasn't much else to say. Being a reporter, Morante probably wanted to ask questions like, "How does this affect your mission?" Being more professional than some reporters and more experienced, he asked a better question. "Can we do anything to help?"

The automatic answer from the ISS crew could have been something sarcastic, and the words almost came out, but through the shock of watching friends die on the launchpad, they all saw one thread that still tied them to humanity. At least they still had one connection with someone who wasn't in the midst of chaos...at least not yet.

"Mr. Morante, we need to ask a favor. We need to keep this line of communication open for as long as possible, and maybe you could have some of your people try to raise one of the Mission Control Centers by conventional means. We can send you the complete list."

"We would be glad to help, Commander, but we've already been trying to contact your people. We can use your list to be sure we haven't left anyone out, but the only site we were able to talk with was somewhat unusual."

"What's that mean?" asked Natalia.

The Canadian sounded like he wasn't sure if he should even mention it because the contact had been very short, and it had only been made as a result of an intercepted broadcast from an unconfirmed source.

"We had a brief conversation with someone who claimed to be involved with NASA, but the communication was cut off before we learned anything. I have an intern checking the information now."

Natalia struggled to keep her impatience from showing, but at a time when everything was unusual, including cannibalism and space missions blowing up on the launchpad, she wanted direct answers to direct questions.

"Mr. Morante, when you ask us questions, we tell you what we know. We'd like the same thing from you. We don't have time for cryptic answers."

Adam and Henry both cringed. They didn't have to remind Natalia that the Canadian had been their only live Earth contact, but they couldn't have him get offended and hang up.

"I'm sorry, Comrade Lebedev. You're correct, of course. We were monitoring broadcasts from the Space Centers and gradually losing contact with all of them when we heard one say they are now unable to communicate with the ISS or the other space centers. It was a US Army radio operator, and he said something about Operation Paperclip and someone named Gentry Campbell. We were cut off immediately after that, and we have been attempting to regain contact since."

Being students of space history, all three of them knew exactly what he was talking about. It would have sounded unusual to anyone who wasn't in the space program or someone who wasn't a World War II history buff, but to them it was like stepping back in time. The name Gentry Campbell in the same sentence as Operation Paperclip couldn't be a coincidence, and the only thing they both had in common was the US Space Program.

Operation Paperclip never became a household name, but it changed the shape of the world. If the Russians had gathered up all of the German rocket scientists at the end of World War II instead of the United States, the Cold War might have become more than cold. Even Natalia Lebedev understood that it had been better for the world that they had been employed by the United States rather than forced to serve the Soviet Union. Yes, the United States improved its attack capabilities, but it had proven that the technology would also be fostered to develop the space programs while creating stronger defense capabilities.

"Gentry Campbell must've survived somehow in Huntsville," said Natalia.

"Yes, but what would that have to do with Operation Paperclip?" asked Adam.

Henry was deep in thought and had a furrow running across his forehead. "Does this have something to do with protecting the scientists and their families if the Russians attacked Huntsville? I remember reading that they built bunkers to keep them safe, but they never used them. There were rumors of an upgrade to the facilities, but I never heard of anyone who could confirm them."

"Whatever it is that's going on down there, at least one NASA facility is still operational, and someone from Mission Control is still alive," said Adam.

5

Resurrection

Guntersville - Year Seven

Word spread quickly through the population of Green Cavern. The news that someone might be alive inside Fort Sumter was met with skepticism because there had been no actual communication with that shelter, but deep down inside, all of us were thinking the same thing. It could mean Captain Miller was still alive.

Jean and I followed Bus to the infirmary. We were eager to hear anything from the two soldiers. One wheelchair was being pushed by Bus and the other an Army medic. They had insisted that they could walk, but Bus wouldn't hear a word of it. They had managed to travel over five hundred miles through a hostile environment, and they were in rough shape.

As soon as we arrived at the shelter hospital, they were helped onto beds and made comfortable. I managed to ask a few questions over the objections of Bus, and the soldiers were insisting that time was important. Their names above their pockets said Trapp and Legato, and their stripes showed they were both Private First Class.

"I know you guys need food and rest, but what's happening in Charleston? You said someone is inside Fort Sumter?" I asked.

Private Trapp answered first, "Things are really different, Sir. It's weird, but you have to make a lot of noise just to be able to find any infected dead around Charleston."

"You can call me Ed, Private. What's your first name?"

"I'm Matthew and this is Rick, Sir. I mean, Ed."

"I heard there were more of you when you left Charleston."

Private Trapp lowered his eyes and shook his head before he went on.

"There were eight of us, but we got too close to Atlanta. We didn't know how bad it was until too late."

"The infected?" asked Jean.

"No, ma'am. We could have handled them. Our squad was real smart that way, but we didn't figure the militias would be ready to kill people in uniform. I mean we ran into survivalists who wanted to make trades and get information, but that one group near Atlanta came out shooting."

Hearing that they were attacked made my blood boil, and I made a mental note that we would be visiting Atlanta to even the score.

"Back up a bit, Matthew. Why were eight of you trying to reach Guntersville, and why didn't you use the helicopters?"

"The helicopters were just bad luck," said Rick Legato. "One broke down, so we used it for spare parts to patch the others up. The other two were doing okay until something went wrong with the fuel. We were still refueling at the Air Force Base, and our guess is that water got into the tanks. The maintenance guys have stripped the engines down to nothing but parts, but there's no guarantee that we'll find fuel for them after they're repaired. Captain Harrelson decided it would be better to send us on foot."

"You lost six people in Atlanta?" asked Jean.

I could tell by her eyes that she was thinking the same thing I had. Atlanta would need to be dealt with at some point in time. Militias were understandable, but they didn't have the right to attack legitimate US forces. It didn't matter how far gone the country was. These soldiers had risked their lives to hold together a small part of it.

Trapp and Legato both nodded.

"We'll talk more about that in a bit," I said. "What was it that made you guys hit the road in the first place?"

Private Trapp said, "When the last helicopter broke down, we had to use boats to patrol Charleston. We set up a small base on Castle Pinckney so we could keep an eye on the whole harbor. Things are still dark on the Yorktown and in the city, but we picked up a radio signal for a few seconds, and the guy that heard it swears it sounded like Captain Miller. We haven't been able to raise the signal again, but we know we have to find out for sure. I mean if the Captain's alive, we have to get to him."

We knew exactly what he meant. The soldiers all felt an attachment to Captain Miller the same way we felt about the Chief. If he was alive, then we had to help. The problem was that the Chief had left along with our best team of fighters. Wherever they were, it would be hard to catch up with them because they had left on fast transportation.

"Has anyone gone over to Fort Sumter and checked topside?" I asked.

They both shook their heads from side to side, and we thought we knew what they were afraid of.

"What about the spiders and the stuff the people from the Yorktown planned to use on the infected?"

"That white powder? That got washed away with the first heavy rain," said Private Trapp, "and the spiders got washed away with it."

Private Legato added, "The powder worked on the spiders too. It didn't kill them as well as most pesticides, but the spiders didn't want to make a web or breed anywhere that the powder touched."

"It was used on the spiders?" asked Jean.

"There was a fire on the Yorktown," said Private Trapp. "We don't know how it started, but it was about two days after you guys left. Our ordnance guys think that the powder was so fine that it could explode if something caused a spark. Whatever it was, the whole thing blew up, and the smoke cloud from the fire left a white coating on everything. Over the last few weeks we noticed there are less spider webs, and there aren't any on Fort Sumter."

"I'm confused," said Jean. "If there aren't any spiders on Fort Sumter, and the powder got washed away by the rain, then why hasn't someone been sent there to see if the Captain is alive?"

The pair of soldiers hung their heads as if they were too ashamed to make eye contact. We waited for them to answer instead of pressing. When Legato lifted his eyes toward us, we saw that they were wet.

"Captain Harrelson asked for volunteers, but no one wants to go in and see Captain Miller dead or worse."

"Worse, meaning dead and walking around?" I asked.

They both nodded.

"So, your dilemma is no one wants to go on a rescue mission if it's actually a recovery mission, and you also don't know if the powder is still active inside the shelter."

"There's a third reason," said Legato. "The entire coast is covered with crabs. The food supply was so large that the crab population exploded. We know that it will go through self-correction just like the rats did, but right now it's hard to even go outside the shelter on Mud Island. The crabs come right up on the beach after you. When we left Mud Island we had to make a mad dash for the boats and get moving before they caught up."

"That means we have to wait at least a month before we send someone to Fort Sumter," said Jean.

Legato asked, "It took us that long to get here, so won't that be long enough?"

I thought back across the years to a time when people ate she-crab soup and crab dip. I tried to remember what time of year they were more plentiful, but my memory of that time was failing me.

"What are you thinking?" asked Jean.

"I'm thinking we should get on the road and catch up with the Chief and the others. Our best chance of getting to Fort Sumter would be him."

Bus interrupted and said it was time to let the men get some rest, and he told us we could make plans without them. Jean and I agreed and left the infirmary, but as soon as we pulled the door shut behind us we were making plans.

We were quick to agree that there was only one way to catch up with our friends, and that was motorcycles. Dirt bikes were more vulnerable than the RZRs, but they could cover more ground in less time. We had at least thirty men and women who were skilled riders, so it would be easy to recruit volunteers. As a matter of fact, it had become a favorite hobby of mine, and I went into Guntersville on bikes whenever I could. I had to admit, the idea of riding a bike further than Guntersville appealed to me.

Jean could read the expression on my face like a book.

"You're having a hard time hiding the fact that you are at least a little bit excited about this, aren't you?"

She knew she would get a smile out of me by saying that because we had used the same words as a prank on the Chief's last birthday. A shop in Guntersville was raided for clothing, and someone found a tee shirt in his size that said the hardest part about a zombie apocalypse was hiding the fact that it was at least a bit exciting. The best part was getting a shirt onto the Chief with anything written that included zombies. He had been a good sport about it, though.

"I guess I am a little stoked about the idea of going on the road on a motorcycle," I said.

"As long as it isn't because you need to get away from the wife for a little vacation."

"Maybe you could remind me what I'll be missing while I'm gone," I said in a low voice.

"As if last night was that long ago," she answered.

We kept teasing each other until we got to the cafeteria where we focused on the small groups that were gathered there and picked who would be best to send with me. We figured four of us would be enough, and if Captain Miller was really still alive, he had already waited long enough to be rescued.

******

Six Weeks Earlier

Walking wasn't as much fun as riding in the all-terrain vehicles, but it did give them time to appreciate the beauty of North Alabama. The humidity was low and everything was green. It would be hotter once they reached the valley where Huntsville was located, but for now it was a pleasant hike. The terrain was relatively flat until they reached the bottom of the mountain that separated them from their goal of reaching Huntsville, and they made good time up until then. Walking up an incline made their legs burn with the added exertion, but it wasn't like they were in a race or out of shape. They kept a steady pace and agreed among themselves that they wouldn't stop until they reached the crest of the mountain. They would be able to see the city from there, so they could make camp and then walk downhill in the morning.

They made it in time to watch the sunset, and the angle of the sun across the city almost made it appear to be untouched by the infection. It lit the buildings and cast long shadows that made it shiny and dark at the same time. They wouldn't try to cross it at night no matter how inviting the shiny areas were. Setting up camp on a scenic overlook gave them the advantage of a long view and steep sides if anything attempted to reach them, but they would still post a watch throughout the night.

Hampton settled in on a large granite slab on an outcropping a few yards higher than their camp. It was the perfect place for him to see past them and spot anything coming their way, and at the same time it would give them somewhere to fall back to if they had to move in a hurry. He hung his legs on the edge and watched them setting up camp, but his eyes were constantly scanning the city on one side of the mountain and the countryside they had just crossed since the tornado.

It was remarkable that they had just crossed twenty miles of trees and fields without seeing the infected, but there was no shortage of theories for why they weren't around. There would never be a time when there were so few that they could go to sleep in the open without posting a watch, but the group was in agreement that there were far less of them because they weren't the surprise they used to be. In the beginning they killed so many people that it was hard to avoid getting trapped. Now it was the other way around. Survivors had become more experienced as people adapted to the dangers.

That was the basis for the main theory, but it wasn't all good news. The original Mud Island group was dangerous to the infected population, but living people could always count on them for help. The same wasn't true of all survival groups. Some of them were far worse than the infected. Given time and the means to become lethal, some of those groups succeeded in clearing large swaths of territory of the infected, and then they set up their own little kingdoms. As Hampton watched his friends below, he knew that they had done the same thing, but the difference was that they had always kept their doors open. There were groups who kept their doors closed and kept to themselves, and there were some that broke down the doors of other survivors. He couldn't help wondering which kinds of survivors they might find in Huntsville.

Sunset caused the area they had crossed to be plunged into darkness sooner than the city side of the mountain, and he concentrated on the long stretches of roads that were framed by heavy forests. If anyone had followed behind them, they would be at the base of the mountain waiting for total darkness before making their move. Hampton was experienced in the woods long before the infection had begun, so he knew better than to ruin his ability to see into the darkness that washed away the landscape. As much as he wanted to look toward Huntsville, it would only make him blind when he looked again toward the other side. He also knew not to move. If anyone was down there, they were either brave, stupid, or already dead, but with the sun behind him, Hampton would be a dark silhouette against the sky. Any movement by him would be easy to see.

He willed his senses to keep watch over the other directions and used his mind to fill in the details of the road they had used less than an hour ago. It was as if he was focusing night vision goggles, to see what would be there if someone was following them, and there it was. There was the movement he knew he would see if it was still daylight. It was hardly a change between black and gray, but he saw it. He counted four changes before it stayed black. Whoever they were, they didn't know the value of wearing dark clothes at night.

The short-range radio Hampton wore on his belt had a full charge because they hadn't needed to use them on the road. He put one finger to the ON button and pressed. With his other hand he tapped the cover over the microphone four times. He paused and then tapped it twice. Below him he saw the small camp light near the Chief go dark. Shadows moved for only three seconds, and then everything was still where the Chief had been.

In those few seconds the sun had finished its descent over the horizon, and total darkness filled the valley behind him. Hampton lowered his body to a prone shooter's position, but his eyes never left the place where the tiny light had been. They had practiced this in the woods over Green Cavern, and it was a simple plan. If anyone tried to sneak up on them at night, they would be focused on the spot where they had seen the tiny white light. What they wouldn't know was that it hadn't been turned off. It had only been covered.

In the darkness of the campsite, the group had moved as soon as the Chief had covered the light. With hardly more than one whisper and a series of taps against the barrel of his semiautomatic pistol, they knew how fast to move and where they were going. Hampton had signaled that at least four people were coming, and then he signaled that they were moving fast. The metal ring the Chief wore on his right hand against the barrel of his 9 mm pistol told them to split into two groups and move fast. He whispered the number of intruders. In seconds they were in covered positions where they could make out the dark shapes of the sleeping bags they had left behind.

Local survivors had a big advantage over people who were new to the area. If they grew up on this mountain, then they knew it well. If they lost their patience, they would lose that advantage, and this group appeared to be overconfident, willing to throw caution to the wind in order to claim their prizes quickly. The only question that remained was how dangerous they would become when they realized they had made a mistake. That's where Hampton came in.

When the Chief signaled for them to split into two groups, each group knew to move together to cover they had selected before the sun went down. Once behind that cover, they would keep their heads down until they knew how out of control the situation would become. They would surrender their camp to an unknown group of survivors, but they wouldn't know if they were enemies or just people trying to protect their territory. They would learn which they were without firing a shot if possible.

Even though he couldn't see them, Hampton knew the first group of his friends was below and slightly to his left, and the second group would be about fifteen degrees beyond them. That way they would form a semicircle around the campsite, and they couldn't accidentally fire on each other. He carefully placed his flashlight on the rocks as far away as he could and still reach it, and he waited. Ten seconds, twenty seconds, and then a half minute went by before the camp light winked on in the blackness of the night.

The man who uncovered it made a startled grunt, and one of the others cursed at the stupidity of the man. They knew there was something wrong, but guns made some people careless, and they spun around noisily searching for the people who were supposed to have been caught by surprise. If they had been the friendly type, they would possibly have called out for someone to come out of hiding. Instead, they opened fire in all four directions.

The rifles were all semiautomatic and sounded like AR-15s. Short bursts of shots blasted the surrounding rocks and trees, but none of the rounds came close to the two groups in hiding. While the men wasted their ammunition on ghosts and shadows, Hampton took aim. Whether or not he would pull the trigger was still up to them.

They finally stopped shooting at nothing with the presumed leader of the group screaming at them to cease fire. Even though he had done his share of shooting, he wanted to know what the others were shooting at. There was a flat, wet sound as he slapped one of the others across the face and screamed.

"What'd you turn the light on for?"

The slap almost knocked the man down, but he managed to blurt out his best defense before he could get hit again.

"I didn't turn it on, Joe! It was already on under that blanket."

The Chief's clear, deep voice seemed to come from all directions at the same time.

"You can decide how this goes, Joe! Are we walking away from this tonight without leaving somebody on the ground?"

Knowing the man's name gave the Chief a slight psychological advantage because the man would actually consider whether or not it was someone he knew. Then he would take a moment to make Hampton's decision for him. Unfortunately for Joe, he made the wrong one.

The man opened fire again in the direction where he thought the Chief's voice had come from. He was so wrong that he was facing almost directly away from Hampton. The other three men turned that way and fired their weapons into the same area, so they didn't see the muzzle flash from Hampton's deer hunting rifle. All they knew was that Joe's head exploded.

That was pretty much what Hampton had expected to happen. A friendly group would have tried to make contact before sunset, or they would have waited until the next day. He also saw from their behavior that they were aggressive, and he was glad to know which one to shoot. He had grown up in a small town where they were considered to be country folk, and country folk always knew who the ignorant bullies were. Joe wasn't in charge because he was smart, but the others would fall apart without him around.

As soon as Joe hit the ground the other three stopped firing. They spun around aiming their rifles into the dark and screaming a variety of threats and curses. Mostly they were just scared and didn't know what to do. Hampton stretched out one arm and hit the switch of his flashlight. The beam was pointed more or less at the spot where they stood, so it blinded them for a moment, and they didn't see that Hampton was at least four feet from the light.

When the light hit them, they all spun that way and pointed their rifles. One of them yelled, "You shot Joe!"

The Chief's voice was louder, and this time it seemed like it was right on top of them.

"Drop your rifles on the ground!"

Two of them did, and even though they weren't told to do it, they shot their hands straight into the air above their heads. The man who had yelled at Hampton took quick aim and shot the flashlight. Hampton could see them because the flashlight had been pointed their way, and as he ducked down he was almost laughing because he saw the Chief step into the circle of light. The sharp sound of a fist hitting someone in the ear echoed up to Hampton.

If the men had realized they were up against so many well-armed people, they might not have tried to get the drop on them. If they had seen the size of the Chief before making their attack, they definitely would have thought twice. The two men who had their hands in the air didn't lower them even after they were told to. The third guy cried as soon as he woke up. He had his hand cupped over his ear as if he was protecting it from something, but it would probably sting for a few days. He stayed on the ground and scooted away from the giant man that hovered over him.

Everyone descended on the trio and got their weapons first. Then they were patted down and generally pushed and turned in different directions. Every time one of them said something it came out as a half of a word and was interrupted before the rest could come out. They were either spun around or told to shut up.

The men were underweight, and their clothes seemed to just hang from them. All of them were in need of a bath, judging by their smell. Kathy wrinkled her nose as she searched them, and she detected something familiar in the smell from a long time ago.

"Someone's been cooking meth," she said. "There's only one way that your type survives during an apocalypse."

The Chief said, "I don't want to know who you are, so don't bother to tell me your names. I don't want to know where you're from or if you have someone waiting for you at home. You shouldn't have tried to jump us at night, and you certainly shouldn't have shot at us."

By the time they had collected their weapons, there was a surprising pile of hardware on the ground. The two who had kept their hands in the air were taken to a tree out of earshot and tied together while the third was kept at the camp where he could be interrogated.

Kathy handed the Chief a variety of small items for him to examine, and she could see he was interested. None of them had any importance to survival. In their experience they had found that almost everyone who survived carried some piece of the past with them. Most were faded photographs of family or friends. It wasn't strange to find someone wearing a Rolex watch or a piece of jewelry worth thousands of dollars before the infection, and it was often a clue about the nature of the person that they would be wearing them. Sometimes it was a symbol of the lifestyle they had lost, and sometimes it was a symbol of the lifestyle they had always wanted. Now they could pretend to be somebody important by taking what they wanted.

This collection spoke volumes about the men. They all had expensive watches and jewelry, and they all carried thousands of dollars in rolls in their pockets. Besides the bags of wedding bands, there was also a large bag full of teeth with gold and silver fillings.

The Chief held one up in front of the man's face and didn't even bother to ask a question. It was obvious what he wanted to know, and the expression on his face left little doubt that he was probably too angry to speak. The men were scavengers, but unlike people who went out in search of prizes such as stainless steel cookware or ammunition, these men went after the things that used to mean material wealth.

The man eyed the tooth and made the mistake of thinking the unspoken question was related to the value of the tooth.

"That's real gold, mister. That's one of the biggest ones we got."

Kathy saved the man from getting hit in the ear again.

"You might want to think about what he wants to know before you speak. Why are you collecting teeth with gold in them?"

"Because they're worth a lot?" he answered. He made it sound like he was asking her if it was the right answer first.

She shook her head at him and waited.

"I ain't got nothin else, lady. They're gold. They're worth a lot. We get more food and stuff if we bring back more gold."

"That's a start," said the Chief. "You trade the gold to someone else. Someone else collects things that used to be valuable."

The man nodded. "We get them out of the biters after we kill 'em. Then we trade 'em to the Sheriff. He gives us supplies for the gold and a bounty on each biter we kill."

"What does he want the gold for, and I hate to ask, but how do you prove you killed an infected?" After a pause the Chief rephrased the question. "How do you prove you killed a biter?"

The man seemed amused by the question and laughed, but his smile faded under the Chief's gaze.

"We cut off the ears."

Before the Chief could react to the answer, the man started talking again in the hope that he could change the subject.

"The Sheriff says gold will be worth somethin again one day, and he plans to be sittin on a mountain of it."

"Where can we find this Sheriff of yours?"

The man gestured toward the dark city down below.

"That's Huntsv'lle down there." The name of the city was clipped by his southern accent. "He owns all of it now, but he lives back that way. Got himself a big ranch house. He told us to catch up with y'all and find out what you were carryin'."

He pointed in the direction of the road they had used to come up the mountain.

The Chief motioned for everyone to come together in a circle while Hampton stood watch over the prisoner.

"We'll keep them here tonight while we get some sleep then let them go in the morning."

Cassandra asked, "You don't think we should be worried about this Sheriff or their friends?"

"I didn't say we shouldn't. As a matter of fact, at least now we know we can expect to run into more of them in the city. The map we've been using shows we have at least twenty miles between us and the Marshall Space Flight Center. We have to go right through the middle of the city to get there. These guys can't be the only tweakers around here if someone is cooking meth."

Everyone gathered up their gear and relocated the campsite to the bluff behind Hampton. It wasn't as comfortable sleeping on rocks, but the Mud Island group hadn't gotten soft living in the shelters. Sleeping through the night had very little to do with comfort and a lot to do with security. They dragged Joe's body over to the trees and Tom stood guard over the other three while they dug him a grave. It was probably more than they would have done for him if it had been up to his friends.

When they were done, Colleen collected their shoes, and they were allowed to bed down for the night. Hampton resumed his post on watch above the former campsite, but Kathy added one last touch that was very entertaining, especially because of the amount of complaining from the three men.

A short length of rope was tied across their ankles so they could walk but not run. Then another rope was used to connect them to each other like they were entering a three-man sack race. Hampton explained to them that he would shoot the one in the middle if he saw anyone picking at the knots while everyone was asleep, but not in the head. That way the other two would be tied to a biter after he died.

As his friends went to sleep behind him and the stillness of the dark night on the side of a mountain descended over them, Hampton could hear the three men whispering at each other not to touch the ropes.

******

A few hours later Hampton was joined by Colleen, and it was such a cool night on the mountain above the city that he sat with her for a while rather than to get some sleep. If this had been a night before the infection, it would have been the perfect time and place for a couple with so much love for each other, but they were still some of the best hours they could remember in a long time. It was hard to believe what had happened in the years since the infection had begun, but they were able to block it out for a bit. At sunrise Hampton woke up with his head across her lap, and they were able to enjoy the cool breeze.

The others stirred behind them as they woke up one at a time. The morning routine was always the same when they were on the road. It didn't matter if the trip was one day, a week, or like this one that had no time limit. They were always quiet. People rolled out of their blankets and went about their business without conversation. They knew firsthand, and they had heard stories from other people about the infected walking into their campsites because they were drawn to the noise or clatter of equipment. The only reason they needed a fire was to make coffee, but that didn't make noise.

Without a fresh stream nearby, they had to use water from their supply, so there would only be one cup for each of them. The smell was a torment to their prisoners, but a morning cup of coffee was not how they would start their day. The Chief and Kathy only went down to them below when it was time to break camp and descend into the city. He explained to them that they could leave without their weapons or their shoes, but they could keep their gold teeth and other such junk. When they complained, he told them that the remaining option was to come with them as prisoners, and they would walk up in front on point. Not surprisingly, they chose to leave.

Everyone started down the steep highway toward Huntsville except Tom. He stayed on the outcropping of rocks and watched the three men through a set of binoculars until they disappeared a couple of miles back down the road. Then he jogged to catch up with the rest of them. The city sprawled out ahead of him, covered in strange shades of green and brown where the hearty trees and vines of the South had reclaimed the land. Once the home of almost a quarter of a million people, it was a city that had hot summers and mild winters. The perfect environment for bugs, scavengers, and the infected dead.

6

Operation Paperclip

Marshall Space Flight Center - Beginning of the Infection - Day Two

Gentry felt like she was living in a real-life version of *Alice in Wonderland,* and she knew exactly where the rabbit hole was because she had gone straight down inside it. The day before had begun with her being asked to do something that was way over her head, but she had accepted. She wasn't sure at the time why she was moved from the role of a Mission Specialist to the role of a Flight Director, but she knew they wouldn't have put her at that desk without a good reason. Knowing what came later, not understanding it but knowing what happened, Gentry wondered when things stopped being real. When did the fiction start?

When she woke up in the dim little room where the soldier had left her, she thought maybe she had a dream, but she was on an Army rack with curved metal ends that were straight out of a movie from 1945. The coarse material of the olive green blanket had a big stenciled label down the middle of it that said US ARMY. This was either real or one seriously deep dream, but either one seemed like it meant she had gone crazy.

Yesterday she had watched coworkers bite each other. There was blood everywhere she looked, and she had seen soldiers shooting people as she had been hustled to safety by a young soldier who, under the worst of circumstances, seemed attracted to her. She had met plenty of guys in odd places like the grocery store, the library, definitely bars…which wasn't so odd…but during a race for shelter? She wondered, what was all that anyway? Was it an attack of some kind? Biological warfare?

A faint rap on the door snapped her out of a half awake state. It was faint enough that she thought she might have imagined it, but the second time was just a touch louder. She realized it had to be MC, and he was too young and polite to let himself in even though she didn't remember locking the door. That bothered her for some reason. Her usual self would have checked to see if the door was locked, and if it didn't lock, she would have found a way to barricade it the way she had done in the visitors' gallery. She realized the events of the day before must have drained her, and when she had been left sitting on the rack, she had put her head down on the pillow and blocked it all out.

She made it to the door just as MC was about to give up, and the sight of a tray with food on it surprised her. She didn't know she was hungry until she saw it.

"It's not much, but it'll start your day better than going without anything," he said. His smile gave away the fact that he was glad to see her, and despite her melancholy thoughts when she woke up, she couldn't resist giving him a smile in return.

"You call scrambled eggs, bacon, hash browns, toast, orange juice, and coffee not much?" she asked with wide eyes.

Her stomach growled loud enough for both of them to hear. She took the tray from him and headed for the little folding table that served as a nightstand next to the rack. She turned around and saw MC still hadn't encroached past the door.

"Oh, I'm sorry, MC. Get on in here! You ate already?"

"Yeah, I've been up for a few hours."

Until he said it, she hadn't thought about the time, and she was shocked when she checked her watch. It was already past ten in the morning.

"Seeing something like you did yesterday can sometimes do that to you," he said. "You kind of escape by sleeping. I did that when I got sent over for a tour a couple of years ago."

She wasn't sure what she saw in his face, but her guess was it was something like what someone would see in her eyes today. He knew that look because he had seen it in a mirror before.

Gentry ate fast at first like she was afraid someone was going to take it away from her, but eating without talking made her start to think, and she chewed more slowly. She swallowed and asked, "What was that? What happened?"

"No one knows. The intelligence people say it has to be some kind of biological agent."

"You mean we were attacked?"

"Not necessarily," he answered. "If it was an attack, they don't know who did it or how. There wasn't a bomb or anything. No one is claiming credit for it, and it appears to be everywhere, in every country. They're not ruling out extraterrestrial."

Gentry stopped chewing on her toast and just sat with the bread about an inch from her face. For some reason, she hadn't even given the Space Station a single thought since she had to bail out at the Mission Control Desk. There were three people up there who probably saw a lot more than she would have wanted them to see given their circumstances.

"We were attacked by aliens?" she said.

"Like I said, they aren't saying it was or wasn't an alien attack. At this point, they just know that people are dying and then getting back up. After they get up, they try to bite people, and I guess eat people."

For a split second, Gentry wondered about herself. Why was she still hungry enough to eat after seeing what she did yesterday and sitting here remembering it? Something inside her, some instinct said to finish her food because there was no guarantee she would get another meal the next time she was hungry. Maybe it was knowing there were people in space who had no one looking out for them.

"MC, do I remember something about the people not getting up again if they were killed by … ?" the words escaped her, and she just left it as an incomplete question.

He finished for her, "Yeah, by getting shot in the head or hit hard enough on the head to do real damage. We learned the hard way that you have to go for the head."

Gentry finished eating and savored a sip of the coffee. MC was a lifesaver in more ways than he knew. She was a coffee addict, and not having coffee this morning would have been the last straw.

"The higher-ups want to meet you," he said.

"Who?"

"There's a Colonel in charge, and he wants to meet with you to see if you can help him identify who was the highest civilian type to make it out of there yesterday. He figures since you worked there you would know who the boss is."

"I don't think the Director made it," she said.

"They already know that. Someone who worked in the cafeteria on the first floor was drafted to help make chow...I mean breakfast for the civilians down here, and she said she saw the Director, and he was one of them."

"One of them?" she asked before it suddenly dawned on her that they didn't have a name for what those people were.

"The news channels are calling them infected dead," he said. "They're infected but already dead."

"What are they called before they're dead?"

The question would have been funny if they were in a bar and already a little lubricated, but at the moment they were both serious.

"How do they get infected?" asked Gentry.

MC was young and had a smooth face, but he felt older than his years, and the seriousness on his face seemed to exceed his ability to say something that was beyond his experience. It was incomprehensible, but he had to say it the same way he had heard it on a news broadcast.

"I heard that you get infected if you get bitten, and after you get bitten you get really sick, but you're still alive, so I guess you could say you're an infected living. When you die you get back up, and that's when you're an infected dead."

"That's ridiculous," said Gentry. She said it with a straight face, and it wasn't funny, but it felt like one of those times when you had to laugh if you couldn't cry. "Who came up with that? Why don't they just say someone who got bitten is infected, and then after they die they become zombies?"

"I don't think anyone on the news wants to be the first one to call them zombies," he answered.

"Well, they should get over themselves, because right now there are worse things than looking bad on TV."

"You mean like getting bitten or becoming a zombie?"

"Exactly," she said. "Thanks for the breakfast. Let's go get that Colonel so I can help him find out who's in charge, and we need to talk about what we're going to do about those three people up at the Space Station."

******

* * *

There seemed to be no shortage of surprises in the last two days, and Gentry had to admit she was surprised when she saw how many people were inside the shelter. The size of the shelter was impressive, and it wasn't like it was crowded, but it was definitely meant to hold a lot of people.

From the moment she stepped out of her room behind MC, she felt the weight of the population around her. It was the same way she had felt on her first trip to New York. The tall buildings made her feel closed in, and everywhere she turned there was another face. The low ceilings inside the shelter were undoubtedly intended to allow for more levels, and more levels meant more people.

"I don't remember it being this crowded last night."

"After I dropped you off in your room I went topside with a squad to see if we could find stragglers who hadn't made it inside. We found more people than we could believe. It seems like everyone in Huntsville had heard the rumors about the secret shelters for the NASA people."

Gentry stopped walking and watched a group of people she assumed was a family. The father was sitting in a plastic chair with a stack of papers on his lap. He was dutifully filling out the forms required to receive aid inside the shelter. Bureaucracy was alive and well. The mother was doing her best to keep three young children under control so the man could get everything done. She heard him say about how they wouldn't get to eat until he finished. Gentry felt a touch of guilt because she didn't have to fill out forms, and her food had been delivered to her.

The same scenario was in progress all around them as they waded into the flow of people who seemed like they had somewhere to go. There was a steady stream of families and single people going in both directions. Some of them had folders of paperwork, and some were following directions to destinations already given to them. There was a hum of lowered voices not at all what one would expect from so many people. Gentry saw the explanation on a sign that was prominently displayed on a large marquee. It blinked a message in bright orange letters.

DUE TO THE NEED FOR ORDERLY PROCESSING, NOISE MUST BE KEPT AT A MINIMUM. PLEASE KEEP VOICES LOW TO AVOID DELAYS.

* * *

They went down two levels of stairs, followed a narrow hallway that was only wide enough to walk single file, and then up one flight to a level that had more spacious rooms. Gentry noticed there were more people in uniform on this level, and judging by their insignia, she figured they were getting closer to the Colonel.

Gentry caught MC by a shirt sleeve and slowed him down enough to whisper a question to him.

"I saw people with new bandages. Did they come from a hospital?"

"No, there's an aid station on the first level. If anyone comes in with an injury they get treatment before going any further."

"What about serious injuries?"

MC apparently didn't see what Gentry was getting at because he hardly glanced back at her as he answered.

"There's a hospital on the main level up top. I heard it's full, but every shelter out here has the same setup, and they can send people over to the hospitals that aren't full yet. Here's the Colonel's office."

MC pulled aside a curtain and stepped into a small office where an orderly kept guard over a second door. MC told the orderly why they were visiting the Colonel, and the sharp young soldier quickly disappeared behind a second curtain to announce their arrival. He politely held the curtain aside for them to enter.

The officer that greeted them was dressed like the others in BDUs, or Battle Dress Uniforms. He looked every bit the part of a combat officer who was ready for a fight, and his rough face sent the message that he had been in plenty of fights before. He confidently stood up from his desk and greeted them with a warm smile. He even greeted MC, and Gentry sensed the pride and confidence MC felt in his boss.

Colonel Rayburn towered over her, and the hand extended to her was large, but the silver hair and blue eyes made her feel like she was being introduced to a kindhearted father figure.

"Young lady, I hear you're somewhat of a celebrity around here." His voice was deep and soft. If it hadn't been, the statement would have alarmed her.

"I'm sorry, Sir. I'm not sure what you mean," she said hesitantly.

"Oh, I guess you wouldn't know," he answered. He lifted a piece of paper from his desk and handed it to her. "We managed to access the Human Resources computer and establish a chain of command for the Marshall Space Flight Center. We've also managed to locate the whereabouts of everyone on this list, and as you can see, things haven't gone so well for your superiors. As far as we know, there isn't anyone alive above your pay grade."

She recognized every name on the list from the Director on down to her own. Each name had a brief comment next to it that said where the people were located. The locations weren't the same, but the dispositions were. It said they were all deceased. It was odd to see what was written next to her name.

"Shelter 204 - Orientation."

Gentry tried to speak past a lump in her throat and found she couldn't. The Colonel handed her a bottle of water and said, "This should help."

After gratefully accepting the water and taking a sip she tried again.

"I feel like I'm supposed to keep saying I'm sorry for something. I'm sorry everyone else is dead. I'm sorry for what's happening. I'm sorry there are families out there who are hungry, and I'm sorry I got fed before them."

She would have gone on adding to her list of apologies, but he gently guided her to a chair. He leaned back and sat down on a corner of his desk so he could comfort her. MC remained standing but took up a position next to her. He was protective, and if anyone had asked, he made her feel safer because one of the things she felt sorry for was how much danger she felt like they were all in.

"Young lady, survivor's guilt is normal. You lost a lot of colleagues in the last two days."

"I'm sure that has something to do with it, Sir, but you don't understand. I don't think it's over."

The Colonel and MC wore the same expressions. Neither was sure what she meant.

"Of course it's not over, Ms. Campbell. Whatever is happening outside these shelters is far from over, but the Army can deal with it. Our job is to keep everyone safe down here. Has MC told you there are over three hundred shelters in this complex? Each one can house about two thousand people, keeping them safe and fed for a year. I'm sure our military will have everything under control within that time."

As he spoke, he kept his face in front of hers and tried to let his eyes reassure her. She had a feeling like she didn't want to disappoint him, but there was something he seemed to be forgetting.

"Colonel, MC said there are hospitals treating the wounded. Have there been any problems in the hospitals or aid stations?"

"What kind of problems?" he replied.

"When MC told me the shelters were all connected to each other, I didn't know there were over three hundred shelters, and I was already worried about the wounded. Don't you know what happens to them after they die?"

"We have security at the hospitals, and so far no one being treated has died."

Gentry felt the tiny hairs on the back of her neck move. It felt like someone had blown lightly on them, and the goosebumps arose between them. She shivered visibly because she had another question to ask the Colonel, and she didn't think she wanted to hear the answer.

"Young lady, you seem to be terribly afraid of something. I know this is a lot to take in, but we're going to need your help in the next few days in particular. You're the one person in authority at the Space Flight Center who can help us get those astronauts home from the Space Station, so tell me what it is that has you so on edge."

She knew there was only one way to get him to understand what was terrifying her, and that was to come right out and ask, even if the answer was unthinkable.

"Sir, what are you going to do with the patients who die?"

The question hung in the air for such a long time that she began to think he wasn't going to answer her. Just as she was about to repeat it, he broke eye contact and walked around behind his desk. He sat down in his chair heavily and lost a bit of the fatherly kindness she had seen in his eyes. Now she was also afraid she had offended him, and her earlier fears grew.

As he answered, Colonel Rayburn linked his fingers of both hands together and propped his elbows on the desk. He rested his chin on his hands and didn't meet her gaze as he spoke.

"Ms. Campbell, as a scientist, I'm sure you can understand the need to gather as much information from this phenomenon as we can. It may well be the information we gain that in the end will determine the fate of mankind. I would think you would want to be part of that scientific discovery."

"You're going to keep them in a lab and study them, aren't you?"

Gentry could sense MC as he stiffened next to her. He was a soldier and not a high ranking one. He wasn't used to seeing anyone put the Colonel on the spot.

Her question also earned her a direct stare from the Colonel that she couldn't quite read. He didn't get to the rank of Colonel by being transparent or stupid, so he had a poker face in his bag of tools. Gentry saw something flicker in his eyes that wasn't menacing, but it was calculated. He only let her see it so she could understand him well enough at this moment.

"Of course that's what you're going to do with them, Colonel Rayburn. What else could you do?"

She saw that it was the concession he needed from her because she could read the relaxed expression that crossed his face next. It was the logical alternative, but something still scared the hell out of her. She just hadn't put her finger on it yet.

He gave her a brief smile and said, "Ms. Campbell, if you're concerned about how we plan to do it, why don't you just leave that to me and my men? That's the part we're trained for. What I need from you happens to be another skillset entirely. As a matter of fact, you wouldn't expect any of those thousands of other people out there to have a say so in what you do, would you?"

It was his question that finally triggered her fears. When she thought about all of those other survivors, she also wondered how many soldiers there were. There were undoubtedly soldiers in every shelter, but they were likely to be outnumbered by the civilians. Then she thought about how many of them, civilians and soldiers, had been bitten before coming inside.

He must have seen the change in her own expression because he dropped his poker face and said, "Out with it, Ms. Campbell."

Gentry sighed and decided she had to trust the Colonel, or mistakes would get made just like the one they had made in the viewing gallery on the previous day. Letting someone in the door had been a fatal mistake, but it paled in comparison to the possibility that there were already hundreds of possible bite victims inside the shelters.

"Colonel Rayburn, MC said this is happening everywhere, so I'm sure you're communicating with other military units. If all of them took in survivors the way this place did, I'll venture a guess that tomorrow you will lose contact with some of those units, and the day after that, you won't hear from someone else. Why? Because it's inevitable that there are survivors in each place who were bitten, but they haven't sought medical treatment. You could have the best isolation unit in the world where you keep the ones you know are infected, but how can you protect yourself from the people you don't know are infected?"

The Colonel knew there was a time for poker faces and a time to play cards. He yelled for the orderly who appeared so fast he could have been standing in the room the whole time.

"Get a message out to all shelter Commanding Officers. Connections between all shelters are to be locked down immediately. There is to be no traffic between shelters of any kind. I want every shelter to give a status report once per hour, and I expect to know within one minute if someone doesn't check in."

The orderly was gone as fast as he had arrived, and the Colonel turned to MC for the first time. MC doubted that the Colonel missed the half smile on his face when he gave MC his orders.

"Soldier, this young lady is your responsibility. If you haven't already found her quarters suitable to her status, then do so. Get her to Communications so she can establish contact with the Space Station. Those people probably think NASA forgot about them by now. Then be sure the Office of Civilian Personnel gets her everything she needs from Supply. Clothes, computer, and anything she needs to be comfortable. We have a meeting scheduled for 0900 hours tomorrow. Escort Ms. Campbell to the meeting on time."

Gentry had been around military officers enough in her short time with NASA to know that the nod he gave her meant she was dismissed. She also saw that she had struck a nerve. The worried expression on his face was almost a mirror reflection of her own. She could only imagine what other orders she had set in motion, but her imagination ran wild. If she was in charge, she would be taking drastic measures to find out who fits into that group of people she had been talking about. Everyone had to be checked for bite wounds, and her guess was they were already too late. Their only advantage was that they were armed and trained soldiers, and the first thing they needed to do was learn who within their ranks had been bitten.

She nodded back at him and whispered a barely audible word of thanks, but he was already on his phone. She had a pretty good idea why. MC held back the curtain and let her go through ahead of him, but he took the lead outside. He was excited and started talking as soon as they could do so without anyone else hearing what he said.

"I've never seen anyone light a fire under a Colonel like that, Gentry. You got a way of getting to the point, don't you?"

"Colonel Rayburn has probably had the same worries tickling the back of his brain since yesterday but hadn't been able to figure out what it was. All he needed was someone to coax it out of him. He poked me until I said what he needed to hear."

MC regarded her with a quizzical look. "Are you a Psychologist too?"

"No, I can just tell when someone is smart enough to ask the people around him for ideas. Your Colonel is a leader. I can tell he's had his hands full setting up this operation in one day, and he could probably use some sleep, but leaders can't think of everything. That's why he had you bring me in. Is it true that I'm the senior NASA person?"

"Seems like it. You're right about Rayburn. He had people beating the bushes for NASA people all night, and every time we found one they were either eating someone or being eaten."

It was the first time MC had slipped up around her. Maybe it was because she had shown the Colonel a little of her determined side in front of MC. It made MC treat her like he would any of the other men or women in his unit, and he had forgotten that she wasn't military. He wasn't insensitive, and she wasn't being overly sensitive, but she wasn't ready to hear what could have happened to her if she hadn't thought quickly enough on the previous day. She could have ended up the same way as the others just as easily as they did. If she was the senior person, that meant a damned lot of people were dead. They were either eaten or being eaten.

"Hey, I'm sorry. I didn't mean to say something that stupid. Those were people you worked with. Those were friends."

"It's okay. I know it's easier for you if you separate yourself from it all and not see them as people."

"No, it's not okay. They were people, and no one has a right to forget that. It won't happen again."

Gentry knew that he meant it. Part of being a good soldier was knowing when to turn off and on the things that separated soldiers from civilians. It was just a matter of respect.

"Well, it's forgotten as far as I'm concerned. What about those new quarters, things I need, and getting me an open line to the ISS?"

She could see that he was happy to talk about something else, and he visibly brightened up when they reached her new home. He had taken so many turns, and they had changed levels so many times that she would need a map to find her way back to the Colonel's office. MC opened a door, and she was surprised to see her new quarters were much bigger than the room where she had spent the night. As a matter of fact, they were better than the apartment she had leased a couple of miles from the Space Flight Center.

"This is where I live now?"

She walked into the room as if she would interrupt the people who really lived there, taking in the furniture and decorations. Other than the lack of windows and lower ceilings, she considered it to be spectacular.

"This is it unless you want something nicer."

"That doesn't even deserve an answer," she said.

MC left her to explore the room and to make arrangements for communications and to inform the Director of Civilian personnel where to find her.

******

The crew of the International Space Station had come to the conclusion that things had to be far worse than they had imagined at first. Otherwise, they would have been able to make contact with someone, anyone in their vast network of systems. Three world class space agencies didn't all go dark at the same time unless it was a catastrophe of apocalyptic proportions. They decided there wasn't anything they could do to help, so the best thing they could do was keep their own house in order.

They had a full schedule of work to keep themselves busy, but the radio was always within reach. When a voice filled the module asking them to respond, all three of them were propelling themselves in the same direction. Natalia was there first.

"This is ISS. Is that you Gentry?"

It was hardly proper radio protocol, but that had been abandoned hours ago.

Gentry was excited to make contact with them so quickly, but for her sake, she had to break the news to them gently, if that was at all possible.

"Yes, Natalia this is Gentry at the Marshall Space Flight Center Ground Control. I'm sorry for the delay in contact." She already felt like she had her foot in her mouth all the way to her ankle because she had started with such a lame apology.

"Delay in contact? Is that what you call it? We've tried reaching every known space agency for the last day, and you call it a delay?"

Adam and Henry had arrived only a split second after Natalia and both were attempting to pry the microphone from her hand. In the weightlessness of the module, she managed to get a foot into Henry's chest and push him away. Adam was behind her, and her push propelled herself and Adam away from the radio. She used the cord to pull herself back in without either of the men interfering.

With an angry Russian accent she said, "Cut the crap, Gentry, and get right to the facts. What the hell happened down there, and don't sugarcoat it."

It was pretty much what she had expected. If Gentry could have broken it to them gently, she would have, but even from outer space Natalia made it clear that she wanted the ugly truth in as few words as possible.

Gentry took in a deep breath and leaned her forehead onto her hands. She put her face over the microphone and said, "It's bad. It's really bad. It's some kind of plague, it's worldwide, and it spread so fast there was no stopping it. The virus, or whatever it is, causes death within hours, depending upon the extent of the injury. The injury is caused by being bitten by an infected person who has already died."

"Stop," said Natalia. "Did you just say…?"

Gentry interrupted her, "Yes, I said an infected person who has already died. The dead reanimate and then attack uninfected people. They bite them…actually they try to eat living people. The people they bite are infected whether they die or not. Wash, rinse, repeat."

In the silence that followed, Natalia simply handed the microphone to Adam and drifted away. She whispered, "I'm sorry," to Henry as she went by.

"Gentry, this is Adam. How're you holding up?"

Gentry didn't expect the question. She had been so worried about the astronauts, how to tell them the details, and how to answer questions about their future, that the last thing she expected was for the Commander to worry about her. Before she could stop herself, her voice broke and she sobbed into the microphone, choking on tears.

The crew of the ISS gathered together and listened without interrupting, realizing that there were possibly worse things than being stuck in outer space. They could use the resupply ship to return home at any time in the next six years, but right now it was more dangerous to be on Earth. If they left, they were more likely to be killed on Earth.

After several minutes, Gentry was gradually able to compose herself. The key must have been pressed because they could hear someone comforting her. If they could have reached out from two hundred and fifty miles away to comfort her, they would have. They would all need some time to just let it sink in.

Gentry's voice sounded tired as she spoke again…tired and resigned. "I'm sorry ISS. I'm sorry that I have to give you this news, but if you were able to watch any news broadcasts, you already know that the two launches from the Cosmodrome were tragic losses of all crew members. We have relocated from the Mission Control center in the Marshall Space Flight Center to an underground bunker or shelter. It's a massive complex of shelters that have been maintained since World War II as a place of safety in the event of a nuclear war. There are thousands of survivors in over three hundred bunkers. There is a large US Army presence, so we are safe for now."

"So are we," said Adam Callaway. "We'll get back to you tomorrow. Hopefully, you will be able to give us some updates on our families."

All Gentry could say was, "Roger that, ISS. Huntsville out."

7

Huntsville

Year Seven

The sign said, "Welcome to Huntsville - Watercress Capital of the World." Colleen spent the next fifteen minutes explaining to everyone what Watercress was and why people would eat it. She couldn't explain why she was the only member of the group who even knew what it was. It turned out that Iris knew but wouldn't admit it because it was fun watching everyone tease Colleen.

If Watercress had been farmed in Huntsville, it certainly would have a bumper crop now judging by the way plants had taken over the city. The road they walked along sloped down the side of the mountain and gave them a good view of the valley. The Chief was able to spot the Marshall Space Flight Center in the distance because the rocket test gantries were still housed inside one of the biggest buildings south of the administration center and mission control. The massive building still stood as a testament to the determination of mankind to build a rocket that could get people to the moon.

"We have a long walk ahead of us if we have to reach that building," said Kathy. "It's mostly jungle between here and there. Can anyone see an easier way to get there?"

The Chief had his map laid out on the cracked pavement. Grass and trees had pushed up the road in so many places that it was hard to get it flat.

He said, "If the plant life on this road is any indication of what it's like between here and there, we've got a hard trip ahead of us. Remember what that baseball park was like in Charleston?"

Everyone remembered the ballpark in downtown Charleston. It was like a well-cultivated field of crops. The drainage system under it was perfect for allowing it to hold the perfect amount of water in the ground for plants of all kinds to grow. The wind and birds were always carrying seeds and dropping them in places where they could sprout new plants, and then they would grow within the protection of the walls that surrounded the ballpark. Huntsville was like that.

"Tom, you lived not far from here. What kind of wildlife can we expect?"

"The usual small predators are my guess," he answered. "Bobcats, skunks, possums, snakes, and mountain lions if we're unlucky, but they've had enough time to establish themselves again north of here in the Blue Ridge Mountains. Our biggest problems are going to be the ones that walk on two legs. There's a lot of cover for an ambush by friends of the sheriff those guys were telling us about."

"We don't have much choice," added Hampton, "but at least we're far enough from the Tennessee River so we won't have to worry about alligators or big snakes."

No one brought up the fact that everyone was worried about the spiders. As far as they knew, the spider population was normal again, but everyone had the habit of checking inside their shoes or sleeping bags before putting body parts inside. It would take a long time to get over seeing spiders everywhere and watching the way they had become so aggressive.

Everyone gathered up their gear, and they formed up in a line to take the final steps into the city. The highway leveled out at the base of the mountain as they entered the city between rows of businesses that were either completely hidden under vines and trees or had collapsed under the weight of debris and weather.

They had entered so many cities that had shown the scars of time. New Orleans was so flooded, and the tropical climate had given birth to a new variety of alligators that were more like crocodiles and an abundance of pythons as big as anacondas that belonged in the Amazon rain forests. Columbus, Ohio had been a frozen wasteland when they arrived. The city was buried under so much snow and ice that the buildings were like ice tombs. In many ways Huntsville resembled Charleston. The streets had become more narrow as the plant life had encroached so much that it wasn't long before they were stepping over new growth, and the sun was being blocked out above.

It was fair to say that everyone in the group of eight survivors was experienced with living outdoors after so many years, so it wasn't a surprise when they all stopped to listen even before Hampton had raised his hand with a closed fist. He was on point, and he sensed the danger before he saw it. His right arm went up, bent ninety degrees at the elbow, and his hand closed tight to let them know they should be silent.

No one took another step or even moved their feet as they swiveled at the waist and searched the green jungle surrounding them. Everyone had their M4s unslung and pointed outward, and fingers were putting pressure on triggers.

What had assaulted their ears wasn't a sudden noise. It was the sudden silence. Up until that moment the sounds of insects, birds, and small animals had filled the air. They had even heard the familiar sounds of formerly domesticated animals and monkeys that had undoubtedly escaped from a zoo. Now it was as silent as the surface of the moon.

Their eyes found each other as the silent question was passed from one to the other, and each was answered with a slight shake of the head. No one had spotted anything unusual. Hampton stayed where he was while the rest of the group eased closer to him. Cassandra was bringing up the rear, and she had been particularly mindful of the fact that there were humans in the area who couldn't be trusted. She wasn't going to let anyone sneak up on them from behind. She signaled that she was negative for contacts, but the trees were still quiet. That meant a threat had moved somewhere, and the animals, birds, and insects didn't feel safe.

The Chief held up an open hand to get everyone's attention, and he pointed at a spot about twenty or thirty feet away. The others saw that he was pointing at a pole on the corner, and it had a weathered traffic light sitting on top of it. They understood that he was telling everyone they had entered an intersection. The growth of trees and vines was so thick on their left and right sides that they could easily have believed there were no roads at the intersection.

"This place reminds me of the entrance to the shelter on Governors Island," said Iris. "If you didn't know a road was there before then you wouldn't think to look for a road there now unless you saw the traffic light."

"Everybody listen up," said the Chief in a conversational voice. "Keep looking around like you're trying to find something, but on the count of three we're going to dive for cover on the left side of the intersection. If someone shoots at us, it's going to come from the right. Return fire in that direction. One, two, three!"

The shots that came from the invisible street on the right were a split second too late, and by the time the shooters adjusted their aim, Hampton was pouring his own bullets into an enemy he couldn't see. A man dressed in hunting camouflage fell out of the bushes onto the street.

The problem with people who didn't practice weapons discipline was that they reacted rather than anticipating. As soon as the man fell to the asphalt, his friends focused their attention on him. The Mud Island survivors had been trained by the Chief, and he had told them a thousand times if a comrade gets hit, expect to be hit next because the shooter who got your friend was already adjusting his aim to a new target while you were worrying about your friend. That meant you should find the shooter before he found you.

With all eyes from the other side of the street aimed at the man who had been hit, there was a two or three second pause. It was more than enough time for the Chief and the rest of them to turn the tables on the ambush. With deadly accuracy, they put round after round into their targets, and four more people fell to the street.

Before the last one had even reached the pavement, the Chief was on his feet and moving across the street. The others saw that he was advancing, so they broke cover and moved with him. In their training he had also told them battles weren't won by merely holding your position, and it wasn't like the cover they had found was where they wanted to be. It was only where they had gone temporarily.

All eight of them moved forward as they fired a deadly blanket of bullets into the green jungle that hid the intersection. The bullets that didn't find bodies found tree branches, vines, and leaves. The air was filled with greenery as if a landscaper was cutting it all down, and gradually light poured through the opening. They could see that the dense jungle was actually a very clever disguise that was used to hide access to the road behind it, and as the disguise disappeared, they saw why the three men on the mountain were so afraid of the Sheriff.

Through the gate they saw a row of four pickup trucks parked with their beds facing the intersection, and in the back of each was a weapon that made the Chief instantly stop. He quickly held his hands out at his sides and dropped his rifle. The rest of the group saw what he did, and they didn't have to be told what to do. The Chief easily recognized the multiple barrels of the M134 mini-guns, and he knew they could shred a man's whole body before the pieces hit the ground. At an incredible rate of up to six thousand rounds per minute, none of the survivors would feel a thing after the first few seconds of firing.

Behind them on the other side of the intersection, a voice yelled out. "Put your hands on top of your heads and drop to your knees. If anyone reaches for their weapon you'll all die."

The Chief risked a quick look over his shoulder in the direction of the voice and saw a gate like the one they destroyed had been rolled aside. It was a tall, chain-link section on wheels. An intersection that appeared to have been reclaimed by nature was an ambush set to capture anyone who entered the Sheriff's territory. He didn't have to see it open all the way to guess what was behind them.

"Did I say you could turn around, big fella?"

The deep voice asked the question in such a matter-of-fact way that there was no doubt that it was the man they had heard about. The confidence in the voice was clear.

"Ladies and gentlemen, let's get something clear from the start."

The southern accent was heavy, but there was no mistaking that it wasn't that the man was just a country hick. It was a smooth and practiced accent that tended to fool enough people, and the man liked it that way. It made him that much more dangerous.

"I am J. Horton Crim. I am the Sheriff, and the great city of Huntsville is mine. If you do as you're told, you'll be given a job. If you do your job, you'll be fed and have a place to sleep. If you don't, you'll be punished. If you have to be punished again, you'll be shot."

The Sheriff didn't wait for an answer as a group of men and women came into the intersection from all directions. The Mud Island survivors were helpless to do anything but watch as their weapons were gathered up and carried away. One by one their hands were tied behind their backs as they were searched and relieved of ammunition and knives.

"You people have some pretty nice gear," said the Sheriff.

He was closer now and walked through the group to the other side of the intersection where they could see him. Being a former police officer herself, Kathy showed the most surprise to see that the man was fully dressed as a Sheriff would be. For some reason she had expected the hat and the badge but not the whole uniform. The second surprise was that he wasn't very tall. His voice was deep and smooth, and fit someone the Chief's size, but the Sheriff was no more than five feet two inches tall. His wiry frame told her he was the kind of man who was used to being underestimated, though. On the streets she had been more cautious around his type than she was the big guys because they were always trying to prove how tough they were.

He stopped in front of the Chief, and it was almost comical to see him eye to eye with the Chief on his knees.

"My oh my, you are a big one, aren't you?"

The Chief didn't answer. He knew this was the challenge phase of the encounter, and the Sheriff would love nothing more than to take out the leader of the newcomers to put the rest of them in their place. As a matter of fact, he was likely to do it regardless of how the Chief responded to him. Across the intersection one of the M134s was aimed straight at him, and he could see the man behind it grinning from ear to ear in the hope that he would be given the signal to open fire.

The Sheriff let out a low whistle as he looked the Chief over, then he moved on to Kathy. She gave him her best stare that sent a clear message, but it was obvious he was inspecting other parts of her and was oblivious to what her facial expression was saying.

"Now that is what I call beautiful," he said. If his voice had sounded smooth before, this time it put silk to shame.

One by one he walked around them, inspecting and making occasional comments to no one in particular. He was almost finished when a commotion broke the silence a block further into the city. A small group of the infected emerged from a side street and stumbled in their direction.

"I am so sick and tired of those things," he said. With more emphasis on the first word it came out as if he said, 'Ah'.

"Every time you need to get something done, they show up."

This time the Sheriff sounded like he was explaining something to his captives as if they were new to the world of the infected dead.

He turned to the pickup trucks and snapped his fingers at the men behind the guns. "What are you waiting for?"

The M134s rotated away from the intersection. Even to the members of the Mud Island group who had seen automatic weapons fire before, the display of destruction was impressive. Over the next five seconds, which was four seconds longer than necessary, the infected disappeared into small pieces.

"What do you plan to do with us?" asked Tom.

The question seemed to startle the Sheriff. He was standing only about two feet past Tom's left side, and he spun around putting all of his weight behind a punch that connected with Tom's ear. The four automatic weapons had left everyone just a little deaf, but they still heard the impact. Tom fell over on his right side and didn't move. Without his hands to break his fall, hitting the asphalt with his head only made things worse, but it was doubtful that he felt it because he was knocked out by the punch.

The Sheriff stood over his limp body for a second too long, and that was all the time Kathy needed to get her feet under her and launch herself at him. If her hands had been free, she could have killed the Sheriff before he got any help from his men, but with them tied behind her back she could only do damage with her right shoulder. She drove it as hard as she could into his lower back, and there was a sickening crunching sound that rivaled the sound of the Sheriff's fist when it connected with Tom's ear.

There was chaos in the street as the Sheriff's men converged on them. They were most likely used to easily intimidating and handling survivors caught foraging around their city, but they had never run into a group of people quite like the Mud Island survivors. More than one of the Sheriff's men found out what happened if they let this group get behind them, and by the time shots were fired there was a big pile of people in the middle of the road.

When the shots rang out the Mud Island survivors froze where they were, hoping they wouldn't see a member of the group in a pool of blood. One of the Sheriff's men stood above everyone with a rifle pointed in the air, and he swept the barrel lower to make it clear the first shot was the only warning. Everyone got the message. There were curses and groans as everyone separated themselves from the pile, but the most prolific cursing was from the Sheriff. He was leaving very little doubt that he was both angry and in pain.

Kathy had a personal motto that was well known to the rest of the Mud Island crew, and their own doctor had agreed with her more than once when he had to treat minor injuries. Doctor Bus put his stamp of approval on the motto every time he said, "When your back hurts, everything feels miserable, so you're lucky you didn't hurt your back."

At that moment the Sheriff would have agreed with her motto. He had both of his arms stretched around to the middle of his lower back so he could press his palms against it, and he was in agony with every step he took as he tried to walk off the pain. His head was thrown so far back that his hat had come off, and one of his men was following dutifully behind him just trying to put it back on his head for him. The satisfied expression on Kathy's face would have gotten her shot if he had turned her way. She backed away from someone with the barrel of a rifle only inches from her face and dropped down next to Tom to see if he was breathing.

The rest of the group had tried to create as much havoc in the pile up as possible, and the results were almost what they had hoped for. Once bodies started colliding with each other, there were opportunities for them to get their hands under their feet and around in front. Even though they were tied, they got the upper hand on the Sheriff's men. If one of them had gotten to a gun first, they might have gotten complete control because the M134s couldn't fire with the Sheriff in the middle of the dog-pile. Now that they had lost their chance, they could only sit back and wait for the punishment they knew was coming. The only thing delaying it was the obvious misery the Sheriff felt in his lower back.

The Sheriff's walk of pain had taken him in a long circle around the intersection, and he and his entourage were working their way back around to where it had all started. He had yet to be able to straighten his body up and walk normally. Every time he tried, a fresh string of cursing started, and he would stretch out his back and duckwalk a little further.

Cassandra and Sim had started out at the back of the mayhem, but when Kathy made her dive into the Sheriff the reaction by his men was to rescue him. They were all so spread out that Cassandra saw their chance, and she launched herself into Sim. They fell together through the foliage behind them. She almost magically rolled over Sim and at the same time slid her hands over her feet to get them in front. She grabbed Sim just as he got his feet under him and gave him a second shove that carried them both out of sight behind a row of cars that hadn't moved in over six years. Their rusting hulks were disappearing in the overgrown bushes along the street, and the two escapees were able to crawl a long way without breaking cover. They only stopped long enough for Cassandra to help Sim get his hands in front too. They could untie them after they put some distance between themselves and the intersection.

There were shouts behind them, and gunshots were fired wildly but missed high. They could both tell that whoever was shooting was doing it blindly without any idea of where they had gone. They were just grateful that they didn't hear the sound of the M134s, and they felt that dread until they made their first turn behind a building. As they crossed under an overpass that seemed out of place because there was no road under it, Sim took a hard fall when his foot caught on something solid. The good news was that he wasn't hurt, and the grass was so deep that it hid them from view. The bad news was the trio of infected dead that were standing in the shadows of the overpass. Any hope that they weren't spotted by them disappeared when they groaned.

Cassandra gave him a hand, but he stumbled again. He saw metal under his hands, and he realized why he kept tripping.

"Railroad tracks!"

"I can see that," said Cassandra. "We can use them to put some distance between us and trouble without using streets."

She helped him up for a second time, and being veteran survivors, they ran right past the three infected dead that were making slow progress in the tall grass. They ran on the tracks for at least a hundred yards before they decided it was safe to slow down. The tracks led them to the back of a long building with a loading dock and single doors spaced wide apart.

"If this is what I think it is," said Cassandra, "it's just what we're looking for."

"What is it?"

"I think it's a mall. These doors are wide apart like the fire exits of stores. I don't think we're likely to find one that's unlocked, but one thing about malls is that I've always found something useful inside them."

They followed the back of the building until they came to the parking lots, but Sim saw something familiar. There was a metal ladder on the side of the building a lot like the one he and the rest of his flight crew had used on the roof of the airport in Columbus, Ohio.

"Hey, check it out. Let's find something to cut our hands loose so we can climb that ladder."

There was no shortage of sharp debris around the cars that still littered the huge parking lot. The pavement was cracked between the cars where small trees stubbornly pushed up to get their share of sunlight. The mall must have been open when the infection broke out because there were so many cars, but one mistake some cities made was to use malls as emergency treatment centers. Judging by the ambulances that were clustered together in one place, someone had made that mistake.

"Be careful with that thing," said Sim as Cassandra sawed at the rope on his wrists. "That metal has some serious rust on it."

"This isn't my first rodeo, Sim. If you want to you can cut mine off first."

Sim knew when to back off, and if he was going to trust anyone it was Cassandra. Besides being in love with her, he recognized her survival skills. Not everyone could survive on a ship that was packed with infected dead the way her ship was. She had been the only survivor, as a matter of fact, and the ship was a hotbed of infection.

With their hands free to move, they were able to work together to pile debris under the ladder. It wasn't designed for easy access to the roof. It had been installed on the side of the building to allow work crews to reach it from below if they had a tall ladder. As a fire escape, it was only intended to allow a person to get close enough to the ground to drop safely the rest of the way without breaking a leg. A few shopping carts piled on top of each other were enough for them to catch the bottom rung, and an easy chin up was all they needed from there. Cassandra went first, and he didn't waste any time. Until they were on the roof, they would be a highly visible target.

Her feet disappeared over the edge of the roof, and Sim was following as fast as he could when he heard the distinct sound of an engine. It sounded like it was coming from the direction of the railroad tracks, and he was tempted to throw a glance that way, but he felt Cassandra's hands grip his shoulders and pull. He cleared the top ledge in the air, and they fell together to the rough surface of the roof. It felt like a hot road with the sun beating down on it, and he pulled his hands away to keep from getting burned.

The sound of the truck came closer, and even with the ledge around the roof protecting their hiding place, they were afraid to move. They had no idea if they had been spotted climbing the building, but with nothing more than their knives for defense, they didn't even want to make a sound.

Cassandra whispered, "Get close to the wall by the ladder. If anyone comes over the edge, they'll be leading with a gun."

As if she had predicted it, the sound of boots rapidly hitting each rung carried to where they were, and they scurried closer to the low wall where someone would appear at any moment. By the sound of it, there were at least two people climbing at the same time.

Someone's right hand cleared the top, and Sim's eyes went wide when he saw it was gripping a 9 mm semiautomatic pistol as the man used his wrist to keep his balance. The left hand grabbed the top of the ledge as he pulled himself into full view. He undoubtedly expected to find he had a clear shot as someone ran from him, and his right arm came up to take aim. Cassandra and Sim were directly below him, and the last thing he expected was to have someone grab his wrists.

Cassandra pulled his arm with one hand and grabbed the gun with the other. Neither of them wanted the big man to fall on them, so they rolled aside as he dove nose first. Sim rolled away from the wall as Cassandra rolled toward it. They pulled downward as hard as they could, and the man hit the top of the ledge with his fat stomach. He made a loud grunt as the air was knocked out of his lungs, but it was cut short by the sound of his face hitting the rough asphalt surface of the roof.

The second man stood to his full height and rested one knee on the top of the ledge, his eyes immediately locking on Sim with the body of his partner between them. He leaned his weight forward as he raised his gun. If he had lowered his head, he would have seen he was so close to Cassandra that she disappeared under his shadow. The gun she had grabbed from the first man was pointed straight up, so the bullet easily found the soft spot below his chin and made its exit through the crown of his scalp. It seemed to both Sim and Cassandra that he was gone before the sound of the gun stopped ringing in their ears.

Cassandra stayed low, but she moved quickly to the side of the first man and got a good grip on his jacket at the shoulders.

"Give me a hand! We've got to dump him over the side before he comes to. If we're lucky they won't be missed for a while, and if someone comes looking for them maybe they won't make a connection between the ladder and these guys being dead."

The man was heavy, and they had a tough time lifting him high enough to get him over the ledge, but once they had him perched on top they only had to give him a shove to make him roll off. They watched him drop to the pavement below, and he sounded like a wet sandbag when he hit. His partner had landed further away because he had been driven backward from a standing position when the bullet had punched into his head.

"How does someone stay that heavy during a zombie apocalypse?" complained Sim. "Most people at least lose weight from all the running, but this guy must've found a snack food factory."

"I don't know, but we have to do something about the truck. That machine gun sticks out like a sore thumb."

The parking lot was full of weather worn and damaged cars. Some had been burned on the first night of the infection. Others had simply sunk lower to the ground as their tires rotted through the years of being parked in one place. As the air escaped unevenly, cars listed to the sides until the other tires did the same.

Then there was the grass. The impact of thousands of dead bodies left to rot on the asphalt was something that always amazed Cassandra. As a survivor, she was an observer of the history that followed the fall of civilization. Seeing buildings crumble wasn't a surprise, nor was tall grass or trees. Wherever man had held back vegetation it was bound to encroach abundantly. What did surprise her was the way people had become the fertilizer of a new crop.

Decaying bodies were fed upon by an untold variety of wildlife and insects, and their populations grew, but in some places the gases and the body fluids had escaped into the cracks and crevices and nourished the unseen roots of plants in parking areas. The plants tenaciously wedged through the cracks and grew until they forced the cracks to widen. The asphalt was pushed upward until the cars sitting on it were further tilted at crazy angles. Where the seeds of trees found the rich soil, their roots grew larger and wider. From above Cassandra and Sim could see trees that had literally forced themselves against cars until they had penetrated openings and grown through them. A pickup truck in good condition holding an M134 in its bed might as well also have a spotlight on it.

They didn't know how much time they had, so they moved quickly and climbed down to the parking lot. As a team, Cassandra was the better choice for combat, but Sim had been a flight navigator before the infection, and mental calculations were his strong suit. Cassandra wanted to remove the M134 or at least disable it, but Sim had a better idea. He suggested that it might come in handy later.

"Imagine that thing in the hands of the right people," said Sim.

As soon as he said it, Cassandra understood. "We're not going to be able to rescue the others using our good looks, but where do you hide a Silverado?"

Sim scratched at his chin. From above the truck was big, but standing next to it made him realize just how big. There were plenty of big stores in the mall, but none had entrances big enough to drive a vehicle inside without crashing through the glass. He turned and let his eyes follow the names of the stores in the mall until he stopped at one on the opposite end. A familiar blue and yellow sign with big white letters reminded him of something.

"There's a possibility. If those people search for the truck, they would probably think to check stores that have big service centers that sell tires and do oil changes, but that store only has a small garage for installing car stereos."

Cassandra beamed at her man. "You're a genius!"

Sim added to her excitement by reminding her there would also be an entrance to the store inside the service garage, so they could get inside the mall easier. They might not find something useful in the mall, but it would at least give them a place to hide while they figured out how to rescue their friends.

8

Farley

Huntsville - Year Seven

The chaos in the middle of the intersection made some of the Sheriff's men unsure of why the others were shooting at the row of rusty cars. Bullets tore through old walls and glass windows that were hidden behind the years of foliage that grew over everything. The shards and chips flew in every direction, but no one knew if they had hit anything worth shooting.

Two of the men closer to the far side of the street gave halfhearted pursuit, but neither of them could see where the fugitives had gone, and neither was willing to venture into that jungle. One of the pickup trucks roared past them and disappeared after making a sharp left turn a block away.

Tom rolled onto his side, blinking his eyes and stretching his jaw left and right. With his hands tied behind his back, he wasn't able to reach his left ear, but it had turned a bright shade of purple and would have been grateful for a bag of ice cubes. Kathy was on her stomach in front of him. She was saying something, but he either couldn't hear her or couldn't understand her because of the weapons firing over them. The smile on her face was because he at least had his eyes open.

Before the Chief had been tackled by four of their captors, he had gotten to his feet long enough to cripple three of them. They had stopped directly in front of him to take aim at Cassandra and Sim as they dove for the bushes. His size sixteen boot had most likely crushed one man's ribcage and punctured his lungs, but the force behind the kick had driven him into the other two. All three went down under the Chief's full weight as he followed them with his heel planted in the first man's armpit. He literally walked on the man to stomp on the second, and the third one hit the tailgate of a pickup truck so hard that he was unconscious before he hit the ground.

Colleen, Hampton, and Iris had all been too close to the row of pickup trucks to cause any real mayhem and had been forced to fall to the cracked pavement to keep from being shot. Iris couldn't take her eyes off of the Chief. Despite learning to expect him to be like a wrecking ball, it was still a sight to see. Hampton and Colleen were watching the Sheriff put on a show just trying to walk while standing up straight. Someone who was most likely the Sheriff's version of a doctor was walking with him and asking him questions while he probed at the Sheriff's lower back. He must have touched the wrong spot because the Sheriff let out a yell and took a swing at him. It obviously hurt the Sheriff more than the doctor because he went down to his knees again.

When it was all over, the Sheriff was loaded into the back of a pickup truck and taken away. There were a few moments of quiet before another man walked into the intersection and took charge. Unlike the Sheriff, he was much taller than the others, and he was more like what Kathy expected at the start. He stood over them and surveyed the survivors without speaking. Kathy's instincts as a police officer told her that this man was possibly more dangerous than the Sheriff, but there was something else about him that told her she could be wrong. The difference between one group of survivors and another was often only the person who was in charge. If that leader kept everyone alive and fed, the followers were inclined to put up with almost anything.

The man wore a badge and had a holstered semiautomatic pistol, but his comfortable stance and easy demeanor made all of them feel like they were less likely to be shot now that the main guy was gone.

"My name is Deputy Howell. You can call me that, or you can call me by my first name, Wesley. I don't care. What I do care about is keeping some kind of order. You may not like the way we do things around here, but we didn't ask you to come to Huntsville. Now that you're here, you'll earn privileges just like everyone else. After you've been here long enough, you'll earn the right to get your weapons back, and you'll be able to do more jobs like hunting biters. If you try to leave, you may get away, but the next time we see you will be the day you die. The penalty for leaving is death."

On a signal from Deputy Howell, several men moved into the intersection and helped everyone to their feet. Tom was a bit unsteady, but after swaying then catching his balance, he managed to stay upright. Kathy tugged against the rope that cut into her wrists wanting to help him, but the best she could do was give him someone to lean on.

The Chief moved without protest when the man pointed in the direction of the trucks, so the others followed, and they were loaded into the bed of one that had a rail running along the sides. Always watching for an opportunity to escape, they all knew it had to be a good chance or someone would die, but any thoughts of escaping by jumping from a moving truck were put to rest when each of them was tied one by one to the rails. A short length of rope was looped through the bonds on their wrists and then wrapped around the rail. The other end was then tied to the hands of the person next to them.

The last thing any of them wanted was the black hoods that were pulled over their heads. Not being able to see where they were going wasn't what bothered them because they could all navigate back to the intersection just by spotting the mountain they had crossed to enter Huntsville. It was the feeling of being defenseless that made them all pull at their restraints from time to time as the truck bounced along to wherever it was they were going. If they encountered a horde of the infected, they wouldn't be able to do anything to save themselves.

It was over two hours later when the trucks pulled into an area where there was more noise. Through the hoods they could hear the sounds made by people in a large camp. There was smoke in the air that carried the smell of greasy food, but there was also the unmistakable odor of petroleum fires. Rubber tires were being burned somewhere, and the smoke was blowing straight across them. For a few moments they were grateful for the hoods.

They were all thrown forward as the truck came to a stop. The doors opened and slammed shut, and there was increased activity all around them. Not being able to see made the Chief feel like attacking the first person to come within reach of his legs, and that's exactly what he did.

The tailgate dropped down heavily and banged into place, and they all felt the rear of the truck drop lower under the weight of someone big climbing into the truck with them. The Chief couldn't see anything, but he had fought in the dark many times, and his situational awareness was good enough for him to know the man was passing between him and whoever was tied up across from him. He was reasonably sure it was Kathy because their boots had bumped against each other during the long drive. They had tried to tap out signals, but there were so many incidental bumps as the truck bounced that they kept messing up the messages. If it was Kathy, the Chief knew she was likely to kick the man too.

The man wasn't as big as the Chief, but he was big enough that most people gave him room when he walked by. His shaved head was beet red in the sunlight, but the lower half of his head was covered by a dense beard. His tank top shirt was stretched tight across layers of fat that hid muscles that used to be as hard as stone, but the loss of civilization had ended his promising football career, and he had let himself go. What he lost in conditioning he had gained in meanness, and the toothless smile on his face meant he was enjoying his job as the camp foreman.

From where Gordon Breedlove stood on the tailgate, he liked what he saw. He was aware of the three men in the back of the truck, but his eyes lingered on the three females. One was long and lean, but two of them changed his smile to a lecherous leer. He was especially drawn to the athletic body of the first one on his left.

"Lady, if you're half as good looking under that hood as the rest of you, then we're getting to know each other real soon. Let me get a peek under there so I'll know what I've got."

Kathy felt one hand tug at the corner of her hood, but his other hand had trailed across her body from her waist up to her chest. She forced herself to breathe slowly and not react because she could tell he had put his back to the Chief and had bent over at the waist. That meant the Chief would have a great target that he couldn't miss even with a hood over his head.

She saw a little daylight creep under the edge of the hood and felt the touch of the Chief's foot as he pulled the big boot back toward his powerful body. She had seen him using a leg press to workout in the shelter, and she knew his legs were strong enough, so she resisted the temptation to shoot her own foot to where she guessed the man's groin would be. He must've thought she was totally helpless or he would never have stepped across her the way he had, but for all she knew, the man would see it coming and block her kick.

More daylight appeared, and Kathy could see enough to know she had been right to give the Chief his shot. With her back pressed low against the inside of the truck, she could see everything, and her smile was impossible to stop. Gordon even thought for a moment it was intended for him because he returned the smile.

For the second time in one day, the Chief had the opportunity to really hurt someone with his foot, and it must have hurt bad. His leg shot forward like a piston, and his boot heel found the center of the big man's buttocks. Kathy ducked lower as he flew over her head first and landed on top of something made of metal, judging by the incredible sound of the impact. On top of the racket was the wail of pain that meant the Chief had scored a direct hit on something delicate, and the raucous laughter all around them was a signal that Gordon wasn't too popular in the camp. He kept wailing long after the last piece of metal had landed, but then the wailing changed to screaming. If it was possible to go higher, the man was shrieking.

The truck lurched forward from where it had been parked, and the Mud Island survivors all listened for clues about what was happening. The wailing, screaming, shrieking, and laughing was punctuated by the yelling as people shouted instructions. Someone had yelled to move the truck, and someone yelled something about a fire. They felt their hands being cut loose from the rails, and the hoods were yanked from their heads.

They were surrounded by chaos. They were in a shantytown of some kind, and they were surrounded by hundreds of people in dirty clothes. The Chief immediately saw his handiwork because he was a little higher than all of the people who had gathered to watch Gordon die. He knew he was going to hurt someone, but even he was surprised by the results of his kick.

The people had only moved the truck to keep it from catching on fire. They had originally stopped in front of an open air blacksmith tent because Deputy Howell had decided someone as big as the Chief would make a good blacksmith. Gordon worked there as well, and he was happy to have someone to boss around, but his status as the head blacksmith was short-lived because he had flown directly from the truck into the immensely hot forge. When he landed on the coals, his clothing quickly burst into flames, and the laughing crowd was happy to let him burn.

Gordon Breedlove flopped around in the hot debris of the blacksmith shop. He was trying desperately to put out the flames that grew even higher when he rolled into a bucket of gasoline that was used to raise the temperature of the super hot forge. It splashed onto him, and the screaming stopped as his beard caught fire, and his mouth was no longer able to produce the sound.

The scene drew people from all over the camp, and they watched as if it was the best entertainment they had seen in a long time. At some point during the show, Deputy Howell showed up next to the truck and stood behind the Chief.

"That was dumb, mister. You killed the guy who was going to at least do some of your work."

The Chief had been sizing up their new situation, and he could see that life in the camp was a matter of survival. Otherwise, Deputy Howell wouldn't be able to walk so freely into the middle of it. Like any prison camp, retribution from the guards was all the protection he needed.

"I guess you're going to have to put one of these guys in the blacksmith shop with me."

He nodded at Tom and Hampton.

The deputy let out a snort. "Do you think I'm stupid? You may have gotten rid of Gordon, but he wasn't your worst nightmare. The Sheriff might not be standing up and walking too well, but there's nothing wrong with his voice, and he's been cussing about blondie for hours. I'm splitting you guys up. This is a big camp, and there's work for all of you. From the looks of these people with you, they're all heathy and will be put to good use somewhere."

"If he hurts any of my people, I'll kill him."

Kathy couldn't recall ever hearing the Chief voice that threat. He was a good, gentle man, but the years had changed him just like it had changed all of them. She saw the expression on Deputy Howell's face, and if she read him correctly, he not only understood that the Chief meant what he said but maybe he would welcome it himself.

"Let's go, mister. You have a mess to clean up while we situate the rest of your friends."

He clapped a strong hand down on the Chief's shoulder in an almost brotherly gesture, and the Chief wondered if Howell wasn't trying to tell him something. The message he thought he was getting was almost a sign of appreciation for what he had done to Gordon. He decided there wasn't much he could do under the present circumstances, so he swung his feet down from the back of the pickup truck and dropped to the ground. He felt someone tug at his hands, and the rope slipped off. Then he was amazed to see the truck just move away slowly, leaving him standing in front of the blacksmith tent.

His eyes fixed on Iris and then quickly to Kathy. The message was clear. He wanted Kathy to look out for Iris, even though he knew Iris was also a survivor. Whatever happened to them, he knew that together they were safer.

With the truck gone, the crowd began to break up, leaving the Chief standing in the town as if he had been dropped into a third world country before the apocalypse. The deputy gave him another slap on the back and disappeared as if he had never been there. The Chief rubbed at his wrists and surveyed his surroundings. From what he could tell by the way people moved freely around him, he had achieved a higher status by disposing of Gordon, but they weren't afraid of him because he wasn't being aggressive toward them. As a matter of fact, he received a few appreciative nods.

"Could you use a hand with this?"

A man was standing next to the smoldering ruin of Gordon's body.

"Even without all of his teeth he's going to become one really ugly biter any minute now. Want me to take care of that?"

The Chief decided to accept any offers of help and realized, just like any prison, there would be alliances. He mumbled a "thanks" to the man and took a couple of tentative steps into the tent. The man pulled a hot poker from the coals and easily inserted it into the back of Gordon's head. The smell from the smoke that drifted from the body was acrid, but the man didn't move until he was sure he had been thorough. He dragged away the body and was gone for about an hour, but the Chief noticed when he showed up again and just sort of got comfortable against the pole that held up one corner of the roof. He didn't know if he was someone looking to make a friend or someone left by Deputy Howell to keep an eye on the new blacksmith.

The Chief had played around in a forge when he was younger. It didn't take him long before he had noticed how it improved his grip, and how muscles that should have been sore from his workouts were feeling a bit different. He decided to incorporate working at the forge into his exercise routine, and for good measure he spent equal time using each hand.

A soft voice interrupted his thoughts.

"You have the appearance of a man who knows his way around a forge, and you're also different."

He hadn't seen the woman until she spoke. In another place and time, she would have been someone he expected to see at a news desk on television. Now she wore clothes that were cleaner than most of the people in the camp, but only because she put effort into washing them. She held out her hand to shake his, and even the way she did that was out of place in the drab surroundings.

"Claire. What do your friends call you?"

"Chief," he answered.

"Chief? What kind of name is that? Oh, wait," she said. "Ex-military, right? We don't get many sailors around here, but you should feel at home this close to the river."

It was the first time he had paid attention to the area outside the camp. He had been so focused on the immediate surroundings that he had ignored things in the distance. He immediately made note of the position of the sun to mark the direction as west, and then he located the mountain northeast of the camp that appeared to be the one they had crossed. That meant they had been carried southwest for two hours. Before the roads had fallen into disrepair, it would have taken closer to an hour.

Behind Claire to the south was a long row of thick trees, and it was easy to guess that on the other side of the trees was a river. Since he had studied maps of the area, he knew it was the Tennessee River, and it was an effective barrier for one side of the camp.

Claire watched him take in his surroundings and gave him a half smile.

"Not planning on hanging around long, are you?"

"It should be obvious. Why would I want to stay here?"

"You didn't fool the deputy either, but everyone has that look in their eyes when they arrive in Farley. After a while the fire behind the eyes goes out and everyone gets used to staying alive even if it isn't great living conditions. At least there aren't any biters in here."

Seeing an opportunity to get information, the Chief showed just enough interest to keep her talking, and Claire felt like there was something in it for her too. Her full auburn hair had seen better days, but she knew she was still attractive, and for the first time in years she had a man standing near her who wasn't making the first move.

"Your friends will get good jobs too. If they behave they may even get weapons."

The Chief was known for his strength, fighting skills, and courage, but people who knew him also valued his analytical prowess. It wasn't lost on him that Claire was quick to mention the part about his friends getting weapons. If they were going to get out of the camp, weapons would be a great idea, but one thing none of their captors would have guessed was the fact that weapons weren't a priority.

"What kind of job would get them the use of weapons?" he asked.

"Hunting for biters. Why do you think this camp is so safe? The river makes it safe on one side, but the biters seem to pop up out of nowhere, so they send out patrols and have guard posts all over. One time a guard post was surrounded by over a hundred of them, so they sent out a bunch of people to shoot them. We never saw so many biters in one place."

"Hundreds?"

The Chief couldn't believe that the biggest hordes this woman had heard of had hundreds of infected dead. Maybe the coast hadn't been the best place to live after all.

"Hundreds," she repeated.

The Chief made a turn toward the northwest and saw something above the trees that he hadn't noticed before. A big building stood alone with a slightly smaller building to the right. The smaller building resembled any corporate office, but he couldn't see any windows on the big building. It was about fifteen miles away, but the distance didn't make it appear any smaller.

"What's that over there?"

She followed his gesture and said, "I didn't think you were from around here. I haven't heard you say y'all yet. You really don't know what that is?"

"No, I'm afraid not. Is it famous or something?"

"I guess you could say so if you're into that sort of thing. It's history if that's what you mean by famous. That's the Marshall Space Flight Center on the right, but that big building was turned into a museum before the biters showed up. That's where they built the moon rockets. You know, the really big ones called Saturn or something like that. I heard that when they tested those things inside that big building it caused houses as far away as Farley to need construction work to repair cracks between walls and ceilings."

The Chief had stopped paying close attention at Marshall Space Flight Center. He didn't even tune back in when she explained there were supposed to be some Cold War fallout shelters there with lots of supplies in them, and the Sheriff was always talking about sending an exploration party over there to try to get into them. The Chief and his team of survivors were way ahead of the Sheriff with plans to explore the Cold War shelters, but what they were really interested in was the big shelter underneath them…the one built by Titus Rush and his survivalist group. After all, one of the best places to build a secret shelter was under hundreds of smaller shelters that everyone else knew about.

******

The Beginning of the Infection - Day Three

Gentry was glad to see MC when he arrived early because she had no clue how to find the Colonel again. He wanted to meet at 0900, so MC came for her over an hour early so he could show her where the mess hall was located. Once again she was surprised to see so many people inside the shelter, and if she told the truth, she had not slept well thinking about what she already suspected. She suspected it was too late to prevent what would happen soon.

As they got in line with trays, there were already well over a hundred people in the dining area, and MC explained that there were four mess halls in every shelter. That meant there were twelve hundred large groups of people gathering in the shelters for breakfast. Her eyes scanned the room, and MC thought she was looking for a friend or colleague. Then he remembered what she had said the day before, and he saw it too. In the crowd there were plenty of bandages on forearms, right where people would be bitten if they put up their arms in defense.

"I'm not really hungry, MC. Could we just go straight to the meeting?"

"Sure, that might be a good idea. I'm not hungry anymore either."

They returned their trays to the holding area by the door and watched as more people came in. One man had bandages on both arms, and he was sweating heavily despite the fact that the air conditioning in the shelter was keeping the temperature at a cool seventy degrees. MC couldn't stop himself from asking the man if he felt okay, but as soon as he did, the man turned and walked away.

"How many more are like him?" asked Gentry.

MC asked, "Do you think I should have him detained?"

"That's my point!"

Gentry didn't mean to shout, but if they detained the man it would cause panic to spread like wildfire.

"I'm sorry, MC. I shouldn't take it out on you, but there's no way for us to randomly go through the shelter and find everyone who was treated for a bite wound. We have to meet with the Colonel and convince him that we have to systematically find everyone who might already be infected with this thing, whatever it is."

"We still have almost an hour until the meeting, but it wouldn't hurt to get there early. Maybe we can catch the Colonel and see why they kept letting people come down from the hospital level after we already got him to cut off access to the other shelters."

There was almost a constant flow of people going in both directions, and it was easy to get caught up in the current as people went about their business. Most were still being processed in one way or another, and both of them saw that patience wore thin as tempers flared. People wanted to get settled into the safety of their quarters. They wanted to get something to eat. Most of them just wanted to get some sleep.

"Has this been going on all night?" asked Gentry.

"As far as I know it has. After I dropped you off at your new place, I reported back to the squad room and wound up standing a four hour watch."

Now that he mentioned it, Gentry thought she saw a little swelling under his eyes. She realized it had been two nights since he had saved her outside, and he probably didn't get half as much sleep as she had.

The administrative level had been busier the day before, and neither the Colonel or his orderly were in the office when they arrived. Two medical personnel came in right behind them to attend the same meeting, and Gentry saw her chance to get first-hand information about the infection getting inside the shelter.

They were both nurses wearing a shade of Army olive colored scrubs, and they introduced themselves as Lt. Karen Sessions and Lt. Wanda Kerns. Even though they were of the same rank, Karen Sessions was at least twenty or thirty years older than the rest of them. That made her forty-five or fifty years old. She was more of a motherly type with a few extra pounds, but she carried herself well. Nurses tend to spend a lot of time on their feet, so she had strong legs. Gentry sensed their anxiety before they even started talking. They were both fidgeting and Wanda had red rimmed eyes.

"What's the situation like in the hospital?" asked Gentry.

She was surprised by their reaction as they visibly recoiled from her. They didn't even bother to hide their defensiveness as they stepped away from her and physically placed MC between themselves and

Gentry. They most likely didn't expect Gentry to have the clearance to speak with them about military matters, but it felt like more than that. The nurses were terrified.

"Hey, I'm sorry, but why can't you answer my question?"

Gentry had been worried before, but now every fiber of her being told her she should be alarmed. She felt bad about what she was doing to the nurses, but if someone didn't speak up there was going to be an even bigger crisis than what they knew…or maybe there already was. If she was going to get ahead of the problem, someone had to tell her how bad it was, and if it was too late at least she would know.

"Maybe I should start by introducing myself. I'm Gentry Campbell. I'm the senior civilian representative of the Marshall Space Flight Center. You know, the place where you were allowed to shelter."

She hated herself for pulling rank on them. A few days ago she was near the bottom of the totem pole, and the only reason she had climbed higher was attrition. Everyone above her was dead, and she didn't want to end up like them. She could see that they were uncertain about what they could say, but strangely enough they were also reassured to be able to voice their opinions to someone who obviously had the authority to do something about the mess upstairs. Karen gave a quick glance in the direction of the door to be sure the Colonel hadn't walked in as she answered Gentry's demand.

"When the order came to close off the connections with the other shelters, there were some that didn't have enough personnel. Captain Pearson said he had the authority to make health related decisions."

Gentry and MC wore similar expressions on their faces. They didn't like where they were sure the nurse was about to go.

"He pulled rank on the guards who were posted at the connection gates and ordered them to allow people who had already been treated to go to other shelters to be reunited with their families."

"Treated for what?" asked Gentry. She felt like she already knew, but she wanted to hear it said.

"Almost everyone needing treatment had bite wounds. He also made the guards let people come into this shelter who were searching for relatives. Some of them had been treated in hospitals for bite wounds."

"The Captain made the guards disobey the Colonel's orders. How does that happen?" she asked MC. "I thought a Colonel outranks a Captain."

"You thought right, Gentry. The Colonel's going to come unglued when he finds out they didn't follow his orders, but don't blame the guards. One thing enlisted men are taught is to follow the last order given to them by an officer. If the order is wrong, you can question it later, but you can never get in trouble for following a direct order."

"That's stupid," said Gentry. "What if the order gets someone killed?"

"Hey, you're preaching to the choir, remember? It might be stupid, but it's an insurance policy to us enlisted types."

"Good luck cashing in that policy. If it's as bad as I think it is in this shelter, the only thing you can be sure of is more bite wounds."

"We were right? Is it true that everyone who gets bitten will get sick, die, and then come back like one of those people out there?" Wanda's voice shook so much she was barely understandable.

The Colonel chose that moment to burst into the room, and the anger on his face was more powerful than anything he could have said. The bloody towel wrapped around his left hand stunned everyone into silence. There was nothing anyone could say to make it better. Gentry knew beyond a shadow of a doubt that her worst fears had come true.

9

Decoy Shelters

The Beginning of the Infection - Day Three

MC carried his rifle with him everywhere he went, and as soon as the Colonel went into his office he pulled the magazine out and replaced it with a new one. Gentry didn't know what made him do it, but she could see something on his face that made her get goosebumps on her arms.

"Don't panic," said MC.

The nurses turned their heads to follow the Colonel when he went by, but neither of them made a move to help him. It was their instinct to run toward an injured person just as it was a soldier's training to run toward a firefight, but there was something about the Colonel that made them freeze right where they stood.

"What do you mean?" asked Wanda.

MC answered with only, "Wait for it."

"Wait for what?" she asked.

A single gunshot from the Colonel's office made Wanda scream. She grabbed for both Karen and Gentry as if they could protect her, but MC was already moving toward the door. For some reason, he had read the Colonel's face correctly when he raced for his office. He had heard the unmistakable rack of the slide as a round was chambered, and after what he had seen outside, it had already crossed his mind that he would eat a bullet if he was bitten. He had only checked his own ammunition because he wanted to be ready if the Colonel didn't go through with it.

"Stay here," he said to the nurses and Gentry.

MC went to the door and pushed the curtains aside. He pulled it shut it behind himself and was only gone for a few seconds. When he came out, he had the Colonel's service pistol and a handful of extra magazines he was tucking into pockets on the legs of his uniform pants. He also had a small black book that fit easily into his breast pocket. Gentry thought about the little address book her father had always carried.

"I haven't seen one of those in so long that I had forgotten they ever existed," she said. She pointed at MC's shirt pocket as she spoke.

MC acted like he didn't know what she was saying at first, but then he seemed to make a decision since she had commented about it. He stepped around them and pushed the curtain to the hallway shut, but not before he stuck his head outside and took a look to the right and then the left. He was acting like someone might be listening, and he lowered his voice before he let them in on a big secret.

"The Colonel called me to come to his office last night. He told me he likes you, and he said that I should make sure nothing happens to you."

"You're scaring me, MC. What do you mean make sure nothing happens to me?"

The nurses were still frozen into that shocked state some people went into when the fight or flight conflict kicked in. Some people were so unable to make the decision between fight and flight that they could do neither. They just froze and waited for their turn to die. They were lucky MC was there because he wasn't the kind of guy to leave anyone behind.

He shouldered his M4 and used both hands to pull Gentry and Wanda closer to him. She was still holding onto Karen, and she dragged her into the huddle too.

"Listen up, ladies."

His voice was just loud enough for them to hear, and that made all of them aware that there were shouts in the hallway. It was starting.

"Last night the Colonel told me that someone has to stay alive who can help those astronauts get back down to Earth, and Gentry was the only person alive who could do the job."

Gentry held up both hands in front of MC like she was going to push him away, but she just waved them around like she was erasing what he was saying.

"Hold on a second. It takes a lot of people to get them up there to the International Space Station. I mean a whole lot of people from all over the world. It also takes a whole lot of people to get them back down because they need to receive a steady stream of information that changes as they make the descent. Computers make constant adjustments to keep them from coming in too fast or too slow. They need the right angle, and they need to make changes in less than a second. Without that data, they will die, and I can't feed them that data fast enough by myself, especially without a computer."

"You've got a computer, Gentry. That's what I'm trying to tell you. The Colonel gave me instructions on how to keep you alive and access to a computer that would help you get the astronauts back to the ground."

"I'll get them back to the ground all right," she said. "If they don't burn up in the atmosphere, I'll give them so much bad data they'll punch a crater in the Earth a mile deep."

"The Colonel said to tell you to have faith in yourself, and he said to tell you he was very sorry if he wasn't here to tell you this himself. The Colonel told me that he doesn't believe in zombies, but he believes in what he sees with his with his own two eyes, and if he got bitten by one he wanted me to shoot him in the head if he didn't do it himself."

Karen and Wanda didn't have a clue what was going on, but they had the sense to watch and wait. Until a few minutes ago they didn't know anything about Gentry, but they knew the Colonel. They were in the right place at the right time if the Colonel had given MC a way to keep Gentry alive because it meant they were going along for the ride.

"What can we do?" asked Wanda.

"Just stay close and follow me. Which one of you is good with a gun?"

"We both had to qualify on the range," said Karen. "Is there another gun around here?"

"We don't have time to search. Let's just try to pick one up along the way."

"Wait a minute, MC. Where are we going?" Gentry felt like she was going down the rabbit hole again.

MC didn't answer. He handed the service pistol to Karen, and it seemed to galvanize her. She ejected the magazine to check how many rounds were in it and then checked the chamber. "Ready," she said.

MC eased the door open a few inches then slid through the opening.

The overhead lights were out, and the only light in the hallway came from the emergency red lights spaced about fifty feet apart. Everyone appeared to be going in one direction, but MC turned to the left and went the other way.

"Don't the red lights lead the way to emergency exits?" asked Gentry as she followed him against the current of a steady stream of people going the other way.

"Yeah, that's why everyone's going that way," said MC.

They moved at a brisk pace following one right behind the other, but on the stairs MC had to use his M4 to intimidate people who were coming up from lower levels as they went down, and when they reached a door where he had to enter a combination in the lock above the handle, he thought he would need to fire warning shots to keep from being pushed away from the door. The hall was so packed with people that he got shoved every time he turned his attention to the lock.

He finally gave up and used his body to shield Gentry while he called out the combination to her.

"I haven't seen a lock like this one since I had a locker in high school," she said.

The door opened into a stairwell that didn't go up, and as soon as they all got through the doorway, MC pushed the door shut behind them. It was much quieter with the noise from the hallway blocked out, but there was still a muted echo from somewhere below. The landing was a bit cramped for four people at one time, but Gentry was hesitant to go down the stairs ahead of MC. She squeezed to one side and glanced over the railing and could hear that echo just a bit better.

"Are you sure this is the right way? I don't like the way that sounds down there."

It reminded her of the way sound carried when she was in the underground parking garage and she could hear the distant sounds of the battle being fought outside.

MC did his best to navigate through the three ladies, but Wanda wasn't nearly as shy as he was and even seemed to enjoy the close quarters. Gentry saw the wry smile she gave MC from only inches away and strangely felt a little jealous. She had only known MC for a couple of days, but she felt a bit possessive of him. Maybe it was because he had been her knight in shining armor, but it didn't hurt that she thought he was cute. She was fairly attractive herself, and she had noticed MC checking her out, but Wanda was going to be some stiff competition with her bouncy black hair and tiny frame.

Once MC was on the stairs he turned back toward them and said, "It's about to get a little worse when we get to the bottom of the stairs, but this is the only way out of here."

"Worse? What do you mean by worse?" asked Karen. "We don't have to go outside, do we?"

"No, we're going deeper from now on, but we have to cut across two shelters as we go down."

That brought all three women to a complete stop just as they had moved as a group down the first two steps. MC kept going until he realized he was alone. He stopped several steps below them and turned around to find three pairs of eyes wide open and staring at him. Somewhere below them it sounded like a crowded subway station.

Gentry spoke for the women. "Is there some reason why you haven't told us where we're going?"

MC felt pinned to the spot by their eyes, but at the same time his anxiety level was going up, and he was shifting his weight uneasily from one foot to the other.

"I'm just worried about getting there in time. I think things have gone sideways like you expected."

"What does that mean?" asked Wanda. "What does sideways mean?"

When he didn't answer, Karen answered for him. "Things aren't so good, right MC?"

He shook his head slightly, but his worried expression said it too.

"Containment didn't come close to working, and the Colonel already knew it was too late last night. He gave me this, and he told me where to take Gentry if he got bit by one of those infected things. He also said he would shoot himself in the head before he would become one of them. You know the rest of that story."

MC reached into his pocket and pulled out a folded map that was so thick it had to have at least forty or fifty folds. He handed it to Gentry who stared at the size of it with open shock. She tentatively opened just a couple of folds, remembering the maps her father had in the glove compartment of the family car. If you ever unfolded it, you never could get it folded back the same way again. Now you just had to tell your phone what address you were trying to find, and it would tell you how to get there. If her dad was still alive, she knew he would still have the maps in his glove compartment as some sort of rite of passage to adulthood.

"He gave you this? Did he also tell you how to get where you're going? Is there an arrow that has *YOU ARE HERE* and another that shows where we need to go?"

"No, but that's why I memorized it last night after he gave it to me. I already know where we're going, but like I said, we have to cross two shelters before we get there."

"You still haven't said where that is."

"He said it's a special shelter that only NASA people will be able to open. He was supposed to take the Director of the Space Flight Center there, but that's only you now. He said you would know how to get the door open."

Gentry felt sick to her stomach without even seeing the door to this special shelter MC was talking about because no one had ever told her about it or how to get inside. Maybe it was part of the training she would have gotten if she hadn't been rushed into the job just that morning.

"Let's cross that bridge when we come to it," said Karen. "The first thing I want to do is get out of this stairwell. I feel like any moment someone's coming through that door. It sounds worse out there, and I even heard someone scream."

None of them could resist giving the door one last, fearful look before practically running down the steps. When they reached the door at the bottom, they listened to the tumult on the other side. The women nervously turned to MC with doubt on their faces because it didn't sound any better than it did in the shelter they had just come from.

"Get ready to close the door fast if I say so," said MC, "and if I say go, then we go fast, okay?"

They all nodded that they understood, and MC got himself into a position where he could see out through the door when he cracked it open, and he would also be able to slam it shut if anyone tried to come through from the other side.

He turned the handle and eased the door open about an inch and saw a small, rectangular alcove with a drinking fountain on the wall to his left. He was directly across from another door exactly like the one he was holding open. It had a small sign on it that said *MEN.* He pulled his own door open just an inch more and saw that there was a sign on it that said *WOMEN.* It was the typical layout for the entrances to restrooms found almost anywhere, but there was one exception. Both doors had combination locks on them identical to the lock Gentry had said reminded her of her high school locker.

Even as MC watched, a muscular man rushed up to the other door and pushed on it. The door didn't budge, and the man backed away a short distance. He stood with his hands on his hips and let out a string of profanity that would have made a sailor proud. He was undoubtedly wondering why the restroom had a combination lock on the door, but he made a decision that obviously meant he considered his needs to be greater than the privileges that earned someone the perk of a private restroom. He drew back his right foot as high as he could and drove it into the door beside the combination lock. The end result of that effort was going to be a lot of swelling in his ankle. The man went down hard on the concrete floor and resumed his colorful expressions of gratitude for someone's stupidity.

MC shut his door quickly because he knew what he would do if he had been that man. He heard the latch click into place, and judging by how soon the door was hit from the other side, the man must have thrown everything he could into it. The first boom was followed by a series of them as the man struck the door repeatedly.

The ladies all backed away from the door and were ready to bolt up the stairs if the door opened. If the man got in, he would be expecting a women's restroom, not a set of stairs and four people. They waited for several minutes with every muscle tense, but the pounding stopped, and MC motioned them to come back to the door.

"I think he's gone, but according to the map, I have to cross the alcove and enter the combination in that lock. There's no way I can do it without being seen, but if everyone is gathered around me no one will be able to tell what I'm doing. Is everyone ready? Make sure this door shuts behind the last one through. If we have to come back this way, we don't want other people in here with us."

They strolled out into the alcove and tried to appear as natural as they could. Karen stopped at the water fountain as the rest of them went to the other door and crowded around the combination lock. MC twirled the dial while the three women watched the tangle of people go by in the hallway. They were all going in one direction with the exception of armed soldiers forcing their way against the current. Whatever was happening in this shelter was probably happening in all of them. The shelters had been a great idea, but no one planned for this kind of crisis.

The tumblers inside the lock all fell into place, and as soon as MC pushed against the door it opened. They practically fell through the opening in a bunch and only barely managed to stay on their feet. Gentry was the last one through, and she turned the handle as soon as the door was in place. She heard a loud click from the lock and drew a deep breath in relief.

The small area where they all stood was just another landing by some stairs. Just like the last stairwell, it didn't go up. They were going deeper and deeper below ground. MC leaned over the railing and tried to see how far the stairs went, but he couldn't tell anything from where they were. He immediately went down the steps taking them two at a time. The women were all wearing flat soles on their shoes, so they kept up easily.

They went down flight after flight until they came to the bottom, but this time there were no doors, just another long hallway. It was more like a tunnel, and it was clearly intended as a passageway to take them deeper into the complex of shelters. Above and around them were three hundred shelters and thousands of people, but they were starting to feel alone.

When they finally came to another door, MC leaned against it and listened intently for several seconds. He held up an index finger and put it across his lips. For some reason, he didn't think this time it would be a good idea to peek through an open door. When he lifted his eyes toward the women he had a worried expression on his face.

"I don't know what's happening in this shelter. I heard gunshots somewhere far away, and then it got quiet. Now there's just random noise. Nothing close to the door, but I can't tell if it's a lot of people or what they're doing."

They each took a turn and listened at the door, but no one could make sense of the sounds. As MC had said, they didn't seem to be close to the door, but one thing was noticeably different. There were no voices of people frantically trying to reach an exit.

Gentry said in a voice hardly above a whisper, "You would have told us if it was like the last shelter. What's on the other side of door number one?"

MC chewed on the inside of his lip and shut his eyes. He opened them a few seconds later and asked, "Do you remember what Colonel Rayburn ordered about cutting off the shelters?"

Gentry had been impressed by the Colonel's quick response at the time, so she easily recalled what he had said.

"Cut all connections with the other shelters and report in every hour."

"Right, and this is one of the shelters that didn't report in a few hours later. When we didn't hear from them the Colonel had gotten really upset because this shelter is the deepest public shelter and the last one before the special shelter."

MC pulled out the map and spread it out on the floor. Karen let out a low whistle as she read some of the connections to other shelters.

At the end of the whistle she said, "So, this is one shelter out of three hundred, and each shelter is that big. First we packed as many people into the shelters as we could, but every shelter is full of those infected people, and everyone who was inside has been trying to get back outside. It must've looked like ants escaping from an anthill. But the people who don't escape stay inside and eat the people who couldn't get away."

Karen turned to face the door out of the tunnel. "This shelter quit checking in last night, so anyone left inside is probably … " She trailed off rather than to state the obvious.

"Yeah, and that would put us right about here," said MC. He put his finger on the map, and they saw that there was an atrium of some sort on the other side of the door, or it was some kind of room with a high ceiling.

"What is that?" asked Wanda.

"If we're lucky, it's empty," answered MC.

"And if we're not lucky?"

"If we're not lucky it's full of infected soldiers … the dead kind."

******

The night before when the Colonel had ordered the connections to the other shelters cut, it was far too late to stop what would happen in every shelter. In a few of the shelters, the officers in charge anticipated issues surrounding the spread of the disease. For the most part they just underestimated how violently it would spread. It wasn't like anything anyone had ever seen, so they treated the wounded and gave instructions to the families to report any strange behavior or worsening sickness. If a victim died the family members were not to touch the body and should get in touch with someone in authority quickly. No one expected the victims to begin attacking so soon after they died.

The armed soldiers who had the job of disposing of the dead became spread out in the vast shelters within the first hour. They were in teams of two, but with so many people dying from their wounds, there weren't any teams close enough to each other to help if a team was attacked. By the end of the second hour the armed teams were dead, and they were attacking people who had come out of their quarters seeking help. It was doubtful that anyone escaped from the shelter.

MC and the three women sat around the map so he could explain what the Colonel had told him they would need to do when they reached this place. The big room on the other side of the door was the last obstacle they would be forced to cross, but it could be the worst. The Colonel had stayed up late with MC to give him the details they would need to know.

The highly secret shelters that were built by the Titus Rush group of survivors were built right under the noses of the general population, but the entrances were always designed as if they had brought in a master puzzle maker as a consultant. They had the main entrance, and they had a back door somewhere. The main entrance of this shelter was hidden beneath some sort of memorial to the men and women of the Space Program.

Every shelter had extra areas built into them that were intended to appear educational or necessary for the continuity of civilization. They were built according to the specifications of a member of the survivalist club, but in return for the government money that was spent designing the shelters, they were required to save the lives of someone important. The shelter in Columbus, Ohio was the one where the President would be safe. There was one in North Carolina where ambassadors and their families were to be taken. This shelter was intended for people from NASA, so in the true spirit of the people who risked the dangers of outer space, the hidden lock that would open the main door to the shelter was somewhere in the middle of a planetarium.

When MC said it was a planetarium, something made sense to Gentry. The Colonel had told MC she would know how to open the lock to the shelter door, and she had assumed it was a combination of some kind. Now she was sure of it. One thing everyone with the space program had in common was math. Everything was done with some form of math, and the basic math of space travel could be anything. She felt like she would know what was expected of her when she saw the lock. All she had to do was live long enough to see the lock, recognize the patterns, and input the numbers that were required.

"I can do this," she said. "Let's check out this planetarium."

There was more light on their side of the door than there was in the planetarium. They realized that little problem as soon as MC opened the door a half inch. He closed the door faster than he wanted to, and he might as well have slammed it. The click of the latch inside the lock sounded much louder than it really was, but it was amplified by their nerves.

"Do you think someone heard you?" whispered Karen.

None of them answered because the others were holding their breath, but the answer to the question came soon enough when a dull thud made them all jump away from the door. The thud was followed by a low moan, and it sounded like something slid across the other side.

"Where's the map?" asked MC.

He was so nervous that he didn't remember he had it tucked into a pocket on the front of his leg. Karen pointed down at it, and he sheepishly dug it out.

"I have to see how the room is arranged. The last time I was in a planetarium was when I was about ten years old. It was a school field trip, and I think it was fun because everyone got their own big recliner."

Gentry added, "They're still made that way, but they're all a bit different. What specifically do you need to know? There's a planetarium on the main floor for the tourists, but I don't know if this one is nearly the same. It seems smaller."

"Is there an aisle straight to this door?" he asked.

"I can't swear on it," said Karen, "but I think that's a fire regulation or something since it's dark in there. They have to make it easier to get to the door if there's a fire."

"That's what I was thinking," answered MC, "but is the door close to the seats or down an exit tunnel?"

"Now I get it," said Gentry. "If there's an aisle between seats, we can at least dodge those zombies, but if there's a tunnel we're going to be face to face with them as soon as we open the door."

Wanda had been quiet and hanging back from the rest of them a bit, and no one wanted to say it, but they were all unnerved by her silence. Some people showed their nervousness by talking more, and that made everyone else nervous. It worked the other way around too. At the start of their journey from the Colonel's office, she had been outgoing and even found the courage to be flirtatious with MC. She had become withdrawn as they went deeper into the shelter complex, and the quiver in her lower lip was getting worse.

"Can we go back?"

It wasn't until she spoke that everyone saw that she had passed being nervous a long time ago. The shaking in her voice gave away the fact that she was absolutely terrified, and before anyone could answer, she turned and walked back the way they had come.

"Whoa, wait a minute," said MC.

He caught her by the sleeve of her scrubs and tried to slow her down a bit, but she escalated fast. She went from nervous and shaking to struggling and all the way back to numb and limp all in a matter of seconds. The sound of her voice echoed back at them as it rose, and there was no doubt she was being heard on the other side of the door.

"I saw this happen in combat," he said to the other two. "Some people were fine up to the last moment, then they fell apart."

Karen and Gentry rushed to catch up. They surrounded Wanda, and all three of them held her in the middle, talking her down from being frantic.

"I thought things were about to get to her up in the hospital ward," said Karen. "There were just so many cases of bite wounds, but she just kept cleaning out the bites, stitching, and bandaging. The whole time we kept telling the patients it was going to be okay. We kept saying that maybe this one would live. Maybe they didn't all die."

"Did anyone live?" asked Gentry.

"No," said Wanda.

When she spoke that single word, it was like someone had flipped a switch. She was calm again. She still stared off in the distance at nothing in particular, but with the terror gone she felt bad about losing control.

Thumps shook the door as if there was a crowd on the other side. The groaning went from one to two and then to three different levels. It was hard to think of them as voices because they sounded more like animals than humans.

"My God," said Gentry. "I've never heard anything like that."

"I have," said Karen. "It sounds like a room full of surgery patients that want more morphine. The only thing different is that no one is begging."

"How're we getting through now? I'm so sorry I made all that noise."

"No," said Gentry. "It's dark in there, and at least we know what's in there now."

MC spread the map out on the floor and found the planetarium. He circled its perimeter until he found the door that separated them from the big room.

"Hey, everyone help me out here. I think this is where we are, and this is where we need to be." He traced his finger from the door to the center of the circular auditorium. "This place is big judging by how it compares to this last tunnel we came through. I would estimate it to be at least one hundred feet across."

Gentry said, "I agree, so it's a round auditorium with six to seven hundred seats. That's big but not as big as you think. If the zombies, or whatever they are, are spread out in between the seats, we can dodge them because they're slow, but that all depends on where they are and if they're coming in through an open door. Wait a minute. What's this?"

She put her finger on a spot that could only be one thing because it had an arrow printed next to it, and similar arrows led all the way to the upper floors of the shelter.

"That's a ladder that goes up to an emergency exit," said MC. "Is there a way to intersect with that exit above the ladder?"

Gentry followed the exit with one finger while using her other hand to backtrack along the tunnel they had used. As her hands converged on the same place she said, "I remember this. There was a big red arrow pointing at it, and it opened like a cabinet door in the wall. We can use it to reach the ladder and then climb down into the planetarium."

"Then what?" asked Karen.

The prospect of climbing down a ladder into a dark room was not what any of them considered to be a good plan, but it was all they had until it occurred to MC that they didn't all need to go that way. All they really needed was one person to keep the dead away from Gentry while she figured out how to open the hidden shelter door. That was under the best of circumstances, though. The Colonel said she would figure it out, but no one said anything about doing it in the dark.

They decided that MC would go with Gentry. Karen and Wanda would listen at the door and try to tell when the dead were leaving the door. That would most likely be when MC and Gentry climbed down the ladder because there was no hope that they could do it without attracting attention. All Karen and Wanda really needed to do was pound on the door from time to time to keep the dead from leaving.

Gentry rotated the map and MC saw that she had her forehead wrinkled up like something had caught her attention.

"What is it?" he asked.

"This is odd. We're here on this side of the planetarium. If we had come in through the main door, we would have entered here through these double doors."

"What's so odd about that?" asked Wanda.

"Well, planetariums cost a bundle, especially big ones because the projectors are intricate machines with thousands of fiber optic lines that do those pinpoints of light on the ceiling. Anyway, since they cost so much it's not unusual to name planetariums after someone who made a large cash contribution to the construction of the place. This main entry over here has a label on it that says the name is The Neil Armstrong Planetarium."

"That doesn't sound so strange to me," said Wanda. "So they named it after the first man to set foot on the moon? Sound like a good idea."

The others chimed in their agreement, but they were guessing that there was more to it than Gentry had said.

"Sure, Wanda, but there's already one named after him in Altoona, Pennsylvania. There's an asteroid named after him and I'm sure lots of other things. I guess I didn't hear about this one because it was supposed to be a secret, or maybe that's why it seems odd to me. Why name a secret planetarium at all?"

"What's that caption under the name?" asked Karen.

Gentry adjusted the position of the map to get more light to hit the spot and peered closely at the tiny print.

It says, "You can find Tranquility here."

10

Tranquility

The Beginning of the Infection - Day Three

It had been a long day, and it had taken a long time for them to reach the hallway outside the planetarium, but none of them were ready to spend the night in the hallway at the last door. They had a few supplies with them, but there was the question of more basic needs, such as a bathroom. Wanda had brought it up, but Karen and Gentry both admitted it had already crossed their minds, but they were trying not to think about it. MC didn't admit to it, but he had probably been thinking the same thing. They decided they had to get inside the planetarium before stopping for the day.

Synchronizing their watches they agreed they could backtrack the way they had come, get inside the emergency exit, and crawl to the top of the ladder in thirty minutes. Karen and Wanda would start pounding on the door in twenty minutes. That would allow the zombies inside enough time to get to the source of the noise before Gentry and MC climbed down the ladder. Hopefully, any noise they made wouldn't draw the zombies away from the doors.

"I'm not sure I can hold it thirty more minutes," said Wanda.

If looks could kill, Wanda would have been dead meat, because the others all stared her into turning away from them.

"I'll just sit over here and wait," she said.

Gentry and MC set off at a light jog back the way they had come.

They overestimated the amount of time they would need to reach the hatch with the arrow next to it, but they lost a little time getting the door open. It was apparently intended for people inside the planetarium to get out rather than the other way around, so the latch was locked in the hallway. MC beat on it with the butt of his M4 until it popped apart and the hatch opened. Their watches said they had taken twenty-five minutes to crawl into the hatch, so Karen and Wanda had been pounding for five minutes.

The inside of the hatch was dark. The last thing either of them wanted to do was climb through a dark tunnel, and Gentry had been convinced from childhood that dark places always meant there would be spider webs. No one had probably crawled through this particular tunnel in years, so in her mind it was the perfect place to run into the really big webs you would find in caves or horror movies.

A beam of light came on behind her as MC leaned forward with a flashlight. The light shone on a shining metal tunnel with a sandpaper-like surface on the bottom that was supposed to make it easier to crawl. She rubbed a hand across it, and Gentry felt like the person who made that decision had never crawled on it before. It was rough, and she didn't think she would have any material left on the knees of her pants from rubbing as she crawled. At least she could see that everything appeared new, and there were no multi-legged creatures hanging from webs.

After five minutes of crawling, she was facing a hatch similar to the one they had come in through, but fortunately the latch was on both sides of it, and MC didn't have to beat on it with his rifle. They had been concerned about that after seeing the first hatch, but there was no turning back since there was no other plan for getting inside the planetarium.

MC crawled up next to her. "Let me open it. We don't know how big the landing is at the top of the ladder, and we have to switch off the flashlight. If it's dark in there the light from the tunnel might be all we need to give away where we are."

When he switched off the flashlight, the darkness was so complete that Gentry felt herself second guessing this decision. If they were wrong, the hatch might open into a room full of zombies, or the ladder might be gone, and they might fall through the hatch and fall far enough to break their necks. MC moved the hatch out of the way, and Gentry felt like they were outside. The moonlight didn't take away from the bright stars that twinkled in the night sky, and the sound of thunder rumbled somewhere in the distance. For a moment it was all real because the last thing she expected was for a program to be running. The projector was on, and it displayed a real time view of the night sky. The thunderstorm was the sound of Karen and Wanda pounding on the door.

MC had been right about the landing. It was hardly big enough for one person. He carefully set aside the hatch cover and cringed at the slight thump it made, but it was nothing compared to the steady thumping on the far side of the big room. With the door out of the way, he was able to lean out across the landing and let his eyes adjust to the dark. There were no lights other than the projector, and none of the tiny nylon filaments were bright enough to affect his vision. He could only guess at the number of zombies in the theater below because there was nothing to light up the aisles. His eyes went to the place where the sound of thumping was the loudest, and he could barely make out the outline of an alcove, but it was pitch dark there.

He eased back into the tunnel with Gentry until their knees were touching.

"Don't turn on the light yet," he said. "There aren't any lights on the aisles, but at least we can reasonably assume all of the zombies have been drawn to the sound of the pounding. Even without light they've had enough time to find their way to the door. I'll get on the landing and take aim into the short hallway by the door. Reach over my shoulder and aim the flashlight that way. When you turn it on, I'll pick a target. If we're lucky, I have enough ammo to get all of them. Ready?"

In the dark tunnel he couldn't see her nod that she was ready, but he felt her warm hand on the back of his.

"Be careful," she said.

MC quietly got himself into a sitting position outside the tunnel on the landing and sighted his M4 on the dark patch across the theater. Gentry held the flashlight over his shoulder on the right side above the rifle while she rested her chin on his left shoulder and pressed her chest against his back. She thought she felt his heartbeat speed up, but then she realized it was her own. His muscular back felt strong and reassuring right where it was, and for a moment she forgot what she was supposed to be doing. MC had to whisper twice for her to turn on the light.

She flipped the switch, and the beam was slightly to the right of an alcove that formed a short hallway to the door. She adjusted to the left, and they saw a group of people clawing at the door and jostling for position with each other. They didn't even react to the light shining on them from across the auditorium.

"Only six by the door," she whispered.

"This is going to be louder than you expect," he said.

It was a good thing he warned her because the first shot was enough to leave her temporarily deaf. All she could hear after that was a long, steady, high pitched tone that seemed to go on forever. She felt the rifle buck with each shot after that, but the sound was no louder to her than the sound of fingers tapping on a keyboard. That was a blessing because the sight of each bullet striking the head of a target was enough to make her nauseated. She had to watch in order to keep the light on the targets, but she had expected the sound of the gun more than she remembered what it would look like. She had seen it happening outside on the first day, but somehow she had managed to push the memory deeper down inside. One by one they exploded while she was forced to be a witness, but MC didn't miss.

"Let me have the flashlight," said MC. Gentry didn't give it to him because she didn't hear him speak. He reached up and gently took it from her, but her hand stayed where it was and she didn't move her chin from his left shoulder. He didn't mind even though it did restrict his movements a bit as he used the flashlight to sweep across the aisles.

From where he was sitting he was able to check the entire circular auditorium, and he didn't stop until he had checked it twice. The aisles were all clear, but he wasn't happy to see the main entrance to the planetarium was a pair of double doors, and they stood wide open. The sound of his rifle could be drawing dozens more of the zombies to their location, and he didn't have enough ammunition for that many.

Feeling a touch of regret along with his fear that he wouldn't be in time, MC separated himself from Gentry and stood up on the landing. He slung his rifle across his back and caught the ladder in one hand as he swung his feet down to the rungs. He climbed down as fast as he could, and when he reached the bottom he ran blindly across the aisle to reach the door. He unslung his rifle as he ran and didn't stop until he brought his rifle up to snap off another shot. His eyes focused in the only light in the lobby outside the planetarium doors, and all he saw was a red, glowing sign that told him where the exit was. Below it and to the left was another sign that said RESTROOMS.

MC couldn't help smiling as he scouted the small lobby and discovered that there was another set of doors beyond the lobby that had to be what prevented more zombies from getting inside. A scuffling sound beyond the doors told him there were more. A quick survey of the area revealed that besides the restrooms, there was a concessions shop and a storage area with cleaning supplies. The storage area also held a variety of construction supplies undoubtedly left behind by the electrical contractors who had installed the projector and computers needed to run it. Computer networking cable was exactly what he was looking for, and he happily grabbed the big spool and ran to the double doors that opened to the rest of the shelter. A few minutes later, and the doors were tied together so well that no one would be able to open them from the other side.

Once he was done, he was finally comfortable enough to test the light switches he had spotted over by the concessions area. When the lights momentarily blinded him, he brought up his rifle and took aim before realizing Gentry had braved the darkness to follow him. She shrieked and dropped to the floor. MC rushed over to her and scooped her into a hug. It took a while, but she finally quit shaking and believed him when he said he didn't come close to pulling the trigger.

MC helped her from the floor, and as the tension was finally released from them, they laughed for the first time. Gentry saw the sign by the restrooms and said, "Oh, thank God. I almost didn't make it before, but after I saw that rifle pointed at me, I came close to not needing a restroom."

She let go of MC and scooted across the lobby looking for the world like she wasn't able to take anything more than short steps. She disappeared into the one marked WOMEN before he could stop her. The white lights gleamed on the tile walls and floors, and she barely made it to the stall in time. She shut her eyes in relief and let out a long sigh as she emptied her bladder. She was barely aware of fact that her feet were sliding away from the toilet. When she opened her eyes and looked down, there was a hand firmly gripping her underwear and pants between her feet and tugging them toward the door of the stall.

Seconds later the screaming seemed to come from everywhere, and at first MC thought it had come from someone on the other side of the doors he had tied shut with the computer wire. The second scream sent him running toward the restroom. He burst through the door and saw two of the dead people, the zombies, at the first stall. One of them was ramming its body against the stall door, shaking the flimsy construction of the dividing walls and the door. The second one was on the floor trying to slide underneath the side wall of the stall. Gentry was inside kicking at the head of the zombie and alternately at the hands that grabbed at her ankles. She screamed for help as she kicked.

MC took aim at the first one and easily put a bullet through the side of its head. He couldn't get a clean shot at the second one, and he couldn't risk hitting Gentry, so he grabbed the zombie by the ankles and dragged it out from under the wall. Once he had it in the open, he was able to shoot it from point blank range.

"Are you okay? You weren't bitten?"

MC could hear Gentry stifling a couple of sobs, but she managed to tell him she was fine. He left her to finally be able to finish relieving herself, and he stopped by the other restroom to do the same, but it also gave him the chance to check out the other rooms so there would be no more surprises. Both the restroom and the concessions area were free of inhabitants, so he finally went to open the door for Wanda and Karen.

Wanda scooted past him and the bodies surrounding the door so fast that MC barely got the chance to tell them to go into the Men's restroom to avoid the two bodies. He noticed they were both walking the way Gentry had when she ran for the restroom. He wished he could get a video of it to prove it to them later.

They passed Gentry at the doors to the lobby, and she warned them for a second time about the bodies in the Women's restroom. MC found another panel of light switches and brought up the lights in the auditorium. He did a quick sweep of the rows of seats to be sure they were alone, and once he was satisfied that there wouldn't be any more surprises, he met up with Gentry at the projector controls.

"It took us a while," he said, "but we're finally here. According to the Colonel there's an entry to another shelter somewhere right under this thing. You think you can figure it out?"

His eyes scanned across the panels of switches, displays, and settings, and knew he didn't have a clue about where to start. Gentry was doing the same thing, but she was mumbling astronomical terminology as she ran her hands along the controls.

"You understand this stuff?" he asked.

"Uh huh," she said. "It's all pretty basic compared to the number of things you have to watch when you're at a control console in Mission Control. In there everything is moving at once, you know what's happening as you watch it. This thing is all about a stationary point in time or a progression of events that have already happened. It's a program of what did happen, while a launch is what you want to see as it happens. This is something that has already taken place."

He felt like he understood, but a practical demonstration would help.

Wanda and Karen drifted up to the console, both walking considerably more at ease than they had been when they came into the Planetarium.

Wanda said, "I went to a planetarium one Christmas, and they told us they were going to run back the clock on the star calendar and show us what the night sky looked like on the night when Christ was born. The stars started going by really fast, and then they were just streaks of light. When they stopped them, there was one star in the sky that was really a lot brighter than the rest."

"That's the most popular kids' show," said Gentry. "It's not really accurate, but it's a good way to get kids to understand the relationship between stars and a given date in time."

"Maybe that's what you're supposed to do," said MC. "Maybe you're supposed to set it to a specific date."

"I'm impressed," said Gentry as she flashed him a smile. "That's exactly what I was thinking, but what date?"

MC rubbed at his chin. "The Colonel said you would know, or you would figure it out, but I'll bet it has something to do with Neil Armstrong since this place is named after him."

"That's too easy," said Karen. "Not everyone knows the date, but a lot of people do. People could try dates until they get it right."

Gentry nodded her head, "I agree, but it's a starting point. There's also no rule that says there can't be more than one combination. It could be a series of inputs that have to be entered in a specific order."

"I'm confused," said Wanda. "Why do you think there would be more than one combination? I mean, I get it. This hidden shelter is like King Solomon's Mines or something, and they don't want just anybody stumbling into it, but I don't see a scanner for a thumbprint. There isn't a retinal scanner or a facial recognition camera, or is there?"

Wanda leaned over the control console until her face was practically touching it.

"Is that a camera? No, I'm sorry, it's a screw. I was just being hopeful."

"The reason I think it's more than one thing is that there are more controls on the projector console than just a place for the time and date," said Gentry. "People would get bored fast if the only thing you could do at a planetarium is a show about where the stars, planets, and constellations will be on a given date. I think I'll just go with the obvious for a start."

Gentry pressed a few buttons, and the projector silently raised and rotated, then it lowered a bit. The night sky above them grew brighter as the moon appeared with brilliant clarity.

"July 20, 1969, ladies and gentleman. You're standing below the night sky when Neil Armstrong set foot on the moon," said Gentry.

MC had his head tilted backward and asked, "What time is it?"

Gentry couldn't stop herself from giving him an approving look. She answered, "That would be the second part of the combination."

Karen wandered around to the other side of the projector and called out, "No secret doors opened over here."

Gentry realized they hadn't given any thought to where the door might be, so Karen was right to check. What if the door had opened somewhere, and they didn't realize it? For all they knew, it could be like one of the hidden doors in that magic and witchcraft school she had seen in a movie. Maybe a toilet moved over in one of the bathroom stalls. They had to watch for changes inside the planetarium because they might be subtle at first.

"Did anyone see anything move when I put in the date?" asked Gentry.

MC said, "Just the projector. I think you're right that it's going to be more than one thing, but if they have to be in a specific order, I hope it's not too many different things."

Gentry nodded again, "The number of permutations would go up with each required combination."

"I don't follow you," said Wanda.

Gentry flashed back to her early days in math classes when professors had given the classes busywork. Calculating the permutations was required learning because it helped to develop an understanding of logarithms.

"Assign a letter to each combination. For instance, call the date A, and the time would be B. There would only be two ways to enter that. Enter A then B, or enter B then A. If you need a third combination and use the letter C, then the permutations would be ABC, ACB, BAC, BCA, CAB, CBA. We started out with two permutations for two inputs. Even though we added only one input the possible permutations jumped to six inputs. If you add a fourth or fifth input then you can spend all day trying permutations."

MC couldn't help but add to the explanation, "Then you have to worry that some of the inputs were intentionally supposed to be left blank, so you could have an AB_D."

Wanda covered her eyes and said, "That makes my head hurt."

He grinned and said, "Or it could be as simple as the day, the time, and the place."

Gentry's head came up from the control console.

"Of course! You're a genius, MC. There are four inputs that appear to be obvious, or at least the first three are. The date of the first landing, the time that Armstrong set foot on the moon, and the Sea of Tranquility."

Karen, Wanda, and MC all crowded close to Gentry to watch her put in the information. She already had the date displaying on the console monitor, and her fingers punched 22:56 in for the time. She saw that none of them reacted when she used a twenty-four hour clock and remembered they were military, so they were used to it.

"You knew what time Armstrong did his moon walk?" said MC. He held a palm up at her. "Of course you did."

"I heard something," said Wanda.

That immediately caused them all to act like an alarm had gone off. Their feeling of safety and security was comfortable considering the fact that there was a pile of dead zombies by one exit door, and the main entrance was only tied shut with computer cables. They spread out across the auditorium trying to see if there was a threat they had missed, but everything was still and quiet. Something was different, though. All of them noticed it, but no one could put their finger on it.

Other than the seats and the projector, they didn't see what else could change. Whatever it was, it had to be something obvious, and sometimes that was the best way to hide something.

"I have an idea," said MC. "Start over. Clear the board and then reenter the date and the time. The rest of us will watch the auditorium."

While Gentry cleared the information, the others stationed themselves around the projector and faced outward. The night sky whisked back to where they had been, and the auditorium was darker.

Gentry entered the date of the moon landing for a second time, and as the lights went up with the full moon above them, Wanda, MC, and Karen all called out that they saw the seats move. The row half way up toward the middle had shifted one seat to the right.

"Was that one row or two?" asked Wanda. There was a note of excitement in her voice that was echoed in Karen's as she answered.

"It was one row! I saw one whole row move!"

MC asked, "How'd we miss that the first time?"

"We were all looking up at the moon," said Gentry. "And they didn't make any noise when they moved. At least that time they didn't."

Gentry reached for the clock settings and reentered the time of the moon walk. This time they were all paying attention to that one row, so they were all watching as the same row moved one seat to the right, and the row in front of it moved two seats to the right. They also heard a faint grating noise as concrete slid across concrete.

MC couldn't resist the temptation, and he ran up the sloping aisle to the rows that had moved. Wanda and Karen hesitated, but then they followed. All three of them stood in the area that had been vacated by the seats and searched the floor for signs of a hidden door.

Gentry was just as excited as they were, but for some reason she didn't expect to see the entry to the hidden shelter partially open just because she had input two of the combinations. Like any safe door, she knew the door wouldn't appear until all of the codes were entered.

"Nothing," yelled MC. "No seams in the floor or anything."

She yelled back, "You three look like someone searching for a dropped wallet or cell phone."

"Don't keep us waiting! Put in the next part of the combination!"

Gentry eyed the next set of windows where information could be entered. It had a label that said *Coordinates*, and that was clearly why the Colonel expected Gentry to figure out the codes. The casual observer would think the coordinates were a point in the sky, maybe a planet or a star's position, but Gentry had noticed the caption under Neil Armstrong's name had a subtle clue. The sign read, *"You can find Tranquility here."* Since *Tranquility* was capitalized, it had to be the Sea of Tranquility because that was where Apollo 11 landed. She entered 0°4'5"N latitude, 23°42'28"E longitude as easily as most people would enter their phone number.

Her three partners were standing on the section that moved. Both Wanda and Karen let out surprised screams, but it was more from excitement than fear. This time the original row moved over one seat to the right, the row in front of it kept up with it by moving one seat to the right, and the row in front of it moved three seats to the right. The end result was a large blank space nine seats had been. There was still no sign of a seam where a door would be, but the anticipation on their faces was impossible to hide.

The others looked at Gentry for the final code to be entered. They didn't know what was going to happen, but the idea of the floor dropping out from under their feet crossed MC's mind, and he quickly shepherded the two nurses away from the blank spaces in the rows of seats.

Gentry stared at the console as if she was willing it to surrender the last thing she needed to enter. The small windows where the numbers would appear remained blank because she didn't have a clue what they should be. Just like the last code for the place where Eagle had landed in the Sea of Tranquility, the label said *Coordinates,* but coordinates to where?

"What are you waiting for?" asked MC. He tried to keep impatience from showing through in his voice but failed miserably.

"If you're so smart, come down here and tell me what the last code is supposed to be." Just like MC, Gentry didn't mean to snap at him, but it had been a long day, and she was feeling the pressure. She didn't want to let them down, especially since the Colonel had all but given MC a written guarantee that she would be able to open the hidden door to the shelter.

MC felt the sting of her sarcastic comment, but he knew he had started it. Instead of rushing back to the projector console and acting like it had to be the easiest thing in the world, he walked back slowly, and when he got there, he gently got between Gentry and the console and put his arms around her.

"I'm sorry," he said. "I was a jerk."

Gentry put her hands on his chest and pushed him away, not angrily but with enough firmness that he got the message.

She glared at him and said, "Is that some piece of advice your dad gave you, or maybe one of your Army buddies? If you ever get a woman mad at you just tell her you're sorry, tell her you were being a jerk, and give her a hug. Works every time. She'll be eating out of your hand."

She took a couple of steps backward and added, "I don't need hugs, a piece of chocolate, or to take a pill. I need some solid suggestions about what this second set of coordinates might be!"

Her voice had risen with each word, so she was shouting by the time she got done.

MC had his back against the console and both hands raised palms outward in self defense. It was easy to go from hero to goat after a long day and too many challenges to overcome. The two of them made a pretty good team, but Gentry had carried too much on her shoulders over the last few days, and oddly enough she felt like she had left nothing but a long trail of failures. There were still three astronauts in orbit that she couldn't help, everyone in Mission Control had died except her, and for some reason the close call in the bathroom hadn't upset her nearly as much as it should have. She suddenly felt like there was no reason why she should be able to figure out the coordinates that would complete the combination of codes. As a matter of fact, she felt like she didn't deserve to be in the planetarium with a chance to survive.

When her nerves finally broke and her internal rubber band had been twisted as far as it could go, she snapped. The only thing that she could think of to scream at MC was, "How did I get here?"

The words had barely escaped from her mouth when the first long laughing fit followed behind it. Instead of letting loose a torrent of sobs and tears, she laughed so hard her stomach hurt. MC didn't know if he should laugh with her, try to hug her again, or rejoin Karen and Wanda. They had reacted to her outburst by taking seats in one of the rows that had moved to the right. They didn't want to be part of the meltdown that Gentry was having with MC.

Just as MC made the decision to put some safe distance between his body and Gentry's, she stopped laughing and let out a heavy sigh.

"Thank you for letting me get that out, and to think all I needed to do was scream a little to be able to think of the last code."

MC froze in his tracks, but he didn't want to spoil the moment by forcing it. He clamped his mouth shut and waited for Gentry to go on.

"Don't you see? The code is *here*? How did I get *here*? I could have been anywhere else, but the connection between Tranquility Base and *here* is what brought me to this spot." She sounded absolutely overjoyed as she dug her cell phone out of her pocket. She had hardly given it a thought, but she was so used to carrying it wherever she went that she hadn't abandoned it.

Like most smartphones, there was an app for GPS coordinates, and there was also a built in app used to locate a lost phone. It would automatically send the GPS coordinates to a linked phone being used to find the lost phone, and it displayed what it sent in the phone's setting. Gentry knew it wasn't enough to look up the GPS location of the Marshall Space Flight Center. She didn't know how far away that was, but after a couple of days traveling underground with MC, she knew they could be miles from where they had started. She opened the settings and stepped past MC to the console. He dutifully gave her room and watched as her fingers played over the input keys.

The monitor displayed 34°34'29.4"N latitude, 86°38'58.9"W longitude, and Gentry pushed the *ENTER* key.

There was no way of knowing how many years it had been since the door had been opened the last time, but it had been long enough for the heaviest parts to feel the strain. The low rumble sounded like a distant freight train running along rusty railroad tracks, but it was close enough to feel the vibrations come up through their feet.

Gentry spread her hands wide and leaned her body across the projector console. When the vibrations reached her knees, she got a slight case of vertigo and fought to keep her balance. She could see that it was hitting MC too. His head turned left then right as he tried desperately to see what was moving. So far his eyes didn't see anything, but that was because no one could have expected the door to appear the way that it did. They had seen three rows of seats move so far, so their minds were naturally expecting a fourth row to move.

Wanda and Karen saw it first, but both of them grabbed the armrests of their seats thinking their rows were moving again. It was the same reaction people have when they're standing on the deck of a large cruise ship. It moves away from the dock with so little feeling of movement under their own feet that they lose their frame of reference, and it appears that the dock and the land behind it are moving away from the ship while it remains stationary. Wanda and Karen were sitting still in one of the four rows that had moved when the first codes were entered into the console. All around them, hundreds of seats in the planetarium moved four seats to the right. It was difficult for their eyes to interpret what they were seeing, and the sound was as if every seat was occupied, and they all hummed at once. The sound came from everywhere, and they saw movement everywhere.

When it stopped, the quiet and the stillness assaulted their senses. They weren't frightened, but it took a few moments for them to figure out what they had seen. They were still bathed in the light of the moon that was projected above them, but the room had taken on an entirely different feeling. The stillness hadn't just come from the seats stopping in a new place. The exits were gone too. All around them the walls had rotated within the domed building, and the planetarium had been sealed.

MC's eyes fell on a spot behind Gentry, and she turned her head while still holding onto the console. She didn't quite trust her balance yet. Behind her and halfway up through the seats, there was a black rectangle on the floor where sixteen seats had been. No light came out of it for her to see inside, but she knew if she got closer she would see the steps that led downward. It didn't take a rocket scientist to know that it was the entrance to the hidden shelter, but since she was a rocket scientist she announced with certainty, "We found it."

11

Shelter

The Beginning of the Infection - Day Three

The very idea that the entire floor of the planetarium had to move in order to reveal the entrance was startling. From the moment that the first chair moved they expected the entrance to be a door right there, but it was like those few chairs had been the latch on a giant lock. Once they were moved, the door was unlocked and free to open. The four survivors approached the lip of the dark opening and were in awe of the perfection of the smooth surfaces. The steps and walls were so black that they seemed to absorb all surrounding light, yet the precision of the construction was so perfect, it could have been machined by a diamond cutter.

"Why do I feel like this thing was expensive to build when I haven't even gone inside yet?" asked Gentry.

MC answered, "It's not military."

"What makes you say that?"

"It practically screams quality over functionality. Does that make sense?"

The row of steps that went downward wasn't steep, and there were only eight of them. They were wide and a bit broad, but everything was so black and smooth. The sharp angles were precise, and the flat spaces were reflective like glass or obsidian, but they were so black it felt like the four newcomers would fall into them instead of walk onto them.

Karen went down the steps ahead of the others and put a hand on the cool surface of the wall. She said, "Not entirely, but I don't disagree with that feeling of quality. These walls are so perfect."

It had been a long day, and it had taken hours for them to reach the hallway outside the planetarium, but none of them were ready to spend the night in the hallway at the last door. Even though they couldn't see anything beyond the bottom of the stairs, there was no way that they weren't going inside. Gentry, Wanda, and MC followed Karen.

"My flashlight still works," said MC. "Maybe I can find a light switch."

"I found something," said Karen. She had continued to run her fingers over the smooth walls and had almost disappeared in the darkness at the bottom of the stairs. "It's strange the way it feels so warm to the touch, but it doesn't feel hot in here."

MC aimed the beam of his flashlight at her. She still had her left arm extended, and her fingertips were lightly playing over the shape as if she was blind and was forming a picture in her mind.

"What is that?" he asked.

"I'm not sure, but it's like a calculator or a keypad of some sort."

Before he could stop her, she depressed several buttons. They all froze where they were and listened to the whirring sound of hidden machinery. Somewhere inside the darkness there was movement. They could hear something moving, and whatever it was, it was getting closer.

Because of the absolute blackness of the walls and the low lighting of the planetarium, it was difficult to see movement, but they could feel it under their feet. The vibrations increased gradually and the stairs melted into the smooth walls. The area at the bottom of the stairs was like an open mouth, and they were being forced inside. The floor under them was solid, but there appeared to be less room to stand as the walls grew higher until they could no longer see the auditorium beyond them. For a few moments longer they could see the stars on the ceiling above them, but then they too disappeared as the walls arched inward to form a new ceiling. It was all an illusion because everything moved so seamlessly. The walls didn't grow. They only appeared to grow because the floor had descended like an elevator without a ceiling. When the floor slid into place above them, it was so far away that the stars just seemed to disappear.

They were swallowed by the entrance to the new shelter, and although they couldn't see it happening, they wouldn't have been surprised to learn that the appearance of the planetarium had returned to the way they had found it. The rows of seats rotated, the doors reappeared, the light show on the ceiling ended, and the overhead lights came on. The projector retracted into its protective casing, the data in the control panels reset to all zeroes, and the power at the control console switched off. If someone walked into the room, they would see nothing more than an empty planetarium waiting for the next show to begin.

Inside the entrance the four new occupants of one of the most sophisticated shelters ever built stood rooted to one spot. They had opened the entrance because they were trying to, but closing the entrance was an accident. It wasn't even really obvious to them that there was still enough light to see each other, but the light wasn't coming from anywhere in particular. It was coming out of the walls themselves.

Gentry said in a low voice, "Don't press buttons, Karen. If we come across more buttons, don't even touch them."

Karen mumbled an apology, but even though it was barely audible, they could still hear her voice shaking. They also heard Wanda whimpering softly. There was enough light to see, but they were still having to adjust. Nothing was clear enough for them to know where it was close or far away, only that some places were darker than others. MC took a tentative step toward a darker area, and the light smoothly increased in front of him. He took another step, and the passageway became visible.

He sounded far away when he said, "I think we have to go this way whether we want to or not."

"Why is everything different here," asked Gentry. "The lights, the sounds. It feels different. It looks different. It's like they come from every direction instead of directly from a source. The light is everywhere yet it's nowhere specific."

"I know what you mean," said MC. "Is it because everything is so perfect and smooth?"

"Science," said Gentry, "tends to remind us that the properties of something might all be properties, but they might not have anything to do with each other."

MC regarded Gentry as if she had spoken in a foreign language that he had never even heard before.

"I remember that from a nursing class," said Karen.

Wanda had gotten over her fear when the lights had become a bit brighter. A zombie outbreak had done very little to help her get over her fear of the dark. Now that she could see everyone, she was also feeling more like they were safe.

She added, "I remember that class too. It was the one where we studied symptoms and how not to necessarily associate them with each other. What Gentry is saying is that the light is strange because we can't see its source, the sound of our voices is strange, and the walls are incredibly smooth and warm to the touch. Those things are all strange, but they might not be directly related to each other."

That moment made them all feel another new sensation. They all felt more like a team that was determined to survive and less like fugitives from the chaos happening outside. Gentry felt a new measure of respect for the nurses who seemed like they were just tagging along with her and MC.

"You're right," she said. "Whatever it is about this place, so far it's just different. It's cool the way the lights work, but in the end it's just technology. My guess is that the really cool stuff is somewhere up ahead."

Even Gentry was surprised by the extent of her understatement. Walking through the obsidian tunnel with the smooth walls and comfortable lighting was close to her daydream about doing an EVA outside the International Space Station. Ever since she was a little girl and had seen her first videos of astronauts floating in space, she had wanted to someday experience the thrill of floating weightless outside the protective environment of a shuttle or walking on the moon. She hadn't made it into the astronaut program, so she went for the jobs that would get her as close to it as possible. That job had led her to this tunnel, and if she closed her eyes just a little, she could imagine herself walking on the hull of a spaceship in the emptiness of space.

Her spaceship was suddenly thrust into the sunlight, and when she opened her eyes, she was amazed to see where the tunnel had ended. The walls had changed from black to a shining, creamy white. They were incredibly brilliant without being blinding.

"How deep underground should we be by now, MC?" she asked.

"Several hundred feet at least. Maybe a thousand," he answered.

The room resembled launch control. There were rows of computer stations set up with three screens at each station. They were arranged facing in one direction where giant displays dominated the view. The only difference between this launch control center and her own was that this one appeared to be untouched. Every chair was perfectly straight. Every desk had the appearance of just being cleaned. There was no dust or scrap of paper on anything.

"Don't tell me there was a second version of Operation Paperclip," said MC. He studied Gentry's face for any reaction that would give away the fact that she knew this was here all along, but he could see she was as surprised as he was.

"Is this NASA?" asked Wanda. "Is this part of the Marshall Space Flight Center?"

Gentry just shook her head. She didn't know what the others expected her to say because this was a total surprise to her. She didn't think about where she was going until she had walked almost to the center of the room, through the computer stations, and to an elevated back row. When she saw the sign that said Flight Director, she knew what she was hoping to find.

The screens were all blank, but they gave the appearance of a flight control center that was waiting for the people who would light it up. Gentry reached toward different panels of switches that lined the back wall and located anything to do with power. There was no delay as one by one the giant screens at the front of the room lit up and displayed their incredible images. Satellite views from around the world filled the room as computer stations blazed with color.

MC immediately walked to a series of terminals and sat down. Karen and Wanda saw what had drawn his attention and followed his lead. They pulled rolling chairs over to his, not distracted by the images at the other stations. On his three screens were the recognizable images of their own shelter. To Gentry it could have been any of the three hundred shelters, but the others recognized the hospital level, and captions on the monitors identified it as the shelter they had escaped.

The chaos and destruction of human life were far too apparent. If anyone remained alive in the shelter, their only hope would be to reach the outside above ground without being detected. Judging by the number of stumbling dead in every corner of the hospital, escaping from the shelter wasn't likely.

MC located the menu options on the main display and changed the views to other sections of the shelter. The mess hall was displayed on one screen, and they watched as the dead wandered between upturned tables and chairs, coming and going through one open door.

Another monitor showed what must have been a recreation center for the children in the shelter. Karen and Wanda both openly sobbed when they saw the number of small victims in the room. Some had been older than the others, but they had been victims just as quickly as the youngest of them. MC switched the view off as quickly as he could. They all knew what had happed in the shelter without having to confirm it.

"Here's what I was looking for," said MC.

The view on the screen was a tunnel that connected their shelter with another. If it had been closed, MC would have held out some hope that there would be survivors, but the security door at the checkpoint was wide open. Even as they watched, the dead walked clumsily through in both directions.

He stood up from his chair and walked the length of the row, stopping only for a moment to check the monitors. Each station was tuned to a different shelter, and the loss of life was complete. He didn't see a single view where a living person was trying to escape.

Karen had taken over the search menu when MC left, and she called him back to see what she had found. When he saw the screen he was surprised that he hadn't been curious enough to find a view of the planetarium.

On the screen there were several men and women, all alive. They had apparently gotten the doors open in the area outside the main entrance but hadn't secured them well enough to keep the dead out. There were dozens of zombies filling the auditorium as if someone was about to start a new show. They entered the rows from both ends as the living people dodged left and right. Fleeing people climbed across the tops of the chairs, and one man had even reached the ladder at the back of the room. He had only managed to climb a couple of feet before being dragged down. He kicked and fought furiously, but eventually the fighting stopped as more and more blood soaked into his clothes.

It was hard not to feel guilty knowing that people were dying in the place they had just left. It was also hard not to feel guilty about watching them die and not turning on the sound. One woman successfully dodged her attackers so many times that it seemed like she would survive if she could only find a way to reach the ladder, but every close call took just a little more out of her. She eventually became resigned to her fate. She sat down in the center of a row, put her elbows on her knees with her hands covering her face, and waited for her fate.

They watched the monitors until it was over. They saw people die in the same seats that were directly above the entrance to the escape route. Above them people didn't know how close they were to complete safety.

Karen switched off her monitor, and MC did the same to the ones that showed other shelters. Gentry turned to the rows of power switches and turned off the rest of the computer stations. Then she turned her attention to the theater sized screens at the front of the room. Satellite views of metropolitan areas around the world showed the horror. Fires burned out of control in every city. Swarms of people moved through the streets, and they could tell the living from the dead only by how they moved. Great hordes of the dead moved like the slowly moving lava flows from volcanoes. Smaller groups of living people ran ahead of the hordes, and far too many ran straight into the dead as they came from the other direction.

Familiar landmarks made it easy to identify cities. Rooftops of buildings in Manhattan were jammed with people who waved frantically at helicopters that hovered above landing pads or roofs with wide enough spaces. All of them were having the same problem. They wanted to land and rescue as many people as they could, but every group of frantic people was too large, and any helicopter that landed would be swarmed. They had weight limits, and there was no one on the landing areas who could organize the rescues.

One helicopter lowered a chain ladder so only one person could climb at a time. At least that was what they hoped to accomplish, but as soon as one climber was high enough for a second climber to follow, the spot was filled with several people fighting to be next. With two sides to a ladder, they quickly found themselves with five people climbing at the same time, and when the helicopter dipped lower under the weight, the pilot got too close to the building, and several men jumped high enough to grasp the strut on the right side. The helicopter tilted further to the right, and the pilot wasn't able to get control soon enough. The spinning rotors cut a deep swath in the crowd, sending people flying over the edges of the building. Living people and body parts rained down the side of the building to the street as the helicopter slipped to the left, dragging the chain ladder across the rooftop with people still clinging to it. Somehow it cleared the end of the building and ascended as it disappeared into the distance.

Helicopters attempting rescues over other buildings had seen the events as they happened. Others undoubtedly were in radio contact with each other because one by one they lifted away from the buildings. There was no way to rescue anyone if it meant risking the lives of the flight crews. As they lifted higher and all flew generally to the west, people rushed toward the western ends of the rooftops and literally poured over the sides.

On the next large screen there was also a helicopter hovering over the White House. MC had already told Gentry two days earlier that the Army had been kept informed about the President and his whereabouts. As far as they knew, he had made it safely to a shelter, but they didn't know the exact location. The helicopter over the White House was military, and it appeared to be dropping heavily armed Marines by ropes.

"It makes sense," said MC. "They would want a squad to protect the White House until this is over. There's probably a squad in every major government building."

"You think this will be over?" asked Wanda.

MC acted like he was surprised by the question, but neither Gentry nor Karen appeared to be fazed by it. They regarded MC with dulled expressions as if waiting for an answer either way. If he said it would be over the reaction would be the same as if he said it wouldn't end.

"Of course I do. We have a good military, and they're probably in control in some cities, especially the ones with big bases."

They didn't react. They simply turned their attention back to the huge screens.

There was more military activity at other historic landmarks, but there were also the fires and the huge crowds of the dead. Troops who were either National Guard or Army were pouring a withering rain of bullets into the advancing hordes, and in some places they were actually making a difference. Survivors were being carried from the buildings and loaded into trucks that drove away in the opposite direction.

"They're transporting the wounded out with the healthy people, but it doesn't appear that they're doing any better than we did," said Wanda.

Karen disagreed.

"You can tell that from these satellite views. By now they have to know they can't save bite victims."

Gentry backed Wanda with a sarcastic answer. "Oh yeah, I'm sure all those people with bandaged arms and legs on stretchers were just injured. They're probably leaving the bite victims to fend for themselves."

Karen felt stung by the answer, but the fact that she couldn't make eye contact with Gentry told everyone that she was just doing some wishful thinking.

London was on a big screen, and it was in the middle of a heavy storm. The gray clouds blocked the view in many places, but they could see well enough to know that it was similar to Manhattan. The Thames River was jammed with boats of all kinds as people escaped the carnage in the streets by water. The problem was that the bridges were also jammed, but the crowd was moving too slowly to be living people. The people in the boats fought desperately to keep from being pushed under the bridge, but the river was so crowded, and the current pulled at them.

Boats tied themselves together and dropped anchors. There was a straight line of small boats across the river upstream from the bridge, and the people on the boats could see that the dead were falling into the river as the crowd on the bridge grew. The dead reached their arms out for the boats, and even though a steady stream of them fell into the water, they were replaced immediately. It appeared that there was no resistance from police or the military, and the grounds of nearby Buckingham Palace were very much like the grounds of the White House. Snipers were behind guard posts, but they weren't firing at the dead that were pressed against the iron gates. No one really knew what to do.

It was dark on the west coast of the United States, and the satellite views were a mixture of darkness and bright orange tinted with yellow. San Francisco and Los Angeles were displayed on large screens, and they were both burning. Where the resolution was sharp enough to see what was happening under bright lights, people behind barricades could be seen shooting at crowds that marched uncaring straight toward them. The four survivors were getting a good idea of what it was like outside, and although none of them felt particularly tranquil, they did feel like they were the only people in the world who had a chance to survive.

Gentry used her knowledge of the console in front of her to locate the controls that would allow her to task a satellite over the Russian Cosmodrome at Baikonur. Before she made the connection, she glanced at the time in Los Angeles. It was a few minutes after nine at night. It was a twelve hour time difference, so she knew she would have a long view of Baikonur if there wasn't any cloud cover. She wasn't really prepared for what she saw.

Whatever happened to mankind after this worldwide crisis was over, it wasn't likely that there would be a launch from the Russian space center again. Seen from above it was a mass of twisted metal with large craters where the rocket fuel had ignited. The explosions must have killed everyone that was outside at the time that the launches were in their countdown, and the launch pads were overrun by the dead. Now it was a barren landscape of destruction and debris.

"It looks like the cover of a science fiction book about an apocalypse," said MC. He caught the quick sideways glance from Gentry and saw Karen's raised eyebrows. Apparently, he wasn't the only fan of the genre. Some of his buddies thought of him as a super-nerd, but he didn't care. He was already thinking that his long interest in survival stories was an explanation for why he was still alive. He also felt a short pang of guilt over the possibility of his buddies being dead, but it was exactly that. It was short. He would take being alive and feeling guilty over being dead.

Wanda's head turned from one screen to the other as if she was searching for something specific. Not finding it, she caught Gentry's attention and asked, "Can you get your astronauts on that thing?" She gestured toward the control console as if it was the brains behind the mission control system. It was almost a grand gesture like it was a supercomputer.

Gentry didn't bother to tell her that had been her intention from the start. The only reason she hadn't was because the images on the screen were so distracting. Studies had been done by marketing experts since the dawn of the television commercial on how to get consumers to stop in front of a "boob tube" long enough to hook them, and if they stayed hooked long enough, they would buy the product. What they had learned was that reality tended to hook people faster than anything, and nothing was more real than a tragedy.

Gentry replied, "Let me see what I can do. I'm sure they'll be glad to hear from someone on the ground."

It didn't take long for her to locate the communications panel that would put her in touch with the International Space Station, but the moment her finger put pressure on the correct button, the room went dark. Even the screens on the work stations and the theater sized monitors turned off. There was ambient light from power indicators and illuminated switches, and in the gloom everyone turned their eyes to Gentry as if she was responsible for the sudden blackout.

The center screen up front became brighter, and the image of a man faded in. Gentry felt like she had seen him somewhere before, but she vaguely thought to herself he could have been any hippy from the sixties. Maybe it was the resemblance to Willie Nelson. He was just an old guy with long gray hair hanging loosely to his shoulders, but when his voice filled the room, she felt like he was expecting her.

"Well, hello. I'm glad you made it out okay. The world is falling down around you, but you made it. Welcome to your new home." His voice was relaxed and friendly. It occurred to her that her parents would have liked this guy because he was a little bit country with a spark of keen intelligence in his eyes. His giant face looked down on her from the big screen, and he smiled as if he knew she was trying hard to figure out what the hell was going on.

"Of course he knows that," she told herself. "Who in their right mind would be able to figure this out?"

The view panned outward to show more of him, and he was standing on an empty stage. He took a few steps forward to a chair that was facing her. He sat down and said, "I suppose I should start at the beginning and assume one of two things. You're either the person who's supposed to be here, or you're someone else who just happened to be in the right place at the right time. Either way, congratulations are in order because you're in the safest place you could be. If you're the first person, the one who should be here, then you know everything, and you can just turn off the show. Get settled in, and be happy you were among the chosen few. If you're the second person, just someone lucky, then you're going to need the ten cent tour. Along the way I'll tell you everything you need to know."

He laughed as if he had just told a private joke, but Gentry and the others were hoping he would say something useful.

"You know this guy?" asked MC. Wanda and Karen moved up next to him and waited for her to answer.

"I doubt it, but he'd be at home in Texas." As an afterthought she added, "In 1965."

"My name is Titus Rush, and I wish I knew who I was talking to, but that would be a little miracle I couldn't quite pull off. You're in the control center of a shelter that has survived some kind of apocalypse. Whether you're supposed to be here or not doesn't matter. You're here, so make the most of it. Don't leave, and you'll survive as long as you need to or want to. This place won't run out of supplies before you die of old age. Everything you need to know is on the drive of that computer at the Flight Director's desk. It's also on every computer you'll find as you explore the shelter. Just check the shelter directory and use the HELP menu to find what you need. There's information about me, the shelter, and just about anything you need to know to survive. If you're really lucky you brought a doctor or a nurse with you, so you won't have to access the medical database."

Watching the prerecorded broadcast was a lot like having someone tell you what card you had picked from a deck, but it was still a bit amusing. When the man said the last part, the four survivors couldn't help but laugh. They had two nurses with them, so they were definitely lucky according to this guy.

"This room was intended for someone from NASA, so I hope that's you. At least you'll have an appreciation for what you've been given. From here you'll be able to task any satellite in orbit as long as there are satellites up there. If it really is an apocalypse out there, then you have a front row seat. You should be able to see everything as it happens. Not all at once, but you know what I mean. In case you're wondering, I'm not out there trying to get in. If things worked out the way I hoped they would, I'm inside a smaller shelter off the coast of South Carolina, but who knows if I even lived long enough to see this day."

"I wanted this guy to get to the point at first," said MC, "but now I'm enjoying this." He pulled up another chair next to Gentry and sat down. Wanda and Karen did the same, and for the first time in days, they didn't feel like they had to look over their shoulders.

Wanda said, "I wish I had some popcorn."

"There's probably some around here somewhere," said Karen.

"If you haven't turned me off yet, then I better get on with that ten cent tour. So you can keep up, go ahead and turn on that high powered computer sitting in front of you, and let's get started. The government folks told me it's expensive, but I'll leave it to you to decide how good it is."

Gentry powered on the computer and was mildly surprised that it didn't ask for a password, but it seemed to her that they were beyond the stage where the puzzles were necessary. According to the old man with the long hair, all they needed to do now was enjoy the safety of their new home.

"It can't be," she said out loud. The others leaned around to see the trio of monitors in front of her, and they all had the same reaction. The floor plan of the shelter was displayed across all three, and the legend in the upper left corner said Level One.

"How many levels are there?" asked MC.

"I don't have a clue."

"If you have the computer on, you're probably asking yourself just how big is this place anyway? I'll just tell you this much. We hoped to get a lot of you egghead types in here just like they did back at the end of World War II in Operation Paperclip, so there's room enough for you. If there aren't many of you, then you won't need all the space. There are twelve levels with eight rooms on each level. I suggest that you explore the place and get to know what makes it tick. Learn about the power system, the plumbing, the supplies, and the weapons. If you take my advice and you don't leave the shelter, you'll find there's plenty to keep you busy. Turn on the main computer on each level, and leave it open to the floor plan until you don't need a map anymore."

"Weapons?" MC didn't leave any doubt about what he was interested in.

"I want to check out the medical facilities," said Karen.

Gentry used the mouse to navigate to different levels, and she saw that it was like the first day of class in one of the courses where you really had to learn the stuff to pass. There was no faking it. There was a lot to learn, and they were all going to have to learn it. She found one room that was labeled ARMORY, so she showed it to MC. Before the old hippy went on, she found a room that said MEDICAL.

"If there's at least one of you who's an egghead, I imagine you don't need me to tell you how to use the equipment. If none of you are eggheads, well...I guess you're out of luck because I can't explain it anyway." He had himself a pretty good laugh before he settled back down and went on.

"Okay, enough of that. I'll get serious and let you get on with your lives. I'll just take a few minutes to explain who I am and where you are."

It took closer to an hour because the old guy couldn't resist making a story out of it, but when he was done, they appreciated him and the gift that he had given them. Actually, they had the Colonel to thank, but whatever good luck had brought them to where they were, they were doing something that few people were able to do. They were staying alive.

12

Forge

Farley - Year Seven

The shantytown was as dirty as any of the overpopulated cities in the poorest third world countries before the infection. The smells of greasy meat, sweat, and raw sewage were evidence that the people of Farley had given up. They valued being alive over the quality of life, and the Chief didn't understand why they made that choice. He would have preferred to be out on his own out in the world rather than to be safe if for no other reason than to be free to make his own choices. There was no way to know how many people lived under the protection of the Sheriff, but this was the biggest settlement the Chief had seen outside of their own town in Guntersville.

It took a week of hard work and following rules for his captors to stop watching his every move. He could always tell who they were by the way people gave them their space. They tried to blend in, but there was always just a little more room around a member of the establishment hiding in the crowds.

Claire kept hanging around, and the Chief didn't openly encourage her, but he needed information, and she appeared to think she could score some points with him even if her relative beauty didn't. He was glad for the meals she brought him, but it wasn't long before people began making him offers in trade. He could hammer out a weapon in minutes and trade it for almost anything, so he acquired a handful of useful items when they were offered. He didn't ask for anything specific because it would draw attention to his plans, which were to get out of Farley and take his friends with him.

The blacksmith shop was little more than three walls and a roof. It kept the weather out, and with the forge up front there was a place where the Chief could sleep. When he surveyed the contents of the living area, he didn't have to think twice about whether or not he would sleep on the stained mattress used by the previous occupant who had lost his job and life when he made the mistake of putting his body between the Chief and the red hot forge. The Chief grabbed the big set of tongs hanging from a hook over the anvil and gripped the mattress in its jaws. He dragged the mattress, blankets, and nasty brown pillow into the street. Before he could even get back inside the shop there were people fighting over the treasure.

"You could've traded that stuff for food," said the man who had disposed of Gordon's body.

If there was one thing the Chief used to his advantage along with his size, it was his facial expressions. He could make anyone laugh, but his cold stare was something no one could face. There wasn't much value in scaring the guy off, but the Chief also wasn't going to let the man get away with thinking he had made a mistake by throwing away the garbage. He put the glare on his face, and the man took a sudden interest in his own feet. The Chief went inside and came back out with an armful of miscellaneous junk that had belonged to Gordon and dumped it in the street. He kept the glare on the man the whole time, and other than one quick glance, the man got his message loud and clear. He showed he understood by returning his eyes to his feet.

At the end of the first day at the forge, it was obvious that people were crawling into tents and shacks for the night. Claire waited for her opportunity and appeared in the back corner of the shop almost by magic. Blankets and pillows that were considerably cleaner than the ones he had thrown away were arranged on the floor. The intention was obvious.

There was also a spread of containers on a wooden box that served as a table, and Claire immediately busied herself with dishing out a meal onto plates. Sharing food had become a sign of friendship, and to turn it down would be an insult, but he was also hungry. He could settle the question of sleeping arrangements while he ate. She handed him a plate, and the smell was surprisingly welcome. Claire had come across as seductive, but the Chief saw that she could also influence him with her resourcefulness.

It was some kind of fish with a generous helping of small potatoes and some kind of greens. Judging by the thickness of the white meat, he guessed it was a largemouth bass, and the greens tasted like spinach. He hoped his friends were eating as well tonight.

The glass of water Claire sat down in front of him had an odor to it like it came from a swimming pool, and he figured he could do better after eating. It was hot being by the forge all day, and he needed some water, but he didn't want to take the chance. She saw his nose wrinkle when he sniffed at it and laughed.

"It's the water purification tablet I added. You don't think this place smells bad enough already, just try drinking the water without using these."

She tossed a blue and white bottle to him, and he saw that the label said one tablet would make a gallon of water safe to drink. Too bad it couldn't do something about the smell, but he was thirsty and gave it a try.

He shoved a piece of fish into his mouth and was still surprised by how good it was. "You cook this yourself?"

"My mother told me I wouldn't always be pretty, so I'd better be able to cook."

The Chief wasn't ready to let his guard down around anyone, and he certainly didn't plan to abandon Iris for the first woman he met in Farley, but there was something about Claire that made him feel like he should meet her halfway. He didn't mind taking her under his wing if it meant getting her help, and maybe she would settle for protection.

"You're a great cook, and I appreciate safe water over good tasting water, but the rest of this," he nodded toward the blankets and pillows, "ain't gonna happen."

"The blonde." Claire said it without hiding her disappointment. "I could tell you were close."

The Chief wasn't slow, but when it came to women, he wasn't always the first one to figure out what was going on. He didn't quite understand what Claire was talking about, but he had always felt more like a father figure or big brother to Kathy. His blank expression was the result of his confusion, and Claire figured it out before he did.

"It's not the blonde? It's the one with the freckles?"

The Chief felt like he was trying to catch up with Claire. He had just caught on and was about to tell her it was the woman with the silver hair when Claire switched to Colleen. He held up his hands to get her to stop.

"Wait. Before you start describing everyone else, Iris is my wife. The tall woman with long silver hair."

The understanding that passed across Claire's face was more than just clarifying who the Chief's mate was. It was complete comprehension of how well the Chief handled himself around his enemies. Claire sat back on her heels and regarded him with a new appreciation. He started eating his food again, partially because it hid his facial expressions.

"You're good at this," she said. "Anyone would have expected that one of the women was your girlfriend or wife, or whatever, but you did just enough acting in front of Deputy Howell to keep everyone from knowing who. That way he wouldn't be able to use it against you. Why would you prefer that everyone thought it was the blonde?"

He considered not answering, but at this point it didn't matter because she already knew Iris was important to him in a different way from Kathy.

"Because Kathy, the blonde, is as dangerous as I am."

Claire seemed to consider that for a moment, and he thought she would say she wasn't buying it, but he could see the moment she accepted it. Claire nodded her head and just knew she had run into someone quite different from any other survivors she had met.

"So, how can I earn myself a ticket out of Farley when you leave if I can't use my charms on you?"

"The cooking will do, but I have a feeling you're good for something else."

"Oh, like what?"

"You've already started. I'll need information and someone who knows how things work around here. I need people on my side. Let's start with what you know about Mr. Friendly out there. What do you know about the guy who's been trying to get close to me by getting rid of Gordon's body and offering me advice?"

"Him? There's not much to tell. Everyone calls him Stew, and if you want to know if you can trust him, the answer is that no one does, but he can be bought. Gordon always protected him, so when you killed Gordon there were a lot of people ready to kill him."

The Chief had to laugh. "You mean he made friends with me as fast as he could because Gordon was his only friend?"

"That's right, but the Deputy gives him so much leash that he must be on the Sheriff's payroll too."

"That's the kind of information I need," said the Chief. "Now, before we get some sleep, let's talk about what you know about those bunkers over by the Marshall Space Flight Center."

They talked until late into that first night before dividing the blankets and pillows evenly and setting up their beds a couple of feet apart. The Chief didn't mind people thinking Claire was his girlfriend as long as it was to their mutual benefit. It would protect her from the constant offers of men who she wanted to avoid, and it gave the appearance that he was quickly settling into his life in Farley. That would make the Sheriff's men back off just a little sooner, and he hoped Iris and the others were doing as well.

"You sure I can't tempt you to reconsider?" Claire had her head resting on her pillow and was facing him. The way her hair fell around her face and spilled onto her shoulders made her even more attractive, and her natural curves weren't hidden by her blanket.

"I think you know the answer to that already, but don't let it hurt your feelings. If you knew what Iris and I have been through, you wouldn't be insulted. As a matter of fact, you would think less of me if I was the type who took advantage of this situation."

Claire gave him a smile that showed him she did understand, and he saw an expression he recognized as respect. She rolled over and faced away from him and let out a contented sigh. His eyes lingered for a moment longer than he wanted, and he felt a brief but familiar desire that only made him miss Iris that much more. At least he was consoled by the thought that she was with some pretty protective friends.

The first week went by fast as Claire kept him fed, and she had free rein of the town to find out where his friends were. It took her a few days, but she was able to learn they had been kept together for three days before the Sheriff had shown up. He had blustered and threatened them the way he did everyone else, but he had things to deal with and would get back to them later. He left people in charge to watch them, but people were lazy in Farley. It wasn't likely that they were guarded too well.

She said there was a rumor that he had Kathy chained and taken away, and Claire could only guess where, but she said she couldn't find anyone who witnessed it. The Chief knew if the rumor was true that the Sheriff had most likely bitten off more than he could chew, and he used that knowledge to reassure himself that Kathy would be okay until he was able to make his move. He also knew that as much as he wanted to rescue his friends, he had to trust that they would be doing everything they could to stick to the original plans of reaching the Marshall Space Flight Center, with or without him.

As he worked his forge and hammered out a variety of tools and weapons, the Chief became somewhat of a fixture around Farley, and he noticed the guards in the towers and along the fences didn't show him anything more than passing interest. When he asked if he would be allowed to go down to the river to do a little fishing, he was simply told he was free to do anything he wanted as long as his work was done. Getting access to the river was a big part of his plan.

Stew had become useful as somewhat of an agent for the Chief. Instead of making a handful of nails in return for something trivial, Stew had bragged about the Chief's skills and gotten him a few bigger jobs. According to him, the Sheriff liked to entertain guests at his plantation style home, and Stew had lobbied on the Chief's behalf to get him the job of building an iron fence around the spacious pool and cabana behind the house. Even though there were still plenty of hardware stores that could be raided for chainlink fences and barbed wire, the Sheriff wanted the ornate wrought iron that gave it a more majestic appearance. After all, he didn't want his parties to look like they were being held in a prison. For some reason, the Chief felt like Stew was making up the whole story.

The Chief decided he would take Stew and Claire with him on his first fishing trip. He still didn't know if he could trust Stew, and spending some time with him away from camp would be a chance to see if he behaved differently. If he got the chance, he could even feed him some private information and then see if Stew reported it back to the Deputy or the Sheriff himself.

The Chief was surprised by the amount of gear they were given for their fishing trip. After all, they were expected to catch fish and contribute to the overall feeding of the shantytown. What also surprised him was the number of other people from Farley who were at the river. He had considered the possibility of escaping to the northwest by water. That way he could get to the Marshall Space Flight Center without the Sheriff behind him. The options were beginning to narrow to the point where he would have to find a way to escape at night. While he would have the benefit of the darkness as a cover, so would the infected.

They each got a complete set of fishing tackle and assorted items he would have taken with him if it was just for fun. He was also handed a decent knife and an old carbine that he trusted less than Stew. When he inspected it he found it was likely to blow up in his face if it wasn't cleaned first, and he found the same was true for the rifles that were given to both Stew and Claire. It delayed their start by an hour, but the Chief insisted they waste some time cleaning the guns back at his shop before they left. Claire was an eager student when it came to field stripping the weapons, but Stew seemed like he thought it was a waste of time. He complained that they wouldn't get good spots to fish by the time they got to the river, and the Chief made a mental note that it might be better to leave him behind the next time.

It was still morning when they reached the river, and the Chief saw that there was a steady stream of people either going to or coming back from fishing. Catfish were plentiful in the muddy water and were a major part of the town's food supply. Claire explained that it was better to go every day and catch a few than it was to catch a lot and try to make them last a few days. The meat didn't keep well, and a catfish stew could feed a lot of people. The Chief was amused to learn that was how Stew got his name. He always had some catfish stew around, and he had gotten the nickname from the Sheriff.

The main road to the river was four lanes, and it was no surprise to see the bridge from a distance. What did come as a surprise was the big gap in the pavement almost in the middle. Stew explained that it had been blown up by the Army to keep the biters from crossing from the other side. In the early days before the pandemic spread like wildfire, the biters came out of Birmingham toward Huntsville by the thousands. The Army blew up the bridge and then drove the dead out of Huntsville by making a sustained push toward the river.

The Chief had found himself only half listening to Stew at times because he tended to rattle on about nothing, but this topic had intrigued him. The infected didn't retreat. They didn't know what it meant to retreat, and he wondered how the Army had driven them into the river. Stew was like a little kid who had gotten his dad to listen to what happened at school that day, and he explained excitedly that it was a sight to see.

The explosion on the bridge was enough to get the biters walking in that direction from both sides of the river, and a few thousand of them had walked right over the edge. Those that couldn't reach the road to the bridge just fell into the fast current of the Tennessee River and were carried away. The Chief had seen it often enough in South Carolina. Bridges were a great place to kill the infected.

The explosion didn't last long enough, though. When the rumbling was done, the sustained groans of the biters had kept them moving toward the river for a while, but after a few hours they began to slow their pace and become distracted by other sounds. With their backs to the river, the biters found themselves facing troops who had served in combat and didn't know how to quit or retreat. The soldiers had the advantage of superior weapons, but they also had good supply lines with the Army base behind them. They didn't give up an inch, and as the infected moved toward them, the river kept the infected from being reinforced by the dead that had marched up from Birmingham.

By the end of the second day, the Army was doing mop-up work along the northern banks of the river and were able to begin their push in the other direction against the infected that had swarmed through Huntsville. Stew even knew some of what had happened over at the Marshall Space Flight Center, and the Chief was surprised to hear him describe it in detail.

Stew said that some of the soldiers who had set up the perimeter around Farley had come from the northwest side of Huntsville where things hadn't gone so well, and the Chief was all ears.

"It was a bloodbath," said Stew. "There was a whole battalion over near NASA, and their job was to get as many civilians into the shelters that they could."

"Shelters? What kind of shelters?"

The Chief didn't think Stew could possibly know about the secret shelters built by Titus Rush and his survivalist group.

"Yeah," said Stew. "There are hundreds of them up there." He gestured in the general direction of NASA. "I heard it was some kind of plan left over from World War II. You know how the military can be. Sometimes they have a hard time letting go of the things they build. They'll close a whole Army base and let it sit empty for years while they fight over what they should do with it. Sometimes they move back in and start up like they'd never been gone."

"Paperclip," said Claire. "It was called Operation Paperclip."

The Chief was surprised that she knew about it. He only had a vague knowledge about it himself, and that was because he had been in the military long enough to become somewhat of a historian about the war.

"America wouldn't have won the space race to the moon if not for the German rocket scientists the Army captured at the end of the war," she said.

As they talked they drew closer to the river just above where the bridge extended out over the water like a long pier. There were dozens of people on both sides of the bridge with fishing lines swaying in the breeze like long spider webs. There was a squad of soldiers at the bottom of the bridge standing guard. They were bored, but the Chief could see they were also holding their weapons properly and maintaining military discipline.

The Chief considered the differences between this protected area and Charleston. The only military presence that had survived there was likely to be considered deserters by whatever forces remained intact. Their Captain, Jim Miller, had been a good friend, and the Chief figured he had plenty of good reasons to take his soldiers and set out on their own. The forces they had left behind were likely to be dead because of their own stupidity. The way Captain Miller had seen it, there was only one way it could end if you brought the infected dead onto Navy ships at sea. Sooner or later the infection would get loose, and everyone would die.

This protected area around Farley was one of the largest safe zones the Chief had seen since the start of the pandemic, but apparently there had been some form of agreement between the Sheriff and the Army. The question was whether or not they were separate entities or if one or the other was running the show.

"Who do those soldiers report to?" he asked both of them.

"The Sheriff," said Stew.

The Chief raised an eyebrow in Claire's direction, and she gave an affirmative with a nod.

"Why? What happened to the command structure at Redstone Arsenal?" The Chief couldn't believe they had just handed over authority to the local sheriff.

Stew seemed amused by the question and laughed like he had just heard a private joke. Claire apparently preferred her version of it over Stew's and interrupted before he could get started.

"Officers are people too," she said, "and they wanted to keep their families safe. The way it all went down, it's amazing there was anyone left to be in charge. The real sheriff even died inside those shelters along with the base commander and everyone else."

"Wait a minute," said the Chief. "Are you saying the officers tried to take their families to the shelters too?"

"They did. Wouldn't you have done the same thing?" said Claire. "You have all these shelters, hundreds of them, and the civilians at

NASA are supposed to take their families and get inside, but there wasn't time. The shelter doors were open, biters were everywhere. Officers saw the chance to get their families out of base housing and into the shelters, so they did it. I got left behind because there were already biters in our neighborhood, and they couldn't wait for everyone stupid enough to grab the family photo album."

The Chief felt like he should have guessed. The way Claire talked about the chaos of that first day was as if she was remembering it, not as if someone had told it to her, but as someone who had seen it with her own eyes.

"The last I saw of my husband and our baby girl was the taillights of the bus that took them away. I don't even know if they made it to a shelter or not. All I know is what I've heard since then. The shelters were crowded, but there were at least three hundred shelters, and there was plenty of room for more people, but they didn't know what the infection was. They took it inside with them and shut the doors. Two days later, there was an underground version of what happened outside the shelters, but there was one difference. Outside you could still get away. You could run. Inside the shelters there was nowhere to go."

The Chief could tell that Claire was picturing her husband and daughter inside the shelters. It must've been hell for them to be trapped underground with the infected…to become the infected. They reached the water's edge below the bridge, and no one spoke for a few minutes as they got their fishing gear ready. Since they were after catfish, almost anything would do for bait. They were using chicken livers, which would just about guarantee they would have some luck.

The Chief noticed there was a marina downriver on the other side of the bridge, and people were fishing from the docks. He thought about the first time he had seen a marina on the Stono River and how the people who lived there were catching blue crabs by dropping the infected dead into the river. The crabs would feed on the dead, and the marina people would pluck the crabs off the bodies of the infected. Catfish were bottom feeders, and he suddenly had concerns about eating catfish. The problem was, he had already been eating catfish for at least a week. When he considered the question about whether or not it was safe, he could see that Claire and Stew had been eating catfish for years without side effects.

The Chief made a mental note to bring it up with Doctor Bus the next time he saw him. Bus was one of the original members of the survivors club with Titus Rush, and one of the smartest people he knew. As a matter of fact, they had talked about why some species ate the infected and then passed along the infection if they were eaten by people. Bus told him there were other factors to consider, such as the digestive tracts of the animals. So far the survivors knew that crabs and seagulls could transmit the live virus to humans, but there were countless other predators out there that were eating the infected dead. The best answer Bus could come up with was to give up most foods and become a vegetarian.

After they settled in on the riverbank and cast their lines into the water, the Chief asked them if they could tell him more about that first day, and how the Sheriff came to be in charge of US Army soldiers.

"The Golden Rule," said Claire. "You know, whoever has the most gold makes all the rules. The Sheriff had gotten himself elected to the State Senate after graduating from the University of Alabama, and in these parts, that's pretty much all the meal tickets you'll ever need. Of course he used his daddy's money to get the job, and then made plenty of his own. He owned more car dealerships than anyone else around here, and he got the Army to put machine guns on the pickup trucks."

"What's his weakness? Everyone has a weakness that can be exploited."

"Unlike you," Claire said under her breath.

That earned her and the Chief a curious glance from Stew. He had assumed the Chief and Claire were intimate, and so had anyone else who saw the last of them in the evening and the first of them at sunrise.

Claire realized she might have raised a suspicion that could cost the safety of Iris and the Chief's other friends, so she quickly added for Stew's benefit, "The Chief has unlimited stamina, and he only needs half as much sleep as the average man."

The Chief felt his cheeks grow warm, and he mentally hoped none of this discussion got back to Iris. He decided to get the subject back where it belonged.

"We're not talking about me right now. Who would like to tell me something useful about the Sheriff?"

"His parties," answered Claire, "are something like those big events we used to see on television. If you're invited, you're automatically important, and being important means better food and housing. There's one neighborhood that looks just like any rich neighborhood from before the infection. His house is there, and if you're one of his chosen few, you get to live there too. It's not Farley, that's for sure."

"Have you ever been there?"

"Once, about three years ago. I didn't live up to their expectations."

The Chief didn't press her for an explanation of what she meant by expectations. He had a pretty good idea. Instead, he turned to Stew because he wondered if it was possible that everything Claire had just said was for Stew's benefit. Something didn't ring true about where the Sheriff lived, and maybe Claire knew that Stew didn't know if what she said was true or not. The Chief hadn't seen a neighborhood hold up against the infected yet.

"What about you?"

Stew seemed like the question took him by surprise. The idea of him being invited to one of the Sheriff's parties was inconceivable.

"The Sheriff never had a reason to invite me, so I couldn't tell you anything Claire couldn't."

They fished in silence for a few minutes, but the Chief's mind was somewhere else. Somehow he had to locate his friends and get them all out of the clutches of the Sheriff. Then they had to reach the shelters that sat on top of the real shelter, and if he understood correctly from the bits and pieces of information he had gathered, they would have to cross terrain that was totally under the control of heavily armed soldiers. They were the US Army, but they were at the Sheriff's disposal.

Another problem was the shelter built by the survivalist group that was run by Titus Rush. The Chief only had a vague idea of its location, and even if he found it, he wasn't entirely sure how to get inside. He had the codes because he had gotten them from Doctor Bus before leaving Guntersville, but finding the door was always an issue when it came to the shelters. If the doors were easy to find, they wouldn't be as well hidden as they needed to be.

The shelters built by the government for Titus Rush had one unique characteristic that made them stand out from any other shelters. They were hidden by placing smaller shelters in close proximity to them so survivors would be distracted away from the possibility that there was something better. In this case, hundreds of shelters intended for Operation Paperclip would have been a dream come true for most people, but from what the Chief had been told, they had become populated by the infected to such an extent that no one had ever bothered to salvage them. Even after seven years, they were likely to be death traps filled to the brim with the infected.

A question occurred to the Chief, and he was sure Stew and Claire would both know the answer.

"Has the Sheriff found a way to tap the supplies in the Paperclip shelters?"

His question earned him a round of laughter from both of them. He waited for them to settle down because he knew they would be glad to tell him what was so funny.

Stew wiped the back of his arm across his eyes and caught his breath. "That would be something described as a failure, or it seemed like a good idea at the time."

Claire added, "They tried, but they lost too many men. They got a few good things out of them, but it was like getting into a crowded elevator in the dark and finding everyone inside was a biter."

"The Sheriff sent twelve of his best people inside, and only six came out. They refused to go back in, and even the threat of a firing squad didn't change their minds. Some young guy from South Dakota who claimed to be an Indian said he could go in and scout it out. He was inside for over a week and would check in by radio. From the way he described it, the only way to clear out the biters was to open the doors and let them walk out. The shelter had thousands of them inside, and they could overwhelm a direct assault."

Stew yanked back on his fishing rod and set the hook on something big. The Chief had to wait while Stew reeled in their first catch of the day. It was a large catfish that would take care of their supper. Once he had it on a stringer and his line back in the water, he continued his story.

"The Indian took a second group inside because the Sheriff didn't want to wait for the biters to come out on their own, but this time they lost everyone but the Indian. They made it down several levels, though. The Indian said the shelter was loaded with supplies and plenty of weapons, but that was about it. They thought they would find something more valuable, and even though the supplies were worth going after, it wasn't what the Sheriff was looking for."

"I'm confused," said the Chief. "What's more valuable than survival supplies?"

Claire said, "Gold. The Sheriff thinks when civilization comes back to the way things were that money will be based on gold again. He says it always is."

"He thinks someone put gold in the shelters? Maybe it's just me, but I don't think people had time to move their gold reserves to secure locations. It's probably all in the same places it was before. Besides, civilization as we knew it won't be back to a currency system for a long time."

Claire shook her head and said, "The Sheriff said he's going to make sure the gold standard comes back faster by requiring people to use it. He plans to find the gold, but he's going to sell the supplies from the shelters to get to it. If he needs the supplies he can keep what he wants, but by selling them he's also creating a gold market. The word is that he's also been in contact with other places that want to buy from him."

The more he heard the more the Chief realized what the Sheriff was doing. Three hundred shelters built to hold thousands of people meant an incredible inventory. Rumors of gold in hidden places persisted throughout history, and many times they had been true. He had to wonder if someone hadn't tried to move their wealth into the shelters with or without the knowledge of NASA. It wasn't an absurd idea, but short sighted people wouldn't have bet on this kind of apocalypse. His bet would be that the Sheriff would eventually find a ton of cash somewhere in the shelter complex, but it was doubtful there would be a treasure trove of gold. In the meantime, the rumors of gold would drive his market as he sold off an inventory that rivaled the pre-apocalyptic Walmart.

13

Hank & Hazel

Year Seven

Sim loved playing with tech, and it was one of the things he missed the most from the pre-infected world. The electronics store at the end of the mall had proven to be more than just a great place to hide the pickup truck. It had also been a surprise treasure trove of missed survival gear. The store itself had been ravaged just like every other store, but somehow the stereo installation service bay had been missed. The televisions and computers had been picked clean, but it appeared that someone had used the small garage as a depot for more useful supplies that had probably been looted from the neighboring sporting goods store.

Getting inside had taken some imagination, but that was likely to be the reason why the supplies were still there. There was plenty of evidence that others had tried and failed to get the heavy steel door open, but between the two of them it was their ability to think outside the box that had paid off.

Together they had come to the conclusion that the failed attempts with blowtorches, hydraulic jacks, and power tools meant there was something inside that was keeping the door closed, and if that was true, that meant they should try to find another way in and then find a way to open the door.

The glass front doors of the store were shattered, and they marveled at the short-sighted minds of the people who had looted the store. Someone had tried to get a hand truck with two seventy-five inch flatscreen televisions on it out the door over all of the debris, and right behind it was a twenty-seven cubic foot side by side refrigerator freezer.

Cassandra shook her head sadly as she regarded the evidence of the long ago traffic jam at the door.

"You know what's really amazing about this?" she asked Sim.

"You mean besides the obvious?"

"Yeah. I mean, we know some idiot was just trying to get something he had never been able to give the little woman back home, but what's really sad is that there was some poor dude in his store polo shirt standing up here at the door trying to stop the guy with the refrigerator. I'll bet if he thought it through, he would have been down there at the sporting goods store checking out a shopping cart full of stuff he needed more than his job."

"You gotta remember," said Sim, "half the people didn't know what was happening, and the other half thought they knew. None of them had it right."

The inside of the store had seen seven years of Alabama weather and a variety of wild animals had made it their home. Birds flew from the steel rafters above, and the store smelled of animal droppings and urine. Plenty of people and animals had died inside the store, and the smell of decay was overwhelming.

The pair covered their mouths and noses and worked their way through the gloom to the back corner of the store where they should find the door that led to the car stereo installation department. Just as they expected, the door wasn't where it was supposed to be.

Sim said, "This store has the same layout as every other store in the chain, and the stereo installation place is supposed to be along this back wall, but check this out. Nothing but shelves where a door should be."

They stood back and studied the rows of car stereos. Nothing seemed to be out of place until Sim saw the loose wires hanging from the ceiling.

"Sloppy job. Whoever thought of this must've been in a hurry."

He pointed at the wires and then at the tile floor where they stood. The floor was carpeted to the right, so they were standing on an aisle that ended at a shelf, and above the shelf were the wires that used to come down to an exit light.

"It took more than one person to move those shelves," said Cassandra. "Do you suppose they're still inside?"

Sim shook his head, "No, I didn't hear anything on the other side of the garage door when we tried everything except explosives to get the door to open."

They followed the carpeted aisle to the right, and when they came to the end they could see where the heavy shelves had left their grooved indentations from sitting on the same spot for years. There was also a gap at the back of the shelf that was barely big enough for one person to squeeze through along the wall if they turned sideways.

Sim never felt like he had to go first when Cassandra was with him. Her hand to hand combat training in the Army was better suited to this situation than his flight navigational training. He did a gentlemanly bow as she pulled a long knife from the back of her waistband. She had found it tucked into the waistband of one of the men who had chased them to the roof of the mall. She held the knife out in front of her as she put her back to the wall and slid into the dark gap behind the shelves. Sim gave her a short lead and then followed as he watched to be sure nothing came up behind them.

It didn't take long to reach the door that led to the service bay. It had a big glass window on the door, but someone had taped heavy paper or cardboard over the inside. It was a smart move to keep any light from giving away the hiding place. There was a sign that said Employees Only in the middle of the glass.

"Darn, we can't go in there," said Cassandra. "It says Employees Only."

"I spent enough money at one of these places to be an owner," said Sim. "I think that qualifies me to go in."

"In that case…"

Cassandra turned the lock, expecting it to resist, but it turned quietly in her hand until she felt the familiar tick inside it. It was unlocked, and she felt like that might be a good sign.

She pulled gently and watched as a small gap appeared along the edge of the door. It was only going to open a few inches, but it appeared to be enough space for her to squeeze through. No light escaped from the room on the other side, so she expected something to lunge out of the darkness at any moment.

"This is stupid," she whispered. "If I squeeze into that gap I'll be an easy target for anything that might be on the other side."

"What do you want to do? Go back?"

Cassandra was quiet long enough for Sim to think she hadn't heard his question, and he was just about to repeat it when she made a small noise for him to hush.

"I smell something."

Sim thought back to a few years ago when he had missed a smell that should have warned him of danger. He was on his own in a hotel in downtown Columbus, Ohio. The weather had been brutal. The cold, snowy air hid the smell of decay, but in the back of this store in a southern city there would be no way to hide it.

"What is it?" Sim couldn't disguise the tremor in his voice. The darkness beyond that narrow gap in the door was so complete that he could imagine something rancid moving toward Cassandra, and at any moment she would begin screaming as it used its teeth to strip the flesh from her arm.

"Coffee…I smell fresh coffee," whispered Cassandra.

There was a faint shuffling sound in the far corner of the dark room, and Cassandra made her decision. She went through the gap and with her left hand she grabbed Sim by the material of his shirt and pulled him through with her.

"Go low," she said just loud enough for him to hear.

Out of instinct, he put one hand out in front of his body as he went low, and his hand connected with something smooth. Then he remembered that there would be a counter inside the door for those rare occasions when a customer was brought back to discuss the purchase and installation. Cassandra must have guessed the same thing because she had put them both in a safe spot. That was when Sim smelled it too. There was no mistaking the smell of fresh coffee, and there were no undertones of decay.

Cassandra rested one hand on Sim's knee and then put a finger to his lips. She whispered, "Let me talk."

"Whoever it is hiding in here, it's okay. You're safe with me. I won't hurt you."

They listened to the silence, but Sim felt more than saw Cassandra leave. He stretched out his arm to the spot where she had been, but he found nothing but the darkness. He knew better than to follow. The last thing he wanted was to run into Cassandra in the pitch black room. It would be a quick death. All he could do was wait.

Cassandra knew that the only way someone could see better than her was if they had some kind of night vision goggles, but they had the advantage because they knew the layout of the service bay. She slowly zeroed in on the source of the smell using every bit of her Army training, and she carefully moved her hand across the top of a hot coffee pot. She felt the warm air above it and knew it was still on. Whoever was in the room, they must have turned out the lights just as her hand had caused the slight tick inside the door handle. She could admire that kind of survival skill.

When the lights turned on, Cassandra was totally exposed. She had no way of knowing what was beyond the coffee pot, but most people put them against a wall. She was surprised to find she was in the center of the service bay, and the coffee pot was sitting on the tailgate of a small pickup truck. The gray haired man with his hand on the light switch had the other hand stretched out in front of him and was holding a semiautomatic pistol. Even though the sudden light had her blinking, Cassandra could see his hand was shaking.

"What do you want?"

The man's voice was shaking more than his hand, and Cassandra could see he was scared to death. She could also see that Sim had the shotgun they had liberated from the two men earlier. He had it aimed at the frightened man, and she knew things could get messy really quick. She hoped no one would pull a trigger too soon.

"I'll settle for a cup of this coffee if you can spare it." Cassandra kept her voice as soft and sweet as she could make it.

The man didn't see Sim yet, but before the world had fallen to pieces there was something almost universal about sitting down and welcoming strangers by offering them coffee. Maybe it was the way Cassandra made eye contact with him rather than to stare at the gun, or maybe the man had just been alone too long, but she could see his shoulders slump before something inside him broke. He lowered the gun as if he was surrendering to someone who had a gun pointed at him. He never even noticed Sim, and Sim discreetly lowered the shotgun and leaned it on the other side of the service counter.

Sim felt like it was time for the man to know there were two intruders, and he took a chance.

"I'm sorry if we scared you. We're just trying to find a place to hide."

He was just as surprised by the motherly voice that came from somewhere behind Cassandra.

"Well, I'm grateful that you decided not to shoot my husband. He ain't much to look at, but he's all I've got left."

The man gave a mock glare in her direction as the woman came out of hiding from behind the truck, and both Cassandra and Sim knew they weren't a threat. The woman came around the truck and produced a clean cup from a box of supplies.

"Here, sweetheart. Help yourself to some coffee, and while you're at it, pour some for your man."

Sim took a quick look out through the door and then pulled it shut behind him. Despite the overwhelming tension they had been through in the last few minutes, that coffee smelled pretty good.

"I've been working on a way to make that row of shelves hide the door better, but every time I start to work on it those biters come around. If it's not them, it's those people who call themselves deputies."

The gray haired man talked to Sim and Cassandra as if he had known them forever. As he spoke he held out his hands to them both and then pulled out some folding chairs. The woman busily got their coffee and then passed over a jar with a spoon sticking out of it.

"I'm sorry we don't have any sugar, but there's nothing like fresh honey to smooth out the flavor of coffee."

"Honey is fine," said Cassandra. She could smell the sweetness of the honey, and she was reminded of breakfasts as a child. She saw that Sim was feeling the same way.

As they stirred their coffee they took care of introductions, and they were surprised to find that this old couple, Hank and Hazel, had managed to hide in the service bay of the electronics store for the last four years. Hank said if they had found it sooner, they would have been there longer. It was surprisingly easy to stay undetected, and there were enough supplies in the mall that had remained undetected by outsiders. Hank had carried case after case of canned foods from a warehouse and hidden it in the ceiling of the electronics store.

As for the impenetrable garage door, Hank had recognized it as a weak spot. If he couldn't find a way to hold the door down, someone would eventually find a way to raise it. The solution had been surprisingly simple.

The bottom of the garage door had a flat lip on it that extended inward over six inches. When the door was in the down position, the lip fit perfectly into a groove on the concrete floor. Hank had maneuvered the small pickup truck until the passenger side doors were against the garage door, and the truck was just close enough for the tires to be resting on top of the lip. If someone tried to raise the door, they had to lift the truck.

Sim told Hank there were likely to be a lot of people out there with back problems from trying to lift that door open.

"When was the last time you ate?" asked Hazel.

"It's only been since yesterday," said Cassandra, "but we lost our gear and supplies when we were attacked by some crazy people. You mentioned deputies?"

Both Hank and Hazel made sounds of disapproval at the mention of the deputies.

"That's what they call themselves. They're only deputies because they work for the Sheriff. I personally prefer the company of the biters," said Hank.

"Do they know you're in here?" asked Sim.

"No, they gave up on this place a long time ago. Not much use for most of the stuff in this store, but they keep a close eye on the sporting goods place at the other end of the mall."

Hazel handed them each a bowl of canned corned beef hash. They were used to better food in their shelters, but they were grateful for the gesture. As it turned out, they were hungrier than they had realized, and they gratefully spooned the hot food into their mouths.

When they were finished, Sim remembered the reason they had come to the small garage in the first place. He sized up the service bay and saw that there was still room for the pickup truck with the machine gun on it.

"Oh no," said Cassandra. "If we're too late, then we've led them right to you."

Hank waved her concerns off, and between the two of them, he and Hazel cleared several items from around the truck as if they had practiced the routine. In less than a minute the small truck was out of the way, and the garage door was going up. Sim ducked under the door and sprinted to the Silverado. He had it inside in seconds, and the door was already dropping into place. Hank rolled the smaller pickup truck back to its original spot and cut off the engine. The engine of the Silverado ticked a couple of times as the engine cooled but not loud enough to cover the sounds that grew louder as they listened.

The roar of an engine rose and fell as a truck drove faster than it should have across the cracked asphalt of the parking lot. Every time the wheels left the ground the engine's RPMs increased as the wheels spun in the air. Hazel turned off the lanterns that had illuminated the garage, and they all listened as the vehicle outside crashed against an abandoned car.

"Where are they? I thought you said you saw them come this way."

"I did, I swear."

Doors slammed, and the voices rose until they had to be right on the other side of the door. Someone didn't sound too happy about the missing truck and the dead bodies at the end of the mall, but they eventually got back in their vehicles and moved on.

"That was close," said Sim. "Will they be back?"

"Not those boys," said Hazel. "None of them should have passed the fourth grade. They'll make the mistake of giving up too soon and reporting back to the Sheriff. He's likely to kill them if he's mad."

"The last time we saw him, I think he was about to get mad," said Cassandra.

A bumping sound caused them to freeze. It came from the other side of the garage door, and it was easy to tell what it was. The moan that followed the random collisions with debris were familiar.

Hazel said, "It must've seen you come in here and started this way. After the others left it finally got here."

"Do you think the others will be curious about it?" asked Sim.

Hank nodded. "Unfortunately, yeah. It used to be that they would lose interest after a bit, but now they seem to know someone's in here."

"We have to go then," said Cassandra. "We'll lead it away from here."

No one argued with her about it, but even though they had to leave sooner than expected, the stop inside the small garage had been worthwhile. Hank and Hazel loaded them up with supplies and some useful weapons. Even more useful was the information they gave.

The old couple had been residents of a slum on the south side of Huntsville in a place called Farley. Before the infected dead had arrived it was a nice place to live, but a large tract of land along the banks of the Tennessee River had been converted into a refugee camp. According to Hank and Hazel, the Sheriff ran the place, and the Army took orders from him. How that happened they couldn't explain, but to their knowledge they were the only people to get out of Farley alive. You either lived and worked as part of the Sheriff's community, or you disappeared.

"You've managed to avoid detection for four years?" asked Sim. "We almost blew it for you. We'd better go before those people see that one infected still hanging around."

"You call them infected, we call them biters," said Hank. "If you get caught, remember that so you can fit in better."

Cassandra said, "Thanks for the advice, but we're not getting caught. As a matter of fact, if you don't mind, we'd be better off leaving the Silverado with you. All that would do is draw attention to us."

Hank studied the dark shape in the dim light and rubbed his stubble on his cheeks.

"Machine gun's pointing in the right direction. If those idiots ever try too hard to come through that door, I could give 'em something to think about before slipping out the back door."

Before sliding out through the gap in the door and squeezing through the tunnel between the shelves and the wall, Cassandra and Sim both shook hands with Hank and gave Hazel a big hug. Hank packed a bag with 9 mm ammunition and gave them each a Smith & Wesson 2.0 semiautomatic. Hazel gave them a few cans of Spam and sleeves of saltines. The crackers were pretty beat up already, but they would taste the same even if they were poured out of the bags.

As Sim was about to follow Cassandra into the gap, he felt a tug on his shirt sleeve.

"Let me give you a piece of advice," said Hank. "If you get out there and you see that you can't lead that biter away without getting caught, don't hang around on account of us. You gotta get away before those guys come back."

"I'm not promising anything, Hank, but we didn't come here to mess up a good thing for you two."

He knew Cassandra well enough to know that it would be someone else's bad luck if they came back too soon because she would never let something happen to the old couple. He didn't know how well Hank could see him in the darkness, so he just gave him a nod. There wasn't anything he could say that would make a difference.

Sim caught up with Cassandra, and they moved quickly toward the broken exit door where they had come in earlier. They didn't pay any attention to the shelves of things that wouldn't be of use in the new world. A cell phone case or a sound system wasn't necessary for survival. Anything that would have been useful would be long gone.

The sun was low in the west as they hurried from the exit into the parking lot. Cassandra wanted to get behind the infected that was bumping against the door so she could draw it away from the building into the center of the lot. They could put it out of its miserable existence and then keep going toward the main highway that would take them to Farley. If that's where the rest of the group was being kept, it was where they had to go.

The lone infected at the garage door was traveling back and forth from the door to a corner and then back again. They waited until it reached the corner before making their move to distract it. Hopefully, it would take the bait and walk far enough along the next building that it would forget about the garage. Cassandra had a pretty good arm, but Sim had played a little baseball and hadn't blown out his shoulder before giving it up. An old beer bottle did the trick. Sim got it to fly end over end to smash into the brick wall about thirty yards from the infected, and it was immediately on the attack.

It turned and raised its head, and even though they were too far away to hear it, they knew it must be moaning. They didn't hear moaning, but they did hear the crunch of tires on debris as a pickup truck swerved around the corner behind them and to the right. It fishtailed as the driver hit the gas in the middle of the turn, and the man at the big gun in the bed of the truck came close to getting left behind. It was only his grip on the gun that saved him, but Cassandra and Sim both heard his curses.

They ducked lower between the cars and hoped they hadn't been spotted. Cassandra was the one with combat training, but Sim had learned enough to know they would both die if they stayed so close together. Using his slender build to his advantage, he dropped to his stomach and slid sideways under the derelict car next to them. If they had to start shooting, he would be a parking spot closer to the building than Cassandra, but if they were between the same two cars, the only thing protecting one of them would have been the body of the other.

The pickup slid sideways as it stopped only a few feet from the infected dead. It had already forgotten the crash of the beer bottle and lurched toward the noisy vehicle, only making it easier for someone in the passenger seat to level a pistol at it from point blank range. The single shot dropped the infected dead before it got closer, and both doors opened on the cab.

From the parking lot Cassandra and Sim, watched in horror as the men from the cab walked past the back of the truck straight to the garage door. The man at the M134 mini-gun only had to face straight over the tailgate. They could see he had a big smile on his face, and he was really going to enjoy shredding the door.

One of the two men reached up and knocked on the door as if he was being expected. He called out in a singsong voice.

"Hellooooo. Is anybody home?"

The silence only dragged on for a minute, but it seemed much longer.

He knocked on the door with the side of his fist even harder, and the booming noise sounded even louder in the stillness of the rusted cars surrounding them.

"I'm only going to ask one more time. You know as well as I do why that biter was hanging around. Now, I'm going to count to three. If you haven't opened this door by then, I'm going to have my friend open up with his big gun, and I know you've seen what it can do. One, two…"

Cassandra and Sim both thought the man in the truck hand jumped the count and opened fire on two. The sound was enough to vibrate the air around them and cause flakes of paint to fall off of cars. Cassandra stood up between the two cars where she was hiding and took aim with her Smith & Wesson. There was very little doubt in her mind that she could hit the man standing at the M134 in the side of the head. Sim had the same idea even though he wasn't nearly as good with a weapon as Cassandra. Neither of them was ready for what they saw.

The two men who had been standing at the garage door were both on the ground, and the man in the back of the pickup truck was lying on his back on the top of the cab. All three were moving, but they were also covered in blood. Two were crawling as if it was difficult to move, and the man on the cab appeared to be trying to roll over on his side. He succeeded and fell over the driver's side door in full view of Cassandra and Sim. Both could see that he had no idea where he was. He had a head wound that was pouring blood into his eyes, but he managed to stand with the help of the door. He staggered straight toward Sim, who raised his pistol and finished the job someone else had started.

At the back of the truck, the other two men were still crawling, but if possible they were moving more slowly than before. Even as Cassandra shifted to where she could shoot them, they stopped moving. Sim joined her, and as they got closer, they saw the row of holes across the garage door where bullets from the M134 inside had almost cut the door in half. They were only a few feet from it and approaching from an angle when they heard Hank's voice yell out.

"Three!"

The silence that followed the sudden burst from the garage was muted by the ringing in their ears. Even from a distance the rapid staccato of explosive rounds had almost deafened them. Hank was also laughing so hard that he doubled over in a coughing fit. Hazel was yelling at him about giving her some warning next time, but even she couldn't stop herself from appreciating his sense of humor.

Through the ringing they heard her yell, "I'd trade my back teeth for a video of that!"

Hank fell out of the truck and kicked at the garage door until it fell away in two big pieces.

"Damn! I sawed off my door. I thought it would only blow holes in those idiots, but I guess that funny looking machine gun is a bit more powerful than my old carbine."

Sim and Cassandra walked up to the big opening and peered under a piece of the door that still hung by the chain from the garage door opener. Hazel was already packing their gear, and Hank was alternating between helping and carrying on about finding a new place to hole up.

"There's another mall on the northern side of town that has one of these places. Do you suppose you two could give us a hand getting there? If I didn't blow up that other truck too bad we shouldn't have any trouble getting there."

Sim was already thinking the same thing. "How close is it to the Marshall Space Flight Center?"

Cassandra's eyes got wider. "My first thought was that we should head for Farley and see if the rest of the gang needed help to escape, but we might wind up being a few steps behind them the whole way. If they escape, they're heading for the shelters. Maybe we should just try to. Be in that neighborhood when they arrive."

"If I know them," said Sim, "half the people in Huntsville will be chasing them, so we need to be on the other side of that chase."

"It's the least we can do for you," Cassandra said to Hank. "Besides, I really like your style."

The old man gave her a smile and tossed her a set of keys. "Help me get this useless little pickup out of the way so we can get going."

While Cassandra helped Hank, Sim checked out the second pickup truck. A few rounds from Hank's surprise barrage had come close to hitting the second mini-gun, but they were in luck. Hank had assumed the truck was parked with its tailgate facing him, and he knew he had to fire first, but with the help of the man's countdown, he didn't have to dodge any incoming rounds. His first pull of the trigger had chewed up the man behind the gun outside and he tried to keep his own gun level on the spot he figured was the most logical place for the other gun to be.

They had all three trucks outside and ready to go in minutes, but they knew they were much too slow. They had to take as much gas out of the truck they were leaving behind and split it between the two larger trucks, but the infected were showing up across the parking lot. They were too far away to be a problem yet, but they would act as a homing device for the Sheriff's men. All they had to do was find out where the biters were going to know what was making all the noise.

If any of the deputies heard the M134, they knew what it was, but they had stopped shooting at biters for sport a long time ago. With ammunition being a premium item, they had been told not to use their M4s and handguns unless they came across a real threat. Anyone who worked for the Sheriff would interpret the gunfire as a threat and already be moving in the same direction as the biters.

Cassandra took the gray Silverado, the one that had just arrived. She didn't have a rear window, so she could talk with Sim as he got situated behind the M134 in the back.

"You sure you don't want to drive and let me handle that?" she yelled.

"Hank made it look easy enough."

"Yeah, but tell me something. Do they look nervous driving behind us?"

She glanced at the blue Silverado behind her and wondered what Hazel was thinking. She saw that Sim took her hint and pointed the M134 straight upward for the time being, but he was elated when Hazel pulled alongside and shouted that she should take the lead because she knew the best roads to take. Cassandra waved her forward and fell in behind her. She saw Hank raise the M134 mini-gun barrel toward the sky, and even though the light was beginning to fail, she could see that he was disappointed.

"Boys and their toys," she said. "Boys and their toys."

14

Survival Skills

International Space Station - The First Week

NASA had a long way to go before they would send a crew to Mars. There were still some barriers that had yet to be overcome. One of them was the long term exposure to space radiation. They were making progress with protective shielding and special space suits, but every space organization in the world would trade their best equipment for one simple answer to one simple question. How long could people stay above the protective atmosphere of Earth before it took its toll on the human body? The simple answer was that there just wasn't enough data for an exact answer. Maybe there never would be now that the program had suffered an unimaginable setback.

The mission of ISS that was going to unfold over the following year was also supposed to fill in many of the gaps in the data, and if enough of those gaps were filled in, NASA and its international partners were prepared to take the next giant leap for mankind by establishing a permanent base on the Moon. From there they would begin what had always seemed impossible, and that was the plan to send people to Mars.

They would get their data, but not in the way they had originally planned it. The three astronauts living in the ISS were uniquely qualified to fulfill the mission, but just like any human being, they wished they had been able to choose how they would do it. Any of them would have signed up for a mission with the plan to have them stay in space as long as possible. They just didn't like having it forced on them.

Besides being uniquely qualified, the three friends had some similar characteristics. After trying desperately to establish contact with ground stations to gather enough information for them to make informed decisions, they turned inward. They had that in common, and that was what made them such a good team. As much as they cared for each other, they all felt like being alone, and the ISS was big enough for three people to find solitude. They spread out, and they kept to themselves, each of them coming to terms with their situation.

Three days later, almost as if there was a thread that connected them to each other, Adam, Henry, and Natalia drifted into the same module. The unspoken consensus was that they only had one choice.

Even though Adam was the Mission Commander, they had all adopted an informal relationship that allowed them to speak freely. Natalia didn't wait for Adam to call the meeting to order or to ask if anyone disagreed with what they knew he was going to say.

"We can't go back until things get better," she began. "From what we can all see on the news reports, no one is in a position to do a recovery. If we land in the wrong place, we might be killed as soon as we pop the hatch."

"I agree," said Adam. "We have enough supplies to last years, and I want everyone to get on a scheduled workout routine so we're not so handicapped by Earth gravity when we do get back."

Adam had more to say, but Henry surprised them both by interrupting.

"We can survive here, and it might be the only logical thing to do, but that doesn't mean it's what we should do."

Adam wasn't ready to pull rank on anyone, but he was caught off guard by the comment. Henry was hard to read sometimes because he had a good poker face, but behind the stoic expression there was a keen mind.

"Henry, we've all had time to think this through on our own, and we want to hear what you have to say, but you know how bad it is down there."

"Yes, I do, but that's my point. It won't get better. We could stay up here for years and still have problems when we go back, so it doesn't make sense to put it off."

There was an edge to Henry's voice that wasn't typical for him. Adam couldn't quite put his finger on it, but that was because he hadn't worked with another astronaut in his entire career who had become hysterical. Natalia had, and she was seeing warning signs that Henry was in the early stage of an emotional crisis. Her mind was frantically searching for the right thing to say that would keep the crisis from overflowing in the confines of the space station. At the moment there was a rational argument being made by everyone, but something about Henry's voice was the only clue she had. It seemed higher than normal.

Adam had already folded his arms across his chest, which was a fairly universal nonverbal message that the topic was open for discussion, but the decision had been made.

"We can't go back, Henry. You saw what happened at the Cosmodrome, and we haven't been able to talk with anyone except that kid. She doesn't have any answers for us, and we can't put ourselves in her hands. Hell, even if we could land somewhere safe, how would she be able to feed us the telemetry we would need just to get into the atmosphere without burning up or bouncing back into space?"

Natalia was trying to think of a way to get Adam to see what she was seeing, and the best thing she could think of was to get the real issue out into the open where everyone could tackle it together instead of Henry doing it on his own.

"It's your family, isn't it?" asked Natalia. "You're worried about them, and you should be, but you know how the ground support people are. They have a duty to those of us who come up here. A duty to protect our wives, husbands, children, parents, and anyone else we've left behind for the good of the program. They're like the Swiss Guards for the Pope, the Secret Service for the President of the United States, or the Queen's Guard for your country. Those people won't let anything happen to your family. They would give their lives for our families."

Adam was beginning to understand. Henry wasn't just taking a logical position on whether or not they should go back to Earth now. He was worried about not being there for his family.

Henry softened a bit, but he wasn't quite there yet.

"If things are really bad, then the program could use my help back on Earth. You two could stay here, and I could use the Soyuz to go back. You could feed me the telemetry using the ISS onboard systems.

I could help keep the program on its feet until they can send up another mission to replace you guys."

Henry made it sound almost logical, especially the part about them guiding the Soyuz from the ISS. It had been done before as a test of redundant systems to see if the ISS could act as a replacement for Mission Control if they were experiencing problems. His argument broke down a little when he got to the part about sending up the next mission. They could see the confidence he had in the first part of the plan, but they could see the confidence fade in the second part.

As an afterthought he added, "You know they would be able to get things under control and send up the next mission before you run out of supplies, and by then you'll be heroes to the program. You'll have all of the records for the duration by then."

Henry was smiling as if Adam and Natalia would be excited at the thought of being in the history books, but the expressions on their faces were anything but cheerful. As much as they would like to placate Henry to make him feel like there was some chance that they would agree, they couldn't bring themselves to do it. He waited for them to see the light, but they could only gradually find their own feet. His smile faded, and his normally good natured temperament faded with it.

"I should have known better than to sign on for a mission with single people. If you had a family waiting for you at home we wouldn't even be talking about this."

Adam had listened to a lot of disagreements and a lot of personal opinions in his career, but he couldn't recall ever being blatantly insulted. Henry Tisdal was respected by everyone who had ever gone into space with him, and that made an insult from him cut even deeper than if it had been from someone else. Adam felt his body tense, and he even clenched his fists.

Natalia was in a position where she could move between them, but the anger on her face had surpassed Adam's. She wasn't married, but she had relatives, just as she was sure Adam had relatives even though they weren't a wife and children. She knew his father still lived in Florida, and Adam had spoken often about his brother's children. There was nothing fair about Henry's implied insult that he had more reason to go back to Earth now because he had children and they didn't.

Adam spoke through clenched teeth but only to keep his voice steady.

"Everyone knows where their personal, private space is. I strongly suggest we go there now. In one hour we'll return to this module with the understanding that this place has been able to function for a long time because everyone has respected each other as well as the chain of command."

There are some moments when time seems to stand still, and this was one of them. It felt like anger had them all rooted to one spot even though they were free of gravity. Natalia was too shocked to move. Adam was too angry, and Henry was too ashamed.

Just as Adam broke free and turned to leave, Henry spoke.

"Wait. Adam, Natalia…please wait. Please don't go."

The sadness on his face was what made Natalia and Adam move toward Henry instead of away toward their private spaces. They could see that he was going to collapse in grief, not only because his family was in grave danger, but because he had turned on them. They were his family too, and he had hurt them deeply. They all pushed themselves away from the places where they had moments before been rooted by their anger, and they floated together into an embrace. Words weren't necessary, but Henry kept saying them over and over as they all cried.

When the emotions finally washed away, they felt spent, but Henry was able to explain himself beyond a simple apology. Natalia and Adam both understood exactly what he was trying to tell them.

"I knew there was never more than one choice for us to make. I just couldn't face it without first denying it. If I didn't push back as hard as I could against making that choice, I would never be able to look at myself in a mirror and say I had done everything I could to save the lives of my wife and children. I couldn't just roll over and accept that we did the right thing so easily."

Natalia tried to tell Henry he didn't need to say more, but he said there was one last thing he had to say. Then he would know they were going to begin surviving.

They waited as Henry gathered his thoughts, and remarkably he said the one thing that Adam had held back before.

"My friends, we're already too late. If they aren't already dead, they will be soon."

******

* * *

The first week was the hardest because it was seven days of being helpless to do anything other than watch. Once every ninety minutes the ISS completed another orbit of the Earth, and during every orbit they saw the landscape of their world change even more. It wasn't just what they saw on the news broadcasts. It was also the world they could see from their windows. The cities that weren't burning on the last orbit were burning on the next one or the next orbit after that. Smoke rushed up to join the clouds in great, dark plumes from city after city. In some cities the fires found so much fuel that they burned brighter and hotter, spreading as fast as the wind could carry them and laying waste to some of the world's most treasured landmarks.

The news broadcasts were delivered by random faces of people who had never dreamt of appearing on television. Thrust in front of cameras with hastily prepared scripts the reports were delivered by frightened workers, young and old, who just happened to be available. The trusted faces of familiar broadcast journalists were somewhere else, often eulogized by their substitutes before they plunged into the tragic updates.

The reports became more and more tragic from one broadcast to the next, so the crew of the ISS received snapshots of what was happening as they passed each location, and they found themselves only hoping that it would be better on the next flyover. The astronauts seldom spoke while a station delivered reports, especially when the news involved the suburbs of London. Natalia turned off the BBC because she feared that Henry would find it too difficult to bear, but he had asked in a gentle voice that she turn it back on.

All three of them were experts in their own special fields, but one thing they had each mastered was the electronics of their environment. So much so that their jobs often overlapped. Each of them had proven themselves capable of working magic with the communications systems, but even with their combined efforts they had been unable to repair one problem. Their ability to transmit had failed.

As much as they depended on the information they received from the television stations, they also had a need to ask questions, and their frustration grew when they were passing within range of the Canadian television station they had contact with before, and they attempted contact. Within minutes they had traveled too far, and they frantically focused on locating the problem as they made another trip around the globe. When they completed the next orbit and tried again, they could hear the station, but the station wasn't receiving them. They tried repeatedly, but they were unable to locate the failures that had occurred in the equipment that should have allowed them to stay in touch with Earth.

They had counted on information from ground stations as well as public broadcasts, but public broadcasts were of no use to them when it came to the scientific data they needed for the inevitable trip back to Earth. Without the coordination of the broadcasts and a connection with NASA, all they could do was witness the tragedy as it unfolded, and they had to wonder if they had missed some clue back when they had originally lost touch with all of their ground stations.

Just after breakfast on the seventh day following their decision to stay aboard the ISS for as long as possible, they received a badly distorted transmission from Gentry. It was such poor quality that there were more gaps in her message than complete sentences. All they were able to decipher was that she was alive, and that was based mostly on the fact that it was a live broadcast. When her transmission ended, they didn't know if there would be another one. It simply faded out. Ninety minutes later their window of opportunity to re-establish contact came and went without so much as static, leaving them feeling disconnected. Natalia took off her headphones shook her head in answer to the question Adam didn't have to ask out loud.

He turned away and used his hands to propel himself to the adjacent module where he had been dissecting a communications module in hope of finding out why they were losing contact with all of the ground stations. It had taken a week to feel like a routine was developing, and they had even begun the first of the experiments they would have done if the launches had gone as planned. Adam had confided in Natalia that he would feel better about Henry if he showed the slightest bit of interest in the original mission. Natalia managed to convince him that Henry was mentally strong enough to survive the loss of his family, and at first it did seem that Henry was coping, but on two occasions in the last day he had slipped up and called Natalia by his wife's name. It showed he was at the very least preoccupied with his thoughts of them.

The sudden burst of static from the radio speaker followed by the last few words of a sentence caused Adam to use his foot as an anchor, and he drew himself back through the door. The message was badly distorted, but he recognized it as a radio call they had heard before. They hadn't paid much attention to it in the past because it was never a good signal and obviously an amateur, but every ground signal had become more important over the last few days.

"Was that the same person as before?" asked Adam. He didn't need to be more specific because Natalia and Henry both knew about this particular broadcaster. It was some guy without much training on shortwave radios. He said something about being in a shelter, but half the time he either pressed or didn't press his microphone at the right time. All they really knew was that he had a shelter somewhere on the coast of South Carolina.

"Yes, but I got the usual information. Nothing useful."

Over the next month, they monitored radio and television broadcasts, but both were becoming more and more silent. Television stations went off the air first, but the last reports were far from encouraging. The world was slowly losing a battle against some kind of infection that was one hundred percent fatal, every day was the same as yesterday.

Most broadcasts began with pleas for help. Mayday calls were received from planes, ships, and ground stations, and every time they heard one they responded with the hope that someone would at least hear their transmission. There were cruise ships that had been overrun by the infected, as they were called by the broadcast media. Planes that ran low on fuel and were forced to land radioed that they had no choice and would be taking their chances on the ground. One courageous pilot managed to land in the calm waters near the Florida Keys. The crew stayed on the air during the entire event, and the last word from them was that they had landed with no casualties. The crew of the ISS cheered for them from the safety of their own craft, but they never heard from the crew of the plane again. If they made it to safety, they would never know.

Military broadcasts were cause for celebration at first, but after they lost their ability to transmit, the broadcasts became a daily exercise in futility that just served as a reminder that they were on their own. The military units that were still interested in them would send out a message every day as the ISS passed overhead. They would respond, knowing that the military wasn't receiving the response, and the military would sign off as they passed out of range. It was no surprise when the military eventually stopped sending messages.

It was also no surprise that the three crew members of the ISS went through varying stages of life on board the spacecraft. They gradually fell into the routines that had been predetermined long before they were sent into space, but along with the various duties that brought them together as a crew, they adopted new roles that seemed to fit their own personal abilities.

It was at one of their morning meetings that the topic came up that the ISS was perfectly positioned for the research project that had been dumped in their laps. Henry was the one who broached the topic, and although Adam and Natalia were always aware that the loss of Henry's family could be the spark that sent them up into flames, they heard Henry making complete and rational sense as he explained it to them.

"Why do we call this our morning meeting?" asked Natalia. "I've been meaning to ask that question for a long time."

Adam and Henry both laughed even though Natalia was at times over sensitive about the male environment of ISS and had accused them of teaming up on her. She scowled at them and waited but finally had to give in.

"Are you two done yet?"

"Sorry," said Adam, "I thought you knew. It's because we always had them with the ground stations while they were all getting the morning briefing from the night shifts."

That was when they realized she had just baited them into laughing. Their spirits had been getting better, but she felt like giving it a little nudge before they got down to business.

"Well, we aren't on ground station time anymore, so I propose we call them something else. I propose the Breakfast Club."

Adam said, "As I recall from the movie, they were all kids who were in some kind of detention hall or something. Are we being punished?"

It was a borderline question that could have been too serious, but the earlier laughter had done enough to keep them from becoming morose again.

"No, I think she's right," said Henry. "I've been thinking about this situation, and doesn't it seem like it was inevitable?"

Adam and Natalia regarded Henry and both studied him for signs of cracks in his behavior. Both saw the relaxed, often hilarious, Brit who used to be able to deliver a punchline without giving away a clue that he was setting you up.

"Zombies were inevitable?" asked Adam.

Natalia shot coffee out her nose, which was even funnier in zero G.

It took a few minutes for them to settle down again, and when they had almost regained their composure, Adam reminded her that the morning meetings were always recorded, and amidst a second round of shouting and laughing he promised to edit out a copy of Natalia and put it on a continuous broadcast for when someone was able to receive from them again.

Henry picked up where he left off, but he was fully aware that Adam was having too much fun to stop now, so he would choose his words more carefully.

"Zombies, rabid unicorns, sparkling vampires, or like Bill Murray said in that movie where they had to catch ghosts and defeat a giant marshmallow in a sailor suit, dogs and cats living together. Something was bound to happen, and it was bound to happen with a crew on board the ISS. Why didn't we plan for this?"

The humor was still there. It was written on Henry's face, and he'd kept it light, but it was still a serious question.

"Maybe we have," said Adam.

"I must've missed that meeting," said Natalia.

"No, Adam is right," said Henry. "We did plan for it. If we wouldn't have planned for it, then we wouldn't have a way to get home. There wouldn't be a Soyuz parked outside. We wouldn't have enough supplies to survive for as long as we can."

Natalia asked, "What, exactly did we plan for that even remotely resembles what's going on down there?"

She hooked a thumb in the general direction of a window where they could see Earth below them.

"It doesn't matter," said Henry. "My guess is they thought they were ready for anything, and they would at least be satisfied to know that we're alive up here, and even though they don't know what we're doing with our time, they hope they trained us so well that we remembered why we came up here. We still have a mission. It's just evolved a little."

Henry didn't notice, or maybe he ignored, the collective sigh of relief from Natalia and Adam. It wasn't a new Henry they were talking to, it was the old Henry who was as important to their mission as any of them.

"Evolved in what way?" asked Adam.

"Aside from communications protocols being shot all to hell, we have new jobs. I don't know what you two have been doing with your time, but I discovered I have been somewhat of a historian with regard to our circumstances."

"We've all been making log entries," said Natalia.

"I realize that, but I have found myself to be chronicling the events of this apocalypse in great detail."

Henry had always fancied himself as somewhat of a historian with the astronaut circles. He was fascinated by the details of each mission. Their dates, times, places, the people, and the smallest of trivia. He said that it fell to the English to be sure that it was properly written, and for some reason, no one disagreed with him. Maybe it was because he was already better at it than anyone else in their profession, but everyone else accepted his expertise as gospel.

"When this mission is over," said Henry, "our agencies will want every detail of how we coped and how we survived. It was inevitable that something would happen, and what we do here today will be part of the training for the next crew to be up here when the whole world goes to hell in a handbasket."

"Or the vampires sparkle," said Natalia.

"I can't say I've found my calling during this particular clown show," said Adam, "but I see your point. If we had planned for this I'm not sure what we would have done differently for the crew already in the ISS, but I would have done a better job on the ground."

"Ummm, yeah," said Natalia. "Those guys sitting in their launch vehicles ready to go deserved better, but I agree with you too, Henry. As a matter of fact, it makes me wonder what the plan said for us to do. Are we supposed to ride this out? If we go back, are we supposed to shoot for a specific target or just hit a general area?"

"Funny you should ask," said Adam. "While Henry's been writing our story, which will undoubtedly make a great movie, I've been working on something. We've been collecting tons of data just by getting broadcasts from different stations. In six years we have to go back whether we want to or not. That gives me six years to gather all the data I need to get us back safely. I've also been working on your question about where to land, and I think we already know the answer to that. Gentry is somewhere in Operation Paperclip, so maybe we're supposed to go there too. If we're lucky, we'll sort out this communication issue, and Gentry will be able to tell me if my numbers are correct."

"I guess that's where I come in," said Natalia. "I know you guys can fix anything as long as you have a rubber band and some duct tape, but I should be able to fix that radio with just the rubber band."

"Now you're talking," said Henry. "There's a reason we're up here and not someone else, or if it had been someone else, it would have been three people with our skillset. So while I'm writing down everything that happens, Natalia will get us back in touch with people on the ground, and Adam will get us home in one piece."

15

In Honor of Titus Rush

The Shelter - The First Week

Gentry had to admit she was feeling the weight of the world on her shoulders, but she wasn't complaining. For whatever reason, fate had chosen to keep her alive. Not only was she still alive, but she hadn't died as teeth ripped her skin from her body. She hadn't seen people chewing on her wounds while she was drawing her last breath. Fate had drawn two converging lines from her and from an old man who wanted to save humanity to a shelter that would withstand the end of the world.

Only a few days ago Gentry had gotten out of bed at 4:00 AM and rushed through a breakfast of toast and coffee. The sun wasn't up yet, but she had stayed up late laying out different outfits to wear on her first day as Flight Director, still confused about the call she had gotten from Flight Operations the previous evening. She still had a nagging fear that someone had set her up for the biggest prank, but none of her friends would pull a prank that would ultimately hurt her that bad. The caller had simply introduced himself as the Director of Mission Assignments, informed her that she would be the Flight Director, and that mission briefing would be at 5:30 AM. She thanked him and hung up the phone, but she didn't take her hand away from it for several minutes.

As far as she could recall, that was the day before yesterday, but she wasn't entirely sure. When she wasted two minutes trying to remember, she came to the conclusion that it didn't matter. What mattered was that she was alive, and she was with three people who openly expressed their gratitude to her. Somehow she didn't believe the credit belonged to her, but every time she tried to say so, the other three came a little closer to making her believe it.

In some ways they had a point. If there had been nothing else but the combination lock to the shelter, they wouldn't have had a prayer of opening it. The fact was, they wouldn't have been in the planetarium with her if not for the fact that she was scheduled to meet with the Colonel. They would have been scrambling to escape from the shelter along with thousands of other people.

After the introductory video by the old man, they had spread out in the control center and explored the equipment. The room was a pristine white that made them feel like they were in a sterile environment. Everything was bright and clean, and best of all, it worked. Gentry was preoccupied, so Wanda and Karen busied themselves with the computer system that responded like a supercomputer attached to the fastest internet. It seemed like there was the world's most extensive medical library attached to the system, and they explored it to their heart's content. As for MC, he was curious about what they would find behind all of the closed doors around the room, but he had been thrust into the role of protector, so he positioned himself where he could see all three women and was content to watch for any danger.

Gentry was so surprised by the message from Titus Rush that it took her a while to remember she had originally set out to contact the International Space Station. It didn't take her long to find the right menus and connections, but there was something wrong. The equipment appeared to be working with one exception. The digital indicator that was supposed to show the modulation of her voice as she spoke remained flat. When she saw it wasn't moving she keyed the switch several times and did a test count into the microphone.

"Testing, one, two, three, testing."

Gentry's eyes automatically went from one screen to the next, and to the untrained eye, MC didn't know that Gentry was verifying several important functions. One after the other they checked out, but the voice modulation indicator stayed flat.

MC moved a little closer and asked, "No luck contacting the ISS?"

She shook her head. "You see that indicator. It isn't a critical piece of equipment, but it's really nice to have. If it modulates, goes up and down with your voice, it gives you a visual indication that you're at least sending your voice."

"It's not moving," he said.

"Right, it either isn't working, or it's not sending my voice."

"Which is more likely?"

"The latter. Even if it is working, it's not a guarantee that my signal is going out, but it's first in line because it's the simplest piece of equipment."

Gentry saw she had lost MC with her explanation, and she knew what she could say to help him understand.

"Even though I'm speaking into this microphone and keying this switch when I speak, the voice modulation indication isn't next in line. Think of it as last. My voice needs to actually broadcast from the antenna array and be verified as sent in order for the modulator to move."

MC nodded in understanding, "You mean the indicator is the last device in a feedback loop."

Gentry gave him a big smile that earned her a smile in return, but they were a bit embarrassed that they were acting happy about the broadcast not working.

"Oh, that's not good," said MC.

"No, it's not, especially since this place is apparently top of the line tech."

Karen and Wanda joined them just as they came to the unhappy conclusion that they wouldn't be able to contact the ISS, and Gentry went through the entire series of system tests again. Each time they all watched the broadcast indicator as if they were watching for a heartbeat.

"I know it's easy for me to say because I'm not up there wondering what's going on down here, but I think we should start exploring this place. I know one thing that works great, and that's the medical library. If we ever need it, and if the infirmary is anything like this computer, we can at least provide medical care. I have to admit, though, right now I'm thinking about the kitchen."

Gentry hated the idea of waiting to solve the problem with communications, but she had to admit, she was curious. She was also hungry, but beyond the doors of the control room was another new world, and she didn't blame the others for wanting to explore.

"I want to try one more thing," said Gentry. The others all gave her room as she stood up and walked over to one of the other stations. She flipped a few switches, and she got what she had hoped to see.

All four of them marveled at the panoramic views as they appeared on the huge screens at the front of the room. One was the feed from a camera mounted on the outside of the ISS. It was in a position that showed the entire space station, and behind it was Earth. It was breathtaking, but more importantly, it showed that they were still in orbit.

The large screen that dominated the wall to the left of the ISS was a view that showed the failed launches in Baikonur. Smoldering wreckage of the disaster was a sobering reminder of what had happened since, but the third screen was the worst. It showed the area outside the Marshall Space Flight Center and the thousands of unfortunate people who hadn't made it to safety. Gentry hit two of the three switches, and the screens went dark again with the exception of the ISS on the middle screen.

"What else can we see on those screens?" asked Wanda.

Karen added, "There's probably plenty more. I doubt there would be any regularly scheduled shows, but the average household gets over a hundred cable channels, so this place should get a thousand."

In a real launch setting, Gentry would never have tolerated someone touching switches just for the sake of curiosity, and the situation had dictated that she should be in a leadership role, but she wasn't going to bury herself in the part. The truth was that she didn't know what all of the controls did either, and she doubted that any of them were self-destruct buttons. Even though she had already told Karen not to push buttons after the elevator ride, she wanted to see what would happen too.

Karen turned a knob that was surrounded by numbers and resembled a kitchen timer. There was an audible click as it reached the first number, and the immense screen at the front of the room next to the ISS lit up like the navigation screen in a car. It was so familiar in appearance that they immediately understood that the small green icon on the screen was a symbol that represented a person. It had arms, legs, and a head, and it was positioned as if it was standing.

The same navigational display appeared on the corresponding third monitor at the computer station, so Gentry instinctively reached for the mouse. She moved the cursor over to the green symbol, and they all watched as the action was repeated at the front of the room. The cursor stopped on the symbol, and a tag appeared next to it that read

CONTROL CENTER.

Karen reached for the dial again, but this time Gentry stopped her.

"Wait, I've got a feeling about this. That dial selects an area, and this menu labeled VIEW probably does this. This should have occurred to me when we discovered that we could see what was happening in the planetarium."

As she said it, she clicked on VIEW and a dropdown menu listed what she had expected. She selected CAMERA OPTIONS, and a side menu gave her another half dozen choices, but she was only interested in one. She selected it, and the computer screen in front of her and the large screen on the wall showed a live camera view of the four of them standing in the control room. They all did what people everywhere had always done. They spun around in the direction where the camera should be and then turned back to see themselves looking at the camera.

"Is that really us?" asked Wanda. She felt stupid for asking, but it was a natural reaction.

The experience was the first thing to happen to them that made them all feel some measure of control. The implications of being able to find their way around in an unfamiliar place gave them a sense of relief, and at the very least the camera meant there would be some security. The next natural question that seemed to occur to them all was where else could they see, and for the first time since they had escaped certain death inside the planetarium, it occurred to them that they had all assumed they were alone.

******

"Twelve levels," said MC. "Eight rooms on each level. We have a lot of rooms to explore. Any suggestions on how we should get this done?"

"Just like in the movies," said Wanda. "This is where someone says we should split up, and the audience is yelling don't do it."

"And definitely don't go in the basement," added Karen. "They've been making movies like that since I was a kid too."

"I'm in favor of letting MC handle this part," said Gentry.

MC would have said it if Gentry hadn't. He didn't consider himself a Rambo kind of guy, but he was the only one with the training.

"If you don't mind, ladies, I think we should stay together at least until we find the armory, but unless someone has somewhere else they have to be, I think we can take our time and stay together. Besides, if I understood Mr. Rush correctly, it's not too likely that we'll run into anyone down here."

"I don't trust him," said Wanda.

MC wasn't much older than Wanda or Gentry, but he couldn't help feeling more worldly. Wanda acted like she had grown up in a small town and had never left even for nursing school. He gave her a sideways glance and a grin when she said she didn't trust Titus Rush. After all, he had given them something pretty big…a chance to survive.

Karen saw the grin too. "She's young, and she thinks all men over sixty are creepy, but I have a feeling she'll think of the old guy differently after we do some exploring."

Wanda had shaken her head at the comment, but only a few minutes later, Karen was proven to be right. As she put it, "This ain't your grandfather's shelter."

Titus said twelve levels and eight rooms, so they decided to go to the top level and work their way down. He also said in the video that the layouts were on the computer, so they spent a few minutes finding out exactly where they were in the shelter. MC particularly wanted to see how far they were from the top of the shelter, and despite assurances from the old man in the video, he wanted to see for himself just how safe they were.

The shelter map wasn't hard to find on the computer, and even though it appeared to be quite an accomplishment, it was something you had to see with your own eyes in order to fully appreciate it.

There were elevators and stairs, and despite the fact they were impressed with what they had seen so far, none of them had the urge to be enclosed in an elevator when the unknown was on the other side of the door. MC made the point that when the door opened, they would have nowhere to go if there were infected dead on the other side. The reality of that situation was even more frightening than a power failure while they were using the elevator.

They found the stairs in the far right corner of the control center, but according to the floorplans there was another set of stairs in the opposite corner. From what they could see in the general layout, the designer of the shelter must have been familiar with safety codes and wanted more than one way out of every level or room. All rooms had at least two doors, and each landing in the stairwell could be accessed from two places.

The stairwell was standard military design right down to the gray paint on the handrails, and although they were tempted to cross the landing and peek through the opposite door, they stayed together and went up. The sounds of their feet echoed from above and below, and they realized they had all been under a misconception about the size of the shelter. They had assumed the levels were going to be the same as the stories of a building, but after about a dozen steps they came to a landing with no doors. The stairs turned and went up, but time after time they came to more stairs, more landings, and not always doors. They decided as a group to pass doors that weren't labeled but were already coming to the conclusion that it had been a bad idea because none had been labeled so far.

"I don't suppose anyone has been keeping count," said MC.

Gentry said, "I'll admit it. I'm a little OCD, and I count everything, but a NASA Psychologist told me that engineers tend to do that."

"So, how many flights of stairs have we climbed?" asked Karen. "You young people can use the stairs. I'm using the elevators once we get to the next level."

"Three so far, but I think that's a door on the next one. We'll call that one number four, but the levels might not all be the same size."

"Some might be bigger," said Karen.

MC got to the landing ahead of the others, and he stopped them outside the first door.

"We have no reason one way or the other to think we're alone here. We should do this quietly and carefully until we know for sure."

"You don't think that movie was enough?" asked Gentry.

MC seemed ready for the question because he had a question for Gentry that stopped her in her tracks.

"Did you expect to be here?"

Gentry realized she had been acting like this had all been meant for her just because she was the Flight Director. She knew that the builders of the shelter had expected someone more important to be in the shelter, but she had figured the Colonel was the only military man who had known, and he had only made plans for MC to get her into the shelter. If the four of them were in the shelter, someone else might be there too.

Everyone got behind MC when he got into position by the door, and he pulled it open just far enough to see through. The smell assaulted their noses, and the source of it was obvious. A dark smear ran along the otherwise shiny floor. It glistened with the light from the ceiling, and the redness was all any of them needed to see to know it was fresh.

MC had learned in his combat tours to shut his mouth quickly when exposed to the horrors of war. It became almost instinctive because explosives were far from surgical in the damage they did. Karen and Wanda couldn't claim to ever be used to what they had seen in emergency rooms, but they had seen enough to be able to control their reactions. The same couldn't be said for Gentry. She had allowed herself to believe they were safe inside the shelter. She wasn't ready for what was behind the door.

When she retched she tried to turn away quickly, but the spasms came faster. MC was distracted from the door for no more than a few seconds, but it was enough time to allow the infected dead to get through the opening. Everyone fell backward onto the landing, and even though MC had his rifle between himself and the infected, there was no time for him to take aim. All he could do was push as hard as he could with the rifle across his body.

The weight of the uncoordinated man seemed incredible to MC. It was like pushing against a wet sandbag, and for a few moments he understood what people were saying when they referred to the dead weight of something. With the barrel of his rifle against the floor, MC used it like a lever and managed to make the infected dead roll away from him toward the lip of the stairs. He gave one last desperate shove, and the man rolled just far enough for gravity to take over. Each time the dead man hit the stairs and began another turn toward the next one, there was a slapping sound.

A second infected dead came through the open door and slipped on the blood that had spread out across the floor. MC was amazed to see entrails around its ankles, and something gave him the strength to reach out and grab them. It felt like a rubbery, wet hose that was too slippery to hold. He pulled hard enough to make the man flip backward and slide head first down the stairs with the first one. The intestines were so long that they uncoiled from the man as he rolled away. MC still had a loop of the greasy organ wrapped around his hand even though the infected was on a lower level than him. He let it slide to the floor, only just then realizing that Gentry was on her knees and her hands retching violently.

Wanda surprised them all by being the first to get to the open door. She slid into the wall and almost lost her balance, but she managed to get it closed. She had to use her feet to kick the rest of the intestines down the stairs. Then she put her hands under Gentry's armpits and lifted.

"Let's go!"

Her yell was much louder in the stairwell than she wanted it to be, but it got everyone moving. The second of the infected dead was already on its feet and attempting to climb the stairs, but the first one was kneeling on a loop of intestine and keeping it from making progress. The smell was worse than what they were seeing. Gentry was the only one in their group who had never smelled a perforated bowel, and even though it was enough to make it hard for any of them to breathe, at least the others could fight off the smell long enough to get themselves moving.

Going up was their only option, but with each labored step, they were further from the stench. Karen switched off with Wanda and pushed Gentry ahead of her, while MC had produced a rag from one of his many uniform pockets and covered her nose and mouth. It smelled like gun cleaner, but that was better than what she had endured.

After what seemed like forever, there was another pair of doors, and there was no doubt that they had to cut themselves off from the smell in the stairwell. MC took more time to open the door nearer to him, and all he saw was a brightly lit corridor beyond the crack he peeked through. There was also nothing on the floor to indicate there would be a repeat of what they had experienced one landing down.

He held the door wide and pushed them through. Once they were by him, he followed so closely that he was shoving them ahead of him, and pulled the door shut. The first thing on his mind was to find a sink with running water. Soap would be good, but the putrid odor clinging to his hands had to go.

The hallway was curved, and there were no doorways on the outer wall, but several yards ahead there was one on the right.

"Stay here for a minute," he said before taking off toward the door.

He didn't have to worry about Gentry going anywhere. She was flat on the clean floor sobbing and heaving. Every time she heaved, her knees drew up to her chest, and then her body quickly straightened again as if she was trying to pump something from her cramping stomach.

"We've got to help her to relax," said Karen. "These are involuntary spasms, and I'm afraid one will be violent enough for her to injure herself."

"What can we do? I've never seen a seizure like this."

"Hope MC finds something that smells better. She needs deep breaths."

Miraculously, MC appeared as fast as he had left, and he must've had some idea of what would help Gentry because he had a towel that he'd soaked with cold water. Karen gratefully grabbed it and began mopping at the back of Gentry's neck and getting as much of the cooling water into her hair as she could. In the meantime, she had the other end of the towel in her other hand and let Gentry bury her face into it. They could hear Gentry gaining control as she drew in deep breaths, each one refreshing her nasal passages and sinuses by replacing the putrid odor of rot.

When her breathing had calmed and her body was no longer trying to pull itself into a big knot, they rested her against the wall and mopped at her forehead and neck with the wet towel.

Karen said to MC, "I don't know what made you think of a wet towel or where you found it, but that was perfect."

"I would've gotten back faster if my hands hadn't been so gross. As a matter of fact, I'm going to go wash them again. There's something like an apartment through that door on the right."

"You sure it's safe?" she called after him.

"You smell anything?"

"Oh, God," moaned Gentry. She gave one minor heave and covered her mouth with her hand.

Wanda took over with the wet towel and told Karen to go with MC. She could also stand to at least throw some fresh water into their faces, but the smell coming off of their clothes was becoming more noticeable now that they were out of the stairwell.

"Can you stand yet?"

Gentry was apparently recovering fast enough to understand that MC and Karen had found a sink, and Wanda didn't have to ask her twice. She pushed away from the floor, and with Wanda's help got to her feet. She leaned against the wall all the way to the door, but they made good time.

The inside of the door was something beyond their expectations. It was a furnished apartment that was modern and tastefully decorated. There was a wide open sitting area with a couch and easy chairs. Each was covered with overstuffed pillows.

Gentry's eyes were wide. "I can see myself in my pajamas just curled up with a good book on that couch."

Wanda said, "You bounce back pretty good, girl."

Beyond the sitting area was a dining room, and they could hear water running in a kitchen that was separated from the dining room by a serving island. MC came out of the kitchen with a wet towel over his head and a bottle of beer in his hand, and he was already minus his boots and his pants.

"Don't get any ideas, ladies. I rolled around in stuff I'd rather forget. There's a laundry room on the other side of the kitchen." They could hear the thumping noise from the washing machine as his boots sloshed around inside.

Gentry didn't pay any attention to what MC said and had already collapsed face first into the pillows on the couch. Wanda and Karen squeezed by MC into the kitchen, obviously grateful that he smelled better already.

"Nice legs," said Wanda. "That wasn't the last beer, was it?"

There was a whole shelf full of beer in the refrigerator, and even though there wasn't any fresh food or perishables, it was obvious they would be able to throw together a meal with little effort. A pantry had everything they needed in cans and boxes, and without giving a thought to more exploring, both nurses began clattering pots and pans with one goal in mind.

MC walked over to check on Gentry and found that she was snoring right where she had landed. He pulled a throw from the headrest of the couch and spread it over her legs. On his way past the kitchen, he grabbed a second beer from the refrigerator and then left the ladies to work whatever magic they had in mind. Whatever it was, it was already enough to make his stomach growl, but if all they would have was beer, he was fine for now.

To one side of the kitchen was a second sitting room, but this one had more than just a comfortable place to sit and talk. A huge television screen dominated one wall, and there was enough seating in recliners and sofas for at least nine or ten people. The small bathroom he had discovered when he had originally charged into the apartment looking for a sink was next to a set of stairs that went up to a short hallway. The doors were all open, and he just took a moment to step through each door and take a glance around.

The apartment was obviously designed for some type of communal living because each room was a bedroom, and each one was equipped with its own bathroom. It crossed his mind that the old man in the video presentation had said twelve levels with eight rooms on each level. It remained to be seen, but it was his guess that every level would offer something different, and this level was where the majority of the people would actually live. It was also obvious that the shelter was designed more for long term comfort of a few people rather than short term comfort for a large number of people. He didn't know why, but he felt a sudden pang of guilt at the thought of saving just a select few instead of everyone that they could.

In a sudden moment of clarity, MC understood something about the shelter, the old man in the video, and the difference between saving a few people or saving mankind. This place was designed for the long haul. This wasn't a place where they could just lay low for a bit. This was the rest of their lives.

When he got back downstairs, Wanda and Karen were already putting out place settings at the dining room table.

"Washing machine finished, so I tossed your pants in the dryer," said Karen. "I hope you don't expect me to make a habit of it. I already got rid of one husband who thought that was my job."

"His loss," said MC with a wink in her direction.

"Oh, I like him. If he was a couple years older…."

"Find anything upstairs?" asked Wanda.

"I don't know what any of this means yet, but it looks like a nice place to live. Anyone try the TV?"

Since he got a round of head shakes, MC went back toward the room with the TV, but on the way he stopped and checked on his pants. They were dry enough, and they felt good going on warm. He helped himself to another beer and found the remote, not really expecting anything except a library of old series. When he turned it on, he was surprised to see a familiar network reporter standing in front of a bank of monitors, each labeled with the names of major cities from around the world. He turned up the volume and watched in wide eyed fascination.

Wanda and Karen were drawn to the open door behind him and then to the sofas. No one spoke. It was enough to see that what they had experienced on a small scale was happening everywhere. Fire, smoke, police barricades, people throwing bottles with burning rags dangling from the open ends. The explosions, the gunshots, and the worst part….the people who didn't fall also didn't run, and they didn't die. People engulfed in flames who walked with their arms outstretched, reaching for and grabbing at people who fought desperately to break free. Some of them did break free only to be caught again, and some were dragged to the ground as if captured by wild dogs.

A camera moved in closer where a group of men and women were doused in gasoline and set on fire, but even as they burned, they caught hold of the uniformed men who had the unfortunate duty of being on the front lines to fight these monsters. It was really a one sided battle because one side had no fear of dying.

"What city is that?" asked Gentry. No one had seen her come into the room, but no one looked her way when she spoke.

"Paris," said MC.

"I lost track of time again, but I'm so tired. I don't even know what day it is anymore."

Karen held up her wrist and showed Gentry it was eleven o'clock.

Gentry shook her head and said, "Then that has to be just before sunrise in France. How long was I asleep?"

"Just a few minutes," said MC. "Karen and Wanda are making supper. You need to eat, so don't go back to sleep."

Karen added, "You were asleep long enough to miss MC running around without his pants on."

"It's amazing what can happen in a few minutes," said Wanda.

For a moment Gentry was confused by the kidding around. She didn't remember much after they came in the door because she had dropped onto the sofa. She had only intended it as a joke, but apparently she had shut out the world for a few minutes. She also felt an odd pang of jealousy. Why was MC running around without his pants on?

MC saw the furrow on Gentry's forehead, and despite having a lot to learn about life, and especially women, he knew that expression.

"Hey, Gentry. Remember getting sick out there on the stairs? That smell? Most of it was coming from me after I got done rolling around on the floor with those dead guys. I found a washer and dryer back there by the kitchen. My boots are still drying." He held up a foot so she could see, and he was relieved to see in return that it all made sense to Gentry. He was also aware of the way Karen and Wanda were all over his hurry to convince Gentry there hadn't been any funny business.

Karen came to his rescue by suggesting that it wouldn't be a great idea to eat supper in front of the TV tonight. They all agreed that they should be civilized on this one occasion by sitting around the table. It might be one of the few times they could hang onto that kind of life.

Gentry and MC got to their seats because Wanda and Karen insisted on serving the food. They said it was nothing special, but it was apparently just what they needed because they could hardly wait. They dished out big plates of spaghetti and passed around the sauce. They had found frozen biscuits that would have to do in place of French bread, but it was about to be a feast to a very hungry group.

"Hang on everyone," said Gentry. "I think we need to make a toast to our benefactor." She held up her glass of beer so everyone at the table could do the same. "This is a toast in honor of Titus Rush."

16

Huntsville Shelter

The First Week

Supper became a time for healing, and if the hot food had come from the kitchen of a five star restaurant it wouldn't have done more for them. It had been very little talk at first as fresh containers from a well stocked refrigerator were unwrapped and served as if there would always be enough food. The truth was that at least for the moment, they didn't care about anything except for that one meal. Tomorrow could be worried about when it arrived.

As they got their fill, the conversation started to increase slowly. The beer helped too. As they relaxed, they realized just how little they knew about each other. None of them were really sure about how much time had passed since their 9:00 AM meeting with the Colonel. The meeting never happened, but they were thrown together by the Colonel as if they had some special mission as a group. Karen said it well when she said it was like they were part of a plan, but no one had explained it to them yet.

"I can understand Gentry, and why she was singled out by the Colonel, but what about the rest of us?" asked Wanda.

"We were in the right place at the right time," said MC.

Karen lifted her glass before realizing it was empty. They laughed as MC reached across the table and gave her a refill.

"Now, where was I?" asked Karen. "Oh, wait. I've got it now. I'll drink to that."

Gentry politely objected, which caused a chorus of cheers from the others. As she drank, she was more polite because she became more careful with her choice of words. She had been the same way at parties because of her work. NASA had more federal employees than civilians, and federal employees were constantly reminded of the sensitive nature of their jobs. Most positions with any authority were exposed to highly classified information, and alcohol tended to loosen conversations until someone had to be reminded they were walking out onto thin ice.

"No, seriously," said Gentry. "Anyone could have been picked to do this job."

"I doubt that," said MC. "If I listed the people I've met who were launch directors for NASA, I could do it on one hand."

MC held up a hand, palm toward his face, and studied it for a few seconds.

"I should've said I could count them on one finger, but that sounds wrong too."

It wasn't half as funny as they thought it was, but they laughed until there were spilled drinks and generally more laughing at their own silliness.

After everyone had caught their breath and things settled down a bit, there was just a touch of seriousness in Gentry's voice as she said it again a little differently.

"It could have been anyone in that control center. Anyone could have been the flight director instead of me. Do you suppose it was already happening when they gave me the job, and everyone senior to me was already dead because every other director I ever worked with had kids my age?"

The question caused the room to go silent as everyone seemed to be watching something far away in their past. In reality it was just two days ago. Gentry got her call giving her the job and had been unable to sleep. When she considered the possibility that she had only gotten the call because it had already started, she had to wonder why they went ahead with it.

"Maybe they didn't know what was happening," she said. "Something was happening, but they didn't know what it was."

Karen said, "I feel like I just came in at the middle of a discussion. Who didn't know what?"

"The only reason they could have made me the flight director for such an important launch was that everyone senior to me was already dead. If there was anyone around to ask, that's what I'd want to ask them. Was it already happening, and they didn't know what it was? There were at least three people ahead of me who could have been called to take the job. Were they called? Did something happen to them already? If they couldn't reach them, why didn't they cancel the launches?"

Gentry wasn't really aware that the others were just quietly watching her. A few moments before they were letting go of emotions by getting drunk and laughing, but people had died. Some of them had died horribly. There was a guy in the stairwell with his intestines hanging out. When reality hit home, sometimes it hit hard.

"I got to launch control, and I just figured I was early because I was excited since I was in charge. The people who were at their stations were complaining. Someone from the shift that had prepped for the launches had called to say there was some kind of executive order or something declaring a curfew, and how could they come in for the launches if they couldn't leave home?"

Gentry trailed off, remembering that she had been so excited only to be met by angry questions from tired people who needed to go home and get some sleep. She was in charge, but the people didn't care. All she knew was that the big screen showed two Russian rockets on their launch pads ready to go, and Houston wasn't answering the phone. Huntsville was going to take over the launch, but she didn't have a full crew, or even a happy crew.

"You guys weren't on the gates yet when I got here, were you?" she asked MC. She hadn't thought about it until that moment, but security had been pretty lax at the main gates.

He shook his head and seemed almost to be studying something on the back of his hand. In reality, the deep frown on his forehead was the clue to what he was thinking.

"I don't really remember it all because it was so weird. We were in school, you know. We haven't been back in the States for long."

MC shook it off like he was trying to get his thoughts together.

"Let me start over," he said. "I was in Afghanistan and was told I got the school I wanted here at Redstone Arsenal. It was a chance for me to make some rank and get into a job I really wanted, so I picked up my orders and got here as fast as I could. I guess I didn't want them to change their minds."

He laughed like he expected them to see the humor in it, but all he got was polite smiles.

"Anyway, I got out of a cab in front of the barracks and was ordered to load up with everyone else and come to the Space Flight Center. No one knew what was going on. The squad leader handed me an M4 and a 9 mm as they dropped me off at the gates. He told me to shoot anyone who tried to get through the gates who didn't look like they were supposed to. I thought he was kidding. We didn't even know what that meant."

"That's when we showed up," said Karen. "It was shift change at the base hospital, but they were calling in all of the off duty personnel, and no one could go home. We thought there was some kind of mass casualty event coming in, but the only thing on the news was something about a big fight at a park downtown. Something about an attack. We thought it was a gang fight."

Wanda took over when Karen paused. "They told everyone to grab emergency medical field packs and to load up on buses. When we got here you guys were shooting people in the parking lot."

Wanda pointed at MC and made the statement as if she was exaggerating, but they all knew she wasn't.

"They unloaded everyone at the bunkers and escorted us into hospitals that looked like something from a war movie. Next thing we knew, you guys were coming in on stretchers with bite wounds. Some were already bleeding out from carotid arteries with big pieces missing. The lucky ones were just missing fingers, but all we could do was dress wounds and stop the bleeding. We still didn't know what was going on."

For the next hour they took turns and filled in the blanks about what they had been through. MC and Gentry shared their story about how the Colonel had determined that Gentry was the last remaining person from the Marshall Space Flight Center who would have a clue how to get into this shelter, and that maybe she could get the astronauts home from the Space Station.

"Well, we're here now," said Gentry. "What do we do now?"

"We still don't know what's going on," said MC. "When I joined up, I was told American soldiers would never shoot Americans. Combat made sense, but I knew why I was there. Then I was suddenly in a parking lot, Gentry was there looking kind of lost, and I had just figured out I had to shoot people in the head if I wanted them to stay down."

MC didn't realize his voice kept getting louder until he was practically shouting. It was like a pressure relief valve had blown.

"There are people eating people out there."

As he yelled the last sentence, he stood up and pointed at the door, and at that moment he would've accepted a reasonable explanation from anyone.

Karen spoke in the calmest of voices, realizing that MC had been holding himself together for all of them. He had been forced to use his weapon in combat, but shooting civilians who were trying to bite him had forced him in an entirely different direction.

"I don't think any of us took the time to thank you for getting us here alive. MC, thank you for being our hero, and Gentry," she lifted her glass to both of them, "thank you for figuring out how to open the shelter door. I think Wanda and I will earn our keep, but you two got us here today. Whatever it is that's happening, it's not supposed to be happening, but it's real. It's real, and I don't want to end up like one of them."

"I think I know what we need to do now," said Wanda. "We need to get some rest, and then we take it one step at a time. We find out where we are, and then we can figure out what we're going to do."

"There's three bedrooms," said MC, "so I'll take the couch up by the front door. It's been a long day, and maybe Wanda is right. We need rest, and we can figure this out tomorrow."

Karen got up just as MC was finishing what he was saying and gathered together some of their dishes. MC held out his hand in her direction.

"I don't know how much our lives have changed, but I know they've changed. That can wait until tomorrow too. Let's break a few rules tonight."

Karen was reluctant, but she sat the dishes down.

"I am tired," she said with a weak smile.

MC took over like a single father making the kids cut the evening short. He hustled them all away from the table in the direction of the stairs.

"You guys can all pick your rooms without my help, so get going."

They all said good night and exchanged hugs, but they knew MC was right. They were exhausted, and they were at their limits. He listened to them as they easily decided who got which room, and he waited where he was until he heard a third door close. As soon as it did, he made his way into the sitting room by the front door. He spun the sofa around and pushed it over to the front door. He got comfortable in a chair facing the door and went to sleep with his rifle across his lap.

******

Gentry had gotten more sleep than MC or either of the nurses since the day they had arrived at the shelters, and even though she was exhausted physically, her mind wouldn't shut down. She drifted in and out of sleep but always woke up with a start, wondering where she was and why it was so quiet.

The bed was comfortable, and the sheets smelled fresh and crisp. She had always hated those trips home to visit from college because her mom never caught onto the idea that sheets and blankets would get stale over time. This room made her wonder how someone knew to put fresh sheets on the beds before they arrived. Somewhere during the middle of the night, she realized that the little things were bothering her. If she noticed the sheets were fresh, what else was she going to notice? That wasn't normally a bad thing, but sometimes it meant you were coming unglued.

All three bedrooms were big, and they had their own bathrooms, so there was no disturbing the neighbors. The neighbors…she knew who was in the other rooms, but there was that odd feeling you get when you don't know what's on the other side of the wall. What's the layout, and who's over there?

She studied the room from her bed, and she had been so disinterested in what might be on television that she had ignored the device for over an hour. It suddenly occurred to her that she could find the news channels, and she frantically searched for the remote. Every channel had the news except those odd channels that showed one syndicated program after the next. She doubted anyone was watching The Western Channel tonight.

Some of the networks were sharing feeds, so they had the same videos with different reporters. Some were also on a loop, and the videos were from hours before. She found one that had the word LIVE in the corner of the screen, and the man at the anchor desk was actually holding a sheaf of papers instead of an electronic tablet or laptop. Even as she adjusted the volume, someone handed the man a new piece of paper. He checked it and went straight into the update.

"Just as a reminder, we can't independently verify some of our information. We've decided to pass it along to you as we get it, and we'll tell you if it came from one of our competitors. This is not a time for scoops or breaking news first. It's a time for us to be sure you get the news as soon as possible so you can make decisions."

Gentry didn't know the middle aged man, but she liked him for what he was doing. If he was as tired as he looked, she would forgive him if he laid his head down on the anchor desk and went to sleep. He had probably not appeared on live news without a shower since his younger days in the field. Now his hair was gray, and he could only push it aside, but his viewers were concerned about what he had to say, not what he looked like.

"We can now give verification from a military source that the Chinese have engaged in airstrikes in several of their major cities. So far there have only been conventional weapons used, and we are attempting to gather a list of the cities for our viewers as the reports come in. So far we understand that Beijing has been one of the cities where the fighting has been more intense."

Gentry discovered she was not nearly as patient as she thought she was. She was only a minute into the broadcast, and she was already angry that the coverage was about China and not the US. She was a split second from changing channels when the man saved himself.

"We have a live feed coming to us from Atlanta. We want to warn our viewers that the video you are about to see will be shocking. If you have children watching at this late hour, you should take this opportunity to move them to another room."

Gentry found herself moving closer to the TV as she assumed parents were hustling their children in the other direction. She glanced at the time and wondered what she would be doing if she had children in the room. She doubted they would be watching the news. If they were still at home, she would have everyone packing their bug-out bags, and then they'd be heading for somewhere safer. She didn't really know where it would be safer, but under different circumstances she felt like she would have settled that question.

The scene on the large TV set went almost totally dark. The reporter apologized for the loss of power at the moment. Apparently, there had been significant damage at the terminal where they were broadcasting, but just as he was about to complete his explanation, rows of emergency lights illuminated a large portion of the terminal and the surrounding runways.

The taxiway just outside the terminal was a beehive of activity. On a typical day, the same thing could be said anywhere at the Atlanta airport, this was different. People moved with efficient purpose before. Now they moved with a frantic fear, and it was obvious that everyone felt exposed. Ground crews ran haphazardly between planes as they rushed to get planes rolling away from the terminal. Gone were the trains of luggage that normally snaked between the planes. If there was any attempt at all to get luggage to the planes before they pulled away, it wasn't obvious.

The reporter was yelling a warning that couldn't be heard on the taxiway, but even if they could hear him out there, it would have been ignored. A group of people, maybe as many as two dozen, were walking into the path of a Boeing 727 with no regard whatsoever for the huge wheels that rolled in their direction. The plane's wings rocked and bounced as if the wheels were passing over speed bumps, and the reporter shouted about the inhumanity of the pilot who refused to stop.

All of this was happening in real time, and Gentry was seeing every detail as if she was right there in the middle of it, but her mind was a million miles away. To her it was bright sunlight outside, and she had just emerged from an underground garage into the middle of the shooting, the screaming, the smells as smoking hot bullets tore through human flesh. She saw herself standing near MC, a soldier she didn't know yet, and she heard someone saying that you've got to shoot them in the head. Gentry was watching yesterday and the day before yesterday and tomorrow all at the same time. It was all still happening. It had never stopped.

She heard the reporter ask the cameraman a completely absurd question, and she heard the cameraman give an equally absurd answer.

"Where do you think you're going? You can't just leave."

"You can stay here and die if you want to. Who do you think is going to be watching this broadcast anyway? If they're watching it today they're probably going to be dead tomorrow."

They argued a minute longer, but it was one sided. The cameraman said the reporter could keep the camera, and the reporter ridiculously said he would make sure that he never worked another day in broadcast journalism. The cameraman only took long enough to say he was pretty sure that was going to be true for the reporter too, and then he was gone. He apparently left with great haste because the reporter was shouting insults at him not so much out of anger as the need to be heard at a distance.

Gentry had immersed herself so far into the events happening at the airport that felt like she was there. She snapped back to reality like she was attached to a big rubber band, and she stifled a scream by clamping her hand over her mouth.

The reporter appeared to be wrestling with someone over the ownership of the microphone. The network logo stayed visible for all to see even as blood threatened to obscure the bold letters. The person who wanted the microphone had resorted to biting the reporter's hands in order to get him to let go, and the reporter's vocabulary had been reduced to exclamations that would have gotten him fined by the FCC only a few days ago.

Several other people joined the fight, and the entire group fell below the range of the camera, although she could still hear the commotion through the open microphone. Gentry suddenly found herself superimposing more believable explanations for what was happening onto what was being broadcast by the camera.

To her the reporter had been attacked by someone, and other people were trying to help him. Her mind was replacing what was happening with what made sense, and she wasn't aware that she had allowed her body to lay over onto one side. Her arm scooped a pillow closer, and she lifted her head high enough to slide it into place. She went to sleep without seeing the reporter stand up between the seats and move away with the others, undoubtedly in search of his own victims.

Across the hall from her room, light shone under the other two bedroom doors as Wanda and Karen both suffered through the same anxiety as Gentry. In each room they had done as Gentry had and searched the channels for any broadcast that maintained any semblance of order. Viewers were used to seeing reporters waiting for their cue, introducing themselves and their network, and then launching into their story. They weren't used to seeing the reporters arguing with camera operators or yelling for help. Station after station was like tuning into a sporting event with no announcers. There was no recap of the score or explanation of what was happening. They found themselves stopping on any channel that did have someone at least explaining where they were broadcasting from, and familiar places weren't familiar anymore.

Airports on the news are always crowded, and occasionally a passenger can be seen running to catch a flight, but airports are mostly people standing in lines. Cameras pan along the lines from time to time drawing a reaction from unfriendly faces that aren't happy about standing in one place so long. Whether it's a line at the ticket counter, security, or boarding, airports are always made of lines. The only places where the lines break down are at the baggage claim area, and people are more than happy to walk right over you if you're between them and their luggage as it circles the carousel.

Airports on the TV had all changed. There was considerably more running, more shoving, more shouting, and if someone was standing in a line, they were generally encouraging the people ahead of them to move faster. Then the panic would start right there on camera. The people in line at the ticket counters reacted as if their flights were on the other side of the door behind the ticket agents. They rushed forward pushing the agents aside and eventually overwhelmed the luggage check-in areas.

Security officers were faced with frantic crowds of frightened people, and their training was what cost them the opportunity of saving anyone, including themselves. They didn't know what they were up against, and they did nothing except expose themselves to their attackers. It was natural for the officers to attempt physical control rather than use firearms. None of the sick looking people wandering behind the screaming crowds was carrying a weapon, so the uniformed men and women rushed forward with nothing more than batons, handcuffs, and pepper spray.

A wall of uniformed men and women bravely created a barrier to protect the fleeing passengers. They were confused by what was coming toward them. The ragged men and women who approached their line looked as if they were the ones that needed protection. They were slow moving and bloodstained, and they moaned like they were in extreme pain.

Extended arms and hands were met by teeth that snapped shut on skin that was protected by nothing more than clothing. The screaming that had faded with the escaping crowds began again.

Across the world it went on in every city and every airport. During the day in half of the world and night time in the other. People fell asleep watching it happen, and people woke up to see it continuing. Some people, the really unfortunate ones, were in the middle of it. Among the fortunate survivors, there were those who managed to find themselves a place to be safe as the virus raged through countries.

All three women in the Huntsville shelter fell asleep with their TV sets on, and none of them bothered to get undressed. Safely below ground and only a few miles from a major airport they gave in to their exhaustion. When they woke up to their quiet rooms, the broadcasts may have continued on other stations, but not theirs. Screensavers on the modern equipment had turned on, and the pictures rotated between pastoral scenery and underwater cameras. Ironically, some of the most popular screensavers were videos shot from the Space Station.

Gentry smelled the coffee as soon as she opened her door and stepped into the upstairs hallway. She walked barefoot down the carpeted stairs and found the others sitting around the table where they seemed to be studying something like a map. Karen put a cup of coffee in front of her before she could reach the table, and she nodded gratefully as she cradled the cup. She wasn't cold, but the warmth felt good anyway.

"Look what we found," said MC. He flashed a big smile at her.

"Is that a map?" she asked.

"Yes, but not of the whole shelter," said MC. "It must be just this level. Get any sleep?"

She nodded again. "I must have. I woke up at the wrong end of the bed. I think I fell asleep watching the news."

"Same here," echoed Karen and Wanda.

They all felt relaxed, but it was obvious to all of them that it was more likely that they were just totally drained. The last few days had been a long time to be under so much stress, and they still had something hanging over their heads. They felt like they had been spared just so they would be able to bring home the astronauts.

"Is there any chance of us getting this place up and running the way it was designed to be?" asked Gentry. "I mean as a flight control center?"

MC shrugged his shoulders. "That's going to depend on what we find on the other levels, isn't it? We don't have an easy way to evaluate the threat."

"What about the way we did from the computers last night?"

Karen said, "We talked about that already. We might be able to use them to some extent, but the only way we could use them for what you have in mind is if we were sure we were able to see everywhere. We might decide a floor is clear, but then when we walk through a door, we might find ourselves face to face with fifty or sixty of those things."

Gentry had missed it when she walked in, but MC must have forced himself to stay awake all night. He swayed visibly, and she wondered how he had managed to keep his eyes open in the silence of the room.

"We also can't go around busting into every room with guns blazing until we clear every floor," said Wanda. "I mean, look at MC. If it's possible to die from lack of sleep, he's well on his way."

The comment caused MC to stand just a little straighter, to open his eyes just a little wider, and to at least appear normal for all of ten seconds.

"Wow," said Gentry. "Did you see that?"

Wanda and Karen both laughed just a little, but it was a gentle, sympathetic laugh. They both got up at the same time and took over as nurses. With Gentry following and giving them her support, they forced MC to give in. They got him to the sofa under a blanket with a pillow under his head, and he was asleep before they could get back to their coffee.

Sitting around the table with their coffee and a light breakfast of powdered eggs and some kind of canned meat, they came to some decisions without MC. With a little rest, maybe they could find their way back to the Flight Control Center, identify areas where there were infected people, and then eliminate them in small groups.

The news channels they had been watching had referred to them as infected dead, so they did the same. They saw that the mistakes made in dealing with the infected had almost been universal. They had been treated as victims who could be helped, but they should have been treated as contagious and dangerous.

"Was there anything else useful besides the map and food in this room?"

Karen and Wanda shook their heads.

Wanda said, "We wanted to go out and check this level, but MC was a little too adamant about waiting. We're not sure what he was waiting for, but we figured he thinks you know more about this than what you've told us."

Gentry was stunned by the comment, and it must have shown on her face.

Karen held out her hands, "Whoa, wait a minute. Don't take that wrong, Gentry. He didn't say it that way."

Karen flashed an angry glance at Wanda. There was no doubt in her mind that Wanda was a little jealous of Gentry, and she saw an opportunity to erode her feelings for MC.

Gentry was still angry about the lack of trust. "How did he say it?"

"With a lot of respect," said Karen. "He said you should be given a chance to rest a bit before we start pushing you to remember everything the Colonel dumped on you so fast. He said you didn't even know about this shelter until just after you guys met a couple of days ago."

Gentry felt herself cooling down, and her eyes met Wanda's. She wanted to remember to be careful of Wanda in the future.

"Well, it's obvious that we shouldn't go anywhere without MC just in case we run into those things. A little more rest won't hurt all of us, and maybe some showers. We can search this level after he wakes up."

MC demonstrated his resilience by waking up completely refreshed only four hours later. At first the women all insisted that he should sleep longer, but it was obvious from the amount of energy he had that he was ready to go. He also had an incredible appetite for field rations because the powdered eggs didn't bother him in the least bit.

After a quick shower, and discussions about an emergency plan which included getting back to the apartment as a rally point, they set out to explore the shelter. Going out the door wasn't the same as their escape from the temporary shelter somewhere above them. Up there they had a feeling like death was all around them. It felt like it was following them, and it felt like it was waiting for them around the next corner up ahead. All the while they kept going downward, and for some reason, they felt like down meant safe. If they went down far enough, then they left death above and behind them.

Somehow death had gotten inside the shelter ahead of them, but this shelter felt like it was supposed to be their place. It was supposed to be safe, and they would make it safe again.

MC led the way for obvious reasons. Karen had the map, and they moved only as fast as she could mark their progress on the map. They had established where their starting point was and then traced backward as best as they could recall to the place where they had entered this level. They felt like it would be easy enough to explore one level on their first time out, but they agreed that they didn't have to make that decision yet. Twelve levels with eight rooms per level meant that they would have plenty of time for decisions in the days ahead.

The curving hallway was clean and as quiet as a tomb, and they noticed that sound seemed to not carry as far as in straight hallways. One of their early theories was that this level was living quarters, and it was meant to give a feeling of privacy. That theory was reinforced by the first room they came to. Just like their place, the door was unlocked. MC eased the door open with his M4 pointed ahead of him, and they saw it was an apartment with the same layout as the one they had stayed in. A quick search confirmed that the only difference was that this apartment hadn't been used yet.

"This search is going to be quick if they're all like this," said MC.

They had all met back in the living room by the front door, and they were visibly relieved as they made their way from there into the hallway. The next door was about as far from them as the last one had been when they started, but this one held a few more answers. It was an office that appeared to be like the office in a motel because it contained odds and ends for rooms. On the desk was a rack for the electronic keycards that could be given to the residents, and there was a backup supply of floor maps next to it.

"Whoever designed this shelter felt like there would be a need for services for the guests," said Karen.

"This place feels like it was designed by more than one person," said Gentry. "You know, too many cooks in the kitchen. It feels like it was designed by NASA."

"Maybe that's why we ran into some infected last night," said MC. "Too many people knew about this place beforehand, and maybe there was more than one way to get in."

17

Missions

The First Week

Natalia's faith in Adam and Henry to be able to fix the radio was well placed, but sometimes it takes more than a rubber band and some duct tape. Maybe two rubber bands would have made a difference, but in the end the radio wasn't the only problem. There were too many things breaking on Earth, and even though the radio had worked for a short time, it hadn't worked long enough.

The three astronauts came to an agreement, and they had circled a date on the calendar. Since they were all pilots, they all knew that there was a point of no return they had to use as a termination point. It would be natural for them to consider an attempt to return to Earth in the supply capsule, but they had to make a decision as to whether or not there were any other options. That was their first option, and it was the option Henry preferred.

Their second option was to establish radio contact with NASA and determine how the mission had been affected. The original mission was to measure the feasibility of a long trip through space. Could they survive mentally and physically? Could their equipment endure the operations requirements, or would there be too much wear and tear? The only thing that had really changed was the number of people involved in the experiment. Six of their comrades wouldn't be completing the mission with them, and the remaining three needed to learn if that was the only change to the mission.

NASA had taken all of these questions into consideration, and during their preparations and training over the years leading up to the launch, the question of survival had been weighed. When the entire crew was killed in a shuttle launch, it was a terrible setback, but the program continued. When it happened for a second time, NASA knew they couldn't continue using the shuttles forever. They continued for as long as they could, but they circled a date on the calendar and agreed that they would not continue the mission beyond that date. Adam, Natalia, and Henry knew they would make their decisions based on that precedent. They would set a deadline for a decision.

The third option would be based on what happened to the second option. If they were to continue the mission, the question became for how long. The original mission had a scheduled termination date which was contingent upon the supplies. When nine people used their supplies, the mission would end, so now the remaining three had to decide if that would be how the new mission ending would be determined. In other words, would they remain in space as long as the supplies lasted?

They had a brief meeting and laid out the changes and the new guidelines, and when they were done, they gave a pledge to each other that no one would attempt to change the agreement. It was hardest on Henry because there could come a time when he would be faced with choosing between the mission and his family, but he resolved within his own mind that he had made that choice before flying into space to live on the ISS.

So, option one became to fix the radio, and if they were instructed to do so, they would continue the original mission with three people. Option two was to go longer because their supplies were enough to last longer, and NASA officially changes the mission. Option three would be that they would return to Earth if ordered to do so by NASA, or if they reach the date they circle on the calendar and have been unable to get a decision from NASA.

"Did we make that confusing enough?" asked Adam.

Natalia said, "You Americans like to make your rules."

"Could be," said Adam, "but we can't have anyone feeling like they didn't have a fair say in the decision."

Adam had pinned a page from a calendar on a wall, and he floated over to it with an ink marker in his hand. With an air of finality, he drew a circle around the last Friday of the month.

"That's thirty days from now," he said. "If we haven't established contact with NASA by then and told to come home, then we're up here until we run out of supplies. Of course they could say to stay up here on a modified mission, but I doubt they would say stay up here for as long as possible."

"You mean six years," said Henry.

"Right. I don't expect NASA to say we should stay up here for six years, but I expect them to say they want us to stay up here until they can do a safe recovery. Things were pretty bad at the Cosmodrome, and we won't have any idea what a recovery area will be like."

"That's another question," said Natalia. "If land recovery areas are too dangerous, they may want us to do a water recovery."

She paused, but they had all been together long enough for them to know she wasn't done talking.

"I know we have already decided what we will do if we do not get instructions, so I am just saying this to reinforce that decision. We need to know from them where the recovery zone will be. If we stay in orbit and we lose contact with NASA, we may have to change our plans again."

Henry was the one who was feeling the most anguish over the uncertainty. Even if they received new mission orders from NASA, those orders would be in jeopardy if they lost contact with NASA again because the recovery couldn't always be decided in advance. If the weather was too bad over a water recovery zone, they would make a land recovery. Land recoveries had just become a bigger problem than they used to be. The landing area could be covered with the infected for all they knew.

Henry said, "I have an idea. It's not a great one, but at least it's a plan."

"Let's hear it," said Adam.

"Well, first we have to establish contact with NASA. When we do… if we do, we can have one determined recovery zone at sea. If the weather is bad, we can still do the recovery. It just won't be as pleasant as a good weather recovery. We can't have a predetermined land recovery site because we don't know how bad the infection will be anywhere."

Adam and Natalia both didn't like the idea of a bad weather recovery. Unpleasant didn't really do justice to how dangerous they were. Rough seas could suck a Soyuz capsule underwater in seconds. When Gus Grissom opened the hatch of his Mercury capsule too soon, it had filled with water so quickly that he had been lucky to escape with his life. Still, it was the only thread of hope that Henry had. One way or another, if they wound up staying in orbit for six years, that was a long time for Henry to have to worry about his family.

Adam felt like he could answer for them both.

"We still have a few bridges to cross before the decision is made, but I can see why you would want to at least give it a try. Let's cross that first bridge and get NASA on the phone. Then we can see if they agree with your idea too."

Henry knew that was the best answer either of them could give him, so they all set to work on their efforts to contact NASA. So far they hadn't been able to find any of the technical reasons for lack of contact. Every time they passed over the exact same places where they had contact before, it was the same thing. No one answered.

One thing they watched for on any orbit was an automated signal. There was no shortage of signals from all of the locations where they were supposed to be. The system had been in place for years and proven to be reliable. As a matter of fact, it was so reliable that the average person took it for granted. GPS had become a household term without most people even realizing how important it would be for space travel. No matter where the ISS was in orbit, its computers knew where they were because they recognized every location on the ground. Now they were checking those ground locations that transmitted marker signals on a permanent basis, and as long as they knew the locations of those signals, they also knew what NASA installations should be broadcasting.

The good news and bad news was that it also meant their equipment was working. It was bad news because they could probably fix the equipment if it was broken, but there was nothing more they could do if no one on the ground was broadcasting. They decided to work in twelve hour shifts the first ten days. Broadcasting but not receiving would become stressful and would even take a physical toll, but they knew that it would be harder for all of them over the first ten days to find other things to do while they weren't broadcasting. Adam and Natalia wanted to let Henry get as much time trying to make contact as possible.

Henry put on a headset so he would hear the faintest broadcast, and he started his first shift. Adam gave him a pat on the shoulder, but he was already making notes of signals and sending out his first call. Natalia motioned for him to go with her into the adjoining module, so he followed her.

"We haven't had a signal from anyone in so long that I'm beginning to think things are far worse than what anyone expected at the start."

Adam nodded in agreement. He knew Natalia was just being as realistic as he was. After the Russian space center was so easily overrun, he had little faith that other less secure locations would fare any better.

He said, "You know the Marshall Space Flight Center has an Army base for security, and they still couldn't fight off whatever is happening down there. If this thing is as bad as I think it is, we won't be making any decisions with NASA."

"So you laid out all of the options just for Henry?"

"I didn't have much choice. I could make the decision right now, but even if it's the one Henry knows it should be, there's always going to be that tiny grain of doubt in his mind about whether or not I did the right thing. At least this way he'll have time to come to grips with the reality of the situation."

At the end of the first twelve hour shift, Adam and Natalia were surprised when Henry didn't wait to be relieved. He shut down the radio and made an announcement.

"I want to thank you both for humoring me. I don't need thirty days to know that no one is going to answer. Commander, it's your decision, but I recommend we make preparations for the longest space mission in the history of mankind. If we had a way of landing on Mars and then coming back, I would say we should do that."

"Recommendation accepted. I hereby order a complete systems check and inventory of provisions necessary for a six year mission. Set a continuous broadcast to ground stations detailing our mission parameters."

******

As the International Space Station circled the Earth high above the carnage that had destroyed their ground network, the only known survivor who could help them make the return trip was embarking on a mission of her own.

It was obvious long before they finished their exploration of the Huntsville shelter that it was designed for different levels of living. There were quarters for the upper echelon, the administrators of NASA. These were the people who were the equivalent of corporate

CEOs. They were used to a standard of living that they intended to continue in the event of an apocalypse.

The quarters where Gentry and the others spent their first night were comfortable, but they were intended for service personnel. That became obvious when they found the apartments that belonged to the Director and his executive staff.

"The Gods couldn't have treated Commander Bowman better," said Gentry.

"Who?"

The question came from Karen and Wanda at the same time, but judging by the blank expression on MC's face, he might as well have asked too.

"Don't you guys go to movies? That one is required viewing in NASA if you don't want to be shunned by everyone else. When Commander Bowman discovers what the monolith is really for...."

Gentry could see by their blank expressions that she wasn't ringing any bells, so she just dropped it and got right to the point.

"Forget it, maybe there's a copy of that movie around here somewhere. I was just trying to say if you were a really important person, and if you were forced to live, someone made sure you wouldn't mind. Everything would still be done for you."

The evidence began to mount up even before they found the executive quarters. There was a laundry room that was laid out like it was in a hotel service area. A massive kitchen that could prepare individual meals, as well as serve banquets, was on the same floor. Another floor had the dining areas for formal service, but there was a cafeteria style buffet on the same floor as the laundry room and kitchen.

"If anyone wants to move into the suites, feel free," said Gentry.

MC was quick to decline. "I'm all for safety right now. I didn't mind the couch last night, and at least I knew who was in the room with me. I would get creeped out in one of those executive bedrooms."

Gentry thought she saw the faintest reaction from Wanda, and her suspicions were confirmed when Wanda said, "Oh, I don't know. You could get used to those fancy rooms if you had the right person sharing one of them with you."

MC did a good job of pretending he didn't quite catch what Wanda said, but Gentry was fairly sure that Wanda's grin was for her benefit as much as for MC's.

"Speaking of safety," said Karen. Maybe she was picking up on the games that were being played or maybe she had it on her mind that the shelter still had the little problem of the infected dead on one level. They not only needed to dispose of them, but they also needed to find out if there was a hole in the shelter somewhere, and plug it. If not, the survivors needed to at least find out where the other door was.

Karen didn't have to finish the sentence for them to know what she had on her mind. They had explored all of the upper levels of the shelter, and just like any other hotel for the rich and famous, the most ornate rooms and the suites were on the upper floors.

"We came in through a lower level entrance," said MC. "The lower levels of the other shelters weren't low enough. We had to keep going lower and lower, and that took time. I think the plan was for someone to lead a large contingent of service workers down to that level and let them in. Then they would get situated in their quarters and the service areas like the kitchen and the laundry while the bigwigs used an entrance higher up."

Karen asked, "Are you saying we missed the other entrance up in the suites somewhere?"

"Yep, and that would mean two things. First, it's secure because no one came in through it. We just need to find it to confirm my theory."

"And what's second?" asked Gentry. She asked MC, but she still felt a little hot and was maybe flushed a little red in her cheeks because Wanda was still grinning like she was itching to find a way to bring the conversation back around to where MC planned to live.

"Second, the infected we ran into downstairs got here through the same entrance we used, but they got here fast. Someone either brought them here, or they were part of the original plan."

Gentry thought for a moment and added, "Makes perfect sense, and if we can somehow find a way to kill them, we should be able to tell by their IDs."

"Why would they have IDs?" asked Wanda, openly poking a hole in Gentry's idea.

If asked, she would have admitted she had a tone when she answered Wanda. She certainly had the attitude to go with a tone.

"This is the Space Flight Center, and it borders Redstone Arsenal. How many people do you ever see around here without an ID of some kind pinned to their clothes? All four of us are wearing them, aren't we?"

The truth was that Gentry fully expected the infected on the lower level to be people with IDs because of two things. Whoever knew about the shelter and had access to one of the entrances had to be someone who was part of the program. They had gotten into the shelter too fast to have been random survivors. She also thought it might be more of a problem for them because she knew what she would have done if she was a lower level service person with that kind of secret. She was willing to bet they had brought their families here when the killing started.

The group went to the stairs and descended toward the floor where they had stayed the night. Earlier when they had searched their floor before going up to the next one, they had used the stairs on the opposite side of the shelter. They were surprised to find there were no more infected, and they already had a working theory they all agreed to because of their own experiences.

Karen had noticed something about the two infected that made their theory a rather morbid tale, but it was highly possible. She noticed that the two infected both had bandages on their forearms in locations that gave them a high probability of being bite wounds. She and Wanda had treated plenty of wounds just like them. For some reason, the two victims were on a different level from a larger group, possibly even separated from the rest because of the wounds. Their theory was that one of them had died and had attacked the other. He eviscerated his companion and had eaten a portion of the man. That's why his intestines were so badly damaged and hanging out around his feet.

As they went further down the stairs and got closer to the landing where they had left the two infected dead, they all pulled masks from their pockets and tied them across their mouths and noses. It was probably the easiest decision they had made so far. When they had put together field kits before spending their day searching, MC had suggested that Gentry might prefer a mask over hurling her breakfast. He had said it jokingly, but she had thanked him as if he was saving her. For good measure, she included a couple of plastic bags she had found in a drawer.

The masks helped, but there was no way to totally eliminate the smell. The two infected were still on the section of stairs between the two landings, and they were both groaning miserably. It was easy to see why they hadn't managed to climb back up the steps to the landing. One was standing in the coils of the other's intestines, and as the group came toward them, the two couldn't coordinate their efforts well enough to avoid tripping each other. It didn't matter which of them tripped first. It was like a sack race on stairs.

"Everyone plug your ears as well as you can. I don't know if hitting them over the head would be easy in that slippery mess."

Everyone put their hands to the sides of their heads while MC leaned as far over the railing as he could. Even though he was an accurate marksman, they couldn't risk a ricochet in the confinement of the stairwell.

Gentry caught MC just in time to stop him from shooting. At first he was upset because he had already put pressure on the trigger, and if he had fired, it could have been a disaster. Then he felt stupid because that much noise would have given an advance warning if there was some inside the next level. If they were alive or if they were infected dead, they didn't need them waiting for someone to come through the door.

MC reversed his rifle and held it by the barrel, and with the ladies holding him by his belt and the back of his shirt, he was able to lean downward far enough to hit the first one hard. It tumbled backward, taking the other one with it. As they let go, Gentry saw that Wanda had gripped MC by the belt to hold onto him, but her other hand was just resting under his side on his ribs. She knew she turned red again, but it was easier to hide it this time because of her mask.

Stepping carefully over the slippery stairs and bloody body parts, they followed MC down to the heap of tangled infected. The second one had no chance of biting them because it was twisted face first into a corner. This time MC was able to dispose of it by doing a hard stomp of his boot to the back of its head. The sound was almost as nauseating to Gentry as the smell. She was grateful when they were able to get by the mess and make it down to the next landing with a door on it.

The designers of the shelter didn't think it would be necessary to have a window on the landing doors. It gave them an advantage because no one could see them coming, but the obvious disadvantage was that they had to open the door to see if the level was occupied.

Once they were lined up against the wall faced with the real possibility that there would be more infected dead on the other side of the door, MC felt like it wasn't the brightest decision to open the door with an army of one soldier, two nurses, and one nerd. It was also at that moment when he realized as he tried to classify them that he had a tremendous amount of respect for all three, but there was something else. It was easy to classify the two nurses, but he didn't know exactly what Gentry was. It hadn't occurred to him, but he suddenly had an urge to get to know her better. He had gotten into protecting her by chance right at the start, but now it felt like his duty to keep her from being harmed in any way.

They had their backs to the wall, and if he opened the door there would be nothing to stop anything that came through from the other side. If he would have had a squad of trained soldiers behind him, he knew the strategy for breaching the door would have been different, but reassessing the situation, he made a decision.

In a low voice he whispered, "Change of plans. Karen and Wanda, which of you qualified higher on the range?"

"Karen beat most of the doctors, even two who graduated from West Point," said Wanda.

"Nice, Karen. Good to know. Gentry and Wanda, I need for you both to go back up the stairs and get out of the direct line of sight of the door. Karen, I want you to take the M4 and go down the stairs far enough to be able to take aim. I'll ease the door open and have my pistol ready. If we're lucky, neither of us will need to shoot."

They weren't that lucky, and it was something they would give anything to forget. When everyone was in position and signaled they were ready, MC pulled the door open about an inch, then two. He moved his head left and right trying to focus either eye into a hallway that wasn't lit as well as the stairwell. That meant anything in the hallway was seeing him first.

He was just about to say something about it to the others when the door burst open with enough force for it to bang when it hit the wall. Karen had automatically taken aim, and she pulled the trigger with cool detachment. She had been taught by the Army that if she ever had to shoot at someone or something, it was not going to be a paper target charging forward on the attack. It wouldn't be the silhouette or outline of a man drawn on a piece of cardboard that wanted her dead. It would most likely be a person.

They had taught her to become detached from the situation. Be detached from the person who was going be her victim because if she couldn't become detached, then she might be the victim. She pulled the trigger, and her aim was perfect. The bullet left a neat little circle in the forehead of the young boy who had burst through the door.

They had learned quickly enough afterward that the boy was also an infected dead, but it was hard to push away that first mental image of the moment when she thought she had shot a child. If more infected had followed the first, she would probably have been swarmed by them because the first thing she did after pulling the trigger was to throw the rifle to the floor.

MC was exposed for a few moments, but he had no other options. He grabbed the light body and threw it further down the stairs while he also got a grip on the door and pushed it shut. In that moment, he watched the darkness beyond and simply hoped that nothing came toward him because he would have been defenseless. Once the door was shut, he became aware of the sobbing behind him.

Gentry and Wanda weren't as shaken as Karen, but they were close. They didn't have to detach themselves the way Karen did, so they realized it was an infected dead long before Karen did. What saddened them was the boy's age. He had probably been only about ten years old. MC went down the steps to Karen and wrapped his arms around her. It was a gesture she needed badly, and it only made the two younger women that much more attracted to him.

The emotions eventually subsided, and MC was able to ask Karen if she was able to continue. She sniffled a couple of times and bravely lifted her chin toward the door. She wanted to say something and show him she was stronger, but all she could manage was a rapid nod of the head. She retrieved the M4 and made a show of checking it for damage, and finding none, she gave MC a second nod.

They resumed their positions and got ready again, but this time they were greeted by nothing but darkness. It wasn't a black darkness, but it was enough that they had to let their eyes adjust. Once they were able to make out details they could see that there were darker patches on the wall across from the door. MC eased into the darkness and got a close enough look to tell they were bloodstains. He backed out of the doorway and motioned for Gentry to come closer.

"That map of this level shows the armory is to the right and two doors down. With only two weapons there's only one way I can think of that we can do this. Is there anything on that map that shows where the light switch is?"

"No such luck, and if your only idea is to have Karen cover you from behind while you walk down a dark hallway, then you need your head examined."

"You have a better idea?"

"Yeah, we don't know how many infected are on this level, so no plan is great with our resources, but I have to think the elevator would be better. We can open it from the bottom floor and send it to the third floor. We give it time to get there, and after the ding and opening doors gets their attention, the light from inside is bright enough to draw them in, and we can summon it back to the bottom floor. You can eliminate them when the door opens."

MC shut the hallway door because he already knew he was going to take her suggestion.

"I have to ask you how we will know when there are any in the elevator?"

"It's not a perfect plan, but I'm an elevator-half-full kind of girl."

Her smile sold him on the plan, but he thought her answer was just too cute. Besides, he really wasn't excited about the idea of asking Karen to stand in a dark hallway and cover him from behind.

******

The whole operation was an exercise in optimism. They didn't know if there were infected dead on that level. They didn't know if the infected would be drawn to or even enter the elevator, and the worst part was the possibility that too many of them would be in the elevator when the doors opened. The last thing they expected was what they got.

All four of them went down to the bottom level and positioned themselves at a safe distance from the elevator doors. MC approached the doors and was reaching for the button to summon the elevator when Gentry yelled to wait, but his finger was already there.

"The elevator was already on this floor," she yelled.

MC was right in front of the elevator when the door opened, and when he backed away from reaching hands, his feet went out from under him. There wasn't time for him to get his gun out of the holster and take aim, so he focused everything he had on keeping himself moving on the slippery vinyl floor.

The infected dead in the back must have pushed hard against those in front because they came out faster than they would have on their own. If not for the tallest one in front, several of them would have gone down on top of MC. It had its back to the door and didn't have the chance to turn around. With one heel stuck in the gap on the floor, it fell out of control with the arms of several more reaching around it for a chance to grab MC. It landed just close enough to MC's feet for him to use his boots to push himself out of the way. MC saw his opportunity and took it. With one boot on top of each shoulder, he pumped his legs like pistons and slid far enough to reach for his gun.

From a sitting position he aimed up at the infected as they fell over each other to get to him, and it was probably a good thing that he didn't have time to think about it. He just aimed and pulled the trigger. If he would have had more time, he would have thought too much about who he was shooting.

It was obvious that these had been families of people who knew about the shelters, and it was very likely that they had died inside the elevator judging by the mess. As the sound of the last shot still rang in their ears, the women moved forward to help MC to his feet, but their eyes were glued to the brightly lit cubicle. The floor of the elevator held several bodies that were mostly eaten, but they still moved spasmodically. There just wasn't enough left of them to make a difference. MC ejected the magazine into his pistol and replaced it as he stepped forward. He quickly shot the ones that were moving while keeping a close eye on the others.

When he stepped out of the elevator, he saw that all three women were pale, and if he had seen his own reflection in a mirror, he wouldn't have been surprised to see he was too. He shoved the gun back in its holster and grabbed one of the infected by the ankles. As he pulled it out of the way, it reached for him.

MC dropped the feet and pulled the pistol a second time, but he stopped himself.

"If we don't reach the armory before we run out of bullets, it could get harder for us to do it."

It didn't take long to find a fire extinguisher, and it was heavy enough to put the infected out of its miserable existence. He sat it aside where he could get at it faster if it was the better weapon to use the next time.

"Everyone watch out for the heads. If you bump into an open mouth and the teeth break your skin, you could probably still get infected."

He went back to dragging the bodies out of the way, and one by one the women joined him.

"When we're done securing the level, we have to figure out what to do with the bodies. I'm open to suggestions, but I think we could close off one stairwell and use the other. We could drop something over them from above to at least contain the smell a bit."

Wanda asked, "Why can't we put them in a room and just not use it?"

"That might work, but it would mean hauling them back up at least one floor, and there's still the chance that the smell will be too much for the ventilation system. I didn't see any vents in the stairwells."

They eventually got back to the original plan and sent the elevator back to the third floor. After waiting ten minutes they summoned it again, and this time it returned with a more manageable group of four infected. MC stood in one spot and shot them without even backing up. They repeated the process until the elevator came back empty four times in a row. The total number was twenty-eight infected in eight trips, and they were glad they hadn't done it with Karen covering MC from behind. It was obvious how that would have turned out.

They had also used their ten minute intervals to search for information about the lights. In a computer database they found that they could control the lights from right where they were, and they happily sent a computer command to turn on every light in the shelter. When they were ready, they knew they wouldn't have to navigate any dark hallways.

It was a long day, but when they finally settled in for another night in their new home, they knew a lot more about the place than they had before. They had forced themselves to clear the third floor, and they had done things that none of them had ever believed themselves capable of doing. The second floor was approached with the same caution as the third, but happily it had been deserted.

The armory and other rooms hadn't been a disappointment. MC would have been glad to stay and do an inventory of the weapons, but he was content to arm himself and the others with their own holsters and semiautomatic pistols.

After long, hot showers and a quiet meal, they said goodnight to each other and dragged their tired bodies to bed. Answers to the rest of their questions could wait until tomorrow.

18

Plan B

Farley - Year Seven

From the moment the truck pulled away without the Chief, Kathy and the rest of the group knew they would have to play the game to survive. All things considered, they thought they were pretty lucky. None of them had been shot despite the daring actions of the Chief to launch the big guy over Kathy. In the brawl that had followed, they had all managed to get the bed of the pickup truck into so much chaos that they even saw some of what had happened, and although they expected punishment, it never came. They heard enough to know that the Chief had killed the guy, and the fact that there was laughter and cheering from the majority of the crowd told them that things could be much worse.

It also surprised them that they were kept together. Kathy was sure that the pain she had caused that puny sheriff would get her some special attention, but from what she learned talking to people around camp, the Sheriff had such a big operation that he was too busy to get involved with everything that made him mad. His territory was so large that it encompassed everything north of the Tennessee River, and he personally took care of day to day operations. He had a half dozen or so captains who kept the small problems from getting to him, and the captain who ran Farley told her to keep her head down if she wanted the Sheriff to forget what she had done to his lower back.

Kathy, Tom, Iris, Hampton, and Colleen were considered to be a prize catch for the captain when the truck rumbled to a stop, but unlike many of the people who worked for the Sheriff, this one recognized them for the dangerous people they could be. Even though they were tied up and unable to see, he knew they had become hardened by the apocalypse, but they hadn't been lazy slouches before it. He saw that this group was disciplined.

That was his biggest reason for keeping them together. As a group he knew they were capable of acting as a team, but if he separated them, he had no doubt that each of them would recruit and run teams of their own within a month. He reasoned that he would rather deal with one good team than five good teams that would eventually connect and make one powerful league.

They were unloaded in front of an old frame house that was big enough for all of them, and to their surprise they were given a few meager supplies. A cardboard box with enough food for two meals, some old blankets, and a couple of jugs of water were unceremoniously dropped next to them by a dirty guy who smelled worse than his appearance would make anyone expect, and that was an understatement. He stared at the women's bodies openly, but he didn't bother to make eye contact with any of them. He didn't even flinch when Colleen decided to test him.

"Take your eyes off of me until you've at least had a bath, Bozo. You smell like you've been sleeping under an outhouse."

None of them saw as much as a grin, but the man walked over and climbed back into the pickup truck's cab. As a parting insult, he spit a big wad of saliva into the air, and unfortunately he was upwind. It sprayed back in their direction and had all of them scrambling to get out of the way. The truck started and pulled away throwing up a big cloud of exhaust.

Hampton said, "This isn't what I was expecting. The way they tried to shred Cassandra and Sim when they ran off gave me the impression that these people had a short temper."

"I hope they're okay," said Colleen. "Did anyone get a good enough look to see if they did?"

Kathy nodded, "I heard someone say they were missing a search party and that more were sent out. That could mean anything these days, but my money's on Cassandra. By now she's armed and hunting for another victim."

Iris said, "The plan is to reach the Marshall Space Flight Center if we get separated. If they get there ahead of us I think they will at least have some time to set up some form of defensive posture for the rest of us."

The one thing that made them so effective, besides their physical training, was that they always had a plan. They had made their share of mistakes over the years, but they had avoided trouble or gotten out of jams by planning whatever they could. This time they had discussed what to do if the group got split up before they reached their objective, which was the massive shelter system near the Marshall Space Flight Center.

They didn't doubt that other survivors had discovered the shelters by now, probably even the Sheriff, but they hoped no one else knew there was a super shelter somewhere in the area. With the clues they had, they planned to find the shelter, escape to the inside, and let everyone else wonder where they went. Hopefully, they would find the shelter to be occupied by the people who were supposed to be inside, but what they had learned so far was that things hadn't worked out that way.

In Columbus, Ohio, the President had apparently made it to his shelter, but the infection had gotten there along with him, and they had all died. Fort Sumter had a similar situation with a Senator. As for the other shelters, people had survived, but the only real success was the shelter in Guntersville. It had been a success because the man who owned it, Doctor Bus, had the good fortune to be inside the shelter at the start of the pandemic. The smallest shelter, Mud Island, was owned by the founder of the survivalist group. Titus Rush had built the shelters but died before the apocalypse. He had left it to his nephew, Ed Jackson. He wasn't exactly inside the shelter when it all started, but he had learned from the mistake, and the people who learned along with him had become known as the Mud Island family.

Now the Mud Island family was using Plan B. Plan A was to arrive at the Marshall Space Flight Center together, locate the super shelter, and get inside. If it was occupied by the people who were supposed to be there, it meant they would find some of the space program's brightest minds were still alive. If mankind was going to survive after the infection that had turned the majority of the world's population into flesh-eating zombies, science and technology had to survive too. With a little help the scientists could direct their energy toward beating the virus that had infected the world, and the Mud Island family felt like they were the help the scientists needed.

Plan A fell apart when they were ambushed by the Sheriff's people. The attack had separated them from Cassandra and Sim, but then they were separated from the Chief. Plan B was what they would do as independent groups or individuals. Rather than wasting energy trying to reunite, they each had specific tasks depending on who got to the target first. In this case, it was probably going to be Cassandra and Sim. If it was them, their job was to secure a rally point and to supply it with weapons and food. From the rally point they would have a base of operations to work from as they attempt to locate the super shelter.

The group would assume Plan B was a success until they had information to indicate otherwise. In other words, if they found out Cassandra and Sim were dead, or if they couldn't locate them, they would eventually move to Plan C. They didn't want to dwell on that until the time came.

Once they were inside and had checked out the house, they made a quick decision that one or two of them should go out into the shantytown and gather information without drawing too much attention to themselves. Kathy's full, long hair made people notice her. It was so blonde and naturally attractive that the Chief had once joked that Kathy could swim in mud, and her hair would still look clean. It was unanimous that she couldn't blend into Farley.

When they talked it over, Hampton said, "No wonder people are always shooting at us. They're jealous of our women. We have a stunning blonde, an eye-popping redhead, and a woman with hair so silver that she reflects light."

"Was that a compliment or an insult?" asked Iris.

Hampton immediately answered that it was a compliment and added, "Your hair is dazzling, Iris. Men and women all find you attractive."

"Nice recovery," said Colleen.

Hampton was the logical choice to go out into the crowds because Tom was so tall and athletic. As a former professional baseball player, his athleticism made him stand out. Hampton was far from being a slouch, but at least he could blend in.

"If I don't come back soon, don't worry. I may be onto something good, and we need information fast."

There was a back door from the kitchen, and they watched Hampton disappear into the flow of people as soon as he reached the street. People either didn't care who he was, or the crowd was too big for them to tell if anyone was showing him any interest.

Staying patient and on guard at the same time wouldn't be easy, so the group kept themselves busy by sorting out the meals. They were surprised they were given anything at all, and they imagined one of the things Hampton would learn was what was expected of them if they wanted more meals.

They took turns at the corner of one of the front windows. If someone was assigned to keep an eye on them, they were good enough to keep from being spotted. The crowd of people in the street didn't seem to be going anywhere in particular, but one thing was obvious. They weren't a cheerful community.

"Let me know if you see anyone smiling," said Kathy as Iris took over for her at the window.

"I noticed that too," said Colleen. "Funny thing, though. They look so serious, but they go out of their way to avoid eye contact with each other."

Kathy nodded in agreement. "They look beaten, like they know they don't have a choice about the way things are."

"But they're safe here," said Colleen. "I guess you could say they're resigned to whatever this is. They aren't prisoners, but if they leave they have to face the infected."

Tom said, "We've seen some hordes that would walk right over this place. What in the world makes this place so safe?"

Kathy answered, "That's likely to be something that Hampton finds out."

A few hours later, Hampton showed up more or less intact. There was a little swelling under his left eye, but his bruised knuckles were evidence that someone else had swelling under their eyes.

He popped out of a considerably thinner but still strong flow of people just as it was starting to get dark outside, and he managed to blend in so well that he was pretty close to the house before he was spotted by Tom from the window. Tom opened the door for him as he made it to the front porch, and Hampton ducked inside without looking behind him.

Kathy had taken over for Tom at the window as soon as he stepped away to open the door. She got to see that three men were searching the faces in the crowd, rapidly changing directions and going against the flow. It was obvious that they were trying to figure out where Hampton had disappeared to. The current of the crowd pulled the men past the house, and Kathy got a good look at all three of them. One had a nasty cut above his eye that was bleeding enough to keep him from seeing without constantly wiping at it. The other two had bruised faces, but one was nursing his arm like he was having to support its weight with his other arm.

"I think you made some friends, Hampton. You didn't invite them over for supper?"

Hampton gave Kathy a mock scowl.

"We had a little disagreement over the ownership of a pair of boots."

Colleen was already inspecting Hampton for injuries.

"Whose blood is this? Boots? What boots? What's wrong with yours?" she asked.

"Those were the boots we were fighting over. The one who got blood all over my shirt claimed they belonged to him and said I stole them."

"They're gone," said Kathy. "You okay?"

"I'm fine, none of them knew how to throw a punch or how to dodge one. I've got a lot to tell you guys."

They got Hampton a plate of food and settled down in the living room of the old house. The ratty curtains were just good enough to cover the windows, so they sat in a circle where Tom could keep watch while Hampton told him what he had learned.

"I got close enough to see the Chief."

Hampton said it to everyone, but he caught Iris by the hand and gave it a squeeze as he said it. Iris had never doubted the Chief could take care of himself, but she worried about him anyway. She returned the squeeze along with a smile.

"Did he see you?" asked Kathy.

"You know him," said Hampton. "If he saw me, he didn't let on. Anyway, he's okay, and I think he would want us to stick with the plan. I got the impression that all we have to do is let him know we're okay, and no one will need to be rescued."

Colleen put a wet rag against Hampton's face, and he flinched.

"Ow! I forgot about that."

Tom said, "Those three guys must want you pretty bad. They just went by in the other direction. What did they want, your lunch money?"

"Oh, we just had a little disagreement about some money they say I borrowed from them last week."

"Had you mixed up with someone else?" asked Colleen.

He shook his head, "I don't think it mattered. I think they just pick someone different every day, but they might remember me for a few days. They were working on someone else when they spotted me, and I must've had that lost look on my face."

Kathy said, "No one goes out alone again. We'll keep you under wraps for a few days, and maybe they'll forget about you."

That got a laugh out of Hampton, but Kathy knew why because she had seen the men. The one with the arm cradled in his other hand wasn't going to do anything that required two hands for a long time, and the other two wouldn't be chewing solid food for a bit. They would probably think of Hampton every time they ate something.

"Like I said, lots to tell you. This is quite a place. The town's name is Farley, and it's shaped like a horseshoe. There's a perimeter that I managed to follow for a long way. That tree line to the south is the river, and it closes the open end of the horseshoe."

"What closes the rest of it?" asked Kathy.

"You won't believe it when I tell you. To the east and the north, there's a road. Guard towers and armed patrols are all they use to keep the riffraff out. Apparently, they have good weapons and some light armor, and they did a clean sweep of the valley and eliminated the infected. Now they just keep it cleaned up. They also dropped the big bridge over the river, so there's no place for the infected to cross the river."

"Wait a minute," said Tom. "What about hordes? We've seen hordes everywhere, and somehow the infected seem to find each other and start another one as soon as one gets wiped out. Are you saying this place ran out of dead people?"

Hampton was nodding in agreement even before Tom finished asking him the question.

"I asked around, and everyone friendly enough to answer questions said the same things. I don't think these people have a clue what a horde looks like. One lady cried when she described seeing them on the other side of the river, and she said she's never seen more than five or six in a group on this side of the river. No one crosses the road because they know that's where the infected live. Not to mention the fact that patrols might mistake you for an infected dead and turn you into one."

By the time Hampton was done describing everything he had learned, it was obvious to them that they had stumbled upon a unique situation. The Sheriff had his own little kingdom because the Tennessee Valley had enough natural barriers to keep the infected from accumulating large enough numbers to overrun the living. The weapons he had inherited from the Army base had given him the means to keep it that way, and the people didn't know the difference between skill and luck. They didn't exactly love him, but they believed he had saved them.

The big surprise was when Hampton told them the famous Operation Paperclip shelters formed the western side of the perimeter. The outer edge of the shelter compound was less than two miles from their house.

"What are we waiting for?" asked Tom. "It's almost dark enough already. We could be there within the hour."

Hampton shook his head. "It's heavily guarded. It seems like everyone in Farley knows that there are thousands of the infected locked inside the shelters. Supposedly there's a treasure trove of supplies in every shelter, and there are three hundred shelters, but no one who has ever gone inside after the supplies has come back out. The Sheriff made it off limits, and the word is the Sheriff's men caught someone violating his rule and hung them in front of everyone to make it clear."

They talked it over for the next two hours and came to the same conclusion every time. The Sheriff had a pretty good thing going for him because he had solved the problem of getting inside the shelters and raiding the supplies. If he could keep everyone else from finding out, then he had food and weapons to keep a small circle of friends happy. The biggest clue Hampton saw was in plain sight all over the camp. There were MRE packages everywhere, and even though that was to be expected with an Army base so close to Farley, there was no way they would have lasted six years with so many civilians eating them.

Hampton explained that there was a community food program that required everyone to contribute by fishing, but there was no way that catfish could feed everyone. He told them about the little bartering shacks near the river where anyone could take the loan of a rod and reel along with an assortment of tackle. There were plenty of people taking advantage of it, and a lot of catfish caught every day, but then he discovered other bartering shacks where people were trading catfish for MREs. Some of the shacks had other items such as soap, clothing, blankets, and toiletries. Most of those things could be looted from department stores in malls, but there seemed to be an overabundance of military issue products.

"What about weapons?" asked Kathy.

"I didn't see any weapons except on Deputies, but there were a few talkative folks who told me they actually hire deputies. If you stay out of trouble you can get a job patrolling outside the perimeter for the infected."

Kathy asked most of the questions because she seemed to already have a plan. The rest of them were used to the way she would get this faraway look in her eyes when she was seeing something play out in her mind.

"When you say that you can land a job and even get a weapon by staying out of trouble, exactly how do they keep track of your behavior? There are way too many people for them to do that. I can see how the Sheriff might remember me, and I'm sure those three guys will remember you for a few days, but Colleen, Iris, and Tom haven't done anything. How would they know if they were even still here?"

Hampton said that he had begun to wonder that himself. He had managed to get close enough to the perimeter all the way over by the place where the highway used to cross the river, and then he worked his way north until he could actually see the rolling hills of the shelter complex. There had been patrols in that direction, but from what he could tell, there were tremendous gaps in the perimeter to the east. There were guard towers, but a halfway decent woodsman could sneak past them and the patrols.

"I think I've got it," said Kathy. That faraway look was replaced by resignation. "What did the Army do at this base? Soldiers do more than carry rifles and shoot things. What was their specialty here?"

"The Army had an electronics school here," said Iris. "They're neighbors of the Space Flight Center, so it shouldn't surprise anyone to find out it was a guided missile school. I'll bet they have enough electronic signals around here to fry your brain."

"Signal Corp," said Tom. "I don't know if they called it that anymore by the time the world fell apart, but the surveillance network was already in place long before the infected dead showed up. If you saw a fence along the perimeter to the west, it was only part of the package. Farley probably has more cameras per square inch than any town in the world."

Iris asked, "How far are we from the perimeter?"

"From what I could tell, they put us as close to the middle of Farley as they could. If they put new arrivals too close to the outskirts of town, it may be too much temptation for them to try to escape. We would be seen if we tried to leave in any direction."

"Well, I don't think we need to push our luck," said Kathy. "Does everyone agree that we need to let this play out a bit before we make our move?"

Colleen nodded and said, "We're alive, we have a roof over our heads, and we have access to food. I don't sense any immediate threat, so if we aren't in a hurry, I think we should let the dust settle a bit before we make our move."

"I agree," said Iris. "I don't like being anyone's prisoner, but I like it better than dead. Besides, Colleen is right about one thing. It's not like we have a deadline to meet."

******

International Space Station - Year Seven

It was a clear night, and the Space Station was visible with the naked eye, but the tiny silver dot that crossed the sky above Farley went unnoticed. After so many years it was still a testament to mankind that their technology was so good that it still circled the planet nineteen times per day. When people did look up at the night sky and see it silently travel from one horizon to another, there were some who knew what it was, and they felt the sadness of the loss. Mankind had made so much progress, but obviously progress in the wrong areas. More should have been done to prepare for a pandemic, but the question would always be, could mankind have prepared for this kind of pandemic?

Time was running out for the tiny silver dot, and those few people who looked up and knew what it was all thought the same thing. There couldn't be anyone alive up there now. A few people might see it and think, "I would rather have died like that. I would rather have been up there than to live out my remaining years in constant fear."

"I finished the inventory," said Natalia.

Henry snorted. "That didn't take long."

"Why should it?" she replied. "It's not like it has been a secret to any of us. We knew we would run out of supplies sooner or later, and we stretched them a lot further than any of us thought we could."

She could hear her own voice getting louder and strident with each word, but she couldn't stop herself. The arguments had gotten old over time. There were only so many times they could argue about whether or not to stay aboard the ISS or if they should attempt a Soyuz reentry without the telemetry that would guide them in safely.

"That's enough, you two. How many times am I going to have to break you two apart? You agreed six years ago that we would see this through."

"Yes, we did," snapped Henry, "but you sold us on the idea that before we even came close to running out of food, we would hear from someone on the ground. They would be getting our ticker tape parade ready for the heroes who broke all the records and proved that man could survive longer in space than everyone thought."

"What are you saying, Henry?" Now Adam was the one who was getting louder.

It had come to blows more than once. Six years was a long time for three people to be cut off from any other voices than their own. They never completely stopped trying to hear those other voices. There were times when they had shut off the equipment and cursed and swore at it. They swore they were done trying and stormed out of the module, but a day or so later they always found themselves hoping to hear a response to their broadcasts.

It seemed like it was about to come to blows again, but something made them all shut up at the same time. There wasn't anything that hadn't been said more than once, and as they each searched their minds for new fuel to throw on the fire, they were all quiet just long enough to become weary of the argument.

Henry grunted something that sounded like an apology and drifted through the hatch into the neighboring module. She didn't know if he heard her, but Natalia mumbled her own apology at his back. Adam heard them both and wished as he had thousands of times in the last six years that he could say something, anything that would make it all worth it. Nothing magically came to his mind, so he just turned to Natalia and asked her for the inventory. He saw what he already guessed. They should begin prepping the Soyuz for departure. Whether it was the right thing to do or not, it was the only thing they could do.

"Natalia, please tell Henry to come back. We need to settle this, and I can't decide everything on my own."

Adam wasn't surprised that it took Natalia a few minutes to convince Henry to come back. He could hear them yelling in the distance. After it was quiet for a few minutes, Natalia arrived with Henry close behind. Adam was sure Henry was mad about something and another fight was on the agenda, but instead Henry spoke in a calm voice.

"I vote for a landing zone in Europe since there are two of us who will be closer to home when we land."

Adam did his best to keep his voice calm too.

"That's very generous of you, Henry."

Henry immediately launched into a defense of himself, and it was everything Adam could do to keep himself from yelling that he didn't care about Henry's family anymore. He had certainly heard about them enough in the last six years. It eventually ended the way it always did. The two of them face to face in an angry staring contest.

Natalia was left to be the one to call a truce, but this time she did with some simple facts.

"If you boys are done, I have some news that will make it easier for you to decide what we can or cannot do. I've calculated the fuel requirements and applied weather conditions. It appears that we picked a bad time to run out of food. If we return to Earth any time in the next few weeks, we only have enough fuel for course changes that match a trajectory for water landings or the North American continent."

Henry was vehemently shaking his head before she could finish.

"I knew you would say that, so I ran the numbers too. All we have to do is leave the Space Station sooner and drop to a lower orbit. We would start our descent into the atmosphere later than normal, but since we'll be at a lower altitude, we'll be able to reach the coast of France with less fuel."

Natalia had her mouth hanging open. Henry was on the mission as a Science Specialist while she was a Flight Specialist. It was her job to make those calculations, and letting Henry make them was like letting a Botanist or Psychiatrist do it.

"What you're suggesting is suicide, Henry." She didn't gradually start yelling. This time she went straight to it.

"If we start from a lower altitude, our angle of entry will be far too shallow, and we'll skip off the atmosphere like a stone on a pond, but we won't bounce a second time because we'll be on the longest space trip of our lives. We won't get a second chance to enter the atmosphere because we won't have enough fuel for a second burn."

"We won't need a second burn because we won't skip off the atmosphere. We can use all of our fuel in one long burn and take a steeper angle because the reentry vehicle will be lighter. With all of our fuel depleted, and with less weight, we can take a steeper angle because we won't be traveling as fast."

Adam wanted to make it a safe reentry, so it didn't really matter to him where they landed as long as it wasn't on water or some otherwise unsuitable place.

"Is he right?" Adam asked Natalia. "If he's right, then I don't give a damn where we land. If it's in his back yard, it's fine with me."

"He's wrong!"

Natalia's voice was practically a scream.

"There's a reason you do your experiments up here and I do the flying."

"My numbers aren't wrong," he yelled back. "You can check them yourself."

Natalia took a deep breath and asked in a tone as evenly as she could, "Do your numbers take fuel for the retrorockets into consideration?"

Henry had a frozen expression on his face. Adam knew exactly where Natalia was going with her question as soon as she asked it, but he had to let it sink into Henry's mind before he could support Natalia.

Natalia continued when Henry didn't answer, "Your numbers are based on us making reentry at a steep angle because you assume we will have burned off all of our fuel. We won't be too heavy to burn up, and we won't skip off the atmosphere even though we will be lighter. But your numbers don't take into account the fuel we will still need to slow us down enough for a ground landing. Hell, at the speed we'll be traveling even a water landing would shatter every bone in our bodies."

Henry's cheeks sagged as if he was suddenly no longer weightless. Natalia and Adam both knew he was beginning to understand, but he needed to hear it or he might not totally feel the consequences of failing to think of everything.

In an almost soothing, motherly voice, Natalia continued. She wanted to let him down as easily as she could despite the earlier anger.

"When we enter the atmosphere, we will be traveling at seven hundred and fifty-five feet per second. We need enough fuel after reentry to slow us down to twenty-four feet per second. If we open the parachutes without slowing down enough, our speed will just rip the chutes off of us as soon as they deploy. You know it yourself from previous missions. Even twenty-four feet per second rattles your teeth. Imagine what it would feel like hitting the ground at over thirty times that speed."

Natalia stopped there. If Henry didn't get it yet, he was never going to get it. They all just floated motionless for several minutes, and Adam decided Henry understood but was just waiting for someone to take the burden off his shoulders. Someone needed to tell him how it had to be, so he put the question out there that needed to be answered.

"Natalia, based on your calculations, do you have an optimal landing path that will put us anywhere near a NASA facility?"

"We could try for one of three landing areas, but the first one has the risk of coming up short. If we do, then we would land in the Gulf of Mexico."

"I would prefer something out of the water," said Adam.

"Me too," she said. "The third one has a risk of overshooting the target, in which case we would have a similar scenario except the water would be colder. It would be off the coast of Nova Scotia."

"That leaves the second one," he said.

"Optimal numbers have us landing practically on top of the Marshall Space Flight Center."

They were surprised when Henry added, "I like Huntsville."

19

Quiet

The Shelter - Year Seven

If anyone had asked the four people living in the super shelter left behind for the scientists if they felt like they deserved to be alive, they would have just said they didn't care whether or not they deserved to be. The fact that they were was all that mattered. Someone had decided a long time ago that people were going to survive an apocalypse. They decided who those people were going to be, and as far as they knew, they had been left off the list. It was hard to feel sorry for the people who didn't make it. Maybe it was because no one would have felt sorry for them.

They spent the first month together in the three bedroom apartment. They went out after breakfast each day and searched the shelter systematically. They needed to be sure there was no one left inside with them, dead or alive…or both.

The stairwell where they had put the bodies stunk to high heaven, and the better part of a day had been spent sealing the doors on every floor with duct tape. When they were done, they sealed them again, but the smell got through anyway. In the end they did their best to cover the smell with anything that would smell better. Scented candles seemed to have been someone's idea of a survival necessity, but as odd as it seemed at the time, those turned out to be very necessary, and they really helped.

Because the air was better on the other side of the shelter, they searched that side first. It was a good idea to catalog everything they found, and they were doing a painstaking job of it until they found that someone already had. After they discovered the catalog on the computer system, it was only a matter of verifying that everything was there.

Gentry spent at least an hour every morning and every evening at the radio equipment in the Mission Control Center. She found it to be maddening that someone had left behind a complete control center that didn't do its main job. She could actually track the path of the International Space Station. She could see its track on the big display screens, but she couldn't talk to them. She dreamt about it at night and daydreamed about it when she was awake. She imagined herself sitting at a console and hearing them suddenly broadcasting through her headset.

By the end of the first month, Gentry was depressed and unapproachable. Wanda didn't mind because that gave her more time to follow MC from room to room. Karen spent her alone time in the infirmary and studying the medical files to pass the time. Given enough time, she would at least have the knowledge to be a doctor if not the practical skills.

MC dropped by the Control Center with Wanda in tow and tried to get Gentry to at least find something else to keep her busy, but when he saw she was already working on new projects, he realized Gentry was like Karen. They were both keeping busy. As for him and Wanda, MC would have been content to spend more time in the armory, and there was a tremendous library of movies in the database. It seemed like every movie he could name was there.

Since Wanda's primary interest was MC, she learned about weapons, and she was surprisingly good with them. Less surprisingly she also got the romance she was after. In the second month, Karen said she was ready to move into one of the other apartments, and Wanda said that she and MC had their eye on one of the big suites that had been intended for someone on a really high pay grade. She said the apartment they were living in reminded her of her college dorm, and she felt like it was time to do better.

Neither Gentry nor Karen was surprised by the announcement. Gentry was a little jealous, but it was like waking up from a dream. She didn't realize they had been in the shelter for a month, and she had hardly paid any attention to MC. If she could turn back time, she would, but one thing she did realize was that they were in a shelter under a world that wasn't safe to live in, and there wasn't room for drama.

Gentry was in the Control Center when Karen dropped by to see her. She was curious about one thing, and that was why Gentry was so determined to make contact with the International Space Station. For some reason, Gentry was very worried about them, but Karen thought they were much safer where they were.

Gentry saw the door swing open out of the corner of her eye and waved before Karen got to her.

"Mind some company for a bit?"

Gentry didn't mind the quiet, but Karen had proven to be an easy person to live with.

"Pull up a chair. I'm just going over some numbers."

"What numbers? It isn't like the Agency is getting ready for a launch any time soon."

"No launches," said Gentry, "but there'll hopefully be one more successful landing. The crew that's up there has got to get back down here."

"And they need you for that?"

"They could do it on their own if they had to, but it would be much easier with someone feeding them telemetry from the ground."

Karen said, "Damn it, Jim! I'm a doctor, not a rocket scientist!"

Gentry stared at her for a moment and then got it. She was embarrassed, but it gave her the best laugh she had enjoyed in a long time.

"That's rich," she said. "The nurse pulling the *Star Trek* line on a rocket scientist. Do you know how many rocket scientists I know who've pulled that one on doctors?"

They shared a laugh and then Gentry asked Karen if she really wanted to know or if she was just being nice. Karen said she really wanted to understand it, and maybe she could even help.

"Not unless you can also fix radios that can transmit into outer space, doctor."

"MC can't fix it? No clue what it might be?"

"I have a clue, but if I'm right it will never work."

"That bad?"

"That bad. I think it's got to be the antenna. I don't think there is one. If I were to make an educated guess, there was supposed to be time for everyone to get here, and NASA has always been big on one thing, and that's hand-offs. When a signal is lost by one place, it's picked up by someone else. I think everything was supposed to be transferred to this center from upstairs, and then everyone would have come down here. It didn't get transferred before everything ended up there."

"This may sound crazy, but can we go back, make contact, then transfer the connection?"

Gentry stared at Karen like she was from another planet.

Karen turned more than a little red.

"Don't feel bad, Karen. I was only looking at you like that because I had considered it. I was even going to ask MC if he was willing to try, but then I saw him and Wanda together, and I realized I would be asking all four of us to sacrifice our lives for three people who at least have a good chance of coming back on their own."

"What are their odds of doing it without help?" asked Karen.

"Better than our odds of getting into the control center up top and then making it back here. Honestly, their odds are good, and ours are bad."

"So, if we can't help them, what are you working on?"

"Well, I'm making a guess about what they're doing. One thing I can do is track them, and when the computers give me my data, I can tell that they're still up there. I can tell they haven't left the Space Station. If they haven't left, why not? And when are they going to? And one last question. Where are they going to come down?"

Karen let out a heavy sigh.

"That's a lot of guessing. Have you come up with any theories?"

Gentry didn't realize how much she had missed this kind of conversation. She would probably have been happier in a romance with MC, but if she couldn't have that she was glad Karen had sought her company.

"There was a great science fiction writer who said the longer you had to wait for something to happen, the more options you had for possible outcomes. If you waited to make a decision, some of those options would no longer be available."

"You mean like missed opportunities?" asked Karen.

She was a little embarrassed as soon as she asked the question because the first thing that came to mind was MC and Wanda.

"Good example," said Gentry with a touch of jealousy.

"Anyway," she continued, "if you keep waiting more options will drop off, and you begin to see which options were more likely all along, and in the case of ISS they stayed up there, and the longer they stay up there the more likely it is that they decided to stay up there for as long as they can."

"That makes my head hurt a little, but I think I get it. The more important thing is that you do, but why does that give you numbers to crunch?"

Gentry was more than a little excited that she figured it out, but she showed her work to Karen.

"This chart breaks down their orbits, their fuel, and all of the possible reentry scenarios. If I was up there in the same circumstances, I think the best place to come down blind is right here near the Marshall Space Flight Center. Their last confirmed telemetry was here, and their last confirmed contact. I've just been figuring out how hard it will be for them to do."

"What's your verdict?"

"If everything goes well, and if they calculate the same numbers I have, we should have visitors in about six years."

Karen said she was going to go put out some fresh linens and the good china and left Gentry to worry about the ISS crew.

******

The shelter proved big enough for four people to live more like they were in the same neighborhood than in the same house. They had separate homes, and they had their own separate jobs. The shelter was so large that they didn't need to see each other for days if they didn't want to, but from time to time they made habits that were easily broken when they got tired of them. They made one habit of getting together for supper one night a week. It lasted about six months, but like any other habit, a few missed meals by anyone in the group led to others skipping it.

Disagreements sometimes caused people to skip a meal, and that only made the disagreements go on longer. One of them led to a major fight, and the next time they checked on each other, they found that there were less of them in the shelter.

The fight began when Wanda announced that MC was thinking about going out to have a look around. When Karen and Gentry asked what that meant, she said he wanted to cross over into the other shelters and see if the infection had died out. After all, if they stayed down there in their shelter for the rest of their lives, they might find out someday that it had all ended a month after they had shut the doors.

"I'll fix the problem with outside communication sooner or later," said Gentry. "We might not be able to talk with other people, but we'll be able to listen."

"What if I go into one of the upper shelters and find the problem for you?" asked MC.

"You don't even know what to look for," she snapped back.

MC had gotten angry at the comment and accused Gentry of flaunting her intellectual superiority, and it was all downhill from there. Karen tried her best to smooth the frayed feelings, but Wanda accused MC of being bored with her, and that was the real reason MC wanted to go out exploring. The supper get-together ended when MC stomped out. Wanda stayed behind and got all the sympathy she needed from the other women, and they figured MC would also benefit from some time to cool down. They didn't realize it would give his feelings time to grow, and he decided to do it.

When Wanda got home, she didn't notice anything was missing from their apartment, so she assumed he was just out blowing off some steam. He didn't come home that night, and when Gentry and Karen showed up to check on him the next day, Wanda had gone to look for him.

As far as they knew, none of them had found any of the other exits from the shelter. They had plenty of evidence that other exits were somewhere. The old man who designed the shelters said there were two main exits. One was considered to be the front entrance, and it was the one they had used when they discovered the place. The other was a large entrance that was considered to be the back door. It was supposedly easy to find from the outside but would be nearly impossible to open from the outside if you didn't know how. There were also emergency exits, but they came with a precaution. Some of them were one way. You could open them to get out, and the door closed behind you, there was no way to come back in without going to another door.

Karen and Gentry set out to find out how MC and Wanda had left, but it wasn't easy when they were working from no clues. Over four weeks after they started searching, they found a clue in the armory. The armory inventory compiled by MC out of boredom included some items that were gone, and the realization was there were too many things for him to carry. That meant he had a way to transport weapons and gear, and made them notice the main doors of the armory were far bigger than they needed to be unless they were intended for a vehicle.

"So those are big doors," said Karen. "How does that help us find out what they needed them for?"

Gentry opened the armory doors as far as they would go, and once they were opened the outline on the opposite wall outside the armory could be seen in its entirety. Everyone would expect the back wall of a sealed room to be a hidden door, so that's where everyone would search for one. No one would expect the hidden door to be across the hall from the sealed room.

"There's a gap at the seams of this wall," said Gentry. "It's just a black line, but now that the light from the armory is hitting it, I can see it better."

Karen stood in the doorway and rotated at the hips between the armory and the wall. "That must be what made MC spot it too. If it's a door, I wonder where it goes."

"We'll find out if we can locate the switch that opens it, but if it was easy to find I'll be surprised," answered Gentry.

Karen pulled a rifle free from the rack and immediately put it back. She did the same thing down the row and glanced at the wall each time.

"What are you doing?"

"I'm checking to see if there's a hidden switch attached to one of the weapons. You know, maybe the door opens when one of the rifles is pulled forward."

Gentry shook her head in disbelief.

"What are the chances someone would open the door accidentally if the opening mechanism is connected to the weapons?"

Karen considered the question and had to admit, the shelter occupants would have plenty of accidental openings if moving an object nearby was the doorknob.

"So you don't think MC found it by accident," she said.

"No, I don't. Manuel Calvo is a smart guy. Becoming an enlisted soldier was going to be his way to get his feet under him before he went to college. That bull about his intellectual skills was a stupid discussion, and his leaving the shelter was his way of proving he's smart. He figured out there was a big door here because they would have used vehicles to carry that much stuff into the armory. The ammunition alone needed a truck. Naw, it's my guess that he figured that out first, and the hidden mechanism to open the door isn't so hidden. It's just not that obvious, and MC has a way to see the forest for the trees."

It wasn't lost on Karen that Gentry had regretted her obsessions that made her lose MC to Wanda. It was even more obvious now that he was gone. Gentry was making it more about MC and his qualities than the fact that they had discovered one of the possible hidden exits from the shelter.

"MC would have walked right to the mechanism once he saw that the exterior wall outside the armory was smooth."

"What do you mean?" asked Karen.

"You have the right idea. It's remotely operated from somewhere in the armory, but it wouldn't be buried deep inside, and it wouldn't be something that could be accidentally triggered. It would be secure."

Gentry put herself inside MC's mind. She walked over to the wall opposite the armory doors and stood only inches from it. She shut her eyes and cleared her mind. Thinking only about how she would do it if it was her design, she pictured a lock. She saw a keypad in her mind's eye, and because she had just seen a keypad, that's the one that appeared in her mind.

"Could it be that easy?" she thought.

When she turned around and walked across the hall to the keypad that opened the armory door, Karen said, "No way."

"Why not," answered Gentry, "but what's the code?"

"What was the code to get into the armory?"

"Remember? It was unlocked when we found it. The door was shut, but the lock wasn't engaged."

Gentry had always wondered about the planning that went into the building of the shelter. Because it was located below an immense field of shelters, it was like there was always something happening around it. She wondered how many things had been left unfinished. The lack of communications after a certain point had undoubtedly been one of those human oversights. Leaving the armory unlocked was either human error or it was on purpose.

"What if the lock had never been programmed?" she asked Karen.

"How would that help?"

"I was just thinking about the possibility that the exit code was never programmed either, and if both doors were controlled from the same keypad. If that's true, maybe all you have to do is hit the ENTER key."

Gentry pushed the key, and the display flashed green, but there were no distant sounds of machinery moving, and there was no dramatic sense of discovery.

"This is where tense music would be playing if this was a movie," said Karen.

"Then something triumphant and dramatic as the walls move to reveal a wide open discovery," said Gentry. "Maybe the theme song to *2001 A Space Odyssey*."

"No, I'm thinking more like *Jaws* or *Jurassic Park*."

"I don't remember the scary music from *Jurassic Park*, but you may be right about *Jaws* if I open the door and we find a bunch of infected on the other side."

As Gentry said it she also hovered her hand over the keypad seeking some inspiration. Karen started doing the *Jaws* theme song. She was just hitting the part that picks up speed, and anyone who saw the movie would know the shark was about to attack. Gentry hit the ENTER key twice in rapid succession. It beeped twice, and then there was silence, but they both felt the air around them change. Then they smelled it change. It was a musty odor, like the smell on a sweater that had been in a drawer for a couple of years.

A gap appeared where the black line had been along the ceiling. The wall descended into the floor with only the faintest sound of movement, and the dark gap above the wall revealed a tunnel that gave them no warning of what would be there once it was low enough for them to see beyond it. Before it got to eye level, Gentry and Karen both reacted together by diving into the armory after weapons. The M4 rifles were the closest, and magazines sat at the ready in front of each. They were loaded and aimed as the wall slid past the six feet height. Heads weaved from side to side as they moved steadily toward the growing gap. If Gentry could have stopped the progress of the wall, she would have, but all she could do was take aim.

Karen opened fire before the wall was low enough for the infected to come inside, and that probably saved them from having to lock themselves inside the armory. Gentry joined in, and the extra practice they had gotten with MC paid off. The crowd of infected that had been strangely quiet at the start began the growling and snarling they were known for, and even though they fell in large numbers, the noise increased. Gentry and Karen could see well enough into the tunnel to know that the sound of shooting was drawing in more and more of them from the darkest recesses.

One by one the stack of magazines got smaller. Both women ran out of ammunition at the same time once, and they panicked as they ejected spent magazines and both reached for the same one. Karen slammed it into her M4 and fired just as several of the infected made it across the hallway to the armory door. After that it became a little smoother as their timing alternated. While one was reloading, the other was firing.

It seemed like it went on forever, but it was finally down to a few stragglers that were so far back from the others that they couldn't make it through the pile of bodies. They carefully moved as close to the entrance as they could and mopped up the stragglers from a distance.

"This is going to be awful to clean up," said Karen.

"I don't see why we have to other than the ones that made it into the hallway. We can close this door and let them rot out there," answered Gentry.

"At least we know how they left the shelter. What is this place, though? I remember a back hallway in a mall I went to. I got turned around coming out of the restroom, and I got rudely ushered out by a security officer. This reminds me of that place, but it's a lot bigger."

Gentry squinted into the darkness and said, "Big enough for trucks. I can see at least two. This had to be the delivery tunnel for all of the shelters, but unlike the others this shelter's door was just a blank wall. I can see at least six doors on each side of the tunnel, and most of them are open."

"You think they left through here but couldn't get back in?"

"Yes," said Gentry. "This is one of the exits that can't be opened from the other side. My guess is they pushed the button before it closed then jumped over the wall before it got too high."

Karen had a horrified expression on her face.

"How awful," she said. "Do you think they knew that before going outside?"

Gentry nodded slowly. "MC would have gone out there first to see if they could get back in if they closed it behind them. Then he would've tried to talk Wanda into staying inside, and she refused. It would've been a lot better if they had any idea on how to get back in, but even if they could remember all of the codes in the planetarium, I doubt they could even find that same shelter again."

"I don't get it," said Karen. "Why didn't the crowd of infected attack them when they opened the door?"

"The infected weren't here then. They arrived because something drew them here after the door closed."

"How do you know that?"

Gentry didn't have the words to describe how it made her feel. Wanda wasn't her favorite person, but she didn't want to see her wind up like this. She pointed at the bodies of the infected that were scattered around the hallway. She had recognized Wanda when the door opened and shot her first. The one thing that she kept screaming inside her head the whole time she was shooting was that she didn't want to see MC's face in the crowd. Now that it was over she felt guilty that she hadn't felt more sorrow for Wanda.

Karen recoiled and got sick. She had been too busy to recognize Wanda, and as soon as she recovered enough to stand up straight without stomach cramps, she remembered MC and began going through the bodies.

"He's not there. I already checked. Wanda must have gotten separated from MC and made it back to the wall. The infected had her cornered. He's out there…somewhere."

******

Manuel Calvo

He thought about leaving them a note to explain why he had to leave, but he honestly thought they would figure it out for themselves. It wasn't enough for him to just survive inside the safety of the shelter. He felt selfish for wanting to go outside, but he couldn't push down that feeling that he should be doing more to help. There were people alive out there, and they had room in their shelter. If he could find survivors and bring them back to the shelter, he would feel like he had accomplished something. He would feel like he did on that first day when he had saved Gentry. He would feel like he did when he had helped to get them all to the planetarium. Yes, Gentry had gotten them inside, but he had gotten them to the door.

Wanda wouldn't take no for an answer when he had tried his best to get her to stay behind. When he opened the hidden door, he realized he would be able to get into the other shelters, but it was a one way trip through that door. When it closed behind them, they had watched the light go up to the ceiling and then wink out. They were outside. They were surrounded by thousands of people in the other shelters, but an untold number of them were infected.

MC recalled the argument with Wanda inside the open door with bitterness. He had told her she wouldn't last a day out there, and he wished he hadn't said it because he was right. She didn't last a day. Somehow he had lasted, but she hadn't. He also hadn't been a success when it came to helping other people because he spent all of his time trying to find the next safe place to sleep and the next place where he could eat a meal. He had been on the run for a long time, and as far as he could tell it had been years since he had seen another living person.

He lost Wanda after they left the tunnel. It had seemed like the perfect adventure for a couple in love, and they had held hands as they walked down the tunnel. Their goal was simple. They would pick one of the shelters, go in through the door, and find survivors. They would share their weapons and food with people who would see them as salvation. MC wondered when he had gotten it in his head that he was that important in the grand scheme of things. If he had understood how big this thing really was, Wanda would still be alive.

They picked a door at random, and although they expected to find the infected, they didn't expect to be on the run from the moment they went inside. Their entrance was into a room that must have been some form of a central receiving station. There was a wide roll up door next to the smaller door for foot traffic. The smaller door led into an office where the supply officer kept watch on what came and went. It was a fair guess that he was still there after all this time, and if they had seen him sooner, he wouldn't have cut them off from the exit so easily. He was behind them before they had a chance to be sure the next room was clear, and he wasn't alone.

When MC pulled his semiautomatic pistol, he only saw the first target between them and the door. It was an easy shot that would be loud but effective. The others emerged in the dim light in such a tight group that he had simply followed Wanda when she yanked open the office door and ran into the next room. He followed her across a loading bay where dozens of infected milled around with nowhere to go. She opened another door and went through, and MC had to admit it was exactly what he would have done. He wasn't sure why she went down instead of up when they found themselves in a stairwell. Maybe it was just easier, but when she went through the door on the next level down, the door closed before he got there. When he opened it, she was nowhere in sight.

He was in a long hallway that reminded him of a hotel. Doors were spaced out on both sides for as far as he could see, but as hard as he tried, MC couldn't hear or sense where she had gone. His good sense told him she must have chosen a door close by, but there were four of those, two on the left and two on the right. He chose the first one on the left. That one was locked, so he took the second one on the left. It opened quietly into a stairwell again, and he heard feet clapping on stairs as they ascended above him.

"Wanda!"

The feet stopped, and he thought it might be her, so he ran up the stairs two at a time. He came face to face with a group of infected that had somehow come through onto the landing, and he could only assume it was because Wanda had gone through the door and left it open.

Defeat didn't come easily to Manuel Calvo, but he had to face the fact that he had lost Wanda within five minutes of entering the shelter. There was no way to get through the crowd on the landing, and when they saw him, his only choice was to go backward. In his mind he drew a map of where he was, and where he had lost track of Wanda. He swore a promise to find her again, but to do that he would need to keep himself alive.

In a week of searching, MC averaged thirty minutes of sleep per night. Every time he found a place where he thought he was safe, he was flushed out of hiding by a never-ending supply of the infected. He was bitten once, but as bad as it hurt, the teeth didn't come through the heavy pair of jeans he was wearing. Maybe it was because it was a child who was already under the desk where he had hidden from his latest pursuers.

With red eyes that were only one of the outward signs of his fatigue, he stumbled through a door and found himself in the tunnel again. At least he thought it was the same tunnel, but he had no way of knowing without going back to the starting point. His legs shook with every step, but he forced them to take him to the left. He didn't think it was too far from the end of the tunnel, but even he was surprised when he saw the wall ahead. Three trucks were lined up right where he expected them to be, and two yards beyond them was the blank wall that separated him from safety.

A crowd of infected was gathered around the wall, and he wondered where they had come from. There had been none when they had come through the wall. They didn't see him until he was even with the trucks, and that was when he knew how they had gotten there.

Blue jeans, burgundy sweatshirt, and white running shoes identified

Wanda, and defeat washed over MC. Ten yards from his burning eyes was the woman who wouldn't listen and stay behind. He sank to his knees and watched them wander back and forth along the wall. He knew that Wanda had returned to this spot in a vain hope of getting back inside the super shelter. When she did, the infected followed her, and he knew from the condition of her arms and face that her last few minutes had been awful. She must have been so afraid. She must have been terrified.

He couldn't tell how long ago she had arrived, and the dozen or so infected around her could have all arrived at once, or they could have arrived over time, attracted by the growing numbers. The thing that used to be Wanda took a few steps in his direction, and the guttural sound she made drew the attention of the others. Ten yards wasn't far away, but even at their slow pace, the distance between them and MC was shrinking. He just kept watching her face and trying to see any spark of the person she used to be.

MC couldn't find that spark, but he heard the unexpectedly closer growl behind him. The infected in front of him were much closer, but the ones behind him were already in reach. As a matter of fact, that's exactly what they were doing.

MC didn't even have time to get up. There was only time to move along the concrete floor of the tunnel. He scrambled on his hands and knees toward the last truck in line, and when he was close enough he launched himself upward to the passenger side door. It opened, and he pulled himself inside in time, but the wet hands of the infected slapped at the window.

The truck sat higher than a military quarter ton truck, and even though he was prepared to hotwire the starter, he was rewarded by the sight of the keys hanging from the ignition. He pumped the gas a couple of times and turned the key. He was surprised by how well the engine turned over and started, and MC only wasted the two or three seconds it took to spot Wanda one last time. He regretted getting a last memory of her like that and threw the gearshift into reverse.

The truck bounced as the large tires climbed up and over the infected that had arrived behind it. There was room for him to make a large half circle in reverse, and the infected pathetically chased him at their snail's pace. Once he was facing outward, MC hit the gas hard and drove away. He only watched his mirror for a moment because the darkness closed in behind him, while ahead the tunnel snaked away into a darkness that was only broken by the beams from his headlights. He didn't know how far he should drive, but it had to be until there were no more infected nearby.

20

Descent

International Space Station - Year Seven

Prepping the Soyuz took a lot more work than they had realized it would, partially because they had put it off for years. It wasn't that they neglected it, but there were routine operations that would have made it easier if they had done periodic preventative maintenance on the systems. When they attached the diagnostic equipment to the reentry vehicle, they were surprised by the number of tests that failed. Even the thrust vector control tests failed, and without that system the small thrusters that would fire to start reentry and then slow them down wouldn't be able to rotate. That meant they couldn't aim the thrusters or even rotate the vehicle into the reentry position.

The plus side to all of the extra work was that it gave them something to do as they approached the day for optimal reentry, and they had plenty of time to think about what the last six years had been like.

Henry thought mostly about his family. He tried to picture what his children would look like six years older, but he couldn't do it. Every time he shut his eyes and tried to form the thought, he automatically filled in the information with the images from the one family picture he had taped to the door of his locker. The fact of the matter was that he was having a hard time conjuring up an image of them without first looking at that picture, and in his worst fears he knew that meant he was having a hard time believing they were still alive.

There were long stretches of time over the years when he avoided thinking too much about his wife or his kids. He kept himself busy with experiments that had been scheduled for this mission and even added a few new ones. Then there was the radio. There had been that one time when they had begun receiving a signal from someone who couldn't receive them. His voice coming through the speakers had startled Henry badly, and when he calmed down he tried to interrupt the man with a question, but eventually it became clear that all he could do was listen to what the man was saying.

It was a lot like listening to a news broadcaster, and not wanting to miss anything made Henry give up his efforts to establish two way communication and just listen. Natalia and Adam floated into the module and took up positions nearby. Henry's dejected expression and hand signals were all they needed to know that he wasn't able to communicate with the man.

The man said his name was Tim, and he was transmitting from a small town on the coast of Florida. That was all he would say about his location because there were too many people out there who would try to take things from other survivors, not to mention too many people who would kill you for fun. It made them wonder what kind of world they had missed.

The world they imagined was a world full of resilient people who would use every available resource to protect the defenseless from harm. They knew the infection had spread unchecked, but it sounded to them like the man was saying the battle had been lost. No hospitals, no doctors, no research centers developing a vaccine, and even worse, no protection from people who let their desperation erase every trace of their humanity.

The man said he had been able to receive information from other short wave radio operators, and that he was going to continue broadcasting every day for as long as he could. He said as far as he knew the military was non-existent. At the beginning the bases had done what everyone knew they would do. They went on lockdown, they called up all reserve units, they put ships to sea, and they flew planes to remote locations. The word was that the Air Force had moved everything that could fly to Greenland, Iceland, Alaska, and anywhere else with a cold climate. The rationale behind such a move was simple. The infected dead could be frozen.

Florida didn't get cold enough to stop them, and Tim swore if he could survive the trip, he was going to move to International Falls, Minnesota. He figured he wouldn't make it a hundred miles, but he would eventually try. He said he didn't want to become one of the infected, but if it was going to happen, it was going to happen while he was trying to live and not waiting to die.

Tim said there were random broadcasts that he could only listen to, and there were the occasional connections that allowed him to talk with other survivors. He knew there were people out there who were fighting back because one broadcast described something big happening in Charleston. There were rumors, mostly unsubstantiated, about someone blowing up bridges in South Carolina, but no one had spoken with an actual witness. Something was burning in the harbor in Charleston, and it had been throwing up a cloud of smoke for a week. The ISS crew calculated when their next pass over that area would happen in daylight, and sure enough, they could see the cloud from space.

The thing that the crew found to be most disheartening was the man's broadcast about what had caused everything to fail so completely. Why no one had any success against unimaginable hordes of the dead, and why people who hadn't seen hordes still died. His broadcast was more like a sermon that day as he talked about the need for people to turn their backs on their brothers and sisters if they wanted to live.

Henry remembered Natalia asking what the man was talking about, but all Henry could imagine was his wife being shot at by the police or even his neighbors while she sought refuge or food for their children. The man's sermon said that the insidious infection would beat the best armies and the best scientists because it would get behind their defenses. It would get in with them, and it would kill them in the middle of the night because of their humanity.

Henry had turned to Natalia and explained that when people became infected, anyone who tried to help them would become infected, so they kept it secret when they were bitten. They didn't tell anyone until it was too late. Natalia had asked more out of a curious reflex why people didn't notice who had been bitten. She didn't consider the implications of a parent being bitten while caring for children. If there were no other adults around to stop the inevitable tragedy, parents would turn on their own children.

Hearing what had become of civilization, what had become of their homes, the crew experienced a chilling depression that threatened their stability. Any of them could pilot the Soyuz alone, but the mental condition that engulfed Henry made the others wary of him. Adam encouraged him to stop listening to Tim, but there was a slender thread connecting the man in Florida to the ISS, and Henry couldn't bring himself to cut the thread.

Tim said that he saw ships from time to time. Some came close, but most of them stayed out closer to the horizon. He saw the Coast Guard once, but he was afraid to approach them. He didn't mention it on his broadcast until a few days after they had left because it might give away his position if they were listening. He was afraid of them because they really shot up the place one night.

That reminded him of another chilling aspect of survival during the infection. He saw mutations of wildlife that led him to believe anything that ate the infected would mutate. Tim figured that's what the shooting was all about on the Coast Guard ship. The crabs had gotten bigger, faster, smarter, and more aggressive. He thought maybe the Coast Guard people didn't know that and had been caught by surprise after dark. That was when the crabs came out. He even heard them scraping against his doors some nights, trying to find a way in.

The ISS crew learned a lot about the post-apocalyptic world of the infection, but when his broadcast disappeared and didn't reconnect after a few orbits, Adam and Natalia were glad to see him go. The slender thread that held Henry connected to hope was gone. It was hard for him at first, and he went through some of the classic stages of grief. Adam told Natalia to watch him, but maybe it was a good thing. Maybe he would experience his grief now and get it over with.

They left him alone with his radio and continued their own preparations to leave the space station. During that time Henry seldom ate or slept, but all they could do was wait. When Henry resumed his own preparations, it was without a word, but they could see the change. There was a certain amount of calm about Henry that made Natalia believe Adam had been right. Henry was possibly more willing to accept the possibility that his family could not have survived the infection.

The depression or resignation seemed like it would endure their remaining days in the ISS until Henry experienced something that was a total fluke. It was one of those unexpected things that made him accept the fact that he wasn't the only person in the world who had suffered. As a matter of fact, he realized there were people who had lost more than him. He wouldn't know if he had lost his family forever until he somehow made it back to England in a post-apocalyptic world. There were plenty of people who already knew of their losses because they had been there to see them.

The system checks were finished, and the reentry vehicle had passed the last round of tests with flying colors, unlike the first time. Adam and Natalia put some final touches on the experiments that had amassed mountains of data over the last six years. If their time in space were to mean anything to the future of mankind, they needed to bring back that data. It wasn't likely that people would inhabit the International Space Station in the next decade, so it was tremendously valuable information.

Henry was hunched over the radio again, and neither of them felt like it would hurt to let him relax before they left the station. There was a high probability that the Soyuz would take either a too steep or too shallow angle of reentry, and anything that would relax them before the flight was a welcome distraction. When they heard excited voices and crowds cheering, they couldn't believe their ears. Without a word they launched themselves in the direction that would get them to Henry the fastest.

Henry turned up the radio as high as it would go when they entered the module and floated toward him. The smile on his face was so broad that it made him appear to be a young man again. An announcer was calling a play in a baseball game as a batter hit a ground ball to the pitcher. The pitcher made a clean catch and throw to the first baseman for the final out of the ballgame. The announcer was enthusiastically shouting that the Cubs had just won the World Series for the first time in one hundred and eight years, and that they had done it against the Cleveland Indians in ten innings.

Adam was a big baseball fan, and even though Natalia didn't care for or understand the sport, it was the excitement in the announcer's voice and on Henry's face that made her understand the significance of the moment. It didn't matter that it was a recorded game. It only mattered that someone was broadcasting it. Civilization was alive somewhere.

Henry thought it was a live broadcast at first. He had heard of the World Series and knew how important it was to Americans, but he didn't recognize the game as the final game in the 2016 World Series. He was swept up in the play calling as soon as it started, and the only thing that would have made it better was if it had been a football game. Not that American stuff that was a minute of playing to every two minutes of celebration, but the kind of football played in civilized countries.

The cheering faded away, and a female voice came through the speaker.

"You've been listening to what was probably the best baseball game in history when the Cubs took the 2016 World Series away from the Cleveland Indians in ten innings. If you're going to end a one hundred and eight year drought, what better way to do it, right?"

The crew of the ISS had listened to Tim's broadcasts for so long without their fingers poised over the SPEAK button on the panel that none of them even considered it at first. The woman said listening to that game had really made her more cheerful, but she would be happier to hear a real human voice. All three of them lunged for the button at the same time, and in zero gravity that meant none of them would reach it. One good shove made all three go in different directions.

Natalia used her feet to her advantage and kicked away from the door frame. She went head first at the panel while the men were still trying to reverse directions, but when she punched the button she missed her grab with the other hand and kept going. Adam was the first one to the live microphone.

"Hello, Cubs fan!"

It was silent on the other end of the connection, not because of zero gravity but because of shock.

"Cubs fan, do you read me?"

He said to the others, "Don't tell me we lost that connection already. First voice besides Tim's in six years and we lose it before we get to see if she can hear us."

"I can hear you. I just can't believe it. Where are you? Your signal is so strong."

"It gets like that when we're right above you," said Adam, "and right now we're traveling east over the Atlantic. We just left the coast of Canada behind us."

"No way, it can't be."

That had always been the way people reacted when they found out they were talking with the International Space Station, but it never got old to Adam.

He laughed and asked her, "Why is it that people can accept that their cell phone and TV signals are bounced off of satellites thousands of miles above them, but they can't believe it when they talk to the space station only two hundred and fifty miles away?"

"Wow, this is the ocean-going tug Maggie Mae. Hello up there. I can see you."

"Really?" Adam took the bait.

"No, but I had to get even with you. So, it's really you guys. I always wondered what happened to you. You've been up there all this time?"

Natalia and Henry managed to drift closer to Adam.

"This is Natalia Lebedev, hello. What's your name?"

"Hi, Natalia. I'm Andi Hartford, skipper of this beast. Did you catch the ball game?"

"Yes, we caught the end of it," said Adam, "but you know what they've always said about that game. You only needed to see the last two innings."

"Real fans know that, Adam. I can't believe I'm talking with you."

"Believe it or not, Andi, it's hard for us to believe it too. What happened to all the communication networks? I didn't think anything or anyone could shut them down the way they've been for the last six years."

"It started right after the infection," said Andi. "It seems the networks were far more fragile than everyone imagined they would be. At first I thought it was because TV stations were going off the air, but then it was every ISP I managed to find. The Internet kept working for a while, but then nothing new appeared. Old pages loaded, but there were no updates. A ship at sea can always find someone, but within a month ships weren't even talking to each other."

"What about Maydays?" asked Adam. "There must've been plenty of those."

"Oh, sure there were, but no one was going to answer a Mayday from a ship that had an outbreak of the infection."

Henry was a sailor at heart and even had a boat of his own, and the idea that people ignored the calls for help from other ships at sea was unthinkable, and he said so now.

"I find that hard to believe. What happened to the code? When someone puts out a Mayday, people put aside their differences. All sailors are part of a brotherhood."

"And a sisterhood," she added. "I was out here listening to it, and I can tell you exactly what happened to the code. It got put away in the back of the cabinet along with old food that you would never eat but couldn't throw away. It was still there, but when Maydays started coming in from the ships that had answered Maydays, people started to catch on. You had to be crazy to let the infection get on board your ship. After a while when people called out a Mayday there were answers, but they started with one question. What's the nature of your emergency? I heard it more than once, and I had to ask the question myself."

"You said it was still there," said Adam. "Why the past tense? You still won't answer a Mayday?"

"I probably would now," she answered, "but I'd keep my distance until I was sure of the emergency. There's not a lot of trust out here on the water anymore. It's not like it used to be."

Adam and Natalia were caught off guard by Henry's next question.

"Andi, we're coming down in the next few days. If you made good speed, could you find yourself to be anywhere near the Celtic Sea, possibly south of the Isles of Scilly?"

Henry was thinking ahead to how easy it would be to get from the beautiful little tourist spot to the coast of Cornwall. Not that they blamed him for trying, but they had spent days calculating the right time of departure, speed, and angle of descent for a ground landing in the northern part of Alabama. Recalculating for a landing near England would be a monumental task without the assistance of Ground Control. The answer almost broke his heart and was one more nail in the coffin for his hope.

"Is that Henry Tisdal? I'd recognize your accent anywhere. Why would you want to land there? I know you're from England, but didn't you get any of the news from your country before they went dark?"

They were sure Andi wasn't trying to be insensitive or to hurt him with her answer, but after over six years it was inconceivable to her that he didn't know about survivors and the way they had carried the infection to some of the safest places. Every secluded island paradise in the world had been swarmed by escapees from the infection. Private boats filled with bite victims poured out of every port and every marina in the world. People who lived on islands thought they were safe from the virus, but in the days and weeks that followed the onset of the infection, their islands were invaded by swarms of survivors who didn't care if they were welcome or not.

Everyone thought they had the best idea. Get away from the mainland and ride it out in a little village or straw hut on a sunny beach. Live off the native vegetation, whether it was coconuts and bananas on tropical islands or berries and mushrooms in cooler climates. Some of them were met with open arms at first, but it didn't take long for the inhabitants of the islands to discover that there was more than one kind of death arriving from the mainlands.

As if it wasn't bad enough for the islands to be overrun by bite victims, there were the dregs of society who had no intention of starting all over again. It wasn't their plan to find work to earn the generosity of their hosts. They weren't going to learn how to harvest wheat, mill the grain, and bake their own bread. Not when they could just take it from their dead hosts. So, they arrived, killed, and then were killed in return by the bites of the dead they left in their path. If it wasn't bad enough that people came to islands with the infection or with murder in their eyes, the dead were constantly washing ashore. If they weren't too waterlogged, they wandered inland looking for victims. If they baked in the sun, they became the food for the crabs, seagulls, and sometimes what was left of the wildlife population until they too became food for scavengers.

"No," said Henry, "we lost communications in the first few days, and the only people we managed to hear apparently didn't know much themselves. What happened at the Isles of Scilly?"

Andi was embarrassed when she realized why Henry was asking if she could cross the Atlantic and rescue them when they came down. The gravity of the request was such a surprise that it didn't occur to her at first. Here they were, at the end of the longest journey in the history of mankind. She couldn't begin to calculate the number of times they had circled the planet in six years, and now a matter of miles would separate them from where they wanted to be on land or the water. Of course she could make the crossing, and if they could regain radio contact she could be in the right place to pick them up, but that area was a hotbed of death. If you made the mistake of setting foot on any of the islands, you would survive only long enough to be discovered by the infected, desperate murderers, or hungry scavengers. If you stayed on the water you were likely to be attacked by anyone who wanted your diesel fuel, food, spare parts, and even your women. The oceans were worse now than they had been in the days of pirates.

"Henry, you have to understand, when the infected dead spread out across the countryside, a lot of people escaped to the islands. Reports I was able to intercept said that the Isle of Wight held out for a long time because the military held the island. They stopped infected civilians after taking as many in as they could, but then they closed the island to anyone. Their problem was that they didn't know yet that the dead would come back to life, and they didn't know that the bites were always fatal. Scilly went under on the first day."

Natalia took over at the microphone as Henry gave it up. Adam held Henry by his shoulder and made him face him for just a moment.

"We don't blame you for asking her. I would've done the same thing."

Adam saw that it made a difference to Henry. Henry had expected Natalia and Adam to be angry with him for asking Andi without their consent, but there just wasn't time to debate the issue. They could have lost contact at any second or simply lost the window of opportunity for any number of reasons.

"I'll be okay," said Henry. He gave Adam a weak smile and propelled himself out of the module.

Adam turned back to Natalia and heard her reassuring Andi that Henry was fine. She told the tug boat captain that they planned to make a ground landing as close as possible to the Marshall Space Flight Center, and oddly enough, Andi was able to give them some useful information after all.

She told them that NOAA had been one of the organizations to stay online the longest to those people lucky enough to find their signal, and NOAA had graciously provided the operating frequencies and login credentials that its weather satellites used. With that information the ISS crew would be able to tap into satellites to download critical updates to their data that would significantly improve their telemetry. They would be able to make more accurate calculations and reduce the chance of failure when they make contact with the Earth's atmosphere.

By the time they signed off, it had turned into one of the most vital contacts they had made in their mission, and it had come at the most perfect moment in their journey. If not for the devastating conditions on the islands off the coast of England, they would have been able to recalculate to land close to Henry's home, and the tug that Andi captained was indeed capable of making the trip quickly, but the risk was too great. When they said their goodbyes and wished each other good luck, they also made each other promises that they didn't know if they could keep, but if they could keep them, it was worth knowing each other.

Andi said she had always been a big fan of the space program, and maybe someday she could get their autographs. Natalia laughingly told her she was sure that could be arranged even though it wasn't as easy as it used to be. Andi added that she would be glad to let them use Maggie Mae if they ever needed her.

Natalia said, "Maybe we will."

******

The big day was finally in front of them, and despite being the most seasoned astronauts and cosmonaut in the world, they had been in space so long that the idea of reentry was more than a little frightening. They had butterflies before every trip they had made into space, but they had never gotten this nervous on the trip home. It was always just the last thing you did at the end of the mission. It was always the event that signaled when the fun was almost over. The launch was always exciting and made them nervous, the stay aboard the International Space Station was always the icing on the cake, and the trip home was just the last thing they had to do.

This one was different. Six years of high speed orbits with the best seat in the house for the most beautiful scenery mankind could imagine, but the ride home was not going to be a guaranteed success. It would be the first time anyone did it without someone on the ground talking them down. The first time no one would hold the hands of a crew coming home. It would be the last time a crew would return from space for a long time, and without anyone to ride the International Space Station and monitor its orbital systems, there was no guarantee that it would still be there by the time mankind would be able to visit again. Saying goodbye to their home wasn't easy for a lot of reasons.

"I don't suppose we can find a way to stay here a while longer, could we?" asked Natalia.

Neither of the men answered. She knew they were all ready to go home. She was just afraid of the trip. She couldn't recall ever being afraid before. She remembered wishing the trip was over, but she didn't remember it ever showing on her face the way it did this time.

Even through the bulky visor of his helmet, Adam could see the fear on Natalia's face, and the expression on Henry's face was hard to put into words. Even though they would be landing half a world away from his home, he would feel closer to home on the ground than he did as he passed only a few hundred miles from it in orbit. The expression was probably the closest thing to anticipation that his face could show.

They went through the sequences just as if there was a ground crew guiding them. A series of one or two word questions from Natalia followed by a response from Adam of either check or nominal. They had trained for the return trip hundreds of times, but no one had ever done it with training being so long ago or without ground support.

"You're the pilot, Natalia. You've got this," said Adam.

"What I've got is a bad feeling."

Henry said, "That wasn't the most reassuring thing you could think of to say, was it?"

"Sorry. That wasn't very bright of me, was it?"

They finished the checklists, and the moment finally arrived when Natalia announced that all systems were go and to prepare for separation. Docking rings rotated and if there was motion they didn't feel it. Only the slowly increasing gap between the Soyuz capsule and the dock made their bodies aware that they were pulling away from the station. The instrument panel was a reassuring green and white, and no warnings flashed.

This was the easy part. They didn't have to separate at an exact moment because they would drop down to a predetermined spot below the ISS and then wait until they were at the beginning of their navigational path to the reentry point. They had allowed themselves plenty of time to get there, so there was no rush, and just as they had planned, they completed the first leg of their trip comfortably. As the ISS and Soyuz capsule sped around the Earth together one last time, Adam called out the speed and distance until the moment when Natalia would fire the rockets that would cause them to change their orbit and separate at breakneck speed from their position below the ISS.

When the moment arrived, his voice didn't reflect the anxiety that wracked at every nerve in his body. He called it out, Natalia confirmed the command as she executed the burn, and they were past the point of no return. Until this moment they could have returned to the ISS, but not anymore. Henry stoically watched their home for the last six years as it quickly became like nothing more than a bright place at the end of a long, dark highway. Adam called out the command to terminate the burn. Natalia confirmed the command and cut off the thrusters. Adam confirmed that the thrusters had shut down then reported that they had burned the appropriate amount of fuel.

Natalia acknowledged the report. She was relieved to see that she had calculated the fuel requirement accurately, and that was a good sign because it indicated they would likely be entering the atmosphere at the correct angle and the correct place.

Adam announced, "All systems nominal. Coming up on sixty-seconds until optimal point of atmospheric insertion. Beginning countdown." If they had done everything right, their heat shield was in the proper position to absorb the heat generated by the friction they generated as the Soyuz cut into the increasingly thicker atmosphere. If they were too steep, they would only know about it for a couple of seconds as they ignited into a ball of fire. If their angle was too shallow, they would have plenty of time to think about it as they flew further and further out into the blackness of deep space.

At the end of the countdown, they could see the many shades of red and yellow as they lit up the windows. He called out the temperature readings, and even as Natalia acknowledged him, she knew she had done her job well. They were well within tolerances, and as long as there were no undetected flaws in the spacecraft, it was performing its hazardous job perfectly. She was finally starting to feel good about being the first crew to make the return without help. The thought made her remember something.

"If we were doing this along with ground control, we would be in blackout right now." She had to say it louder because the noise had increased to a roar.

They were silent as they listened to the sound of the oven outside. When they broke through the blackout phase of reentry, they would be traveling at their maximum speed of seven hundred and fifty-five feet per second. The four parachutes deployed in the proper sequence, and Adam called out that indicators had notified him the parachutes were deployed.

They could feel the difference as their speed bled off quickly. When the time was right, and the vehicle was falling at only twenty-four feet per second, the computer would fire the landing rockets, and they would miraculously complete the trip at only five feet per second.

It had been a long time between missions, but everything felt so familiar. The colors at the windows, the commands, the acknowledgements, and the expectation that was felt as they came up on the next crucial moment. It all felt so familiar, and that was why something felt so different.

"Commander Callaway, call out the speed."

Adam had been calling it out at the usual milestones, so his first knee-jerk reaction was to wonder what Natalia could want him to do, but as the Mission Commander it was his job to trust his pilot, so he simply obeyed her order and began calling out the speeds at shorter intervals. That was what made her sure of what she suspected, and it made him see what she had seen. Their speed wasn't decreasing as fast as it should.

He reached up and punched at the indicator that showed the parachutes were all deployed, and the lights flickered behind it....then went out. They all automatically turned in their seats to get a better view through the windows, trying to see the thick risers that stretched out to the immense canopies that were decreasing their speed. There wasn't anything they could do about it even if they could spot the problem, but knowing for sure seemed important. Then they knew for sure, because one of the risers was at an odd angle across a window, and it wasn't supposed to be there.

It could have been worse, but it was bad. Instead of the thrusters taking over at twenty-four feet per second, they were traveling at just over one hundred feet per second when they felt them fire. They felt their bodies stretching at the restraints, and even though there was no way to brace themselves better than they already were, that's what Adam yelled at the last moment before impact.

Henry imagined he now understood what it would feel like to have a car dropped on top of him. The feeling of traveling as fast as a car on an interstate and coming to a stop against a concrete overpass was his next thought. It seemed like everything hurt. His lungs hurt because his ribs had pushed down so hard on his diaphragm. His back hurt from top to bottom because his spine had been compressed. His shoulder joints and hip joints all screamed with so much agony that it made him sure they had all dislocated. Somehow he lifted his arms and twisted the locking ring of his helmet. When he lifted it off, he heard Natalia Lebedev yelling.

21

Sheriff J. Horton Crim

Huntsville - Year Seven

The Chief didn't rule out the possibility that his actions would cause repercussions for his friends, but he knew they would understand. He wasn't the kind of person to just sit on his hands and wait for something to happen. There were times when events dictated his actions, and most of the time he had a plan, but quite often it was both. He made plenty of plans as contingencies. If something happened, then that was a good chance to make something else happen.

The event that fit with one of his contingency plans was the storm that rolled through north Alabama dumping heavy rain and terrific winds. The area was well known for its tornadoes, as he well remembered from the trip to Huntsville. When the sky blackened and he saw the wall cloud in the west, that was exactly what he thought was coming.

The Chief had talked Claire into staying behind at the forge to keep an eye on Stew. He had become increasingly suspicious of Stew and his ability to get anything he needed. Every camp in the world had at least one person like him, and more often than not their abilities were somehow linked to the establishment. He was probably a two-way conduit. He was the means by which the establishment could receive information about people like the Chief, and his power came from the little luxuries he was able to leak into the community. In a perverted sense, he was good for the community, but that was generally the justification used by collaborators since the beginning of time.

Then there was one other possibility. The Sheriff recognized the Chief's talents and knew he could be a powerful ally or a dangerous foe, and maybe the Sheriff needed two sets of eyes on him. Maybe Claire was that other set of eyes. Without being sure, the Chief knew he wouldn't get many opportunities to escape from Farley, especially since the establishment seemed to have him cornered. He was given the most elbow room at the river, so that was where the Sheriff believed he was least likely to find an opportunity, but the Chief knew that sometimes you just had to play the cards that had been dealt to you. If the Sheriff was ready to concede the river, then that was where he would have to make his move. That was where the Sheriff would expect him to try, but that was because it was where the Sheriff also believed he had his best defenses in place to catch him.

Leaving Claire and Stew behind was his best chance of getting a closer look at something he had been studying ever since his first fishing trip down at the river. The small marina on the left side of the highway leading up to the wreckage of the bridge was always busy, but the Chief counted the number of boats and noticed that there were always less boats tied up in the mornings than at night. At first he just considered the possibility that the boats were always leaving before sunrise. To fishermen that was just a way of life. If you were on the water when the sun came up, you were there when the fish began to feed.

Then he noticed some of those same boats as they returned to the marina. They weren't coming in with stringers of fish. They were coming in with boxes and crates, and many of them were a familiar Army green. They were also coming back from upriver, and that was where the river passed the massive shelter complex.

Claire had told him she knew a great deal about the shelters, but most of it was second hand information. What she said she knew for certain was that the Sheriff had placed a permanent ban on any attempts to access the shelters because so many people had been killed while trying. His edict was explained as necessary to ensure the infected inside the shelters would never find a way out into the world. Claire said that mothers told their children bedtime stories about the shelters full of sick people on the other side of those fields. The sick people were just waiting for someone to let them out, and if they did, the sick people would eat them.

It was amazing that the stories being passed on to the children by the parents were then shared with other families who would then share them with their neighbors until bedtime stories became fact. The shelters were definitely there, they were definitely full of the infected dead, and they were definitely a treasure trove of supplies. The one thing that the Chief couldn't figure was why no one knew someone else who had actually been in on the failed attempts to enter the shelters. The Chief had his money on the Sheriff and his mysterious firepower.

The Chief had worked his way closer and closer to the marina until he was between it and the bridge, and he was only trying to be in a position where he could get a closer look at the stenciled crates. To cover his movements he was catching catfish and stringing them, and every time he moved he lifted the stringer high enough out of the water to be sure that curious onlookers would see his successful catch.

Sure enough, workers waiting for the next boatload of supplies took an interest in the catfish and started thinking ahead to their own suppers. They called friendly greetings to the Chief who encouraged them by lifting it out of the water. Some of them offered him trades, mostly things he would have no use for, but in a world where survival meant getting a good meal when you had the chance, a few began offering knives and tools that were useful. He acted excited about a few of the offers and took the opportunity to walk out onto the docks.

He was greeted by hopeful men and women who wouldn't get the opportunity to do their own fishing until their daily work was done, and he took on the role of the generous neighbor by accepting trades of items that he would throw away as soon as possible. It was obvious that he was being a soft touch, but that made everyone like him that much more, and when he hung around just talking after he had given up his catch, he was invited to fish from the marina. He knew an opportunity when he saw it, and he got himself comfortable at the end of the dock away from most of them and resumed fishing. It was helpful that his good luck fishing seemed to pick up right where he had left off. He landed a huge catfish that had new offers flying his way as he put it on a stringer.

The next boat appeared upriver, and the workers went back to their work getting ready to unload it. The Chief wondered what leverage the Sheriff used on this group of people to keep them quiet, but whatever it was they weren't concerned about him. They had probably been doing this job for so long that they were just used to not talking about it when they got home.

It was only a few minutes before the boat would reach the dock when the temperature plummeted, and they all knew what it meant. He heard them commenting to each other, asking if anyone else had felt it. People took cover before it started. They had been through it before, so the small buildings on the docks of the marina became occupied well before the first big pieces of ice hit, but when the big ones bounced in different directions, sometimes they came from unexpected places. Golf ball sized pieces shot like rockets through open windows and connected with heads and hands held up as protection.

The storm pelted Farley with large chunks of hail, and everyone knew that the dreaded funnel cloud could be right behind the stinging pieces of ice. At one point it was not just stinging, it was lethal.

There were screams for help from the boat as it traveled the last few feet to the dock and the crew tried their best to tie off as they protected their eyes from the ice that fell like bullets. Streaks of blood already ran down the face of the man in the bow who was ready to tie off the boat. Getting no help from anyone on the dock, he was left with the unenviable chore of making the jump by himself. His bad timing caused him more pain as he missed the jump and hit face first on the flat part of the dock. He slid backwards into the water leaving a red streak on the wood. The man must have had the rope around his wrist because the bow of the boat turned in the direction of his fall. It listed and rolled to starboard and the top row of crates slid over the side.

The Chief was a spectator because he had done the only thing he could do. He had dropped into the water and ducked below the dock. Even though he was viewed as generous to his new friends, there wouldn't have been room inside any of the small buildings. He also doubted he would have made it to one in time. But that wasn't what he was there for either. The opportunity was putting itself right in front of him, and he was taking it.

In the very short time the Chief had been at the end of the dock, he had found the time to wonder about something that had bothered him for a long time. How deep was the water, was it all this muddy, and what else besides catfish, garfish, and snakes were in this river. On the other side of the river it was still common to see the infected walk off the bridge or the banks, get caught in the current and dragged away downriver. It was entertainment to the people who saw it happen so often that they had lost sight of the fact that the infected had been people. To a large extent, the Chief had lost sight as well, but he had seen millions of the infected, while these people had for some odd reason not seen quite as many at one time.

When the Chief ducked under the dock he got his answer about how deep the water was. He was neck deep, and his toes couldn't find the bottom. The current pulled hard enough for him to need to hold onto the edges of the boards above him, and his fingers were already bleeding from the small cuts. He still considered himself lucky until one chunk of ice hit his ring finger on his left hand right below his wedding band. He was sure it was broken, but he had endured far worse injuries.

As for what else was down there with him, he hoped that question would go unanswered for the time being, and the current was his one saving grace. It was pulling so hard that an infected dead would have to get a good grip on him before it could bite him. He tried not to think about the fact that the strong current meant something was likely to be going by at any given moment. He just had to be ready if he felt a bump that was larger than usual.

The first thing to come his way was the unfortunate man who had made the bad jump to the dock. He was still conscious, and he helplessly reached for the Chief in desperation. The Chief pushed himself from under the dock but kept hold of the wood with his right hand. He hooked his powerful left arm under the man's torso and grabbed as hard as he could. The broken finger hurt just enough to make him grimace, but in one smooth motion he thrust himself upward and tossed the man through the air. He landed in the middle of the dock face down, which was merciful considering the painful chunks of hail that pelted him.

The people on the dock in the nearest building saw the heroic sacrifice by the Chief and even braved the hail to retrieve the man. Two of them dodged unsuccessfully out to him and dragged the man inside. The Chief got hit in the face and across his scalp a few times, but his feat had put him ahead of the now drifting boat, and he was able to slip from view onto the starboard side. His suspicions about the crates were immediately confirmed when he saw the labels were US ARMY, and the contents were MREs.

The hail slacked off and came to a stop, and it was replaced by rain that came down in torrents, but the good news was that rain didn't hurt. The Chief caught the rope and used it to pull himself onto the boat. He immediately saw that the small craft had likely only been carrying the man he had rescued, so he ducked into the seat at the steering wheel and hit the starter. He spun the wheel and headed upriver in a downpour that was so heavy that it was doubtful that everyone at the docks could see where he had gone. Most of them could have sworn that they had seen him go downriver with the boat.

At least that was what they would report later when asked where he had gone, and the delay in accurate reporting was just enough time for the Chief to get upriver to the shelters. Under the cover of very heavy rain, he was able to take the boat along the opposite shore, totally invisible to anyone who might be watching. When he was sure he had traveled far enough and by drawing on his memory of a map he had reviewed a month or so earlier, he eased the boat to the center of the river and cut the engine.

Over the sound of the heavy rain, the Chief could hear shouts, and his old training as a Navy SEAL told him that he had managed to get himself upriver from the soldiers who were watching river traffic. He started the engine again and idled against the current until he got a quarter of a mile further upriver and then headed for shore. He couldn't wait to see the shelter complex for himself.

People who used boats along rivers stayed out from under low hanging branches because snakes were poor companions in a boat. They tended to drop into boats rather than stay in the trees, probably because they were frightened, but regardless of their intentions, the results were usually panic. The Chief needed to hide the boat, and he needed to tie it off undetected so he would have time to get from the boat to the shelters. For that reason he couldn't go ashore at any of the openings along the bank. Instead, he had to pick a spot where the overhanging branches were thick. He felt like he was hunting for snakes instead of avoiding them. Fortunately for him, he could identify snakes on sight and knew that most of the species he would encounter were harmless.

He picked his spot and let the boat coast in quietly under the cover of the rain.

He said aloud, "Well, I know where the snakes are if anyone else wants to know."

His eyes roved over the thick covering of foliage trying to tell the difference between branches and snakes. He was sure he got some of his observations wrong, but he was careful to keep the boat from bouncing against the trunks of the trees. The vibrations would have been enough to make it rain snakes. He heard a thud behind him and knew he had a passenger. He turned in time to see a kingsnake go over the side. He knew that the snake preferred not to be in the tree in the first place because it was a scarlet kingsnake.

The scarlet kingsnake is often mistaken for coral snakes because of their red bands, but the red bands on this snake were bordered by black bands, not yellow. They lived on the ground and this one had probably gone out on the tree branch to avoid something.

The Chief focused his eyes in the dim light, trying to see through the foliage and find a safe place to go ashore. Whatever had disturbed the snake would be disturbing to him as well. He saw tree trunks move and searched around for a boat hook or a paddle. It was too late to push away from shore, but if that pair of tree trunks were what he thought they were, he would be grateful for anything that could be used to push it away from him.

The boat hook was at least six feet long, and the Chief had an idea. Usually, the best way to deal with an infected dead was to get away from it, but there was a good chance that it wasn't alone. Avoiding it might be just prolonging the inevitable. He lifted the boat hook and reached out toward the pair of legs he had mistaken for tree trunks and carefully got the hook around them. If they turned out to be trees, he would at least be able to pull himself ashore.

Before he had a chance to trip the infected dead, it took a step in the opposite direction. That had been the Chief's goal, so he only had to hang on. The infected fell with a crash into smaller branches and flailed its arms as frightened snakes slipped away from it. It didn't have the reasoning power to know it had been tripped by the boat hook, but with the hook around its legs, it was having difficulty getting to its feet. When it rolled toward the river the Chief pulled and directed it to fall into the water next to the boat instead of in it. He got the hook free and used the pole to push branches aside.

Glad to be out from under the overhanging branches, the Chief found himself on the edge of a vast field. Through the gloom and the driving rain, he could see the mounds that held the first layer of shelters. From what Doctor Bus had told him, the shelters were huge, and they overlapped underground. He was probably even standing above one already. Now all he had to do was make his way to the back entrance of the super shelter built by Titus Rush.

******

* * *

The Chief's escape went unreported for a long time because he had saved the life of the man in the boat. He was a close friend of everyone on the docks, and until he regained consciousness, the others tended to his cuts and talked about the big man who had saved him. Most of them recognized him as that new blacksmith with the big smile. Always quick to help someone lift something heavy or fix a broken tool, they had not really been surprised that he had shared his fish with them. He had been known to give his food to hungry children, and when people had something of their own to spare, it was his if he needed it.

The marina workers knew they had to tell someone a boatload of supplies had been lost, and they knew they would have to say it was the blacksmith who took it. Saying they couldn't describe the Chief was pointless, but they decided they could delay reporting until they got help for the boat owner. When he woke up and learned what had saved him, he was quick to suggest that he should remain unconscious for a while longer.

An armed patrol arrived when the rain stopped. It was obvious that another storm would be on them in minutes, so they had been sent to expedite the unloading of the boats. They arrived to find the workers huddled in their protective shelters on the docks and crates of supplies still in the water. Some of the crates were making good speed down the river, and the boss wouldn't be happy about that. Workers were pushed to a boat and sent to round them up while the others were questioned about what happened. Even with their willingness to cooperate, the scene was chaotic, and the Chief gained more valuable time.

When the events were finally sorted out, the story was clear to the guards that the blacksmith had stolen a boat and gone upriver under the cover of the storm. The Sergeant in charge of the soldiers knew that the Sheriff would have his stripes because they had never bothered to post guards upriver. The current was so strong that every attempt to escape on the river was with the help of the current. Around the bend downriver, there was a string of boats anchored and manned around the clock. If anyone came upon the blockade, they were immediately shot with no questions asked.

The guards on the blockade also reported escape attempts immediately, and the blacksmith would have been a big story. No one had gone that way, so the soldiers sent word to the Sheriff that he had most likely gone upriver. Search parties were sent in both directions, but the Chief had a good head start.

As word spread quickly through the security system around Farley, most of the soldiers and citizens assumed the Sheriff had been contacted at his lavish estate. Almost all of them thought the estate was in the big private neighborhoods on the other side of the mountain miles from Farley. That was where the rich people had lived before the infection. It was conveniently far enough away from Farley to keep any of the people from entertaining any thoughts of paying him a visit. In between was wild territory rumored to be infested with the dead. As for the few soldiers who knew the truth, they weren't going to sacrifice their somewhat better existence for anyone outside their circle.

Some people thought the Sheriff lived in the heavily wooded area only a mile or so north of Farley. It was rumored to be surrounded by an electrified fence and heavily guarded. Rumor also had it that escapees from Farley who were found in that area were executed, but the guards didn't dispose of them completely. In other words, they were allowed to turn into the infected and were tied to trees. Some escapees had the misfortune to stumble across the infected before they were found by the guards. In the dark woods it wasn't a good idea to lean against a tree.

The real truth of the whereabouts of the Sheriff had remained a secret for six years because he had control of such a massive stockpile of resources, and with the support of the Army, no one had attempted to take it away from him. The officers who stood behind him had been faced with the decision to expose the Sheriff years ago, and as they delayed taking action against a civilian government, they became complicit in the secrets they protected. Then when he shared his resources with them and they lived better than their own men, it became more and more dangerous to reveal the truth.

Sheriff J. Horton Crim was in his shelter when the word arrived by courier that they had an unprecedented escape from Farley. When he read the piece of paper and learned it was the big man that he had stared at in wonder while walking around him, he felt an uncomfortable but all too familiar stab of pain in his lower back. The officer sitting across from his desk who was sipping at an expensive brandy had a momentary urge to be somewhere else when he saw the grimace on the Sheriff's face.

"Is everything okay, Sheriff?"

He didn't answer. He just slid the sheet of paper across to him. The officer read it and was careful not to react too quickly. He had learned it wasn't enough to deliver promises of a quick response. He had seen that backfire before. With the Sheriff it was best to give him a moment to decide how mad he was.

"Tell your men to send in a squad with a personnel carrier and pick up these people. He jotted names on a piece of paper and the address of the house. I want them brought here under heavy guard. If one gets away, someone will be severely punished."

The officer glanced at the names and knew who they were immediately. The blond and redhead had been all his men talked about, and he had been wondering how long it was going to be before they lost control of some of the young bucks who had never been serving in the military for the right reasons. Service was starting to take on a new meaning after six years. There was an attitude that clearly asked the question, "What's in it for me?"

The soldiers had been well cared for by their commanders, but there had been incidents over the years of increasingly sadistic behavior. It wasn't enough to make sure they got a big steak for supper from time to time. It wasn't enough that equipment was repurposed to ensure the soldiers had a club and a theater. What they didn't have was the freedom to go into town, get drunk, and find a girl. It was like being in a combat zone for six years. That's why the Sheriff and his secrets were becoming an even bigger concern to the officers who were in on them.

"I'll have them here within the hour, Sheriff."

He glanced longingly at the unfinished brandy, but he knew better than to pick it up. Sheriff Crim noticed and was also one to understand when to throw someone a bone.

"Finish it, Captain."

The officer managed to thank the Sheriff, finish the brandy, and be out the door in seconds, and he was gratified to find the Lieutenant waiting with his Sergeants outside. They had anticipated a reaction by the Sheriff one way or another.

Less than fifteen minutes after leaving the shelter complex the officer and NCO's were at the compound where the soldiers lived. They gathered up a squad in a personnel carrier and splattered people in the streets with mud as they raced through Farley.

"Why am I not surprised to see you?" Kathy asked as they pushed open the door without knocking.

Iris had seen them coming and quickly reminded everyone to be on their best behavior. It wasn't that the visit was unexpected. As a matter of fact, the only surprise was that it took so long to happen.

"Shut up and come with us."

Everyone assumed it was a group invitation, and the Captain had to wonder about this group of people a bit. They just seemed so unfazed by what was happening. He couldn't recall ever seeing a group that was so unconcerned about their situation.

"The Sheriff wants to see you."

Kathy said, "Oh, I'm so sorry. Did I forget to ask? Where are you taking us?"

The men all stepped out of the way to politely let the women pass, and from being around Captain Miller's men they knew that some things were universal with American soldiers. Some even exchanged pleasantries with them as they walked to the personnel carrier.

When the back door was closed, it was dark inside without windows, but they didn't feel like they were in any danger yet.

"I guess they don't want us to see where we're going," said Tom.

Kathy said, "Time for that overdue audience with the big guy."

"No," said Hampton, "that may be part of it, but I think that would've been a private party. He didn't need all of us there to teach you how to behave."

"What then? You think this has something to do with the Chief?"

Iris chuckled at the question. "If he's in the neighborhood, there's a good chance it has something to do with him."

There was a banging sound from above and upfront.

"You guys shut up down there unless you'd rather wear hoods."

That wasn't what any of them wanted, so they rode in silence. At one point Kathy held up a hand and tapped her wrist with two fingers. Everyone took that to mean they had been riding for fifteen to twenty minutes. They knew from previous discussions on the topic that men estimate longer periods of time and women estimate shorter, so they had agreed they would always go with somewhere in between.

They also remembered when they began their stay in the little frame house that they didn't think it would be the last time they were taken to a new location wearing a blindfold. They had spent the evening doing a diagram of the shantytown and where they guessed the landmarks were. It was fairly easy to guess a lot of it because they knew where the river was and where they were in relation to the river. They all knew the bridge sat in a bend of the river, and the shelters dominated the landscape to the northwest. They didn't know which way they were going, but they had a good idea of how long it would take to get places. Judging by the long ride and the fact that they never drove on smooth pavement, they knew they were going northwest.

When the personnel carrier came to a bumpy and sudden stop, they could hear above the sound of the idling engine that the rain had started again. The doors flew open wide, and soldiers yelled at them to move out like they were assaulting a beach. There wasn't time to get a good look around because the back of the personnel carrier was so close to a large steel door. The door seemed to be growing out of the side of a hill, and very little light came from inside.

If they hadn't been following a pair of soldiers who led the way, they would have run through the open door and broken their necks in the fall to the bottom of the stairs. The ceiling above the stairs sloped at an angle that perfectly matched the slope of the stairs, and it was so steep that they felt like their eyes were pointed at the ceiling the whole time. It was almost like going down a well standing up.

The rain ran down the metal stairs and rails with them, and they fought not to slip. The soldiers in front moved fast, and the soldiers in back continuously yelled, "Move, move, move!"

When they reached the bottom they burst into a room with a high ceiling, and despite the low light they could see that the room was cavernous. Row after row of crates rose in high stacks around them, and there was no longer any doubt about where they were.

Kathy whispered to Tom, "I thought they couldn't get into any of the shelters."

"It looks like someone is holding out on the people."

"Which means we aren't going back to Farley," said Colleen.

Someone shouted, "No one said you could talk!"

Soldiers moved in close behind them and to the front, and on their left and right were high walls of crates, so this was where things would happen. There was no way for them to fight. They had no weapons, and they had no idea how many soldiers there were. Their only hope was that this wasn't an execution.

The soldiers in front moved slightly to the sides creating a narrow path down the middle, and the familiar face of one of the Sheriff's main men took shape in the gloom as he came closer. He walked straight up to Kathy and said, "Follow me," in a voice she barely heard. As she took a step forward to follow, he turned and said, "Just you."

Kathy hesitated, but there was no use in putting it off. She had probably ruined every good night's sleep for the Sheriff since the day she nailed his lower back. She would be mad if she had been on the receiving end of that kind of back injury.

It was suffocating in the low light of the shelter even though the room was large enough to cause echoes, and there was an untold number of rain soaked soldiers in the narrow path between the crates. Much to Kathy's disgust, that was exactly what they had in mind, and she had to suppress the involuntary sounds that wanted to rise out of her throat as she felt their hands take advantage of the close quarters. As the escort weaved through the dense bodies with her close behind, she wondered if he was even aware of the indignity they were forcing upon her.

Kathy's hands blocked groping hand after hand from both sides as quickly as she could until she snapped. With reflexes honed by her training and by six years of killing the infected, her body went into an automatic mode. It didn't matter that they were armed. It didn't matter how many there were or how big they were. Her left forearm went into the throat of the last man who touched her and her right palm heel drove upward into the tip of his nose.

The man's nasal bones pierced his brain, and he was dead before he reached the floor. The amount of blood that flew into the faces of everyone close around him caused a general amount of pushing with shoulders and rifles rather than any coordinated counter attack. One wall of crates on the right side leaned away and then back toward the crowd. Someone tried to steady the wall and managed to make the bottom crates move because some idiot had stacked full crates on top of the empty ones, probably in an attempt to be organized.

When the wall of crates fell, the wall behind the melee on the other side went over under the weight of people falling against it. Even in the chaos Kathy had time to think that she couldn't be causing all of this, but if she was, it was so satisfying to get back at all of those perverts who violated her, and she had to smile when she saw the man leading her disappear under people and crates. He had lost the advantage.

Shots rang out in the narrow passageway, and people went down. Kathy felt herself leave the floor. She was flung over a low stack of crates, and unbelievably her fall was broken by landing on top of Hampton. Then her breath was knocked out of her when Iris landed on her back. She somehow managed to get her feet on the floor and ready to swing at the next uniform she saw, but the lights went out as she was body blocked into a dark stairwell.

There were shouts and grunts as air was knocked from lungs, and bones collided hard with metal railings echoed up from the darkness, but the mass of sounds of the fighting seemed to be blocked out. Gunshots sounded farther away. Curses and shouted orders were indistinguishable as if they were coming from somewhere else.

Over it all she heard a familiar voice say from only a few feet away, "Is everybody here?"

They were in a tangled pile in darkness, but one by one they acknowledged the Chief. Everyone was there, and they were on the floor at the top of a pitch black stairwell that dropped away below them.

"Let's move it, folks. I don't think it will take them long to find this door."

22

Homecoming

Huntsville - Year Seven

For over six years the skies had been quiet. Most people remembered how quiet the world became during the 2020 Pandemic as airlines canceled flights and the military moved their strategic assets to locations away from their normal areas of operation. There were still planes, but there was a noticeable difference, and it was a long time before people quit lifting their eyes to the sky when they heard a big plane coming in for a landing. So it was six years into the pandemic that had brought the infected dead, except more so. In most areas of the world no one ever saw one of those magnificent flying machines we had come to take for granted.

When the Soyuz reentry vehicle burst into the clear blue sky, few people were aware that they were getting a spectacular view because the Earth had over half a decade with no man made pollutants being added to the atmosphere. There had been some catastrophic events caused by man such as the fire in Charleston that consumed the Yorktown. Nuclear reactors and other man made structures would add their own poisons over time, but all in all, the sky hadn't been so clear in over a century.

The people of Farley were likely to be the most awestruck by the arrival because so many of them had been part of the space program. If they hadn't actually been employed by the programs, they lived alongside neighbors who did. Huntsville's international population had caused the shantytown of Farley to be one of the most highly educated slums in the world. The people lived in squalor, but there were signs every day of innovations that made people live just a little better. Given the materials to improve their lives, Farley had a chance to become a safe haven much like the village over Green Cavern in Guntersville.

The sonic boom reached them long before they saw anything in the sky. People pointed at the spot where something had just become visible, and more and more people found the streak that grew in size as it neared the skies over Huntsville. Then there were the big orange and white parachutes that blossomed against the blue sky. One was trailing behind the object that glinted in the bright sun but was burned black in other places. The chute flailed in the wind and seemed to be spinning like a top. The orange and white sections whirled faster, tightening the ropes that held it attached to the capsule. It was a beautiful but deadly sight because there was no way the chute would open with its ropes twisted so tight.

It didn't mean as much to the people on the ground, but some of them understood. There was nothing they could do to help, but they knew the passengers of the capsule were in for an awful landing. They had often wondered what had happened to the last crew of the ISS, but none of them speculated any likely outcome other than the possibility they had landed six years ago in the Pacific and had safely lived out those years in the sunshine and comfort of a tropical paradise. Some cried because they knew they had been wrong, and six years of sacrifice was about to end in tragedy.

The rockets fired on the bottom of the Soyuz capsule, and a cheer went up from the crowd. Hands were held up to faces in prayer as the crowds begged God to let the brave ISS crew land safely. When the capsule disappeared into the hillsides of Madison to the northeast of Huntsville, all the people saw was a dust cloud that rose with the smoke from the retrorockets that had done their best to slow the descent of the doomed craft.

The crowd in Farley surged forward in a vain hope of reaching the landing site, but the boundaries of their town were surrounded by fences in that direction. Warning signs attached to the wire had always kept the curious from crossing the broad fields that led to the shelters. If the electricity in the fence didn't kill you, the mines would, and if you were lucky enough not to step on a mine, you would definitely be shot. No one bothered to ask where the electricity came from because they weren't likely to get an honest answer anyway.

As the sun slowly made its passage to the west, the crowd settled in for the night on the edge of the shantytown. An all night vigil began as people hoped there would be some word given from the Sheriff's men about the outcome of the hard landing. They waited almost as if they believed they would see the silver and white spacesuits coming walking together over the hills in the distance.

******

"Commander Callaway! Adam!"

Henry Tisdal's ears were ringing so badly that he was disoriented. He recognized Natalia Lebedev's voice screaming the words, but their meaning wasn't registering. He hurt too much to care, and he absently wondered how Natalia had the energy to be screaming anything.

Six years in space without gravity had taken its toll on his muscles. His head felt like it was too heavy for his fragile neck, and all he wanted to do was rest against the restraints that kept him in his seat. He was on his right side, and that was okay with him. It was a restful position, and if it was all right with the others, he would be fine with staying there until everything quit hurting. It didn't sound like it would be all right with the others though.

Because the capsule was sitting on its right side, Natalia and Adam were above Henry. He could see them out of the corner of his left eye, but his head felt too heavy for him to turn the bulky helmet in their direction. It wasn't until the sound of Natalia's voice became more than just words that he understood something was wrong…very wrong.

Natalia felt the crushing impact of the Soyuz into the soft soil of the hill, and it had felt anything but soft. When the obvious had sunk in as they watched the slack risers of the chute bend away at an odd angle just before impact, Natalia had grasped the loose ends of her seat belts and yanked as hard as she could. That quick thinking had pulled her more tightly into her chair just in time, and even though she had felt the same bone crushing impact as the others, she had absorbed it better.

She had seen Commander Callaway reaching for something in front of them of the control panels. She had imagined it was either the fire suppression system or the switch that would blow the hatch from the capsule, and she had wanted to yell at him to wait. Both could wait until they survived the crash, and having an arm extended at the point of impact was an invitation to be injured. She didn't have more than a split second to consider how severe that injury would be, but she had enough time to know it would be bad.

Lifting the heavy helmet to face the visor toward Adam was more than she could manage. Natalia turned her head slightly inside the helmet, but she couldn't see him well enough. She could tell he wasn't moving, but then again, neither was she. It was easier to let gravity help her get Henry into her view, and she could see enough of him to know that he was alive. She saw him do as she had done as he put all of his efforts into turning his head, but she couldn't tell by his reaction if he had succeeded or not.

There was only one choice, and that was to get her helmet off first. She didn't need it anymore anyway. If her helmet was too heavy to move with her neck, she wondered why she thought her arms would be any better. Each one felt like she was moving against a heavy current in a river while holding a bowling ball in each hand. Instead of lifting both of them, she focused all of her strength on her right arm, and it slowly appeared in front of her face. She worked at the locking ring at the base of her helmet, and she didn't realize her left hand was helping her right until the ring disengaged. She didn't remember trying to lift it.

Natalia lifted her helmet away from her head, and she had a wider view of the interior of the capsule. She carefully lowered the helmet letting the new pull from gravity help her, but she didn't let go until she knew it wouldn't bounce off of Henry. Then she painfully turned her attention to Commander Callaway.

Adam's handsome face was pressed against the glass of his visor, and Natalia's first thought was the suits weren't designed to allow that. You could move forward into the bubble of the visor, but the face wasn't supposed to be able to reach the glass. He was staring straight at her, but his eyelids never blinked.

"Oh noooo, Adam."

It came out as a wail, and Natalia somehow summoned up the strength to reach for him. He was hanging a little closer to her because his straps had a little too much slack in them. She was able to reach his helmet locking ring and gave it a hard twist. His helmet came away, and she deflected it to keep it from falling into her face or on Henry. It clattered away beneath them, and she reached for Adam's face. It was slack, and his eyes were still focused on a spot somewhere below her.

Then she saw the lump on his neck where the bones had stopped after they had broken free. He had probably died instantly. Natalia felt the tears well up in her eyes, but they were nothing compared to the feeling that something was trying to push its way out of her throat. She didn't know that she was holding back a scream.

It was a scream of frustration at the horrible loss of such a good man, and it was a scream directed at whatever power there was in the universe that would allow a man to survive for six years in what had been their prison only to snuff out his life when he was finally able to come home. Natalia screamed and screamed until her throat couldn't produce the sound one more time. The tears flooded her eyes and blocked her vision so much that she didn't even see the first movement. It was hardly more than a twitch, but she would have seen it if not for the tears.

Henry didn't see it either because he had faded into blessed unconsciousness and hadn't returned until the screaming had jolted him awake. The pain was still there, and he couldn't move, but he was awake when the screaming changed from anguish to horror. He recognized the change and knew that Natalia was in real trouble. His bruised body resisted, but he had to help her.

The harness holding Henry in his seat was designed for a quick release if it was punched hard enough, but the last thing he wanted to do was punch himself in the chest. That's where the mechanism was located…right in the one place on his body that hurt the most. He watched his left hand raise up in front of him as if it belonged to someone else.

"This is going to hurt," he managed to say just before the clenched fist hit the quick release button. For a second time it felt like the Soyuz capsule crashing into the hillside, and Henry let out a scream as violent as Natalia's. The straps flew away from his body despite the stress he was putting on them, and he fell out of his seat.

The fall knocked the wind from his lungs even though he only fell a couple of feet, but Natalia was waving her arms and screaming, and she needed his help. He didn't know exactly why, but from his new vantage point on the wall of the capsule, it appeared that Commander Callaway was grabbing her pressure suit and trying to pull her closer to him. There was also a new sound. It was growling. It was a mindless, savage sound, and it was coming from his friend.

Henry managed to get his feet under his body despite the pain that lanced across his chest with every move. First one foot then the other, and he was finally able to push with both legs. He wasn't sure why he did it, but as he stood he hooked one hand inside the rim of the helmet that had belonged to Adam and lifted it with him. He still wore his own helmet, but something told him he would need another. From what he had expected, the pull of gravity would be so strong that he couldn't stand, but adrenaline forced him upward. All he knew was that he had to help Natalia.

Standing on the wall of the Soyuz brought Henry almost face to face with Adam Callaway, and Henry saw that his friend had been replaced by a snarling creature that he didn't recognize. He saw the broken neck and the unnatural tilt to his head. His lips were bared, and his eyes remained locked on Natalia until Henry's own face appeared only inches away. Despite the broken neck that should have paralyzed Adam, the appearance of Henry in front of the slavering teeth caused the creature to turn away from Natalia. Henry lifted the helmet. He fended off the hands that grasped with bulky gloves at his own rounded helmet. The curve of his face shield was quickly smeared with saliva, but behind the protection he regarded his friend with sympathy.

For as long as he could remember, Adam had been his American counterpart in the training for a great adventure. They were to be part of the history making mission that would be made up of the largest crew to serve aboard the International Space Station, and from the beginning they had been friends. Adam had been there for the birth of Henry's second child, and little James Adam Tisdal delighted when uncle Adam had visited their country home in England. Henry's wife Elizabeth had commented more than once about their bond being that which brothers rarely achieved.

Now Henry found himself putting the helmet over his friend's head with much the same somber deliverance as a eulogy. He said goodbye as he drew it over Adam's head and engaged the locking ring.

Natalia had stopped screaming, but she was sobbing loudly as Henry pulled Adam's hands away from her and wedged them under the tight chest straps. He wished he had a way to keep the thing inside the helmet from seeing outward, but it helped Henry and Natalia not to be forced to watch their old comrade behave as if his gentle and handsome self had never existed. Once his hands were secure, Henry reached to the crown of Adam's helmet and found the embedded button that once depressed would lower the reflective sun visor. It was like watching the final curtain go down as Adam's face disappeared behind the gold mirror of his helmet. In that instant, Henry's mind allowed him to forget the image of the broken thing inside the spacesuit, and he would only allow himself to remember Adam's half smile. The one he reserved for those moments when he wanted to display the most affection.

Henry turned to Natalia, and their eyes met. He could see that her soul was as broken as their bodies, and he honestly didn't know which pain was worse. They had no way of knowing what they would find once the capsule door was ejected, but they couldn't stay where they were. As much as it hurt, Henry forced himself to take control of the situation. Natalia would need time before she assumed her role as second in command.

Natalia caught her breath between sobs and surprised Henry when she spoke.

"I'm okay. I'm okay, Henry. Adam is gone, and we can't help him. Are you hurt?"

Henry let out a short grunt when he opened his mouth to speak, and Natalia knew the answer.

"Thank you for what you did. It must have been hard."

He was only able to give her a nod, but it was enough.

"Ribs are banged up. Maybe one broken that will need to be wrapped as soon as we get out of here. Let's see if we can get you out of your harness without dropping you on the floor. I promise, that's the hard part. Once you get your feet under you it won't be so bad."

Henry was only trying his best to be reassuring. In all honesty, he didn't have a clue if Natalia was hurt or not. For all he knew, it could be her legs that took the brunt of the collision between the capsule and the ground. It all depended on the way the energy was transferred through the capsule when it hit. If Adam hadn't been reaching for something at the wrong moment, maybe it wouldn't have broken his neck. If Henry hadn't pulled his harness straps tighter, the impact might have collapsed his sternum straight into his heart. Instead of helping Natalia, he would be coughing up blood inside his own helmet. When it came right down to it, he had been lucky, and he needed to accept that.

With Henry supporting her weight, together they were able to release Natalia from the seat and lower her to the floor. Miraculously there were no stabbing pains that would herald the arrival of another crisis.

"I'm good," she said.

They were squeezed into the small space between the seats and the control consoles, and under other circumstances it could have been intimate, but at the moment they embraced it was quite the opposite. The strength of human contact sent a wave of grief over both of them, and they shuttered like two small school children who held each other after a night terror.

"Are you ready for me to open the hatch?" he asked.

There was a long pause, but he didn't press the question. Anything could be out there. It could be quiet and peaceful, or they could have gone straight through a house. There could be people waiting anxiously for them to emerge, or there could be more of them like Adam. They knew where the target had been, but with one chute failing to deploy, they either drifted away from the landing zone, or they had simply hit it harder.

She answered in a voice that was slightly above a whisper, and Henry didn't hesitate. To do so was only adding time that would allow the fear of the unknown to build. With bodies that were weakened by the prolonged lack of gravity and the added insults of their crash landing, they would be forced to face whatever it was that waited outside.

Henry's gloved hand hit the large, shielded button that sent current to a small explosive charge in the seal of the hatch. It was small, but the blast was so close to their heads that it was deafening. The hatch blew away from the area above their heads, and they both averted their eyes from the light as if they expected something to drop through the hatch. When they lifted their heads to the opening, there was only blue sky framed by the blackened metal.

Henry helped Natalia find the seat with her boot, and he lifted her upward even though the pain was enough to make him see white spots dance across his vision. Natalia got her hands over the edges where the hatch had been and pulled as he pushed, and soon she was sitting outside the capsule with only her legs dangling inside.

"What do you see, Comrade?"

Even though the landing had been brutal, and they had lost their beloved friend, Henry used the term familiar to his Russian counterpart as a way of giving her something to celebrate.

"I see blue sky, green trees, and rolling hills, Comrade Tisdal. It is safe for us to officially end the longest mission in space for Mother Russia."

Henry had to laugh despite the tragedy of their loss.

"You mean for the Queen and country, don't you?"

"No, Comrade. You boarded the Soyuz before me, so I was technically aboard the International Space Station longer than you."

Henry recalled that he had also climbed into the ISS ahead of Comrade Natalia Lebedev at the very beginning of their mission, but he didn't say so. He was happy to let her have her moment. Her legs swung away from the hatch as she reversed her position and held her hand down to him. He grabbed at it, and he could swear he felt the strength in her grip that came from the pure joy of being alive. The odds had been against any of them living through reentry without telemetry support from ground control, so they had beaten the odds by having two of them survive.

Henry lowered himself down inside the capsule that had saved at least two of their lives and found Natalia's helmet. He didn't know why, but it belonged with them. He didn't have much strength for throwing something as heavy as the helmet, but he managed to stretch high enough to push it over the lip of the hatch. Natalia saw it roll over the edge and retrieved it as soon as it reached the ground.

As he passed by Adam, he felt rather than saw one hand come free from where he had wedged them. The grip was weak and clumsy because of the glove of the space suit, and it was only enough to remind him to say a final goodbye. There was no telling how long Adam's body would rage on inside that suit, but the capsule would be a fitting tomb. When he emerged from the hatch, rather than to take in the green landscape and blue skies, he glanced around to find the hatch cover so he could return it to the capsule. He would close the door of the tomb for his friend.

Natalia knew what Henry was doing as soon as he slid down the side of the Soyuz. He quickly asked her to stay on her perch by the open hatch while he got the cover. Once he handed it to her and it was in place, she slid down next to him, and they finally took in their surroundings with survival in mind.

"Did we land in the target area?" he asked, still wearing his helmet for safety. It made his voice muffled, but it also kept them from being heard from a long distance. It was a moot point considering the sound of their arrival, but it still felt like a good idea.

Natalia turned in a complete circle before answering, but she finally nodded.

"I would say we did well. Those raised areas should be the shelters we talked about. If anyone is still alive inside them, we won't be outside and exposed for long. We can get some rest and heal up before we decide our next move."

On unsteady legs they took their first steps toward the nearest of the shelters which were also happily downhill from them. They had never seen an astronaut walk away from a Soyuz landing because their muscles would be too weak, but the determination to be safe after the experience of landing drove them forward. They looked back only once, and they understood the finality of the moment. There was little doubt about the future of manned space flight.

******

From the way the trees were bent and broken, Natalia and Henry guessed there had been a violent storm recently. Neither had ever seen the path of a tornado, but if that wasn't what had wreaked havoc on the terrain, they didn't know what had. They were both as weak as newborn children, and gravity pulled at every bruised spot as if it knew where they hurt the most, so climbing over debris made for a slow journey to the nearest shelter. Everything was wet, and they were grateful for their spacesuits.

The blue sky then had been the calm after a storm. That was just one more piece of useful information they would have had if they had been landing with telemetry. No one in their right mind would have tried to time a spacecraft landing with a thunderstorm and probable tornado.

The ground was especially soggy where the sloping ground met with a road of some sort. It wasn't paved and it ran away in a snaking series of curves past the ends of the large earthen mounds.

"Are those tire tracks?" asked Henry.

"Fresh tire tracks. At least two vehicles. Maybe more but different sizes."

They both craned their necks to the left and right trying to see as far as they could down the muddy road, but there was no sign of the vehicles.

"I don't suppose it matters which of these shelters we choose," said Natalia, "so we might as well go into this one."

She indicated with a wave of her arm that she was talking about the one to their left. There was a rusty steel door embedded in the grass covered end of the sloping mound, so they walked up to it expecting to open it and announce their arrival to whoever lived inside. Everything they knew about the shelters included information that people would have used them to survive the apocalypse. They didn't expect a ticker tape parade, but they thought they would at least be welcomed.

Henry reached for the door handle and pulled, but it didn't budge.

"Let me try."

He moved aside to let Natalia get in front of the handle. She positioned both feet ahead of her and pulled backward with all her strength, but she didn't feel the slightest movement.

Henry turned around and walked across the road to the door of the next shelter. He saw before he even got to it that it was slightly ajar.

"Comrade, this one is open."

Natalia followed him over to the door, and she suddenly felt very conspicuous out in the open. Two bulky white spacesuits in the middle of a muddy dirt road weren't something people saw every day.

As if her thoughts had conjured up a living soul, a figure appeared in the road a few shelters away. From a distance they couldn't quite make out the details of the person's appearance, but by the way the man or woman moved, there was something horribly wrong with one leg. Both of them regarded the approaching figure with growing interest, but also with a growing sense of understanding. They had seen plenty of news broadcasts in the early days, but they had either forgotten or had blocked out the horror that had swept the planet.

"It can't be this bad," said Henry. "It can't be like this everywhere."

Natalia stepped past Henry and reached for the door that was open a few inches. She gripped it by the open edge and pulled hard, all the while glancing to her right at the wreckage of what she now guessed was, or rather had been, a woman in her middle thirties.

The door resisted at first, but it squealed loudly at the hinges and opened to reveal a black entry. She had expected a room, so she didn't lower her gaze immediately. Going from the bright sunlight to the pitch dark made it even more difficult for her to realize she was facing a steep drop down a flight of stairs that seemed to go on forever. The light didn't reach the bottom.

The sound that came from the slowly moving woman let Natalia know that a decision had to be made one way or the other. They had to go down the stairs or stay outside, but at the moment she didn't know which was a better choice. Henry made the choice for her.

For all his bruises and broken ribs, he showed surprising agility, especially under more gravity than he was used to. He stepped calmly toward the woman and reached out with his heavily gloved hand, catching her at the back of her neck and rudely dragging her forward. He pushed the woman past Natalia into the darkness and gave her enough of a shove to get her going. The grotesque thing that the woman had become didn't resist, but the nasal snarling continued loudly even as she disappeared into the darkness. They heard her reach the bottom, but the snarling rose in volume. There were more of them down there.

Natalia said, "I guess there are at least sixty metal stairs."

"Do you think all of the shelters are like that?"

"The designers thought it was a good idea to make one that way, so they probably made them all that way. They probably wanted a depth that could withstand bombs. Remember, these are Cold War shelters."

"Regardless, it seems that our newly introduced friend has company down there," said Henry.

"I didn't catch her name," said Natalia, "but after what you did to her, I doubt she will tell us what's happening down there."

Natalia pushed the door shut again, and they shuffled away in their heavy spacesuits, both glad for the extra protection. They didn't doubt that the tough material of the suits would be impervious to the fatal bites of the people.

"What was that the news broadcasters were calling these people?" asked Henry.

"Infected dead," said Natalia.

"They could have come up with something better," he grumbled.

"I can live with it unless you prefer something more catchy," said Natalia. "Let's keep checking doors."

They didn't bother to count how many shelters they tried to open, but they had gone far enough away from their landing site that they didn't see the people who arrived with guns. They would have wrongly thought they were being rescued if they had seen the Sheriff's uniform, and they would have been signing their own death warrants. The last thing the Sheriff wanted was a bonafide hero or celebrity showing up. Someone who represented authority in the past and who would possibly challenge his rights to what he had claimed as his.

As it turned out, they were able to evade detection when one door finally opened easily, and the stairs were well lit by ceiling lights. No snarling noises came from down below, so they began their descent.

Gravity was on their side as they climbed down the steps on shaky legs. They weren't used to the extra pull on their bodies, and it was more tiring than they could believe. When they reached the bottom they were surprised by the enormity of the place. The main room was cavernous, and it appeared to be largely filled by opened and emptied boxes.

"Someone has pillaged this shelter," said Henry.

"I half expected that when the door opened so easily," answered Natalia.

"Should we keep checking the shelters or explore this one?"

She considered his question for a moment. The prospect of climbing that barely sloped ladder wasn't attractive, but her gut was also telling her it was better to be inside. She couldn't put her finger on it, but she had felt vulnerable outside. There was something dangerous out there, and it wasn't just those infected people.

"Let's see what this place is like before we move on. We might need to get some rest before we give those stairs a try."

Henry turned where he stood and studied the steps.

"Why did they build it this way?" he asked. "It must have been difficult to bring provisions down that thing, unless they sent down crates before they put in the steps and the rails."

"I'm betting on multiple exits," said Natalia. "They probably have a loading bay somewhere deep in the complex. If I had designed this, I would have dug one central tunnel that trucks could use, and the tunnel would go to the back entrances of multiple shelters. That tunnel would also be a place where people from the other shelters could connect with each other. There are hundreds of shelters, and that one tunnel could connect all of them. It would be the easiest way to carry provisions to them all."

Natalia walked away into the depths of the structure, and Henry hurried to catch up. Lights were on in some places, but there were dark corners everywhere. It seemed to both of them that there was movement just beyond their peripheral vision, but every time they tried to see what it was, there were just more empty boxes and packaging debris.

Henry reached up and thumbed a button on his helmet, and his external lights came on.

"I have one hundred percent charge showing," he said, "so save yours until mine gets lower."

Natalia nodded agreement and gestured for Henry to take the lead. He stepped past her, and she was spared the second guessing she had been doing. Henry's helmet lights illuminated the dark corners even when he didn't face directly toward them. Henry didn't see the big folded map sitting on a table, but she did. She tapped the back of his suit, and he followed her to it. It was exactly what she had hoped it would be. It was a map of the shelter.

She excitedly spread it out on the table and ran her finger along the corridors in hope of finding what she was sure would be there, and there it was. A central corridor that was colored a deep blue. The red lines appeared to be the barrier wall of the shelter. The green lines were the passages inside, but the blue line only touched a red line in one place and then moved on in the direction of another red line around a different shelter.

"This has to be the connecting tunnel," she said.

"What are these gray squares?" asked Henry. He put a finger on one, and she saw there was a number and a letter on it. It reminded her of something she had seen once a long time ago when she was studying a map.

"It has to be a reference point. Look at the edges of the map. The map is in grids, and that gray square is A26. If I'm correct, A26 will appear on another map, and we'll be seeing a different level in the shelter. This other number on the upper right corner of the map is the level number." She pointed at it and saw they were reading a map of level six, and a big number at the top of the map in the center meant they were lost likely in shelter number fifty.

Henry probably didn't need to tell her that he pointed at that particular gray square because the red line and the blue line touched each other at the gray square. She saw it too.

"I think those are more than reference points, Henry. I think they may be stairwells."

Henry reacted the way anyone would. While they had been studying the map, he had been orienting himself in relation to the different colored lines and how far they had walked. His body rotated at the waist until he saw what he was looking for. A doorway was only about twenty feet away from them, and it was possibly stairwell A26. If it was, it would have an exit into the central corridor that connected all of the shelters.

"Bring the map," he said. She scooped it from the desk, and they walked to the door. It pushed outward easily, and the beams from Henry's helmet shot into the pitch dark blackness of a stairwell. It also revealed another door directly across the landing, and if they were right, it would lead them to the central corridor. For some reason, that felt important. They could worry about why later.

23

Witnesses

Huntsville - Year Seven

People were already watching the skies when the Soyuz capsule came back to Earth because of the storms that had brought destruction to the countryside. The entire population of Farley stood riveted by the sight, but to the people who were most interested, there was no time to waste. The crew had to be captured and dealt with quickly.

"I won't have any martyrs on my hands," shouted the Sheriff. "It's hard enough to keep these people under control. All I need is for them to start having hope again, and no one will listen. Everyone will want to do their own thing."

The Sheriff wasn't far from the landing site, but the tornado had blocked the roads in just enough places to keep him and his men from getting there quickly. If this had been a normal day, maybe he would've already been in the shelter complex, but as soon as the storms had passed through he had rushed in the opposite direction. The reports about the Chief had been relayed to him, and he had dispatched his soldiers to pick up the Chief's friends, but he never in a lifetime expected the Soyuz capsule to return at the same time. He had decided to go to the river and had left minutes before when the capsule appeared. When he ordered his driver to get him to the landing site as quickly as he could, he had made another tactical mistake and gotten their jeep stuck by pushing the driver too hard.

By the time he had arrived on the hill just above the Soyuz, a dozen or more of his men were around the capsule. They were arguing about whether or not to open it, but they hadn't settled the argument before the Sheriff appeared. If they had opened the capsule, he would have shot them.

"Are they inside?"

His question wasn't aimed at anyone in particular, so no one answered at first. He painfully turned to face each of them with the same expression that said he was waiting, and everyone started speaking at once.

"Shut up! You two guys get up there and get that hatch open."

The two men he pointed at didn't waste a moment getting up onto the capsule. They pulled at the door, but it wouldn't budge. Like most people, none of them had a clue how to open it. Someone produced a crowbar and tossed it to them, and they found that it was just stuck. It popped free under their combined weight, and the crowd of soldiers cheered.

The Sheriff didn't know what to expect, but he was worried about his soldiers joining the hero worship bandwagon. He resisted yelling at them to stop cheering, but it was only through willpower that he was able to restrain himself. One of the two men had dropped flat to his stomach and had the upper half of his body hanging inside the capsule. The second man had maneuvered around to where he could hold onto the man's legs.

Inside the Soyuz the soldier was surprised to find only one astronaut strapped into a seat. The astronaut had his helmet on with the sun visor closed, so the soldier couldn't see what was happening inside. It didn't register in the soldier's mind that the guttural sounds coming from behind that visor were the snarls and growls of an infected dead. His lack of understanding of the virus that had caused the apocalypse kept him from realizing that the astronauts had not been immune to the disease. He simply thought the helmet was preventing him from understanding what the man was saying in there. As for the hands that pulled at the soldier as he unstrapped the astronaut, he thought the man was panicking and wanted to be freed from the confines of the capsule.

A second cheer went up as the man emerged from the capsule with his arms wrapped around the upper body of someone in a spacesuit. The man holding his legs slid to the ground and pulled the other soldier with him. All three slipped from the top of the capsule to the ground in a heap, and more soldiers rushed in to help.

Doing their best to ensure the safety of the astronaut, they were too quick to help and too slow to understand the way he grabbed at them. They thought he wanted out, so that's what they did for him. Eager hands reached in and rotated the locking ring on the helmet, and as soon as it was free, other hands lifted it away.

The screams that followed were more like shouts of warning, but one scream continued to pierce the ears of everyone close to the action. The thing inside the spacesuit had ripped away a sizable piece of an arm, and the victim was venting his pain. Blood splashed from a severed artery onto the white spacesuit, and everyone within that circle who had tried to help crawled on all fours in every direction.

The Sheriff stood on the opposite side of the capsule when it started and moved uphill for a better view. With his feet apart and his fists planted on his hips, he very much looked the part of a drill sergeant who was unhappy with his recruits. Inside his mind he was anything but unhappy. He had hoped the landing would kill the occupants, but he hadn't really believed it would.

"What about the others?" he yelled.

It took a minute for anyone to answer, but the man who had pulled the astronaut free finally responded in a hesitant voice.

"He was the only one inside, Sheriff. There's no one else."

The man thought the messenger was definitely going to be shot, and he was surprised by the Sheriff's answer.

"Someone put that thing out of its misery."

As an afterthought he added, "And him too."

He pointed at the man who was bleeding out after getting bitten.

"The rest of you get that thing loaded onto a truck and carry it down to Farley so everyone can get a good look. Be sure to spread the word that only one of them made it back, and he was killed in the crash."

The Sheriff was so happy with the turn of events he almost forgot to ask who it was inside the spacesuit. He called over his shoulder to the man who had just reached down and pushed a blade into the dead astronaut, "Which one was it?"

The man appeared to be unsure at first, thinking back to a day over seven years ago when he had seen pictures of the astronauts.

"It looks like that Callaway fellow, Sir."

That satisfied the Sheriff even more. The other two were probably dead already, but it was worth it to know Adam Callaway was. The Sheriff figured he was the only one he really had to worry about because everyone had loved the handsome astronaut. He didn't bother to hide his smile.

******

"He sure seems happy about that astronaut being dead," said Cassandra. She handed the binoculars to Sim, and he nodded after only a few seconds.

Hank spit out a mouthful of tobacco juice and wiped his mouth with his sleeve.

"We could shoot him from here and not miss."

Cassandra shook her head. "We don't really do things that way. He might be the only person standing between us and the location of our friends."

"Well, I do work that way," said Hank.

If not for Hazel, Hank would have opened up from the back of their truck with the M134. She reached over and pulled the barrel away from its target. He was right that he couldn't miss from that range, but until they knew where the Sheriff had stashed their friends, they needed him alive. It was also useful to see where he went when he left the landing site because he was walking instead of going back to the vehicles.

"I think the Sheriff is using a shelter as his headquarters," she said. "He's walking at an angle toward the dirt road."

Cassandra watched through her binoculars and saw that a messenger approached the Sheriff with a piece of paper. She didn't know what was written on it that could make him so mad, but he did what any bully would do. He smacked the messenger across the face. There was no way she could know for sure, but a wry smile crossed her own face as the thought occurred to her that her friends were probably the reason for his sudden fury. They had a habit of getting people mad like that.

"Something's got the Sheriff worked up," said Sim.

"I can see that. Can you keep him in sight so we can see where he goes?"

"Sure. He's walking again. Whatever it was that got him mad, he's going in the same direction as before."

Sim hopped down from the bed of the Silverado where he had been perched next to Cassandra and ran further up the hill. They had found a nice overgrown cemetery on the side of a long sloping hill, and it had given them a good view of the shelter complex. Hiding the vehicles was easy, and they decided it was a good place for an overwatch when the time came. With two M134s, they had a surprise firepower advantage, and the key to rescuing their friends was not to use it too soon. Shooting the Sheriff would be a loss of their advantage.

Cassandra guessed Sim was going for higher ground so he could watch where the Sheriff went because they couldn't see him between the biggest mounds. Taking the trucks to higher ground also meant moving further away from the shelters, so they had chosen the lower location.

Sim was only gone for fifteen minutes. Either he had lost the Sheriff, or the Sheriff had finally been caught doing what they had hoped. Judging by Sim's smile, she felt like she knew which of the two things had happened.

"He went into that shelter," said Sim. He helped Cassandra locate the correct mound with her binoculars. "Walked right inside."

Cassandra had worked on a fairly accurate map she had drawn that had the mounds in neat rows and shaped like extended ovals, sort of oblong and tapered. She leaned over the drawing and put a big X on one of the ovals.

"Good work. Now that we know where he goes, we can keep an eye on that shelter."

Sim asked, "What if he comes and goes through different entrances? These things are supposed to be overlapping, right?"

"He could be," she admitted, "but he most likely fancies himself as a strategist, and it would be more to his advantage to keep the locations of those entrances to himself. That's what I would do."

Sim had learned a long time ago that Cassandra Gibbs had almost supernatural instincts. If her gut told her the Sheriff limited himself to one shelter entrance, then he probably did.

Hazel tapped on the side rail of their truck to get their attention.

"What's the plan, Honey?"

"We have a good position here. We know where the Sheriff goes now, and we know which direction the astronauts took. I think Sim and I should go after the astronauts. I'm not exactly sure why, but I think that's the thing to do. At the very least, I think the Sheriff was happy that one was dead, so maybe he wants the same for the other two. I also have some small hope that the astronauts will lead us to the super shelter that's located somewhere in this complex."

Hank asked, "Do you think they know where it is?"

"I don't know. Maybe, probably not, but it wouldn't hurt to find out. If they do know or if they can help us find it, then that's where I would expect our friends to be."

Cassandra had no way of knowing if their friends had been kept together or if they had been split up. What she did know was that the Chief had told her a long time ago what to do if they ever got separated. He told her the key to a unit getting back together was for every member of that dispersed unit to assess the terrain and find the best place for a strategic overwatch. If they all thought the same way, Cassandra knew they would all like the spot she had picked. From where they were hidden, they would be able to see anyone who tried to reach their spot.

"That's why we're glad we have you two helping us, Hazel. Sim and I can go after the astronauts while you and Hank hold this high ground."

Hank asked, "What if the rest of your group shows up before you get back?"

"You'll know them if you see them. Trust me. You'll know the Chief by his size. As for the rest of them, Kathy's blonde hair next to Colleen's red hair should be enough, but the silver hair on the Chief's wife is something I would kill for."

Sim couldn't help himself. "That would be a good look for you."

Cassandra tried her best to give Sim a frown but couldn't pull it off.

She said, "Let's get after those astronauts before someone else finds them, and while we still have enough daylight to track them."

As Cassandra and Sim worked their way down the hill toward the highway that separated the cemetery from the shelter complex, Hazel took over at the sights of the M134 in their truck. Hank stayed at their gun and tracked their progress to the highway. If they were spotted crossing the road, the M134s would be able to cover their escape.

The cover was good enough for them to stay hidden until they reached the big drainage ditch that ran parallel to the highway. It was four lanes with a wide median, but seven years of growth and new encroachment by shrubs meant they only had to hurry across the paved portions. They stayed low and crossed quickly. Even though Hank knew exactly where they should be, he lost them as soon as they were into the median, and he didn't spot them again until they popped out on the other side. Just as quickly as they had reappeared, they crossed the next two lanes and disappeared into the other drainage ditch.

When they reached the bottom of the drainage ditch on the far side of the road, Cassandra stayed in the ditch and headed west with Sim following close behind. She didn't want to come out of their cover too close to where the capsule had landed, and the astronauts had used a road between the shelters that also went more or less to the west. After she felt like they had gone far enough to avoid detection, Cassandra signaled Sim with hand gestures to follow her to the fence that bordered the shelter complex.

The fence was old, but it was heavy chainlink with concertina wire at the top. On the other side of the fence, a berm had been raised along the entire perimeter so they couldn't see over the fence to know what was there. For all they knew, the berm was also the top of a shelter.

Cassandra produced a pair of wire cutters and clipped just enough wires to create an entrance that she could pull in place behind them. They didn't need any unwanted company following them through, and they also could save time leaving if they remembered where they had entered.

The whole operation only took a few minutes, and they tied off their escape door with a colorful piece of string so they could spot it on the return trip.

"Do you carry stuff like that around with you or magically pull it out of thin air?" asked Sim.

"You don't?" answered Cassandra.

"You didn't answer my question," said Sim.

"I don't plan to," was all she said back.

Sim mumbled under his breath as they weaved their way toward the only gap they could see in the berm.

When they reached the gap, Cassandra signaled for him to cover her as she ventured into the space between two shelters that sat side by side. Their raised walls towered above her on each side, and she knew she would be totally exposed if anyone used the road that crossed in front of the shelters.

She reached the road and dropped to the ground along the side of the shelter on her left. After listening for a moment she eased far enough out to see left and right. It was all clear, so she motioned for Sim to move up. When he laid down in the grass next to her, he could see the shelters spreading out across the fields. It felt so different being between them than when he had seen them from the cemetery. They were more real somehow.

"We might as well start trying doors," she said.

"I don't think we'll need to try too many," said Sim.

When she turned his way, he pointed at the muddy road. Even from a prone position she could see what he meant. There weren't many footprints that would compete with those made by a spacesuit boot, and there were two distinctively different sets of prints that led straight to the shelter on their right.

"I guessed right," she said. "They must've known they were in danger when they got out of the capsule. Otherwise they would've just waited for someone to arrive, or maybe they waited to go into a shelter after putting some distance between themselves and the shelter they chose."

"There are over three hundred shelters out here," said Sim. "How did you guess this one?" He gestured at the door where the footprints stopped.

"It's just what I would have done. Maybe they know something about the shelters, or maybe they just felt like they were in danger outside. Whatever drove them inside, my guess was they would try doors until one opened and there was no chorus of groans from inside."

In less than two minutes they were at the door and pulling it open. Bright lights lit the stairs that dove downward, and there was no sound. They listened together, but when their eyes met, both shook their heads. They weren't going to learn anything standing at the top of the ladder listening.

"This reminds me of that stupid ship," said Cassandra.

"The hospital ship you were on when it all started?"

"Yeah, steep stairs that seemed to be more for decoration than anything else because they're too damned steep. I think the soldiers probably slid down them by kicking their feet out in front of them while pressing their hands into the metal handrails."

As if to prove her point, that's what she decided to do, and she slid down the long stairs as if she had been doing it her whole life.

"I must be crazy," said Sim as he pulled the door shut behind him and assumed a position at the top of the stairs like a ski jumper poised for a jump.

When he threw his feet out in front of him he couldn't believe the speed that he traveled to the bottom, and his only hope was that he had given Cassandra enough time to clear out of the way. At the back of his mind was also the thought about a line from a movie he had seen a long time ago. It was something about two men jumping from a cliff into a river. One of them said he couldn't swim, and the other one said not to worry about it because the fall would kill him.

That was how Sim felt as the floor seemed to be rushing upward at him. He hit the bottom at a much slower speed than he thought he had been traveling, and Cassandra was there to help him make a smooth landing.

It was obvious immediately that this particular shelter had been picked clean, and the lack of supplies also said unspoken volumes about it likely being free of the infected dead. Whoever had emptied the valuable food and equipment from this shelter would have also mopped up the undead population. There weren't even any human remains to stink up the place.

Cassandra said it for both of them.

"The Sheriff already picked this one clean, which is probably good news for us because we won't have to worry as much about running into dead or live people."

Sim nodded and added one sobering thought that hadn't occurred to Cassandra yet.

"If he's had time to empty this and maybe a few other shelters, then he knows a lot more about them than we do. We want to find our friends and the super shelter, but as big as the super shelter would be, it's going to be like a needle in a haystack, and if the Sheriff suspects its existence, he's been looking for it for years."

"When did you become Negative Nancy? You know how we are. We've got that magic that rubbed off onto us from the Chief. We've already figured out where the astronauts went, and with this shelter already picked clean we can explore a little more safely."

Sim had to laugh at Cassandra's description about life with the Chief. The man had more lives than a cat, and wherever he was, he was sure the Chief was making life miserable for anyone who crossed him and pleasurable for someone who needed a helping hand.

******

The scramble in the darkness to get from one level of the shelter to the next was like a suicide run down a tunnel full of snakes. The dim light they used was only enough for the lead runner on the stairs to see their own feet, but the run had been so fast and reckless that most of them didn't even know who was in the lead.

It was Hampton, and he tried to rely on muscle memory more than his eyes or his feet. He didn't even know how many levels they had run down. He just kept up the pace until the only sound was their shoes on the metal steps. It was like a descent into hell. The Chief brought them to a stop with a sharp but short whistle. They almost piled up on Hampton's back in near total darkness, but they were all glad to stop.

As the Chief came into the huddle they all hugged him with relief that everyone was still in one piece. They were still missing Cassandra and Sim, but they were all hopeful about their safety and would stay that way until there was information to the contrary.

"We can talk more when we get to a really secure place, but I learned the hard way that the Sheriff's people haven't cleared every level of the shelters they have under their control. Some of the levels are just too crowded with the infected. So consider every level as dangerous no matter how safe it seems."

Everyone murmured their understanding, and Hampton asked, "Where to from here?"

The Chief's big hand found Hampton's shoulder in the dark and gave him a squeeze.

"Buddy, you were making some good time in the turns, and I was having a hard time keeping count, but if I'm right we're on a level that I used earlier. If we're not, just be ready for anything. If we're in the right place, we're next to a door that opens into a corridor that's clean."

Standing under a blanket of such total darkness was almost suffocating, and Hampton was happy to turn on the small flashlight he had used to guide their descent. He shone it outward in an arc, not sure if he was facing a wall or the next set of stairs. The door was straight ahead and a little to his right, but it was on the same level with them.

"Is that your door, Chief?"

"They all look alike," he answered, "but we can't keep going up or down. Sooner or later we have to get out of this stairwell before they check here. I'm surprised they haven't checked here yet."

The Chief moved ahead of Hampton and eased the door open. It was quiet in the darkness beyond the door, so he went through. He switched on a much more powerful flashlight and exposed the whole room. It was a lot like a cafeteria with a buffet style serving line and tables scattered around the room. Old food had long ago become the ash colored substance that filled the bins of the serving line. Behind the counter there were still stacks of coffee mugs and glasses for drinks. Whatever happened in this shelter, the cafeteria had been abandoned before everything went crazy.

"There's still power in most of the shelters. Don't ask me where it comes from, but if I had to guess, it would have something to do with the military and NASA working out some kind of deal with the Tennessee Valley Authority. Remember the seaplanes at the country club. The same people had probably worked up here in Huntsville."

The Chief flipped a light switch and temporarily blinded everyone. There were some good natured shouts about warning everyone first, but they were all grateful for the light instead of the darkness that hid so many different ways to die.

"Let's all catch our breath and talk about our next move," said the Chief. He pulled chairs together around a couple of tables, and they all gladly accepted the opportunity to take a break.

"Do we have a plan?" asked Kathy.

"You know me," said the Chief. "Of course we have a plan. I just haven't finished it yet."

Hampton couldn't resist egging the Chief on.

"Everything has gone according to plan. The Chief knew if he escaped the Sheriff would have his people bring us to the shelters where he could help us escape. The only thing I want to know is how he knew which shelter we would be in because there are hundreds of them out here."

"That really wasn't such a hard thing to figure out," said the Chief. "The soldiers use the same routes to get to this shelter. All I had to do was get inside a shelter next door and then work my way over to this one. I have to tell you, though. These things are mazes. They started out with one basic design, but people can't resist modifying spaces. That worked out for me because I could memorize the route I took by little changes."

"How bad is the infected population?" asked Tom.

The Chief let out a low whistle and said, "Really bad. The shelters are so big that they probably haven't even tapped out one of them yet. If they have, they certainly haven't finished looting two. The place is a treasure trove that could support a city if it was distributed properly."

Iris leaned against the Chief, obviously relieved to see him again. She said, "We've seen how they decide who gets the good stuff from the shelters. Officers and a few favorite people get everything while the general population of Farley lives on catfish and cornbread. Not that those two things are so bad for you, but catfish are bottom feeders that prefer rotten meat, so I imagine they eat a lot of the infected that fall in the river."

They had all been forced to eat catfish since arriving in Farley. It was either that or starve. On the plus side, some of the people in Farley had been eating river catfish for years, and none had shown any ill effects from the feeding habits of the catfish.

Colleen added, "From what we've heard, people have been eating better because of your fishing skills, Chief. We heard about the new blacksmith who everyone loves…especially the women."

The Chief put on a mock glare and used a stern voice at Hampton.

"Get your woman in line, Sir. I made it clear to the women folk that I was spoken for."

They all shared a moment of laughter that had been a long time coming. The Chief had counted on them to be patient, and before they had been captured, he had stressed how important it was to wait for an opportunity and not force it. Now it had paid off, but the wait had been harder on them than it was on him. Being solo meant he only had to control his own behavior. The rest of the group had to keep each other in control.

"We spied on you once," said Kathy.

"I know," grinned the Chief. "Everyone around my part of town couldn't wait to tell me."

"Do you think Cassandra and Sim are okay?" asked Colleen.

The Chief nodded. "Remember the plan? If anyone got separated from the rest of the group, they would make their way to the best overwatch position above the Marshall Space Flight Center. They would find some high ground, secure it, and hold it until we need their cover."

Kathy said with a smile, "No one could ever accuse you of being a pessimist. The last time we saw those two they were making their escape with their hands tied behind their backs. At least one or two heavily armed trucks were sent after them."

The Chief nodded in acknowledgment. "If I was one of the guys they sent after them, I would've found a couple of infected that resembled them and hauled their bodies back. You know why? It would have turned out better for them than if they caught up with Cassandra and Sim. Especially if they caught Cassandra. Catching her without getting themselves killed is not on my list of possibilities. My money is on them finding a way to reach the overwatch position, but mostly I have to believe they succeeded because it's one of the things that keeps me going."

"Where are we going to go from here," asked Tom.

"I admit my plans are a bit short term right now, but the goal has to be to get into the shelter, and our biggest problem is not knowing where the shelter is. For now, we have to explore and use our collective brains to figure out this puzzle. If we find the entrance or the back door, then we can go inside and see what we've got."

Kathy had a quizzical expression as she said, "You plan to take down the Sheriff and liberate the people in Farley, don't you."

"It's not going to be impossible," he answered. "There isn't exactly a revolution brewing in Farley, but there will be when they find out what's inside the shelters. All we have to do is make sure we get to the right people, and my guess is that the NCO's are the right people. I saw something in their faces every time I got near one. They're good soldiers, and they don't like what their officers have become."

"You would have been the one to see that," said Kathy. "So, the plan is to get inside the Titus Rush shelter, then to recruit Army NCO's for a little mutiny. I can't wait to hear the rest."

"I do have one idea I haven't told you about. I know where the back door is."

24

Saturn V

Huntsville - Year Seven

Moving such a large group of people through the cramped corridors of the Cold War shelters was a conspicuous operation. Some of the hallways were clearly main thoroughfares, while others were barely wide enough for two people to walk side by side. Nothing in the design seemed to make sense, but a pattern emerged when Colleen spotted a sign that was similar to another she had seen. They had been moving in silence because the lighting was sporadic, and the darkened areas were the worst places to encounter the infected.

The group was strung out in a line with Kathy up front and Tom trailing the pack watching for possible infected closing off their path of escape if they came to an area they couldn't cross. So far they had only come across small groups of the infected, and they had quickly eliminated them. Experience told them it didn't always go that way, and sooner or later they would run into a horde that was too large to fight through.

The inevitable happened when Kathy held up a closed fist and took several steps backward at the same time. Whatever she saw in front of her, it had the same effect as walking into the path of a charging lion. The group bunched up fast, but at the middle Iris pushed open a door into a stairwell, and everyone slipped through quickly. Their rule was that the person who was forced into taking an alternate route would also be the person to take the lead. They had also agreed they would go up whenever possible.

Iris took the stairs two at a time and eased open the first door she came to. She could have kept going, but they had also agreed that it would be more difficult to fight their way out of a stairwell if they were faced with locked doors. So, they always chose the first door that was unlocked. It was Hampton's job to keep track of their upward progress, and he called out in a low voice that they were plus three. It was a slow process that had gone negative twice, but this time they had gained the highest number upward so far.

Colleen went through the door close behind Iris, and she saw the sign by the door. She thought back to others she had seen and realized there was a similarity. She held up a fist and tapped Iris on the shoulder at the same time. Iris immediately dropped to a knee with a closed fist. It would give her a chance to let her eyes adjust to what was up ahead, and whatever Colleen stopped her for would be passed along the line. Colleen turned to the next person in line behind her. This time it was Hampton. The Chief loomed over his shoulder, and behind him were Tom and Kathy. They waited as Colleen explained the signs.

"The first number might be the shelter number. I noticed when we moved laterally long enough that we went through a long hallway that had a sign on it that said 22-3. After we passed the sign there was another sign with arrows on it going left and right. The numbers started with 22, so I think that's the shelter number. It was followed by 3, so that's the level. The next numbers were room numbers because they were in ranges. The sign we just went by in the stairwell said 25-1. I think the stairwell only kept going upward because it connects with another shelter, but if we're on level 1, there will be an exit somewhere on this level."

"Good job. What was the number range on the last sign? Stands to reason that we should go toward the lowest numbers."

"That would be behind us," said Kathy, "but they don't go all the way down to the number 1."

"Remember," said Tom, "sometimes people start with 100."

"The military does that," said the Chief.

"In that case, the main entrance is back that way."

Their optimism about finding the main entrance was enough to drive them forward at a fast pace. They were all tired, but they had the endurance born of years of survival driving them on. It was almost a mistake.

The main floor of level one was the floor where the entrance stairs dropped down to the ground at a steep angle, but before they got to that room, they had to go through what many had found to be the biggest mistake made by the shelter operators. The hospitals were all on the first level, and many people had died in them on the first day. Before Kathy could signal the group to stop, they were all inside the hospital.

The first days of the spread of the pandemic were chaotic and terrifying everywhere, but in the confines of the shelters it was a dark nightmare. The scarlet stains on the walls had turned black over the years, and the blackness seemed to absorb all of the light, but there was no way to hide the apparitions that arose from the floors and beds. It was unusual to see the infected doing anything except standing around in groups or walking aimlessly from one corner of a room to the next. So many of these infected had died in their beds when they were attacked by the others. They were the food that had fed the spread of the infection, and it was their arterial spray that had painted the walls. Because they were so mutilated by the infected that could reach them, their bodies had restricted them to their beds ever since, but the arrival of living flesh within close proximity galvanized even the worst of them.

The infected that fell from their beds crawled on elbows. Those without arms moved almost as snakes would. They were slow, but they also weren't the majority. The majority emerged from every corner, every cubicle, and every aisle. The number of them between the six survivors and the main entry room of the shelter was beyond their guess, and as they bunched up at the entrance to the hospital, the numbers grew.

The Chief reacted first. He grabbed Kathy by her upper arms and pulled her back to face him.

"Get everyone behind me and secure an area a few doors back from the stairwell entrance. If you can control our six, I can deal with everything in front of us."

Kathy had no idea what the Chief planned to do, but she knew better than to doubt him. She pushed the rest of the group to retreat down the hall until they were past the stairwell entrance. The Chief followed until he got to the stairwell, and the infected filled the hallway to follow them. Kathy saw him duck into the stairwell, and her first thought was that he planned to lead the infected from the hospital down the stairs. She wondered what made him think they would follow him when they could just keep walking toward the rest of them, but she had scarcely finished the thought when he reappeared.

The Chief was one of the few people Kathy had ever seen who was a physical specimen even at his age, but despite everything she had ever seen him do, she was still amazed. When he came back through the door, he brought the door with him. Apparently, it was only a minor inconvenience that the door opened into the stairwell rather than into the narrow hallway. Using brute strength, the Chief ripped the door from its frame and brought it back into the hallway. He placed himself in the center of the hallway and held the door up like a shield just as the infected arrived.

Kathy took the liberty of a slightly longer look and saw the Chief brace himself behind the door. The infected built up their numbers on the other side until the door leaned forward under their weight. The Chief put one foot way behind him, and it seemed the door would fall onto him as his feet began to slide. The Chief suddenly gave a great push forward, and as the wall of bodies moved in the other direction, he let the door lean toward the open doorway to the stairs. Infected fell through the opening. Some tumbled down the stairs on the initial push, and some even hit the top rail and flipped over it.

The Chief quickly backed away to let the next wave of the infected pile up against the door. This time he didn't wait as long because he didn't want any to have the chance to come back into the hallway from the stairwell. His second push seemed to clear an even larger number of the infected than the first, and a larger number of them were permanently removed because they tripped over the dead that were piled up on the landing. Some were moving so fast from the Chief's push that they seemed to almost dive over the railing.

Kathy could have watched the ex-Navy SEAL all day long, but behind the place where the Chief was making a stand, the rest of the group had engaged a sizable group of the infected themselves. Kathy joined in with her long knife instead of her machete. There wasn't enough room to swing the big blade. In one motion she drew the knife and shoved it upward through the soft bottom of the chin of the nearest infected that was reaching for Tom. Her blade had hardly left the first one before it was having to be pried from the head of the second. As a group they were all doing it the way they had from the beginning. They used patience and control, and they eventually ran out of targets.

When they turned back to the hallway where the Chief was holding the pass like the Spartans at the Battle of Thermopylae they were surprised to see he was gone. No one had seen him go through the door with the infected dead, but Kathy ran straight toward the opening. He was nowhere in sight, and the landing was stacked at least four deep with bodies at the top. Dozens more were on the next landing down and scattered on the stairs in twisted positions.

"Coming through!"

Kathy dodged out of the way just as the Chief rounded the corner from the hospital. With the door still held out in front, he bumped against a half dozen of the infected that were alternating between reaching around the door and trying to keep their balance. The Chief bumped just hard enough to keep them moving, and as one fell over backward, Kathy caught it by the collar of its ratty sweatshirt and guided it in over the rail. The other five stayed on their feet and kept reaching until they found themselves stepping on bodies and backed up against the railing of the landing. Kathy reached around and thrust at them with her knife until they were all down.

The rest of the group moved past the open stairwell to attack the remaining infected in the hospital, and when Kathy and the Chief joined the fight, they were mopping up the last of them and taking the attack to a few stragglers in the first room at the bottom of the stairs.

"If you had told me your plan, I would've shot you to keep you from doing it," said Kathy.

The Chief put on his best innocent face and said, "It worked, didn't it?"

Hampton was the first to go up the steps, but as he passed by the Chief he said, "If you had told me fifteen minutes ago that we would be getting out of the shelter up these steps, I would've said you're crazy, but I'm with Kathy. That was crazy, Chief."

The others fell in behind Hampton and climbed the steep stairs. When he reached the top the door was locked from the inside, and a rusty steel bar was laid across it in steel braces. It was no wonder that no one had cleared this shelter yet, and if a lot of the shelters were barred from the inside, they would be hard to clear. In the close confines at the top of the stairs, Hampton strained to lift the rusty bar free without making noise. It grated in protest but moved enough for him to get some momentum, and it lifted free.

He only opened the door about an inch, and the first thing that hit him was the crisp, clean smell of the air. He was tempted to throw open the door and just drink it in, but he kept it right where it was and just breathed through his nose. The air was humid and wet, but it was refreshing. He felt a poke from behind.

"Enjoying yourself?" Colleen leaned around where she could see the smile on his face.

"Sorry. I'm just making sure it's clear."

"If you say so," she grumbled.

It was quiet long enough for Hampton to open the door a few more inches, and he put his face through the gap.

"I think we're in business folks."

Hampton flipped the door open all the way, and as they followed him out into the open, they knew they were standing at a place where history had been made. They had traveled far enough underground to reach the Saturn V test gantries. This was where the rocket boosters that carried men to the moon were tested.

The Chief got a broad grin on his face and announced, "Ladies and gentlemen, I give you the back door to the super shelter."

******

The Saturn V test gantry had been converted into a tourist attraction years before the end of the world, and on that day there had been a large number of tour buses surrounding it. Since there was a scheduled launch of two crews on the same day, the attraction had increased the size of the crowd by installing large screens outside. The idea was to broadcast the launch, but what the tourists had seen were news broadcasts about the cannibalistic attacks around the world. The people gathered near the screens had turned to each other for answers and then to their hosts. To their horror, their hosts didn't have a clue about what was happening in either the cities where the attacks were happening on a large scale or at their own launch site at the Cosmodrome.

When the gunshots rang out in the parking lots at the front of the Marshall Space Flight center, people at the Saturn V gantry could only ask what was happening because it seemed so far away. Being located in the southern portion of the shelter complex, they were shielded from the view of the attacks by the tall buildings of NASA, and like anyone who didn't expect the sound of gunshots, they wrote it off as fireworks celebrating the launch. They wondered about fireworks in the morning hours, but it made more sense than soldiers shooting people who were eating their coworkers. They aimed their cameras and smartphones in the direction of the gunshots and waited hopefully to catch something memorable.

What they got on their pictures and videos was memorable, but not for the right reasons. People who weren't ushered toward shelters by the soldiers spilled over into the parking lots and fields on the other side of the fence from safety. Everything they saw happening on the big screens they saw happening only a few blocks away, and it was coming toward them.

Some of the tourists retreated to the safety of the buses while others rushed inside the small information center poised next to the Saturn V gantry. In a matter of minutes the information center was overrun by strange people who moved like apparitions but seemed to possess the will to move forward against all threats. When the security guards at the tourist attraction pulled their handguns from their holsters and ordered them to stay back, they were ignored. When they pulled the triggers, the apparitions were knocked over, but they got back up and continued forward.

Two of the people who had been shot climbed aboard a bus before the driver could pull the door shut. Within seconds the windows and the ceiling air vents were flying open, and people spilled from the sides of the bus. The air vents were too small for the overweight people who had tried to climb through them, and at first they only yelled for someone to help them. One was a man who was stuck in the vent toward the front of the bus. His pleas for help became incoherent screams to stop as people ate freely on the lower half of his body. When he stopped screaming, the woman stuck in the second air vent started where he left off. The man slumped over and hung limply in the vent as the woman screamed at the unseen teeth ripping her bare legs apart. She pounded on the roof with her fists and shook violently, but eventually she slumped over just as the man did.

Some of the tourists ran to the south in the direction of the Tennessee River. Whatever longevity that gave them was dependent upon where they went after that, but some of them realized the same thing a few others around the buses did. There were no cannibals on the other side of the fence around the shelters. None of them knew the mounds were shelters, but the fence was protection, so they climbed. When they reached the strands of concertina wire at the top, one of the youngest men did something incredible. He pulled off his belt as he climbed, and with agility he might have developed doing rock climbing, he ran his belt through several of the loops and then drew them tightly together. The gap in the concertina wire was all they would need for a mass exodus over the chainlink fence, and a large contingent of tourists converged on the nearest shelter door.

That was years ago, and now Hampton stood in that same door with the others all squeezing out around him. The fence was still there, and there was still a gap in the concertina wire. Buses were parked in a semicircle around the information center.

The Chief pointed at the fence and said, "People came over the fence there. They must have felt so much safer if they got into these shelters, and maybe they would've stayed alive if the people running the shelter had kept people out if they had bite wounds."

"The back door of the Titus Rush shelter is in there?" asked Tom. "Do you know where?"

"Before we left Guntersville I sat down with Bus and checked the plans for this one. The information center was labeled as the back door, but Bus said he was suspicious about it."

Kathy asked, "Why? It's probably going to be easy to find because that building is so small."

"When's the last time you saw a back door to one of these things get easy? Even if we walk right up to the door it's going to be something we have to solve," answered the Chief.

Kathy pressed him about it and asked, "Bus didn't give you the combination?"

"He said this one had a note written where the code would be on his original list. It said real survivors would know the code when they see the lock."

"Great," said Colleen. "Another puzzle lock to figure out. Let's do this."

It was downhill to the fence, so they walked at a brisk pace aided by gravity. In the distance they could see Farley sprawled out along the edge of the Tennessee River. Another fence marked the perimeter of the Marshall Space Flight Center, and about a half mile away they could see that it joined up with the fence around the shelters. That fence ran in a straight line right to the river. The Chief was able to make out where he had come ashore, and he was surprised how much distance he had covered in the rain.

"Is there anything you can tell us about this place before we start searching for the door?"

Kathy had noticed something about the Chief that only she would probably notice, but the others had been around him long enough to recognize his familiar grin. It was the one he got when he was amused because he was a step ahead of everyone else.

Hampton said, "I think he has that look the cat gets after eating the canary. He's trying to look innocent."

The Chief gave in as they reached the fence and said, "Okay, I'll give you a little history while we do this, but the clock's ticking everyone. I don't want the Sheriff's people to catch us down here before we've had a chance to get inside."

Tom hit the fence running and used his athletic body to clear the tall chainlink fence in seconds. Kathy was right behind him followed by Colleen who got a leg up from Hampton before he went over. The Chief picked Iris up and lifted her almost to the top of the fence, which gave everyone a laugh. As he scaled the fence with agility that few big men could show, everyone expected the fence to collapse.

As he dropped to the ground and started walking toward the main building he told them what he thought he knew.

"The test area was actually several test gantries, but this is where the static tests were done."

He gestured toward a tall structure that seemed to be a combination of old and new.

"There's a tourist center because there was real history made here. They strapped down the big moon rockets and then fired them to measure their thrust. They were beasts, so this place had to be made like a fortress. Great place to hide a shelter. It's also a great place to build and test new rockets, so private companies have added to the test facility even though most of the other buildings were demolished."

"So the hidden entrance isn't likely to be inside the original gantry because it's been modernized," said Kathy. "I wondered why it was so new and so tall."

"Right," said the Chief, "and the visitor center isn't that much."

Tom and Hampton said almost together, "It's somewhere near the gantry and the visitor center."

Everyone stayed close together, but as a group their eyes searched for possible places to hide the entrance. It was like an outdoor museum with equipment that was all part of the Apollo program. There was a space museum a few miles away that had more displays, so this one was dedicated to the more mundane process of testing the boosters. The most interesting item on display was one of the giant Saturn V thrusters. There were five of them on each rocket, and they were immense. The power that passed through each one had to be strong enough to lift tremendous weight, so individually they were impressive. Since all of them were staring at the same thing, the Chief had to laugh.

Hampton said, "You've got to be kidding me."

They all walked to the big cone shaped thruster that was sitting with its open end facing the ground. They surrounded it trying to find the door that would allow them to go inside. The Chief walked over to the bronze sign that was embossed with a description of the Saturn V engine and the Apollo program. The NASA emblem was beautifully set in a circle at the bottom of the summary. Above it was an image of a Saturn V rocket and a single sentence.

"Mankind worked together for a mission that brought all of us closer to our goal."

The Chief reached for the NASA emblem and asked Kathy, "Remember the lock outside Ambassadors Island?"

He pushed on the NASA emblem. It went in and then came back outward until he could grip it like a knob. He put his hand around it and got a good grip. When he turned it, the image of the Saturn V turned with it. The Chief strained a bit to make it move, so they all knew it was tight, and the average person couldn't turn it without a wrench of some kind. The Chief pointed the tip of the Saturn V rocket at the word *"for"*. He stopped there and renewed his grip, turning the dial to the right. The Saturn V slowly turned until it was pointing at the word *"all"*.

Before he could begin the turn to the next word, everyone else got it. There was a collective realization as everyone waited to see what would happen when he made the long trip back to the first word of the sentence.

"If I'm right, the bell of the thruster will open briefly. Unless there's a control inside somewhere, this thing feels like a big egg timer when I turn it."

Even as the Chief explained it to them, they could see the tip of the rocket was drifting back toward its original position.

"After it opens, the timer will go back to where it started, and the opening will close."

Everyone took it as a suggestion, and they all went over to stand beside the massive engine.

Kathy called out for the group, "Ready when you are, Chief. Just don't move too slow and get yourself locked out."

"Yeah, I'll make sure I don't run over you at the door."

He got a good grip and put everything he had into turning the knob back to the left. He felt it catch on the first word as he went by and could tell it was designed to stop there if it wasn't forced to go further. The door would probably close if that happened, and then the rocket would return to its straight up position again, which was roughly at the second or third letter in the word *"mission"*.

He thought he heard the inside workings of the knob grinding as he got closer to his goal, but finally, the Saturn V rocket was pointing to the left at the word *"mankind"*.

Even from where he stood at the bronze sign, the Chief heard the metal protest as it moved for the first time in years. As a matter of fact, it hadn't moved since the shelter had been constructed around the end of the Apollo Moon program.

The Chief ran over to stand beside Kathy where she and the others stared wide-eyed as the huge thruster got even bigger. It got bigger because the cone grew in height until it was almost twice as tall as it had been. If it was big before, now it was close to the size of all five original thrusters had been together. The group of survivors had to back away as the bell of the thruster spread toward them.

When it finally stopped growing, the cone began rotating in sections, and they saw a pattern appearing. Small gaps in the metal rotated until they arrived next to similar gaps, and the black hole grew in size. The entire time the metal rotated it rubbed against itself, and it sounded like an engine moving without oil. There were groans, scrapes, and the scream of metal against metal until the opening stopped in front of them.

"Anyone need an invitation?" asked the Chief.

He ducked inside, and the others followed.

******

If it was loud outside, it was deafening inside as the metal rotated for a second time. The gaps went by, first as a large door, and then in smaller sections until it was nothing more than pinpricks of light passing by. The metal stopped moving, and it was dark.

No one spoke because this wasn't the first time they had been inside a dark room after entering a shelter. At Ambassadors Island, they had stood on a large platform not knowing when the lights came on that there would be a view over a shelter that was like a small town underground. It was where the Chief had eventually run into Iris again, so the memory of that dark landing seemed like yesterday.

Colleen was the one who broke the silence, but it was a natural reaction that even the most seasoned of them almost did.

"I'm not sure if it's my imagination, but is the light increasing?"

"It is," said Kathy. "I can see something in the outer curve on the floor of this place, so nobody move."

Everyone focused their eyes on the shapes that appeared around them, mainly the rest of the group, but there was something about the floor where Kathy saw something. It was darker and lighter at the same time. No one could see recessed lights, so the glow came from everywhere. The dark patch on the floor became more and more clear, and a railing took shape around it, obviously intended to keep anyone from falling inside it before the lights were high enough.

It was a set of stairs, and there were faintly luminescent strips on them that gave off that eerie glow they had all been able to find in the darkness.

"This is it, folks," said the Chief.

He took the lead and walked down the steps that curved gently to the right in a spiral. Following close behind him were Iris, Colleen, Hampton, Tom, and Kathy. Kathy noticed that the luminescence faded behind her as if the steps knew no one else was coming behind her. In front of them the light increased, and with every bit of brightness they knew they were nearing the bottom. It was only minutes later when they found themselves inside a brightly lit room that faced a door that had a strong resemblance to the bank vault doors on Mud Island and Fort Sumter.

"This part I know," said the Chief. "Bus told me we would need a combination after we figured out where the back door was located." He stepped up to the combination lock and spun the dial. For effect, he laid his head against the door as if he was listening to the tumblers inside.

"Oh, please," said Kathy.

Just as she said it, the Chief pulled down on the big locking lever and pulled the vault door open. The inside was also brightly illuminated, but in stark contrast to the lights, there were two women with M4s raised in their direction.

"Who are you?" said the younger one.

******

Gentry and Karen had no idea what happened inside the shelter, but it was as if it had come alive. Monitoring equipment that had never worked before suddenly turned on, and along with the screens lighting up came the alarms.

They were enjoying a peaceful breakfast of scrambled eggs, bacon, and toast. Coffee was in large supply, so they were sipping at fresh cups when the alarms scared them to death. They had never heard the alarms before, so they had no clue what they meant. All they knew was that they were deafening.

They tried screaming questions at each other over the noise, but they decided it was worthless to communicate until they found the source. Both of them got their weapons and were prepared to repel intruders, but it had been so long since they had any outside contact that they didn't know what to expect. In all their years in the shelter, they had no idea who or even what walked the surface. They didn't know if Huntsville was even still there.

They hurriedly changed from robes into jeans and sweatshirts and ran to the control room, all the while expecting to find intruders whether dead or alive. When they arrived in the room that resembled a launch control room at NASA, they immediately saw the source of the alarms, and they couldn't believe their eyes. The room was fully operational in a way they had never seen. Every screen was bright as data rolled by updating status and telemetry reports.

Unheard by Karen, Gentry asked the question, "Status and telemetry of what?"

Her answer appeared as if in answer to her question when the giant video screens displayed a spacecraft in reentry. At first the view was animated to show the real-time progress of the spacecraft, but they suddenly switched to a live video feed, and right before their eyes they witnessed the return of the ISS astronauts.

Gentry knew instinctively why there were alarms, and she flipped switches to silence them. Karen's expression was a mixture of gratitude for the silence and confusion about what was happening.

The alarms were triggered by the fact that the entry angle was too steep, but then she saw a slight burn had corrected the angle. That told her the Soyuz was being piloted rather than just falling back to Earth.

Mindful of the questions Karen wanted to ask, Gentry yelled over the ringing in her ears that the returning Soyuz must have triggered an automatic response from the main computer. The alarms were caused by corrections that needed to be made to course and entry angle.

"Where are they going to land?" yelled Karen. She was just as deaf as Gentry.

"Here! They're going to land close to the Space Flight Center, practically on top of us!"

Gentry was just as shocked as Karen, and her mind was already racing to answer the question that Karen was shouting even before she asked it.

"How can that happen? How can they get so close without telemetry?"

"The computers must've sent them telemetry even if they didn't know it. They must have decided to land here because they knew we were here. That means they haven't had contact with other installations, and that scares me more than you know."

"ISS crew, this is Gentry Campbell at the Marshall Space Flight Center. Do you read me, over?"

On the main screens they saw the Soyuz grow in size and then the chutes deployed. The cameras followed the spacecraft as it descended, but for some reason they didn't follow the capsule all the way to the ground. It passed out of view at the bottom of the screen, and the last thing they saw was the top of a main chute before it settled to the ground. Gentry felt helpless and hailed the Soyuz repeatedly, but there was nothing. All she got was an alert on a screen that said Contact Terminated.

"What should we do?"

Karen seemed ready to charge outside to the landing site. If anyone was likely to be so foolish, it was Gentry, but she understood the reality of the situation.

"Nothing. There's nothing we can do. We could maybe get the computers to give us the GPS location of the landing site, but it would only be accurate to within about six miles. They could be right outside, or they could be on the other side of the Tennessee River or the Elk River. They're on their own unless they contact us."

It was a day she had hoped for, but she didn't expect to be forced to watch it as a spectator, and she was afraid for the ISS crew. She imagined what it would be like when they ran into the first infected dead.

Several hours went by with the two of them waiting for any contact. Gentry resisted the urge to call out on her microphone, and when Karen asked her why, she said she really didn't know, but she had a bad feeling about giving away their location if someone else is listening.

"Who else would be listening?" asked Karen.

Gentry said, "It's just a feeling."

It was late afternoon when another alarm blared next to her, and this one scared her badly. It said the second main entrance to their shelter was open. She had never even been there. She always meant to at least check it out, but she kept putting it off.

Karen was waiting for Gentry to tell her what was happening.

"Get another gun. We have visitors."

25

Mud Island Survivors

Huntsville - Year Seven

Gentry and Karen had the advantage of knowing their way around the shelter, but neither had ever seen the big vault door open. They each got an M4 from the armory and hurried through the corridors at the back of the shelter that led to the door. They took wrong turns twice, but they still made it in time. They couldn't believe their eyes when they saw the locking wheel on the big door spin. That meant someone had entered the combination and disengaged the locking lever. They lifted their rifles and aimed them at the opening.

When the huge door swung out of the way, both of them found they were aiming too low because the ruggedly handsome man who pulled the door aside was also one of the biggest men they had ever seen. They both adjusted their aim higher, and the man didn't come closer. Instead, he gave them a smile that was one of the most charming, warmest smiles either had ever seen. People stepped up around him, and they weren't afraid of the guns pointed at them, but they all put their hands where they could be seen.

"Who are you?" asked Gentry.

She hoped she sounded menacing with her M4 in her hands and asked her question in a deeper voice than she normally used. The end result was that she sounded like a kid pretending to be older than she was. Even Karen glanced at her as if she was checking to see if Gentry was all right.

The six people standing in the open doorway all had relaxed, confident postures while the two women inside were getting nervous adrenaline shakes. Any one of the new arrivals could have spoken and helped to break the standoff, but Iris did it with a simple gesture. She stood on the right side of the group, and Gentry and Karen watched her take the big man by the arm and hold him close.

"We must be the most frightening things you've seen in a long time, but the big man here is my husband. Please don't shoot him."

Before Gentry or Karen could react, the woman with the kind face and the brilliant silver hair went on.

"His name is Joshua, but we call him the Chief because he was a Navy SEAL. My name is Iris, this is Kathy and her husband Tom. Over here we have Colleen and her husband Hampton. May we ask your names?"

Iris did the introductions so casually that they could have been the neighbors dropping by for tea, and it disarmed the two women mentally, although they kept the guns between them.

"I'm Gentry Campbell. I work, or rather worked for NASA. This is Karen Sessions."

Karen quickly added, "That's Lieutenant Karen Sessions, RN. I suppose I'm still in the Army even though I haven't seen anyone else in the Army for years."

The introductions did a lot to diffuse the tension, but it had been so long since the two women had seen another human being that they were still afraid.

"How did you unlock that door?" asked Gentry. She resumed the stern attitude and adjusted her grip on the rifle.

That made the Chief a bit nervous because he saw that both women had their index fingers inside the trigger guards, and he could see the safeties were off. He wouldn't be the first or last person who was shot just because someone took up too much slack on a trigger.

"I have the combination to the lock, Gentry."

The Chief said it naturally and called her by her name to get her to relax.

"I got the combination from one of the men who had this shelter built. It's a long story, and we can explain everything, but please at least take your finger away from that trigger. I think you'll be glad we showed up after you have a chance to get to know us."

Gentry's eyes moved from one face to the next, and all she saw was kindness. She lowered her rifle and flipped the safety on. Karen did the same with a sigh of relief that visibly spread across the six new arrivals.

"That thing was getting heavy," said Gentry. She thought she sounded pretty lame, but she added, "Welcome to our home." She wondered when she actually started thinking of it as home, but seven years was a long time.

There were a million questions for them to ask, and even though the strangers had come in from the outside and knew so much more about what was happening in the world, they had plenty of questions of their own. There was a strange familiarity about them that Gentry couldn't identify immediately, but within a few minutes of wild, overlapping chatter at the door she realized it was simply that they were all so likable. There was a level of trust and a bond between them that she longed to be part of, and for some strange reason she broke down into tears and buried her face in the big man's chest.

Karen shifted from one foot to the other like she didn't know what to do, but Iris knew what she needed. She stepped over to her and gave her a hug too. Karen didn't realize she needed the hug too, and the tears flowed down her cheeks. It became more like a reunion than a first time meeting. A reunion of human beings who had been starved of contact with other human beings.

"I'm sorry about the guns," said Gentry. "We were just startled half out of our minds this morning, and now you all showed up and actually had the code to the door."

"What happened this morning?" asked Kathy.

"You don't know? You mean you didn't see what happened?" asked Gentry. She felt something drain out of her because the Soyuz must have landed much further away than she had thought. If people outside didn't see it, it must have landed in another state altogether.

Kathy and the others just shook their heads in bewilderment. Gentry seemed to want something from them, but they had no idea what.

"You didn't see the reentry? The crew of the International Space Station came back to Earth this morning. We thought they landed somewhere near here, but if you didn't see them then they must've landed further from here than I thought. Our equipment alerted us to the reentry, but we couldn't get a good GPS location or establish radio contact."

"Wait a minute," said Tom. "Your equipment...you have communications equipment good enough to track a spacecraft?"

Gentry nodded and said, "This shelter is essentially a mission control center, but most of the equipment never worked until today. It all came on this morning, the alarms scared the hell out of us, and the Soyuz showed up. Like I said, we tried to make radio contact with them, but there wasn't an answer. I thought you would have seen the parachutes and heard the breaking thrusters fire. Kind of hard to miss."

The other two members of the new arrivals had been just soaking in the room where they had entered the shelter and had been quiet, but the man who said his name was Hampton had a small town way about him that made Karen feel drawn to him. Colleen stepped between the two when Karen seemed to move closer. Karen got the message but was disappointed. Of course Hampton missed it all.

"We weren't above ground this morning ourselves," said the Chief. "As a matter of fact, from the time that we emerged from below ground to the time that we met you, I don't think we were outside for an hour. If the Soyuz came down this morning, we missed it, but we also didn't see anything near the Saturn V gantry."

Gentry was surprised again. "Wait a minute. You mean you guys came in through the old test gantries?"

"Not exactly," said Kathy, "but near there. You didn't know where the back door is located?"

"No, we came in through an entrance located in the bottom floor of one of the shelters, and we haven't been back outside since."

The Chief asked Kathy, "Remember what Ed always told us that Titus Rush said. If you want to live, go inside your shelter and stay there."

"He also said don't open the door for anyone and definitely don't let them in," said Kathy.

"Well," answered the Chief, "he let us in."

"I think I've met Titus, but who's Ed?" asked Gentry.

"They're part of a long story, Gentry, and if you'll lead us to your kitchen, we can bring you up to speed over some of the good food I imagine Uncle Titus put in this beautiful place."

"He's your uncle?" asked Karen.

******

Gentry and Karen gave the Mud Island group a tour of the shelter, and as they did, the Chief and Kathy related the story of how they met Ed

Jackson, and how that meeting had given them safe places to live through the worst parts of the infection. Learning about the shelters built by the survivor's club run by Titus Rush gave the women some insights into the designs of their own. The shelter at the Marshall Space Flight Center had obviously been intended for the best and brightest people in the US Space Program and their families, but if it was true that each shelter was also the brainchild of a member of the survivors club, they wondered who that member was.

"Someone was supposed to be here," said Gentry. "I mean, I know the shelter was intended for NASA people and their families, but if you're telling the truth, then someone was supposed to be here who didn't make it. I wish they had made it so I could thank them for saving my life."

"One of the original members of the club is in his shelter in Guntersville," said Tom. "He was a friend even before the end of the world. So far, he's the only person we know of who made it to a shelter and lived."

"Maybe we can find out who it was when we talk with him the next time," said the Chief. "For now I think we should talk about what we plan to do with all this."

"What's that mean?" asked Karen.

They arrived in the main kitchen as they talked, and everyone spread out gathering utensils and food as if they were at home. It made Gentry and Karen a little uncomfortable. Even though they liked these strangers who had arrived out of nowhere, this had become their home, and they were hearing talk about what someone else planned to do with it.

"Everyone hold up a second," said Kathy. She noticed the way Gentry and Karen stood together yet separate from everyone else. Their home had been invaded, and now there was talk of what would be done with it.

Kathy said, "We just put the cart before the horse, and it made it sound like we're taking the shelter from you. We're not. As far as we're concerned this is your shelter, and you can make the decisions about it. What we should talk about is how the shelter will impact other survivors."

Gentry said, "I'd like for it to stay a scientific facility. I mean, sure we have room for more people inside, but it was meant for people who would advance the space program."

"I'm sorry if I came across like it was anyone's decision except yours," said the Chief. "We can help you make that happen, but I guess I have two questions about how you plan to do that. First, you have space inside for a couple of hundred people at least. Second, how can this place be a way to preserve any of the space program?"

"There's a third issue," said Kathy. "Someone has to deal with that despot, or whatever it is you call him who's in control on the surface."

Gentry surprised all of them by saying, "Who?"

Tom said, "You don't know anything about the Sheriff? You have kept your heads down, haven't you?"

The Chief explained how they met the Sheriff and how the Sheriff seemed to have gained control over the shelter complex. He had somehow gotten the military to buy into his right to authority, and it was likely involved with the huge stash of supplies. There were a lot of people in Farley, but they could all live within the safety of the shelters if the infected were cleared out, and the supplies inside the shelters could feed and clothe them for years to come. The shelter complex was far bigger than Farley, and the medical supplies alone were important to the survival of the people living along the river. He agreed with Kathy. Someone had to remove the Sheriff from power.

The Chief said, "Listen up, people. There was a time when the world said America will help them, and sometimes we stepped up and told dictators that we weren't going to stand by and watch them violate the rights of other humans. Sometimes we didn't, maybe because we had to pick our fights. I'm not saying it's our job now that the country is gone, but this guy's in our back yard. It's only a matter of time before he sends troops to Guntersville."

"Okay," said Hampton, "but I'm curious about the space program part. There were people who didn't understand that before the infection. My guess is that the space program has suffered a pretty significant setback, so how is this place supposed to help?"

Gentry said, "That's right. You couldn't possibly know what this place is. Do you have communications at all these other shelters? Mud Island, Fort Sumter, Ambassadors Island, Guntersville? Did I leave any out?"

"The oil rig," said Colleen.

"And Columbus, Ohio," said Kathy, "but I don't think that one will be opened for a long time. It's sort of a tomb."

"Okay," said Gentry, "do they have communications? We might not be able to send anyone back up there for a long time, probably not in our lifetime, but we need to get as much of the space hardware operating as soon as possible, and there's a damn lot of it. People don't ever think about how much we need that stuff so businesses can coordinate with each other. Governments, hospitals, and the internet need the space program. Am I the only one that misses online shopping? I've got my shopping cart full on Amazon!"

"This place can improve that?" asked the Chief.

"That and more," said Karen. "Wait until Gentry shows you her office."

Karen had to give her shelter roommate some credit for what she represented. There were people who wouldn't get it, but this shelter could be part of bringing people back together. It might even become the central communications hub that lets labs coordinate on a cure for the infection.

"Gentry's office?" asked Kathy.

"Yep. The tour isn't over. Gentry has a whole gymnasium sized office full of sophisticated equipment that didn't start working until today when the Soyuz showed up. We don't have a clue why, and we haven't even had a chance to test everything to see what else we can do in there."

Everyone waited expectantly for Gentry to give the invitation, and even she was surprised by how protective she was about the mission control center. She gestured with a hand toward the door as if to say, "After you."

They used the stairs to descend from the living levels to the control center, but along the way they stopped by the armory to drop off their weapons. Both Gentry and Karen were surprised when Kathy and the Chief walked along the rows lifting rifles and handguns. They ejected magazines, racked weapons, checked the actions, and inspected them for cleanliness. They were at home in the room the way MC had been.

"This place was where we lost two of our people," said Gentry. "Manuel Calvo and Lieutenant Wanda Kearns. The four of us came into the shelter together. They fell in love with each other, and when MC decided he wanted to do more than spend the rest of his life underground, he figured out how to open a hidden door over here, and they left."

She walked over and put a hand against the wall as if they were right on the other side of it.

"Maybe they made it," said Colleen.

Even as she said it, she knew from their lowered eyes that they knew more.

"We opened it," said Gentry. "If there's a way to open it from the other side, they couldn't find it to get back in."

"We've seen that before," said the Chief. "The entrances and escape doors of all of the shelters are tricky at best. How do you know they tried to get back in?"

The Chief saw Karen turn away, and Gentry sniffed and dabbed at the corners of her eyes before answering.

"We don't know what happened to MC, but we saw Wanda. She was one of them."

Gentry shook it off and said, "You're welcome to arm yourselves. We never saw much reason to carry guns with us. Besides, there's too much important equipment in mission control for me to trust carrying a gun in there."

Karen said, "I've been meaning to tell you, Gentry. I've had your back in there."

She pulled a semiautomatic pistol from her lower back.

Gentry managed a small grin and said, "That's comforting."

The Mud Island group wasn't shy about the invitation to arm themselves. They gathered around the racks like kids in a candy store. They each found at least two handguns apiece and loaded up on extra magazines. Back pockets and cargo pockets were stuffed full, and ammunition packs were loaded with boxes of 9 mm ammo. They all went with the same size ammo to be able to carry as much as possible.

Gentry said, "You guys look like you're getting ready for war."

The Chief nodded, "We have at least two enemies out there, maybe more. Ready to show us your office?"

On the stairs Kathy and the Chief noticed the dark stains that had never completely faded after being washed repeatedly. They exchanged an understanding nod that it must have been bad when Gentry and Karen arrived at the shelter, but it would be a conversation for another time.

There was no way for them to prepare themselves for what they found beyond the door at the bottom of the stairs. Technology in the shelters had always been sporadic. It would work fine for a short time but then quit. There was even a time when they had tapped into a satellite and watched in real time as Cuban gunboats had entered their territory.

The room was immense, but it had to be big to accommodate the massive view screens at the front of the room. Everywhere there were monitors with data streams just waiting for someone to read them and pass the information along. Everything was working, and the prospect of working technology and the ability to communicate over long distances gave the Mud Island survivors hope.

"Imagine," said Tom, "being able to talk with all of the shelters at one time."

Hampton added, "We could have caravans of supplies and raw goods on the roads again and opening trade routes between cities."

"I hate to put a damper on the good things you're realizing," said the Chief, "but Gentry can probably tell you what the first application of this technology has to be."

Gentry nodded. Being a scientist, she had witnessed firsthand the way science had to bow to military application as a means to protect the merchandise because that's what it was. It was a precious piece of merchandise that could be used as a weapon. Therefore, it had value that meant it could be bought and sold.

"Right now it's working," she said, "but it isn't doing everything it's supposed to. We still can't establish communications with anyone."

Kathy said, "That might be a good thing. The Sheriff's people have had plenty of time to reach the reentry vehicle you described. If they heard you calling out over the radio in the Soyuz, then they'll be searching for you next."

"Do you think they've taken the ISS crew?" asked Karen. "They've been in space a long time. They should be under medical observation."

"We've seen the Sheriff's operation," said the Chief. "He could give them adequate medical care, but I doubt he would. The last thing he needs is a real American hero winning over the military from him. Isn't the ISS Commander still a commissioned officer?"

Gentry nodded again, and they could read the worry on her face. The ISS crew was in danger, and they needed to find them if they hadn't been caught by the Sheriff already.

"Where do we start? I mean how can we help?"

The Chief gave Gentry and Karen his best reassuring smile and said, "If I know my friends as well as I think I do, we have help outside. Now all we have to do is make contact with them to see how prepared they are. Let's start by doing a quick check of everything you have in here. If we can open a line of communication with someone in the Sheriff's military support, maybe we can start a little mutiny."

******

* * *

Sim thought about how he had hidden in cars, under cars, in dumpsters, hotel rooms, and an RV. It seemed like he was always hiding somewhere. More recently it was on the roof of a mall and then inside the service bay of an electronics store. The cemetery wasn't so bad. It was creepy, but he had even been in worse cemeteries since hooking up with Cassandra and her friends. Still, nothing compared with the dark corridors of these shelters.

At the moment Sim was expressing in a low whisper his preference to be elsewhere.

"Right now I could be on an island in the middle of a lake just north of the Canadian border. I could be surrounded by friends with fishing poles instead of guns. I could be fishing for pike and bass and whatever else they fish for up there. But no, I'm crawling around in the dark in some kind of tomb, and there's something out there that's hunting for me. I'm the pike."

"Right now you're a bigmouth bass," whispered Cassandra. "Don't you know we're surrounded?"

"That's my point. Why are we surrounded? We've got guns. We've got knives. We've even got these fancy short stabbing poles you made us bring along. Why aren't we fighting our way out of here?"

For the last two hours they hid under furniture in a room that seemed to be attracting more and more of the infected. They didn't know what was drawing them into the room, but whatever it was, it was still doing it. The reason the two survivors were able to talk in a whisper was because of the racket being made by the infected. Something was making them moan and groan like nothing Cassandra or Sim had ever heard before.

Something bumped against Sim's leg, and he involuntarily jumped. His head hit the underside of the table making a sound like a dull gong. He immediately crawled through the legs of infected that tripped and fell like dominoes. That was what saved him. The infected couldn't tell each other from the living as long as he moved like them and didn't make any noise.

Cassandra was close enough to see the pileup, and she recognized a new strategy. Sim was already using it without even trying. She only hoped he would catch on if he saw through the crowd what she was doing.

She wriggled out from under the desk and reached through the legs of an infected that was facing away from her. She grabbed its right ankle and pulled hard enough to make it tumble over to the right, and it took several others with it. Even though it was dark, she could see the infected around her turn in the direction of the disturbance. The groaning increased as they dragged their weak legs toward the infected that were flailing around on the floor. Like magic they formed a dogpile a few feet from her. She laid flat out and didn't move, and the infected that tripped over her and fell began their slow crawl toward the commotion.

Sim was only about six feet away, and he had adopted a similar pose on the floor. He kept his head turned toward Cassandra and was amazed at the calm way she kept her eyes on him. Her mouth was moving, though, and he focused on what she was telling him.

Cassandra knew she had to get Sim away from the room and moving again. The flow of infected from other rooms into theirs was slowly decreasing, and as they came in they were drawn to the ruckus where they were piling up. Without words, she shaped her lips and said, "Go. Move now."

Sim understood, and he also understood she didn't mean to get up and run. Using just his legs, he pushed himself along the floor. The infected crawled by in front of him, but even when they seemed to groan right into his ear, he kept his head flat to the floor and pushed with his knees and feet. He felt his ear fill with something warm and wet and almost panicked at the thought that one of them had just drooled into his ear. Even though Cassandra saw the revulsion and fear in his face, he managed to stay down. When his shoulder bumped into the wall at the corner of the door, he finally felt like he might make it.

There was a tug on both of his legs near his feet, and his eyes went wide when he saw one was an infected dead, and it was poised to bite. He waited for the sharp pain that would follow and wanted to scream, but the tug on his other foot was Cassandra using him for leverage. She pulled hard to give herself the force she needed, and her blade sliced neatly through the skull of the infected dead with the open mouth.

Now it was time to go.

With no words needed, they both sprang to their feet and charged forward. There were only a few of the infected ahead of them, and Sim was grateful that Cassandra had gotten the lead because his own legs felt numb. He forced himself to follow her and was careful not to collide with her back when she stopped to eliminate any that got in their way. Even though it was almost pitch dark in the narrow corridor, she kept them moving toward a light up ahead.

There were two last huddles of the dead in the room where the lights were on, and they were focusing their attention on bloodstained and slime smeared pieces of furniture about the size of recliners. One of the recliners was in the middle of the room covered by the infected that were biting at the tough material. One recliner was in a corner, and it was occupied by six more of the biting and snapping dead. Both of the recliners moved on their own.

Cassandra was like something from a movie script. The moves she made as she unsheathed her new machete were practiced and accurate. Sim would have been happy to watch, but he didn't have time to be a spectator, and neither did the person inside the spacesuit who was unable to get free from the weight of so many infected.

He drew his own machete and buried it deeper than he had meant to into the top of a dirty mop of hair, but he remembered what Cassandra had told him. If your blade gets stuck in a head, use the machete to move the infected before you try to free the blade. He gripped it with both hands and pulled the heavy infected away from the corner. In the open he was able to plant his foot on the back of the infected and yank the machete away. He immediately swung a backhand at the second one and made it more of a glancing blow on purpose. His target fell away, not eliminated but out of the way for now.

By the time Sim finished the remaining four infected and turned to the one he had knocked away, Cassandra was standing over it. She wiped her blade across it and put it away. They both turned their attention to the astronauts who were still down. There was no time to check them for injuries. There was only enough time to get them on their feet and to move as a group away from the scene that was likely to become crowded again.

Another level had proven often enough to be the only way to escape. Once inside stairwells they always seemed to have two options. Up or down, sometimes they were both possible. Cassandra was afraid to go up because there was always the chance of running into a search party. Going down seemed to mean going into unsafe country belonging to the dead. The third option was to at least take a few minutes to recover, and that's what they decided to do.

Some of the stairwells were labeled with the signs that said shelter and level numbers on them, so they picked the first one they came to. It was a bad choice because there were infected dead on the landing.

"I'm not in the mood for this," yelled Cassandra.

She leaned her astronaut against the frame of the door and pushed the whole crowd of reaching arms and faces backward until some tumbled down the stairs, and some went over the railing. She rammed the remaining two and sent them spinning to the floor. Then she grabbed the closer one by the back of the collar with one hand and the belt by the other. She lifted it in the air and tossed it over the railing like a sack of potatoes. Without watching her handiwork, she did the same thing to the second one.

The astronauts watched from inside their helmets as they were rescued, and as they were helped to sit in their bulky suits, they wondered about the two people who had saved them. "Where did they come from? Who are they, and why do they seem to almost have super strength?"

The dim light of the stairwell came from small lights embedded behind steel wires. They were typical military issue and impossible to break. They shone down on the four people and gave enough light for the astronauts to see the smiling faces of the man and woman who rescued them. As for their own faces, they had streaks of sweat running into their eyes, and the dark circles and puffy eyelids made them look like two fish that had jumped out of their aquarium.

Cassandra worked at the collar of the helmet over Natalia's head and finally got it to rotate. Sim was doing the same for Henry, but they were interrupted by the smell in the stairwell as it hit Natalia in the face. She had already lost her stomach once after the reentry, so there wasn't much else to lose, but the sour bile had to come out. Years of smelling the stench of decay had desensitized Cassandra and Sim, but this was something entirely new to the astronauts. Cassandra held her head for her as spasms racked Natalia. She used her other hand to reach inside a cargo pocket, and she produced a small pony bottle of water.

A few sips seemed to help, and as the spasms passed Henry said it was okay to take off his helmet.

"Are you sure, love?" asked Cassandra. "Are you ready for what it smells like in here?"

Henry gave her a weak grin.

"I could really use a swallow of that water."

"Okay, but let's leak a little of this fragrant air into the helmet first. If you start to do what she did, I'll pull the helmet off the rest of the way, and we'll get this over with."

Cassandra took over for Sim after transferring Natalia's head to Sim's hands. He held her cradled against him and reassured her that they were safe now. He didn't bother to explain just how much trouble they were in. That could wait until they knew if the astronauts had any bite wounds that had gone through their suits.

Cassandra talked Henry through opening the helmet locking ring, and Henry was sure he was prepared, but he had been breathing recycled air for years, and the stench was a shock to his system.

"Here it comes," said Cassandra.

She yanked his helmet out of the way, and then she helped him turn his head and held him while he went through the same thing Natalia did. When it was over she gave him a few sips of water to ease his burning throat.

"Better? Welcome to Earth, or at least one of the worst neighborhoods," said Cassandra. "My name is Cassandra, and this handsome guy is known as Sim to his friends."

Natalia's throat burned as she croaked, "Nice to meet you. I'm Natalia, and my comrade is Henry. Is it like this everywhere?"

Sim answered, "We've got a few safe places, but if you mean is it this bad, the answer is yes. You have to make your places safe. If we can get you out of here, we can get you to where we live, and that's a good place."

"Why are you here?" asked Henry. "We didn't know any better, or we wouldn't have come inside this place. What made you do it?"

"We've been trying to catch up with you," said Cassandra. "We saw your Soyuz, and you got away from it as fast as you could. You must've realized that the entire world wasn't going to be there to give you a ticker tape parade, and you cleared out fast. We decided to come after you because someone else is coming after you too."

"Don't tell me," said Henry, "the world has been in ruins long enough for a few bad people to be in charge. We've had some contact with people on the ground, and we've heard not everyone can be trusted."

Sim said, "Some people took advantage of the situation. There's a lot to tell you, and you'll hear everything in due time, but I imagine we have more immediate concerns. Getting you out of here and back to our overwatch position isn't going to be easy."

"Overwatch?" asked Henry. "Natalia and I are both military. Why would you have an overwatch position? Thank you for saving us in there, and thank you for the water, but why should we trust you? Why are you the good guys?"

"Fair questions," said Sim. "I don't have a resume on me, but I was the flight navigator of the plane that got the President out of Washington. Cassandra was Chief of Security on a hospital ship. I think you can judge for yourselves, but to start with, we don't want anything from you. We're only offering to help you."

Cassandra interrupted, "Listen, we can show as we go, but first things first. Were either of you bitten?"

"You bet we were," said Henry, "and even though they couldn't get their teeth through our pressure suits, those bites hurt like hell."

They were all amazed and relieved at the same time as they spent a half hour helping the astronauts inspect their suits for rips where they were bitten. Both of them complained about bruises, but the suits proved to be as tough as advertised.

"I think I can speak for Cassandra when I say these suits will be worth keeping in a world where getting bitten is the leading cause of death," said Sim.

26

The Tombs

Huntsville - Year Seven

Getting out of the shelter by going up was ruled out quickly. Cassandra scouted each level above theirs and was surprised to find they were six levels down. When she returned to the trio waiting for her, they were also confused by how deep they were because they didn't recall going down that many sets of stairs. It finally occurred to them that the shelters overlapped each other in so many places that they must have crossed over from one shelter to another, and they probably had done it more than once.

"When we came into the first shelter," said Henry, "we didn't run into any of those things, those infected. As a matter of fact, we found an empty shelter. The supplies were already gone, and we figured that would be a safer place to hide because anyone searching for us would figure we would bypass an empty shelter."

Natalia added, "The map was the only reason we stayed in the same shelter. We figured we could navigate out when we needed to."

"What map?" asked Cassandra.

Henry tugged open a velcro flap on his suit and fished out the map. Cassandra could read a map as well as anyone with her military background, but she deferred to Sim. As a navigator, maps were like preferred reading to him. He eagerly spread it out on the floor and traced with his finger trying to mentally match their route to the stairwell with something familiar. He found it in only seconds and then located the stairwell.

"This is amazing," he said. "I know exactly where we are, and the only thing the map is missing is notes to show which areas are packed with the infected and which are empty."

Henry said, "Here there be tigers."

He was surprised that Sim understood the reference, but Sim surprised him by answering, "I'm a Ray Bradbury fan too."

"You have two clueless people here," said Cassandra, "and I hate insider jokes so give it up."

Henry obliged her with an explanation that it was widely believed that medieval cartographers used that notation on maps, and it was the title of a Ray Bradbury story. In this case it would be useful if the map had notations like that.

"Well, at least we have a map, so what's the best way out of here?" she asked.

Natalia put her finger on the map and said, "We saw this and figured it was some kind of connector between a large number of the shelters. It passes at least fifty different shelters and appears to go to the surface."

"A supply tunnel?" Cassandra asked Sim.

"Maybe," he said, "but something doesn't make sense. See the way it reaches a dead end? It's like someone decided another shelter wouldn't fit there, but look how big the space is."

Cassandra said, "Are you thinking what I'm thinking?"

"Fill me in," said Henry.

"While you're at it, explain to me what you're talking about," said Natalia.

Sim said, "You asked why we need an overwatch. You were right to ask because the term implies we're working with someone else. We are, but we don't know where they are right now, so we were holding position waiting to see if they would show up."

"How long?" asked Natalia.

"As long as we have to," answered Cassandra.

"But the point is," continued Sim, "we picked our spot to wait because our original reason for coming here was not these small shelters. We're here because somewhere around here is a super shelter that would make these things look like they were dug on weekends by backyard amateur survivors."

"So, you're thinking it's on that map?" asked Henry.

"Not exactly," said Sim. "It's what's not on the map. This supply tunnel you guys spotted goes to this spot, and there's room for three or four more shelters. That doesn't make sense."

From the darkness above them, a new voice said clearly, "There aren't any doors there, at least none that you can see from inside the tunnel."

The voice wasn't threatening, it just wasn't expected. Cassandra whirled and drew her semiautomatic in a smooth motion. All she found to point her gun at was darkness. Wherever the man was who had suddenly revealed himself, he had stayed where he couldn't be seen. Her quick draw also didn't cause him to panic. There was nothing but silence and darkness for so long that Cassandra started to wonder if she even heard him before. When she lowered the gun he spoke again.

"Thanks. You were starting to make me a bit nervous. I can dodge teeth pretty good, but I don't think I can dodge bullets."

They saw the movement then because he stepped forward a few inches. He was young, but anyone who had known Manuel Calvo when the infected had arrived years ago would say he had aged more than most people. He had a haunted look that was disturbing but also sad.

"I didn't mean to frighten you. It's just been a long time since I've seen people this deep who weren't already dead, but I also haven't seen many astronauts."

He said it with a touch of humor in his voice, but there was something else about the way he said it. It was like there was supposed to be more to it. They were all just about to ask him who he was when he asked his own question.

"Do you guys know Gentry Campbell?"

******

It didn't mean anything to Cassandra or Sim, but the reaction from the astronauts was impossible to describe. It was like they were stuck between saying they know Gentry Campbell and asking the man if he knew Gentry Campbell. Natalia finally got the answer out coherently, and then she openly cried. The man took that as an invitation to come the rest of the way down the stairs. Cassandra still had her Smith & Wesson in her hand, but she had lowered it to her side where she had one knee on the floor. If he made a move, she would still have time to stop him.

Natalia asked again, "How could you know Gentry?" She sniffed tears that could only be happy because the smile on her face told how she really felt. This man had just given her a link to their past with NASA, and he had to be a friend.

"I've been trying to get back to Gentry for a long time. I heard you say something about a big shelter. It's true. It's there, but there's no door."

"How do you know it's true?" demanded Cassandra.

"I lived in it with Gentry and two Army nurses."

Something passed over his face that was like he was seeing something in the distance and then remembering something he had forgotten.

"I'm sorry. I haven't been around people in so long that I forgot to tell you who I am. I remember now. People introduce themselves. The last time I introduced myself to someone, he shot at me. I've stayed away from people since."

He walked forward with one hand extended toward Natalia since she was the one who was so openly shaken when he mentioned Gentry.

"Who are you?" she said.

"Oh, man. I'm just a rambling idiot. My name is Manuel Calvo. My friends call me MC. I was in the Army stationed here at Redstone Arsenal when everything started. I ran into this cute NASA lady who was caught up in it, and she turned out to be someone important. The brass made me take good care of her, and the Colonel told us about this super big shelter under the planetarium, and she knew the answers to the codes in the door locks, so we got inside. I shouldn't have ever left."

The young soldier did tend to ramble, but Cassandra saw the almost imperceptible nod from Sim. The kid was suffering from something, and whatever it was, he had been carrying it by himself for a long time. Sim recognized that he had a need to be asked.

"What happened MC? Did you lose someone?"

MC made eye contact for a moment, and they saw his were damp.

"Yeah, man. I couldn't stay in the shelter. It was like so perfect there that I felt bad for the people outside. I wanted to go out and help them."

Sim said, "Hey, I know a whole group of folks just like that. They could stay safe in their shelters, but they're out there somewhere right now because it's not enough for them to just survive. They need to help people too, so you didn't do anything wrong."

"But Wanda would be alive if I had stayed inside. She only came out because I did."

There it was. He was carrying that guilt around with him for years in the dark shelters without anyone to confess his guilt to, and it had grown heavier over the years.

Sim walked over and took the man's extended hand.

"If she followed you it was because she wanted to. Unless I miss my guess, you tried to talk her into staying behind."

They could see the cloud lift from above him and the burden fell from his shoulders. Natalia held up her hand so Cassandra could help her to her feet. Together they pulled Henry up to join them, and they greeted MC with hugs.

They could have stayed in that embrace a while longer because human contact had become so scarce, but a rude reminder of their circumstances came from the other side of the stairwell door. The loud thumps indicated that the corridor had repopulated with the infected dead.

"We spend far too much time in stairwells," said Sim. "You ever notice that?" he asked Cassandra.

"I won't argue with you about that. We've got to figure this out with fewer stairwells. It seems like the shelters were pretty typical 1950's Cold War designs, and there was no imagination. Rectangular designs stacked on top of each other and connected by stairwells at the corners. You can't find your way from one place to the next because everything looks alike. If the super shelter wasn't designed and built until the late '60s, how did they fit it in?"

"I think I know how they got around some of the problems. Could you show me that map you found?" said MC.

Sim put his back against the door for good measure while they spread out the map for MC. In the dim light he had a hard time with the colors of the lines, but with their help he began to see the pattern he was looking for.

"You see these lines? They don't show up in shelters until later. The first shelters didn't have them because they didn't have the same type of HVAC systems in the '50s. When they built the new shelter, they needed to discreetly feed the fiber optic cables for the technology to the shelter, so they included it in the power grid and HVAC."

Cassandra said, "The umbilical cord."

"Yeah," said MC, "you could call it that."

"They did call it that," she replied. "I'll give you the rest of the history later because believe me it's a long story, but the first shelter in the system was on an island. They called it Mud Island, or rather they still call it that. They had an umbilical running from the mainland to the shelter. It got cut when a Russian ship sank onto it, but damned if they didn't have a spare. These super shelters are supposed to have all kinds of redundant systems in case of power failures and such. Are they on this map?"

"Only if you know what you're looking for," said MC. "You see these dotted lines? Unlike the solid lines that indicated barriers like walls, rooms, and stairs, it's the space between the dotted lines that counts. You see how they run parallel to each other? That's because they're conduits."

Sim leaned away from the door and positioned himself above Cassandra's shoulder.

"We used the same things as navigators. Flight paths are more or less straight lines with a few turns, but sometimes you have corridors you fly through. It's rare to see another aircraft in your corridor."

"Same principle on big ships," said Cassandra. "Hospital ships aren't as big as oil tankers, but you need corridors to allow for adjustments."

"Would it surprise any of you to hear that spacecraft use corridors?" asked Natalia.

Henry said, "People drive in lanes everywhere, and you all are acting like you've just solved the DaVinci Code. I've been saying all along that Britons drive in the proper lane, and you Americans don't. Maybe that's why it took you by surprise that the dotted lines are corridors."

It was hard not to laugh. They saw he had a good point about the maps being obvious, but they weren't ready to concede about which country drives on the wrong side of the road.

"If you're so smart, what were you doing under a pile of the infected in the other room?" asked Cassandra. "I'll wager you've been following the map."

"I'll defer to your skills, young lady, especially since it was you who saved us from the creatures."

MC picked up where he left off. "The conduits do some crazy things. They get narrower without warning, they have steep drop-offs that aren't on the maps, and I guess they figured anyone who crawls through them would have a flashlight because they're dark."

"Are you saying that's how we're going to reach the super shelter?" asked Sim.

"No, that's how we're going to get to the tunnel that services all of the shelters. I haven't been able to find a way back to that tunnel since I left it years ago, but the map shows me there's a conduit not far from here that I never found."

Cassandra said, "I thought you said there's no doors there."

"There's one door, but there's no way to open it. That's why Wanda got killed. She went back to try, but I already knew it was only a way out of the shelter."

"What makes you so sure?" said Sim.

"The control that opens the door is on the control that opens the armory inside. You can open and close the exit from there, but I couldn't find a way to open it from the outside."

Sim considered it for a moment then said, "You ever read anything from Robert A. Heinlein? He said one man's magic is another man's engineering. I don't doubt that you gave it your best shot when you searched for a way to open the door from the outside, but one thing I've learned about the shelter designers is that they were a bunch of eccentric, creative nuts. All we have to do is reverse engineer what they did."

Cassandra was more of a warrior than Sim, but she had a healthy respect for his quiet, logical problem solving skills. He had a way of working a problem until the solution was obvious, and there was something about the way he told MC with confidence that he could figure it out.

"You already know something, don't you?"

Sim tried to put on his best innocent expression, but that was a dead giveaway.

"I can neither confirm nor deny that I've solved it, but I have an idea."

MC was stunned. "You see something on the map? I have to know. Is it that easy?"

He had spent years being hard on himself, and if it was that easy, he would be even harder.

Sim wanted to let him down easy, but there really was a major clue on the map. There would be no proof until they reached the end of the tunnel, but to Sim it was literally the big picture that did it for him. He decided to let MC figure it out for himself so he would see it wasn't magic, it was engineering.

"MC, go up the steps a bit so you can look down at the map. Blur your vision a bit and don't focus on small details. Look at the big picture."

MC did as Sim asked, and as soon as he faced the map he saw it. Spread out on the floor of the landing, he could see a pattern in the dotted lines of the conduits that he hadn't seen before. If it had been the lines that defined the walls of the tunnel, he would have seen it before, but dotted conduit lines only roughly surrounded the tunnel walls, and they clearly converged on the end of the tunnel. The pattern was shaped like a key.

"Engineers have an interesting sense of humor," said Sim, "and if I'm right this place was designed for NASA engineers by a member of the survivors club who was also an engineer. The controls that will open the door are most likely inside the conduits. That's where you come in. Do you recall seeing any openings in the conduits near the wall that opens?"

MC thought back over the years and tried to imagine the dimly lit tunnel. Every detail seemed to be covered by the thin film of time. Even Wanda's face was harder to see. Through that film he saw the trucks, he saw the doors, and he saw recessed lights that didn't seem to do more than show the bare minimum. Then his eyes opened, and his mind saw through the film.

"Where are the doors to the other shelters?" asked MC.

Cassandra and Sim both leaned over the map and pointed at the doors, and each one was directly adjacent to where conduits changed directions by ninety degrees.

MC remembered those places. "There was a vent above each door. I remember them now. It's exactly what anyone would expect, but what are you thinking?"

Sim said, "The vents might have controls inside them that open the doors to the shelters. One of them or all of them may open the super shelter door. All we have to do is figure out the code, and since the engineers would have used the same sense of humor to build the thing, they would have wanted to make the code part of the overall puzzle. What code did you use to open it from the inside, and by the way, how did you close it?"

MC grinned. It had been a long time ago, but he still remembered the revelation that the armory door had never had a code programmed into the lock. When he decided that hitting the ENTER key twice might open the exit, he had reasoned that there was no way to unlock it from the outside simply because he had been so smart. He had been blinded by his own success.

"You aren't going to believe this."

He was right about that. Even the astronauts didn't believe it. No program in the lock gave them a feeling that it was going to be even easier than they thought to open the door from the outside.

"And you got outside by just jumping over the wall before it rose up from the floor too far?" asked Sim. "No wonder you figured you couldn't get back in."

"I think I know how to do it," said Henry.

******

All they had to do was find the nearest access panel to the conduit and remove it. They found it on the map in the corridor about eight doors from the stairwell where they had taken refuge. Opening the door again wasn't anything less than they expected.

Natalia and Henry were moved up to the next landing. MC assured them that when he came down from above, the stairwell was free of the infected. He said that he had seen the door open a few inches a few floors up when Cassandra had scouted the levels earlier. She was right that all six levels were heavily infested with the dead, but when she opened the door to where he was currently hiding, it had given him the opportunity to eliminate them and follow her. As soon as the door had opened, it had drawn the infected in her direction, and they had hungrily gone after her. He took advantage of her diversion and started taking them out.

Cassandra had suggested that they should go back up to that level to find a conduit or ductwork, and MC had simply thanked her for peeking through that door. He said there were still dozens of infected on that floor, and he hadn't seen any of the panels on that level. The map showed one on their level, and they were at least in a safe place to fight them off on the stairs.

Sim explained to Natalia and Henry that they had a lot of experience fighting the infected, but never take it for granted that they wouldn't have to retreat. He told them to go up a level to the next landing if they got forced backward.

Cassandra opened the door, and the parade began. During the time they had talked on the stairs, it seemed that every infected dead on the level had been drawn to the groaning of the first few that had followed them.

Standing three steps up from the reaching horde of infected it was easy to split their heads with machetes, but the infected came through in larger numbers than they expected. They had to take down the first wave fast enough to create a barrier of bodies for the rest to be stuck behind.

"Everyone plug your ears," yelled Cassandra.

She pulled her handgun, flipped the safety with her thumb, and rapidly took aim, fired, took aim, and fired again. She had a fifteen round magazine, and she didn't stop until there were fifteen bodies in front of her. She ejected the first magazine and punched in a second. The landing wasn't big enough for her to keep acquiring targets, and they wanted room for the infected to come into the stairwell. Using her long machete, she was able to hit them hard enough to cause most of them to fall down the stairs with one blow. By the time they stopped flowing through the door, the pile down to the next landing below was so deep that they were almost level with where Cassandra stood.

Eventually the landing was so full of bodies that more couldn't come in, and Cassandra, Sim, and MC were forced to step on backs and greet them at the door. Almost an hour later, the weary trio came back for the astronauts.

"Is it like this everywhere?" asked Henry.

Sim said, "I doubt it, but if you're asking if there are a lot of bad places, I'm afraid there are."

He didn't know that Henry wasn't asking because they might have to fight their way out of the shelters. He was asking because he was always wondering how it would be at home.

Everyone stepped carefully through the carnage as they worked their way into the corridor out the landing. There were stragglers, but they were the ones that had suffered the most when they originally died. Most were missing limbs or couldn't stand to be able to attack. In some ways they were more dangerous because they could bite a leg before being noticed.

It was a flashback to enter a conduit for MC because it was just like the panel they had removed seven years ago so they could reach the fire escape at the back of the planetarium. It was a bit wider than that one, but MC told them to be ready for it to become narrow in places. Natalia and Henry were exhausted before they reached the panel, and Cassandra and Sim had to go through their entire supply of water before they even started crawling.

Getting to the tunnel by crawling through ductwork was even more exhausting, but it was the fastest route, and it was by far better than fighting the hordes of infected dead on every level between their starting point and their goal. The metal of the ductwork bent under their weight, and the groan of the metal was matched by groans of the infected in the rooms they crossed. Their greatest fear was that the ductwork wouldn't support their weight and would drop them unprotected into a room full of the infected.

MC had taken the lead because he had been in the shelters for so long. He called them the tombs, and they had earned the name. If the number of infected they had eliminated was representative of the entire shelter complex, there were thousands of them. Sim followed behind MC, then came Natalia, Henry, and Cassandra. Sim and Cassandra carried the helmets from the spacesuits for the astronauts because they were already so tired that the extra weight just slowed them down.

It felt like they crawled for hours, but finally MC stopped and said, "We're here. There isn't enough room for us to do anything but crawl out one at a time. When I drop down, I need backup because there's company down there."

Sim passed the word back to Cassandra, and after giving it some thought, they decided that it was worth wasting some time to have her wriggle past the other and drop down first. As she passed the astronauts, they each thanked her over and over for being there for them. She felt like she was saying goodbye, especially when she got to Sim and he told her not to let anything happen to her.

She pulled herself even with MC, and he said, "I need to get home to Gentry."

The panel fell away with a crash, which was the last thing they wanted to do, and there were groans somewhere in the distance. It was pitch dark below, and Cassandra couldn't even see the floor where she would land.

"Hey, everybody. Listen up. I can't even see the floor down there. For all I know, I'll be landing on something really sharp, or I could break a leg. Does anyone have anything that glows in the dark? Right now I don't care if it's the dial on your wristwatch."

"The helmets," said Natalia. "They have internal lights. They also can take a big shock, so they will stay on after you drop them."

"Awesome," said Cassandra, "but one should do it unless it rolls away under something."

"Think positive," said Sim as he passed the helmet up to her. She found the switch on the side of the helmet and aimed the light at her face first.

"Do I look positive?" she asked with a wry smile.

"You look spooky."

It was meant as a joke, but for some reason it felt for a moment like he was seeing Cassandra as the way she would look if things went terribly wrong. Before he could stop her or say something meaningful, she slipped over the edge and dropped into the room.

******

Cassandra dropped the helmet a split second before she went through the opening, but she held onto the rim where the panel had been attached long enough to see the light reach the floor. She saw the helmet land on a white surface and then bounce away at an angle. The light played across the surface of a vinyl floor, and she knew she could follow the same path. The white surface turned out to be a bed, and the mattress made for a pleasant landing. She let herself bounce and then roll toward the light.

When she came out of her roll she felt the grip of something sharp in her shoulder blade, and it was too late to stop it. She felt hot blood against the left side of her neck and upper arm, and she automatically spun in that direction. She drew her pistol and fired three shots before she could even think about it, but as the last shot was fired she felt the satisfaction of knowing she had hit her target.

Sim watched Cassandra drop over the edge and pushed himself to the opening as fast as possible. He saw her land feet first on something and then roll away. Almost as quickly there was a flash and the deafening crack of three 9 mm rounds being fired. The helmet light shone at an angle across a vinyl floor, and Sim watched with dread as a dark pool of blood spread across the light.

Sim didn't care if he was dropping into the middle of Hell. He knew he wouldn't let her die alone. He went feet first and hit the same spot as her, but he pushed the other way to keep from landing on top of her. When he made his roll, he spotted the light from the helmet and immediately moved in that direction. With his machete held high, he charged across the room and fell over something that tangled his feet painfully and slapped against his shins. He went down hard and hit his right cheek against something metallic.

MC followed close behind Sim, but when he hit the white surface, he grabbed it with both hands and held on. The lower half of his body bounced into the air, but he managed to stay on the bed. The light from the helmet reflected off of a glass cabinet in the room, and he had a brief glimpse of the door. He took a chance that it would be like any other door and made a dive for a spot on the wall to the right of it.

Lights blazed on in the room that was no more than a twelve by twelve foot rectangle. A hospital bed occupied a large part of the room, and hospital supplies were scattered around the room. Sim was wrapped up in an embrace with the lower end of an IV drip pole that stretched past the bed into the corner. The whole thing didn't make sense to Natalia as she leaned down through the opening in the conduit, but it gradually sorted itself out, and she could tell Cassandra was in excruciating pain.

Despite her own body aches, she knew she couldn't be hurt as badly as Cassandra, so she just let herself land. It knocked the wind out of her, but she let herself fall from the same side of the bed as the injured woman. She brought her knees under herself so she could be above Cassandra and firmly pressed down on the back of her shoulder to keep Cassandra from doing more damage.

Sim heard Cassandra scream, but his fall had left him disoriented. He didn't even remember what happened yet. Henry had yet to drop from above, and he knew there was nothing he could do to help.

When Natalia pushed down on Cassandra, she firmly gripped the metal hook of the IV drip pole and pulled downward to ease it out from under her shoulder blade. As the metal tip pulled free, blood gushed out behind it, and Natalia clamped a hand down on the wound. Cassandra screamed again, but as painful as it was, it was not the same as a bite.

It was an hour before Cassandra regained consciousness, but that was a blessing because it gave Natalia time to sew up her injury. She wasn't an expert, but she and Henry both had enough training to know she had probably done some damage to the muscles in her shoulder that would take a long time to heal. The hook had gone under the shoulder blade and pulled everything upward as her own weight caused the damage. When she rotated out of reflex and shot at the pole, she had ripped it out from under the bones, but it was still stuck inside her when Sim fell across the pole.

While she was unconscious Natalia had scrounged through the

drawers of medical supplies and found sutures and alcohol. The wound was cleaned and stitched before Cassandra came around, and the first thing she did was stand up too soon. She fell backward as the room spun around, and everyone rushed to the bed to keep her down.

"Where are we?" she managed to croak out.

The small hospital room actually had a working sink, but they doubted the water was safe to drink after so many years. At least they were able to wet some towels and cool her down.

"We made it to a room in one of the shelters next to the tunnel," said MC. "You were injured when you landed in the room."

"Was I bit?"

Cassandra became frantic on the bed, her eyes searching for the infected dead she remembered shooting after it sank its awful teeth into her. Hatred, disgust, and satisfaction that she had been able to end its miserable existence all washed across her at the same time. Sim caught her just in time or she would have passed out again.

It took a few moments of restraining her and reassuring her, but they finally got her to understand there were no infected dead in the room. She saw all the blood on the floor, and it reminded her of the surgical rooms on the hospital ship. She remembered the restrained bite victims and the slow death of the entire crew. Somehow she felt like she was back on the ship, and these people were here with her.

"We have to get to the galley. That's the only way out of the ship. We can get out through the cargo door."

No one knew what she meant, but she passed out again before they could ask.

27

Codes

Huntsville - Year Seven

Natalia couldn't believe their good luck when she found the morphine in the first aid kits. It would have been better to use it while she was working on the wound, but at least she was able to knock Cassandra out so she would stay still for a while. She had lost a lot of blood and could benefit from a pint or two, and according to Sim there would be medical facilities inside the super shelter that would make it possible. All they had to do was get inside.

Henry was feeling invigorated despite dehydration and still adjusting to Earth's gravity. He felt like he was part of something bigger than him and said so more than once. They had lost their commander, but they had gained three new crew members, and Henry had always enjoyed being part of a mission. He was ready to go out and give his idea a try and open the door to the shelter.

MC scouted the shelter they were in and found they had an unusually clear path from the treatment room to the tunnel, but they would take any favors they could get. After the fight with the large horde in the last shelter, they felt like they deserved a break. He came back and reported to Henry who had worked his way out of the clumsy spacesuit and was ready to go in a set of Army clothes they had found in a closet. It was a typical set of battle dress clothing with insignia that said it belonged to a Colonel Harding. An arm patch identified him as a member of a medical battalion, so this had probably been his examination room. He had left them more treasure than he could have known.

The next time Cassandra woke up, she was more coherent. She wanted to know what happened to the infected dead that had bitten her, and they showed her the IV pole. She couldn't believe she had actually bounced from the bed onto an IV drip pole that impaled her under the shoulder blade. They knew how lucky she had been that the hook went upward instead of straight in, and if the pole had not fallen over, it could have been worse.

"So after I was impaled, you decided to fall on the IV pole?" she asked Sim.

"You're just delirious," he said. "Go back to sleep."

To the others he said, "Did you have to tell her that part?"

MC was at the door, and he announced that he was ready to go. He had located a step ladder which was going to be extremely useful. The three men would go out and locate the access panels that hid the door controls. The idea was to do it while drawing as little attention as possible, but experience told them they would have to eliminate some infected while doing the job.

MC went out first with Cassandra's machete in his right hand. Henry followed with the step ladder, and Sim covered them from behind. Natalia stayed behind in case their patient woke up and attempted to get out of bed. MC had made sure every side door was shut between them and the tunnel, and within three minutes they were easing through the last door. After so much time, MC couldn't believe how the end of the tunnel was still so much the same. The only difference was the pile of long ago decayed bodies along the wall. He couldn't picture what had happened after he had fled from the area, but he imagined Wanda was still there.

Henry gave a low whistle and pointed up at the vent directly above their door. He spread the folding ladder and climbed silently to the top. He worked at the screws quickly using a pair of scissors, the only thing they could find in the medical examination room. It fit into the screws, but a screwdriver would be much faster. When he finally got the last screw out, he pulled off the panel and was gratified to see a keypad. He didn't hesitate, and trusting his suspicions, he pressed the ENTER key twice. The panel displayed a green light, but the wall didn't move.

"One down and three to go," he said to the two men keeping watch below him. He handed the panel and scissors down to Sim and climbed down.

Henry's suspicion was that the keypad was programmed to accept four digits from four separate control panels. In the modern world, hackers would be able to deal with a four digit panel, but since the lock had never been programmed, all they would have to do was hit all four ENTER keys at four locations. They hurriedly ran to the next overhead panel and repeated the process.

With the panel open and a second keypad right before his eyes, Henry felt like Indiana Jones solving ancient glyphs. He hit the ENTER key twice, and once again the green indicator light illuminated.

"That's number two."

They removed the panel over the third door and were disappointed to find it was only a vent, but they had expected it. They weren't happy about wasting time because every minute in the tunnel was another minute that they had to risk being detected by the infected that still found their way into the tunnel from a distant opening. It had been quiet so far, but they had never expected to get it done without drawing a crowd.

They expected number three to be on the other side of the tunnel, and Sim asked a disturbing question as Henry scrambled up the ladder.

"What if the keypads have to be activated in a specific order?"

It was a completely logical question that they had ignored in the hope that the designers of the shelter had overlooked, just as someone had overlooked programming the locks.

"I think we'll just have to cross that particular bridge when we come to it," said Henry.

Each panel had four screws, and Sim couldn't remember a time when screws cooperated so well, but as soon as he thought it, he also thought, "The jinx is out there." If there were four screws, the do-it-yourself rule of thumb was that three would come loose easily and the fourth would get stripped.

Above him Henry cursed, and a piece of metal bounced off the ladder. When Sim retrieved it, he found it was one whole side of the scissors. Henry was cursing because he had broken his screwdriver, but he was still working with the other half. Sim was still holding it when the wet growl of an infected materialized from the side of one of the remaining trucks. It was only a few feet away, and Sim barely had a second to react, but he didn't have to reach for the sheath that held his machete. He swung with a backhand and planted the half of the scissors in the side of its head.

Henry had a good view from above, and he saw what saved Sim. He couldn't help but ask, "Still believe in good luck? Let's get to that fourth panel."

Sim could see from the ground that the green indicator light was on.

MC gathered the ladder and ran with it as soon as Henry's feet hit the ground. Henry ran up the ladder faster than he had believed he could and worked furiously at the first screw. As each screw fell away, their hearts beat faster with excitement, and in less time than ever Henry handed the panel down to MC. He reached inside and hit the ENTER key twice.

The indicator light turned red.

It was so quiet in the tunnel that they could hear the air circulating through the long ago built vents, but the red light might as well have been an alarm system attached to a siren by how it jangled their stretched nerves.

Sim said, "I knew it. I jinxed us."

Henry answered, "My good man, what you say, do, or think had very little influence on what someone did forty some odd years ago. If there is a puzzle here, then there must be clues here. We know this from experience with the engineers who started this charade."

MC almost laughed at Henry's speech because he was already thinking the same thing but in less flowery terms. There was a clue, and he was sure he had seen it already, but it seemed so long ago.

"That's it!"

MC practically shouted in the quiet tunnel, and both Henry and Sim got ready to run for cover.

He lowered his voice down to a whisper, but somewhere in the distance came the familiar call of an excited and unwanted guest. Its groans were either echoes or responses, but they couldn't tell which.

"Sim, you go get Natalia and Cassandra. By the time you get back, Henry and I will have the door open."

He was skeptical, but MC had a look of total conviction on his face, so he did as he said. Getting Cassandra awake and moving would take precious time, so he had to trust him.

As Sim ran for the door that led back to their hiding place, MC ran over and jumped into the cab of one of the remaining trucks. They still sat in the same places with slowly deflating tires, but MC had remembered something about the truck he had taken the last time he had visited this end of the tunnel.

He came back with something in his hand, and as he passed it to Henry he said, "Here's the order you need to use on the keypads."

Long ago MC had started the truck and reached for the lever he expected to be for a manual transmission. He didn't give it another thought as he popped in the clutch and shifted into reverse, but he did find it odd that the positions of the gears were labeled wrong. Instead of shifting where the numbers and lines were cut into the shifting knob, he shifted to where he believed the gears were located. Then he put it out of his mind because he had just lost Wanda.

Henry studied the hard pressed rubber gearshift knob and said, "You Yanks not only drive on the wrong side of the road, you have your gears in the wrong locations."

MC could tell the Briton was as excited as he was and just having fun because Henry grabbed the ladder and ran with it to the open vent that matched with the spot where first gear was written on the knob.

As he climbed the ladder he said, "I'm assuming the direction where the truck is located has something to do with the orientation of the four numbers."

It was as much of a question as it was a statement, and he didn't stop climbing when MC answered.

"You can test that theory, Henry."

Just like the first time, the panel turned green when Henry hit the ENTER button twice. He didn't waste time, but he checked the gearshift knob to be sure and ran to the second panel. It turned green as expected. He already knew where number three was, and he hurried with his ladder across the tunnel to that panel. As he crossed, he saw the shadows down the tunnel as they grew on the walls. They would have company soon and a lot more than they could handle.

The third panel turned green as he had hoped, and even though he knew which panel was number four, he glanced again at the knob. It was definitely an engineer's idea to hide the sequence in plain sight, and maybe they hadn't forgotten to program the lock. It would be so much in the character of an engineer to give someone at least a fighting chance.

By the time Henry had his ladder in place below the fourth and final panel, Natalia came through the shelter door and held it wide for Sim and MC. They were supporting Cassandra between them with Henry's spacesuit draped over her and his helmet on her head. Inside the helmet she was vehemently insisting that she could walk on her own, but they weren't listening. As Henry climbed the ladder to the panel, they went straight past him to the wall. He hit the ENTER button, and it seemed that the entire tunnel turned emerald green to him.

The wall began its slow descent, and Natalia saw tears stream down MC's face. He knew he couldn't have done it on his own, but it still saddened him to know that with time, he could have gotten Wanda back inside.

In front of them bright lights grew across the ceiling as the wall dropped lower. Behind them another wall of the infected was moving inexorably forward. Henry came down from the ladder and faced them. If he had to he would keep them busy while his friends made it to safety.

The brightness grew and the light reached the faces of the infected dead as the horde spread from one wall of the tunnel to the other. Henry backed away a few feet with the knowledge that behind him his friends were probably already over the wall when it was low enough, and at any moment the wall would go up again.

He was just about to risk a glance at them when he felt something grab viciously at his collar from behind.

"Oh no you don't!" yelled Natalia. "You don't get to do that."

Natalia pulled on Henry's collar so hard that both of them practically vaulted head first over the door to the shelter. It was already slowly rising, and inside MC, Sim, and Cassandra were shouting to hurry. MC had hit the panel to close the door far sooner than Cassandra wanted him to, but she understood why as they saw the infected walk into the ladder that was barely two feet away from Henry.

When Natalia and Henry flipped over the rising wall, the others cushioned their fall as well as they could, but all five ended in a pile on the floor. Hands appeared on the top edge of the wall, and some actually managed to hang on long enough to be carried to the ceiling. The forces that propelled that much weight upward were too strong to be denied, and the unmistakable sound of bones being crushed came from the ever shrinking gap along the ceiling. Eventually, there was no more gap and no more sound other than their own labored breathing and crying. It gradually gave way to a few chuckles before they erupted into all out laughing.

The laughing didn't stop until Natalia started beating on Henry's head. He covered up as best as he could, but she avoided his hands and scored some solid blows.

"You fool! You have a family to get home to! What were you thinking?"

The others became spectators and ignored Henry's pleas for help. Not one of them felt like it was worth losing him even if it had gained them a few seconds to get over the wall.

"You're lucky we aren't all kicking your butt," said Sim. "You think there's someone out there handing out knighthoods to martyrs?"

******

In the mission control center of the shelter, everyone was hard at work trying to find the gremlins in the system that were stopping them from establishing a link with a satellite. With thousands of them in orbit, Gentry was sure they could do it, and if they could find more, then they could keep the system running permanently.

Under her supervision, all six of the Mud Island group were at workstations. Karen was at hers, and Gentry floated around the room as data flooded into each station. From what they could learn at each station, there were satellites responding, but they had been unable to create a network. The Chief and the rest of the group knew the benefits of contact with the other shelters. It would be the beginning of a comeback by survivors of the infection.

Concentration levels were high, and Mission Control resembled an advanced university class that was in the middle of a grueling midterm exam. They were all focused on their work when the security alarms cut through the silence. It wasn't like them to be startled, but it was the last thing they expected, and they turned to Gentry for instructions.

Gentry was as startled as the rest of them, but she knew she only had to do one thing, and that was to identify the source of the alarm.

"Armory exterior exit," she yelled.

It was reassuring to her to see the way this group of pros responded. They may have been startled, but that didn't make them run like someone had yelled fire in a crowded theater. In an orderly fashion they split into two groups of three. She saw hand signals pass between them as one group went up each of the opposite sets of stairs, and they were checking their weapons as they went. She could tell that their different routes would allow three each to come up on opposite sides of the armory. Whatever had set off the alarms, it was going to be contained at that location.

Gentry was also happy with the decision to allow the newcomers to arm themselves when they arrived. There would be no time to do it if the door outside the armory had been breached.

"Shouldn't we go with them?" asked Karen.

"We would just be in the way, but we should follow at a safe distance."

Gentry turned off the alarms as they passed her console, and they ran to catch up with the group being led by the Chief. They could hear their footsteps up ahead, but that was all. They knew they could be facing any possibility so they weren't wasting time chattering about what it might be.

The Chief had Iris and Tom behind him, while Kathy was being trailed by Colleen then Hampton. They paced themselves so they would arrive at the wall at the same time, and they were ready to mow down the threat. They suspected either the Sheriff's people or that the infected had somehow gotten inside. They were leaning toward it being the Sheriff's people because they didn't think the shelter had any leaks where the infected could squeeze inside. They also didn't think the tunnel entrance could be opened by accident. Whoever came through that door, they must have done it on purpose.

By the time both groups reached the corridor where the armory was located, they were mentally prepared for the conflict they faced. After all, this wasn't their first time. They had gone into battle together so often that they had lost count, but this was one of those dangerous situations where they were facing an unknown enemy. Oddly, that didn't cross their minds. It was either going to be people who meant to do them harm or the infected dead. Either way, the reaction would be the same.

The Chief's team arrived first, and from their vantage point they could only see far enough around the corner to know the wall was dropping toward the floor. Iris whispered over his shoulder that maybe they could stop it, but he shook his head.

"No time. The controls are on the armory door. The wall will be halfway down before someone could stop it then get clear. If there's someone on the other side with a gun, we would be sitting ducks. Best to let them in then hit them from the front and back at the same time."

Tom said, "There's no cover in the corridor except the curve, and we can't shoot over each other."

"Okay," said the Chief, "if they come our way, then do a leapfrog retreat. When I reload, Iris will move up. When she reloads, you move up. If they go in the other direction we'll use the same plan to advance."

On the other side of the hallway there was a similar conversation in progress, but they had the advantage of an intersection. Before reaching the armory they were able to take cover at the intersection with two of them on one side and one on the other. From their position they could see the wall dropping toward the floor, but they couldn't see past the armory to the Chief's position.

"We have one advantage," said Hampton, "we aren't in a straight line with the others, so we're less likely to shoot one of our own people."

Kathy leaned around from her side of the intersection and watched the dark gap grow larger.

"Whoever they are, they're going to be coming from the dark into a well lit hallway, so they'll have to adjust to the light. Don't be too quick to shoot, and wait for them to start looking for targets. Avoid hitting the outside wall with any of your shots. That thing is metal, and a bullet could skim the surface just enough to ricochet into the Chief's group."

"I hope they noticed the same thing," said Colleen.

When the wall was waist high, both groups could see the dim light from the other side shifting from lighter to darker as shadows moved closer. They could tell someone was moving quickly toward the growing gap, and that meant two things. They weren't the infected dead, and they were going to jump over the descending wall as it came down. It maybe meant they would come in shooting.

There were also shouts from the other side. They clearly heard someone yelling to hurry, and then there was someone hurtling over the wall. From both ends of the corridor, Kathy and the Chief took aim.

A group of three people came over the wall together. It wasn't entirely clear why, but it looked like the one in the middle was thrown over the wall by the other two. For a fleeting moment the Chief thought someone was possibly throwing the infected into the shelter with them.

"That would be new," said the Chief.

The one who was thrown inside also had their arms wrapped around something white and bulky. It reminded him of a flight suit he had worn in the Navy when he had done high G training. The thought was further reinforced when he got a better view of the helmet. The sun visor was closed, so he couldn't see the person inside, but he could have sworn the helmet was from the space program and not military. Whatever the big, bulky gear was in the person's arms, between it and the helmet, the blow of the landing was much softer than it would have been, and he understood better when he saw the big red bloodstain on the left shoulder.

Iris saw the same things and asked, "Is that person hurt, or is someone out there chucking the infected into the shelter?" A second helmet bounced around in the narrow space, its white surface and face visor were streaked with dirt and blood.

Her question was no sooner asked when it was answered because the two people who had thrown the first one over jumped onto the still descending wall and then let themselves fall into the hallway. One of them sprang to his feet and lunged for the lock on the armory door.

The Chief took aim at the man over the sight of his handgun, but the curve of the wall took away his opportunity for a clear shot. Taking a chance, he took a long step across the hall and acquired his target. He was just in time to see the man tap the ENTER key twice and then fall to the floor. That didn't make sense, unless the man clearly knew how the lock worked. It looked like he was closing the door instead of trying to gain access to the armory.

The grinding sound of the wall descending came to an immediate halt, but then the pitch changed as it strained to move the heavy door in the opposite direction. Two of the three people were yelling for someone to hurry, and the Chief could just make out two more people outside. Two more long steps forward, and the Chief could see that there was a military man in a US Army battle dress uniform with his back to the open shelter, and beyond him was a solid wall of the infected moving toward him.

The Army officer spread his arms wide as if welcoming the horde, but his heroic challenge was interrupted by a woman. She was wearing a white flight suit like the one the other person was holding, and the Chief clearly saw the shoulder patch on the right arm that extended toward the man. It was a Russian flag. She gripped him by the back of his collar and put all of her strength into that arm.

When the woman pulled, she yelled something that the Chief didn't understand, but together they fell backward toward the rising wall. It was at just the right height for them to hit it at the knees and flip over. They landed in a heap on top of the other three people.

There were collective grunts as they knocked the wind out of each other, but the immediate concern was the wall not closing far enough to stop the horde from coming inside with the people. The mixed bag of people on the floor appeared to pose no threat to the inhabitants of the shelter, so the Chief stepped further into the open and targeted an infected that was close to clearing the top of the wall. The bullet punched a hole in its forehead and pushed it into the path of several more that had gained a purchase on the wall.

From the other side of the hallway, Kathy's group opened fire, and the faces of the infected disappeared. In a few more seconds the grinding sound of the rising wall was replaced by the crunching of brittle bones as the last of the infected failed to let go of the wall in time. Then it was quiet. At least it was until the people on the floor started laughing.

Sim came out from under the person in the helmet and sat up in the middle of the pile. He pulled the helmet from Cassandra's head with both hands and pushed it over his own. Her hair immediately went in every direction, and before she passed out cold, she yelled something about wanting to do that again.

"Hi Chief," yelled Sim from behind the visor. "Bet you didn't expect to see us in here!"

MC stood up and helped Natalia separate herself from where they had all landed. The armory door was still closed, so they had all been forced to dive over the wall in a much more narrow space as the door to the shelter closed behind them. It was frightening at first, but once they realized they had made it, they all laughed from the excess adrenaline.

Gentry pushed past the Chief and ran to the man who had pushed the ENTER button. She threw her arms around his neck, and everyone realized the man must be the missing soldier who had rescued her.

Karen waded over people she didn't know to get to Cassandra. She saw the ashy skin tone of shock on Cassandra's face before she passed out, but she also saw the large injury the Chief had spotted. She had to find out how bad it was, but she knew she had to rule out an infectious bite. She didn't know this was another of the survivors from Mud Island, but she had to know if she was a danger to them.

Kathy and Colleen moved in to help separate the pile of people, and Natalia felt how helpful their hands were. They were careful, and they asked questions about injuries. Sim was still laughing with relief inside the helmet, but he was also trying to play host by introducing everyone. It didn't take long for everyone to understand the significance of this reunion. They had lost Wanda, and they had lost

Commander Adam Callaway, and despite Cassandra's injury the Mud Island group was together again.

Karen asked Tom and Hampton to get her a stretcher to carry Cassandra to the infirmary, and Sim told her he was sure she was O positive blood type and so was he. Karen told Sim he was a volunteer to donate a bit of blood without knowing that Sim would have given her as much as she needed.

The Chief grabbed Sim in a big bear hug and lifted him off his feet.

"I'll bet you have a story to tell, my friend. I don't know how you and Cassandra got yourselves inside the shelters, but it's good to see you. Do we have someone on overwatch outside?"

"Of course. That's what you said the plan was. Remember that wicked firepower the Sheriff had?"

The Chief heard the accent on the last word, and his eyebrows went up.

Sim went on, "Hank and Hazel are on our side. They have two of the Sheriff's weapons on overwatch. When you're ready to move, they have us covered."

"Hank and Hazel? Sound like wonderful people," laughed the Chief.

After getting Cassandra on her way to the infirmary, the Chief and the rest of the group was able to get proper introductions to Natalia and Henry.

"It's my greatest honor to meet both of you. It's a sorry world you've returned to, and I wouldn't blame you for wanting to leave again, but you're in good hands with us if you want a place to be. Gentry has some things here that you're going to like."

Natalia said, "Gentry. I knew she would be here somewhere. When MC told us he knew her, we felt like we were almost home."

"Speaking of home," said Henry, "do you have any information of what it's like in England? Has anyone established a way for me to get there? I'm sure someone has made the flight or has ships connecting our countries by now."

Natalia felt bad for both Henry and the Chief. She wanted to see Henry find a way home, but she would have preferred to warn the Chief before Henry could blindside him with the request. She didn't know the Chief before this moment, but she felt like she had known him forever by how he eased Henry into understanding the enormous difficulties of such a request. The Chief managed to postpone the answer rather than to put an end to it.

Karen insisted on giving the ISS crew complete physicals before allowing them to do anything else. There was a question of getting their electrolytes balanced, and Karen insisted that they were both at risk of heart attacks or stroke if she didn't get them onto the proper dietary supplements as soon as possible.

When she was through with them, Gentry showed them to their rooms where they were alone for the first time in years and had the opportunity to enjoy showers and clean clothes. They emerged only a couple of hours later, both looking like they had been renewed, but both complaining that they couldn't deal with the total privacy. It would take some getting used to.

MC chose to go to a different room than the apartment he and Wanda had shared. He and Gentry sat in the dining room at a table in a corner and talked for hours, a little about Wanda, but Gentry couldn't believe how difficult life had been for him. He was still the handsome young soldier, but the lines at the corners of his eyes spoke volumes about his sadness.

Sim stayed with Cassandra until she came to, and then he called for the others to let them know they could have a few minutes with her. They all got in their hugs despite her injury, and of course they had to tease her about being taken out by such a formidable piece of hospital equipment.

When Karen broke up the reunion so her patient could rest, the Chief and Kathy stayed behind to work on their plans to take out the Sheriff and to liberate Farley.

28

The Battle of Farley

Huntsville - Year Seven

The Sheriff couldn't explain away what the people had seen. He could tell the people that the crew of the spacecraft had been killed in their reentry, but he couldn't change the fact that the location of Farley had made it key to the survival of a large number of NASA employees. Many people who weren't directly employed by the Marshall Space Flight Center were employed by private companies that were located near NASA because they manufactured crucial systems for the space program. He never realized how much like family they were.

The battle of Farley didn't begin with a disorganized attack. It began by word of mouth. Claire had talked with the authorities about the missing blacksmith, and some suspected that she had collaborated with the soldiers, but those who knew her well spread the word that the Chief was different, and he wouldn't have just run off. The same was true for the quiet group of people who had been brought in with the blacksmith. That they had gone was too big of a coincidence considering that the Chief was missing, and the timing of the reentry of a spacecraft undoubtedly from the International Space Station gave the air over Farley an electric feeling, like something was about to happen.

The soldiers guarding the outskirts of Farley were nervous. They noticed more and more people seemed to be watching them, and they asked for reinforcements. That made the NCO's nervous, which in turn made the officers nervous, and they took their worries to the Sheriff. The Sheriff had never considered public relations to be his job, and he made it clear to the officers that anyone who couldn't control the population would become part of the population instead of an officer. He didn't think they would be happy living on catfish stew like everyone else.

When Hampton showed up in Farley, he was well disguised, but it had always been his small town upbringing that had made him able to blend in. It took him the better part of a day to find Claire, but she told him tension was high in the muddy town along the Tennessee River. She told him people were talking about a rumor that the shelters held food, and that some of the shelters had even been cleared by the Sheriff and his soldiers. Hampton told her it was true. If they wanted to, the entire town of Farley could be moved into the safety of the shelters, and the supplies inside the hundreds of remaining shelters could provide medical care, clothing, and food for years to come, but the Sheriff was keeping it for himself and a select few officers who had sacrificed their integrity for their comfort.

Claire made sure the information was passed to the right people, and Hampton slipped away to let the Chief know the battle had begun. The Chief left with Kathy and Tom through the back door of the shelter in the middle of the night. What they had in mind wasn't easy, but with the help of the map brought in by the astronauts, they had been able to locate the one missing piece of the puzzle to the massive complex of shelters.

One thing in common that the survivors club had in their designs was the fake shelters. Some were more elaborate than others, but the builders had reasoned that any shelter above or near the super shelter would distract from the idea that there was something better nearby. At Mud Island it was a houseboat. At Fort Sumter it was the old fort itself. On the oil rig it had been something along the lines of a bunkhouse the size of a mobile home. Every shelter had another shelter nearby that was more obvious. The nearby shelter in Huntsville was the largest of them all, and the man who had come up with the idea had reasoned that a large number of survivors living above the super shelter was better insulation than a small number.

The designer didn't take into account that a large number of people who survived this particular type of apocalypse would also be bite victims, and they would insulate the super shelter by filling the surrounding shelters with the infected dead. After all, this wasn't the apocalypse that was first on anybody's list. Regardless of what apocalypse happened to decimate the population, the member of the Titus Rush survivalist club who designed the fake shelters realized that every city needed a port. Every city needed a way to resupply or even just a place where they could come and go. So he connected them all with one tunnel.

The occupants of the super shelter already knew where one branch of the tunnel was, but when MC told them about how he had escaped death by taking a truck, he was also able to tell them where the other tunnels were. Using the map he traced out the path he had taken that night, and they were able to learn where the tunnel intersected with at least a third of the shelters.

With Claire's help and the underground that had rapidly recruited in Farley, two dozen people slipped out of the town under the cover of darkness. They were told they had to be brave enough to try something crazy, but when they heard the plan, they were all in.

Everyone involved was fed and rested for a day, but on the next night they moved. Using corridors that were scouted and cleared of the infected, volunteers were led to places in the main tunnel, and they began opening the floodgates. Shelters that had been the tombs of thousands of infected were opened in sequence, and the infected were summoned into the tunnel by a slow-moving parade of supply trucks.

Their destination was the entrance to the shelter that had become the Sheriff's personal residence. All the Mud Island group had to do was make sure the back doors to the shelter were open when the parade arrived, and that any resistance that might slow down the horde was reduced before they swarmed into the shelter.

By scouting that shelter in advance, they already knew that soldiers didn't patrol into the tunnel. They were simply posted at guard points nearby. The Chief had explained to everyone that it wasn't his goal to eliminate the rank and file soldiers. His goal was to eliminate the Sheriff and his corrupt officers. He wanted as many NCO's and enlisted troops kept alive as possible. It began with the guards at the back entrances, and instead of killing them or even taking them prisoner, they were simply relieved of duty.

There were six entrances to the shelter all within thirty yards of each other, so there were only four guard posts manned by two soldiers each. Getting uniforms had been easy, and recruiting people with enough military experience to pull off the disguise, the Chief marched a squad of soldiers up to the guard posts and ordered them to stand relieved. It wasn't the way they were used to doing it, and they were being relieved early, but they didn't care. They saluted the big man leading the squad and ran for the shelter doors.

When the parade arrived two hours later, the Chief already had enough vehicles in place to block the tunnel, and the vehicles had been used to draw out the infected simply doubled up on a few places.

"Now the fun begins," said the Chief. "Remember, these people haven't had regular military training, so self-preservation is going to be a high motivator. I'll lead with Tom, Hampton, Kathy, Colleen, Sim, and MC."

As he called their names they each stepped out in front wearing Army battle dress uniforms.

"We'll go in each door with a squad behind each leader yelling the same thing. Don't let anyone stand and fight. If we run into an NCO, we have to get them on our side fast. I think they'll all get on board, but leave them to one of us. We have a script to follow. Just keep yelling that the infected dead have breached the shelter and to evacuate."

"What happens if we run into an officer?" asked one of the men.

"Tell him that the Sheriff has called for all officers to meet with him in his stateroom immediately, and then watch where he goes. If we get enough officers running in one direction, we'll find the Sheriff."

The groaning of the horde was close, so it was showtime. If everything went as planned, they would flush the shelter out like an anthill. It would be full of the infected again, but they could be dealt with over time.

"Let's go! We have confirmation that the Sheriff is here, and remember," he paused for effect, "I want him alive, but that's optional."

A laugh went up from the small army, and each group ran ahead to their entrance.

******

Only minutes after each group entered the shelter yelling their warning, it became a fact that the infected dead had breached the shelter. They bunched up around the first door, but the tunnel filled to capacity against the trucks causing them to spread across the side of the tunnel until they found every brightly lit open door. If they didn't have enough encouragement, once they were inside they could hear the panicked screams of self-preservation coming from people who weren't even part of the plan.

The Chief was the first to run into an NCO, and the man recognized him immediately. The Chief didn't mince words.

"Sarge, this is going down tonight. If you're with us you'll be alive at the end with a blank slate. We could use your help."

The NCO simply nodded and yelled for everyone to evacuate.

An officer came running up behind the Chief and the NCO, but he only yelled to get out of the way as he went by. The Chief asked the NCO if that was the way to the Sheriff's stateroom. He said it was more like his palace, but that was the way to get there.

All around the Chief there was a flurry of activity as the soldiers and a few privileged citizens made their way to the upper level entrance. He didn't doubt that there was already a sizable number of people outside. An NCO approached him, and he thought he was going to need to do his script again, but the man asked what were his orders once everyone was clear.

"Muster everyone with their squad leaders, Sergeant. Are there any that won't be team players?"

"Yessir. Two of them have been bucking for a promotion, so they've been kissing up to the Sheriff."

"Eliminate them however you see fit. Wait … tell them they're wanted in the stateroom and put someone else in charge of their squads. How many men do we have out there?"

"About four hundred, Sir."

The Chief had a difficult time hiding his surprise. If enough of them had decided to put down a rebellion, it would be over in minutes. He could guarantee them heavy casualties, but there was no way they could have withstood a force that size.

"Thank you, Sergeant. Two more things I need from you. Is there a backdoor to the stateroom?"

"Yessir, it comes out at the end of an escape tunnel in the cemetery across the road from the Space Flight Center."

For a second time the Chief had to hide his expression, but this time it was amusement.

"You said there were two things, Sir."

"Yes, thanks for reminding me. Find me when this is all over with."

The Sergeant ran off to take care of his assignments, and the Chief saw the first of the infected dead arriving at the end of the hallway. It was time to put an end to this.

Working his way across and up the levels of the shelter the Chief gathered together his Mud Island group. Their work was done, so they followed the trail of officers to the stateroom. It was easy to guess which door because it had a large gaudy Sheriff's badge on it.

The officers didn't expect armed intruders, so they didn't have their weapons drawn when the Chief calmly walked through the door. He was tempted to kick it in, but someone may have reacted. There were eight of them, and they were all seated at a long conference table. He was followed closely by Kathy, and she scanned the room for the two NCO's who had been led to believe they were being promoted. She spotted them standing dutifully together behind one of the officers who had undoubtedly questioned their presence.

Tom, Colleen, Sim, and MC filed in behind Kathy and spread out to cover the room while Kathy disarmed the Sergeants. The only one missing was Hampton, and he was busy acting as the liaison between the Chief and the NCO's. He was likely to be outside already organizing the troops and explaining the new order of things.

The only other person missing from the meeting was the Sheriff, and the Chief had a pretty good idea where he was.

"Gentlemen, I'll make this quick because that sound you hear in the hallway outside this room is about a thousand of the infected. I want a show of hands from anyone who wants to live. Point at the location of the escape door."

It was fairly unanimous that the escape door was behind a flag that was as gaudy as the star on the door. One officer stood up to confront the Chief and was surprised by his lightning fast reaction.

The Chief lifted the man by his neck and body slammed him on top of the table where he stared up at the Chief with wide eyes. The Chief didn't let go of his neck immediately.

"I said I would make this quick, so let me answer one question for all of you. If you were an officer at the beginning of the infection, or if someone commissioned you afterward, I don't care. You forfeited your commissions when you let that little civilian wanna-be Sheriff take over. You took an oath, and everyone in this room violated that oath, so you are no longer officers. If you want to live, get into that escape tunnel and run, because we spent too long in here, and we can't go back out the way we came in."

They didn't need to be asked twice, and the two NCO's got moving first.

Kathy asked, "Don't you think they'll just scatter when they get to the other end of the tunnel?"

The Chief shook his head and said, "If they do, Hank and Hazel are asleep."

"Do Hank and Hazel know not to shoot if anyone comes out of that tunnel?"

"I haven't talked with them. No way to communicate the plan. As a matter of fact, if the Sheriff made it to the other end of the tunnel and he was wearing his hat, he might have gotten Hank and Hazel stirred up. At least they'll be ready for the rest of the gang because they'll be watching for them. That's why we're giving them a head start."

The Chief called to Sim and told him to go first since Hank and Hazel knew him, but not to follow too closely in case the old couple was shooting first and asking questions later. Sim flashed a smile and took off through the tunnel.

"Why aren't we leaving with him?" asked Kathy.

The Chief held up a finger and placed it over his lips. He gestured for Kathy, Tom, Colleen, and MC to sit at the table, but before he sat down himself, he whispered, "I'm playing a hunch." Then he pointed at the desk at the end of the conference table.

Everyone waited with their eyes fixed on the area behind the desk. There were more flags draped on the wall, and the Chief knew it didn't matter if he was wrong because there was still time for them to leave through the tunnel.

After only five minutes the curtain moved, and Kathy whispered, "Don't you ever get tired of being right?"

"You're forgetting the times I've been wrong, like the time I pretended to be that guy at the shipping terminal and got captured along with the rest of you."

"It's easy to forget when you pull something like this," she answered.

The Sheriff was so sure he had fooled everyone that he didn't even notice them all just sitting there watching as he came out of hiding from behind a state flag. When he saw them, he bolted for the door.

If he had opened the door, he would have regretted the decision, but the Chief figured it was his choice to make and didn't make a move to stop him. The others followed the Chief's lead and didn't react, but Kathy couldn't resist. The Sheriff still suffered from lower back pains from the last time she had tackled him. A disc in his spine was bulging and not likely to get better, but Kathy hadn't gotten over his rude welcome when they arrived in Huntsville.

It felt ironic to her that she would get a second chance to pay him back, especially since he presented such a tempting target from the opposite direction than the first time. Before she reacted, she had a split second to consider how bad it would be for him, but she couldn't stop herself. She launched herself at him, and her right shoulder drove with her weight behind it straight into his right kidney. He screamed in agony and clutched at his lower back.

"Let's go," said the Chief in a loud voice. The impact from Kathy had driven the Sheriff face first into the door, and even as his right hand had gone to his back, he grabbed the handle on the door and pulled. His hat and most of his head were in the hallway, but his shoulders were pinned against the door and the frame.

Even before they could move for the escape tunnel, something was pulling at the Sheriff's head, but his feet weren't moving. It was quite possibly due to his broken back. He was, however, not completely paralyzed and could feel what was happening to the rest of him.

Everyone scrambled for the tunnel, and unless the infected stumbled into the flag, it wasn't likely that they would follow. There was no light, but they each had a few glow sticks they had brought with them from the super shelter supply room. The walls were damp because the tunnel had never been reinforced, and the Chief was a little more than worried that there would be a collapsed section ahead, especially since the Sheriff had dug the tunnel into a cemetery.

MC was in front, and he passed the word back that there was light ahead. They slowed their approach and had Sim squeeze past everyone. If Hank and Hazel were using their pickup truck mounted M145s on anyone who came out of the tunnel, they had to hope they would recognize him first.

The light got brighter, and Sim saw that the headlights of one pickup truck were aimed at the exit. The other truck had its gun aimed at the row of officers who were all on their knees with their fingers laced behind their heads. The bodies of the two NCO's were on the ground in front of them, and it was obvious what had happened to them.

"Don't shoot, it's me, Sim," he yelled.

"Hey, Buddy," answered Hank. "You got Sandy with you?"

"No, she had a little problem inside, but she's okay. Don't worry. I brought some friends, though."

Everyone filed out behind Sim, and he gave quick introductions.

Their reaction when they saw the Chief come through the small tunnel exit was the usual because it seemed like he was too big for the exit.

"We didn't want to shoot those two," said Hazel, "but they didn't cooperate."

Hank added, "Sorry we didn't stop the Sheriff before he got away, but we didn't know about this tunnel until he popped out."

"Who was that back there?" asked Kathy. "It sure looked like him."

One of the officers spoke up and said, "The Sheriff plans everything. He used that body double routine on us once before. Makes people feel like he can be two places at one time."

"Hampton's out there," said Colleen.

The Sheriff had a good lead on them, and the Chief reminded Kathy that he could be wrong after all. She didn't want to hear it, though, and said the Sheriff had underestimated them. The smirk told the Chief that Kathy had done something, but right now was the time to make up the distance between them and the Sheriff. They piled into one of the pickup trucks with the Chief behind the wheel and drove down the side of the hill through the cemetery. He barely slowed at the ditch along the highway and almost threw everyone out of the back.

The direct route to the front gates was the way the Sheriff would have gone, but Kathy had made other arrangements. While the Chief had organized the parade of the horde to the Sheriff's shelter, Kathy had recruited Hampton to help her with the citizens of Farley. The last thing she wanted to see happen was for them to turn into a mob and to rush headlong into the shelter. They would have learned the hard way the same thing people did on the very first day of the infection. There would be injuries, bites, and the infection would spread through Farley the same way it had everywhere else.

Hampton had stayed behind with the newly recruited NCO's because he knew they were going to be confronted by the citizens the soldiers had abused, and he needed to keep the peace. Kathy had gone on the assumption that the Sheriff had years to plan for an uprising, and he could probably turn his army on the people. So, she made sure that Claire and her supporters had a way to see for themselves that the soldiers had staged a coup, and that the Sheriff had cornered himself.

Before the soldiers evacuated the shelter, the fence surrounding the shelters was cut, and the population of Farley streamed toward the Space Flight Center. By the time the soldiers fled from the infected dead in the shelter, the citizens had reached the Saturn V test gantries and filled the fields between the shelters. They were met by the NCO's and Hampton, and with the promise of the shared wealth and safety of the shelters, the newly appointed civilian leaders kept the mobs under control. There was only one last detail to take care of.

With the help of the NCO's, all of the routes the Sheriff could take were closed off by gates and armed guards. Just like the horde that was led through the tunnel, the Sheriff was directed without his knowledge into the same area where the soldiers stood in formation, and the citizens waited patiently behind them.

The Sheriff assumed he had reached safety and began shouting orders to the NCO's. When they didn't respond, he shouted threats, but then he saw the angry faces of the crowds behind the soldiers and backed away. He also saw that the NCO's were waiting for something. Behind him a pickup truck turned onto the road between the shelters, closing off any chance of escape except one, and the Sheriff took it.

The front entrance of the shelter had been left open on purpose because the infected couldn't climb the steep stairs that had caused more complaints than any other thing about the shelters. They were hard to climb up or down because they dropped down at an angle that made them more like ladders than stairs. The lights were on inside, and a sea of dead faces crowded around the bottom of the stairs. Their dead eyes looked upward at the dark rectangle of the entrance, and as the Sheriff bolted through the door and descended the stairs, they let loose with a welcoming chorus. He stopped halfway down and clung to the rails. When he turned back toward the entrance he saw several people looking down at him. The Chief, Kathy, an NCO, and a woman stood together without expressions of sympathy.

Claire said, "Hey, Sheriff. Remember me? You hung some of my best friends just for civil disobedience. If you come up the ladder now, I promise you'll get a fair trial."

The Chief felt bad for ever doubting Claire. He never knew what her motive was for staying so near him, but he understood now. She had suspected the Chief would be her savior and her path to revenge.

Before the Sheriff could answer, Claire yelled, "I'll take that as a no." She closed the door shut with a loud bang.

Outside the door, the Chief took the NCO aside and instructed him to back a truck up to the door so it could only open an inch or two. He told him to keep the Sheriff on the stairs for as long as Claire wanted.

"What if she never wants the truck moved?" he asked.

"I figure he can hang onto those stairs for maybe two days," said the Chief and left it at that.

* * *
******

Before the real work began, the entire community joined together in mourning the loss of Commander Callaway, and as a tribute to him they held a memorial service at the Soyuz landing site. The capsule was sealed, and a grave marker was placed beside it.

Under the Chief's supervision the NCO's worked efficiently to clear the infected from one shelter after the next, and with each one cleared the treasure troves of supplies inside were distributed to the population of Farley. Work crews followed the soldiers into the shelters, and as rooms were cleared of the bodies and debris from years of neglect, safe rooms were restored to habitable conditions, and families were brought inside.

Within a week there were cafeterias and health clinics operating in the first two shelters, and with those two serving as the headquarters for the newly appointed government, there was an announcement that there would be an election within the year. The military removed officers who had lived in comfort for years and established a detention center on the surface where the town of Farley had been. Their sentence was to provide fresh fish for the community living in the shelters. The people didn't need the fish. They simply wanted the officers to live as they had.

The Chief didn't disclose the existence of the super shelter until all of the citizens of Farley were living inside the safety that had been originally planned by the builders of the shelters. Each shelter selected representatives to attend a meeting inside the planetarium under one of the shelters, and they were treated to a show they hadn't expected.

First they were introduced to Natalia Lebedev and Henry Tisdal who were given a hero's welcome by the excited crowd. Natalia explained to them the sorrowful passing of their comrade and introduced them to Gentry and Karen. The crowd was stunned to learn about the super shelter under their feet but not surprised to find that the two women never knew what was happening above them.

The next big shock to the already elated crowd was the explanation that the process of hiring mission control specialists would begin now that everyone was inside shelters, and that anyone who was hired would be moved into the super shelter. There were apartments for the families of the people who were hired, and former NASA employees could apply for the first positions. There would be other jobs available, including anyone with communications experience. They learned that the new Director of NASA was Natalia Lebedev, and that Gentry Campbell was the Director of Operations. Hank and Hazel were given an apartment, and they gratefully accepted positions as the directors of custodial services. Henry was talking about going home.

Then the doors were opened, and the tour began. To people who had lived in poverty and danger for seven years, it was a return to normal, and the Mud Island group had a front row seat to the building of one of the most efficient communities since the infection began. They only had to protect it as they grew.

By the end of a month, every shelter was free of the infected, and the perimeter around the shelter complex was being strengthened. The Army was operating out of one shelter in order to maintain a certain amount of separation from the general population, but just like any military base, soldiers with families could live in the civilian shelters.

The only thing left for the Chief to do was to settle the issue with Henry Tisdal. The topic of him reaching home had come up several times, but he had always been vague. He would simply say he would figure it out, and one day he would leave for home. England wasn't exactly a short drive, but talking with a man who had orbited the Earth almost twenty times a day for over six years about doing something difficult wasn't easy. As long as the word "impossible" didn't creep into the conversation, he was going to do it.

******

There finally came the day when the Chief and Kathy found Gentry and Natalia to talk about what they were going to do next. Staying in Huntsville wasn't in their plans now that it was virtually a thriving city. They lived underground, but that didn't make them any less of a city.

The technology in the super shelter was proving to be what the people needed to revive the industrial park only a few miles away. With a strong military presence and what was likely to be the largest concentration of scientists anywhere, they could reclaim enough territory in the city to move from one place to another. There would still be problems. There would be the infected and there would be the survivors who didn't fit in anywhere, but now that the right people were in charge and the assets weren't controlled by one person, they could be used more effectively.

The group decided that for the time being it would be a good idea to return to Guntersville to check on the settlement and the shelter in Green Cavern. It would give them some time to resupply and plan a trip up the east coast of America. They grudgingly admitted that Henry had convinced them that they should accompany him as far as New England, and he said he had a plan in mind for how to make it the rest of the way. There was actually no reason not to go with him. It would also give them the opportunity to at least see what had become of Charleston and then make a detour to the shelter under Ambassadors Island. When Kathy mentioned stopping at Mud Island for a few days, it made them all feel like they were going home.

They were better supplied when they pulled away from the securely guarded entrance to the shelter complex than they had been when they left Guntersville. On that trip they had decided to travel light, but on this trip they wanted to make even better time. Henry asked them if they could get him to New England in early spring, and the assumption was that he intended to cross the Atlantic, and it would be far more difficult in the winter.

It had been hard for him to say goodbye to Natalia, but she knew he had always wanted to at least try to get home. She wished they could have landed closer for him, but the way it had worked out for her was definitely better.

As a parting gift to Kathy, Natalia gave her the spacesuit she had worn for so long. She said it would provide protection from bites, but it was also a symbol that a Russian woman had broken all the space records. She told Kathy that she would have made a great astronaut, and Kathy admitted if she could have done anything besides become a cop, that would have been her first choice.

Gentry said her parting gift to them was to get the Space Flight Center completely functional again, and it was her way of thanking the Mud Island family for coming to their rescue, but the Chief wouldn't hear any talk about her owing them anything. It was enough to see yet another piece of humanity taking steps toward survival. With MC back in Gentry's life she painfully confessed that she had put her mission ahead of him, and she had learned that life without human connections wasn't really life.

29

Epilogue

Between Guntersville and Huntsville - Year Seven

Their small convoy of trucks made good time across Huntsville and over the mountain. The Army NCO's insisted on giving them an escort through the worst section. The Chief didn't think they needed an escort, but the soldiers wanted to show their gratitude for restoring them to what they had been before. They were all sporting a new patch on their uniforms. It was shaped like a baseball diamond with an H in the middle of it. They took pride in their work, and with any luck Huntsville would be a good starting point. They certainly planned to send survivors with science backgrounds in that direction.

They waved to their escort and reached the open road by late morning and got their first surprise of the day when they saw motorcycles coming in the opposite direction. They were even more surprised to see it was a familiar face from Guntersville on the first bike. The Chief put on his emergency flashers, and the motorcycles slowed their pace. When they saw the Chief step out of the cab of the lead vehicle, they quickly crossed through the tall grass of the median.

Everyone could see the urgency in the man as they brought their motorcycles to a stop next to the Chief, and they all piled out to hear what was happening. The messenger was Kyle Jeffords, one of the elected constables in the small town above Green Cavern. He had an urgent message from Ed and Jean, and it was a lot to take in at one time.

Kyle didn't know where to start because Ed had been forced to send him in his place, but with a little help from the Chief he got himself together and broke the news. Ed had received word from the Army in Charleston that they believed Captain Miller was still alive inside Fort Sumter. That news alone was enough for celebration, but it was quickly dampened by the second part. There was some kind of militia operating in Atlanta, and they had wiped out all but two people from the squad that had carried the word from Charleston to Guntersville.

The Chief felt himself turn red, and he could imagine his own blood boiling in his veins. He thought of the men and women in that unit as if they were his responsibility. Captain Jim Miller had sacrificed himself for them, and if any of them died, he felt like he had let Captain Miller down.

"What's happening at Green Cavern that made Ed turn back?"

"It's a long story, Chief, but Ed found something on the way to Huntsville. He had to get it back to Green Cavern before anyone else found it, and he said there were only two people he knew who could fly it."

"Fly what?"

"It's a C-130, and they just got it back to Guntersville. Bus said the runway there is five thousand feet long, but he said he could land in three thousand."

The Chief said, "It's called a maximum effort landing. Yeah, I can do that. Is it armed?"

Jeffords handed him a slip of paper with a list of the weapons it carried. Starting with the powerful M134 Minigun, this plane was a serious piece of equipment.

The Chief's head tilted toward the rest of the Mud Island family. Kathy, Tom, Hampton, Colleen, Cassandra, and Sim all knew that grin, but he had it fixed on Henry.

"Henry, I don't know about getting you all the way home, but if you're willing to make a stop in Charleston and let me borrow those spacesuits for a few hours, I think we can work something out to get you closer to home in less time, and when we're done, we can pay a little visit to some people in Atlanta."

ABOUT THE AUTHOR

Bob Howard (1951-) was born in New Jersey to an Army Sergeant from Ohio and a mother from Romania. He was moved from one Army base to the next, and before he began high school in Huntsville, Alabama he had lived most of his life overseas in Germany and Okinawa with brief stays in Maryland and North Carolina. He credits his imagination to his exposure to different cultures and environments at an early age. He began reading science fiction and fell in love with post apocalyptic novels. He still has an original copy of the first one he read in 1966, The Furies by Keith Edwards. He joined the Navy after high school and continued to move from one base to another, including a submarine base at Holy Loch, Scotland. He eventually stayed in one place when he got stationed in Charleston, South Carolina. He graduated with a BS in Psychology from the College of Charleston. He married his wife in 1984 and together they raised a son and a daughter.

It takes a lot of work to get a book of fiction written and then edited. We want the book to flow, but we also want it to be grammatically correct whenever possible. If you see a spot where you think a comma was needed, it may be that I left it out because it interrupted the flow. The same isn't true for typos. If you see one of those nasty little things and would like to let me know, I would be pleased to correct it. I've learned that I've got some really bad habits when it comes to pet phrases, and I make mistakes. I hear from a gentleman in Japan regularly because he has such a keen eye for errors. I'm lucky to have him as an after-editor. That doesn't mean you won't see something that everyone else missed. Please make my books better by telling me.

I would love to hear from you, and I value your opinions and comments. The best way to help an author become better at his craft is to write a review, so please feel free to write one. If you would like to know more about me or get in touch with me, please visit my website at ***realbobhoward.com***. You can also sign up for my newsletter and be notified when the next book is released.

* * *

With gratitude,

Bob Howard

www.ingramcontent.com/pod-product-compliance
Lightning Source LLC
Chambersburg PA
CBHW020639020726
47494CB00001B/266
* 9 7 8 1 9 4 5 7 5 4 0 6 7 *